Conway Moncure

The Life of Thomas Paine Vol. 1

With a History of His Literary, Political, and Religious Career in America

Conway Moncure

The Life of Thomas Paine Vol. 1
With a History of His Literary, Political, and Religious Career in America

ISBN/EAN: 9783337202491

Printed in Europe, USA, Canada, Australia, Japan

Cover: Foto ©Raphael Reischuk / pixelio.de

More available books at **www.hansebooks.com**

Thomas Paine

ÆTAT. 67

FROM A PICTURE BY JARVIS, IN POSSESSION OF THE AUTHOR.

THE
LIFE OF THOMAS PAINE

WITH A HISTORY OF HIS LITERARY, POLITICAL AND RELIGIOUS CAREER IN AMERICA FRANCE, AND ENGLAND

BY

MONCURE DANIEL CONWAY

AUTHOR OF "OMITTED CHAPTERS OF HISTORY DISCLOSED IN THE LIFE AND PAPERS OF EDMUND RANDOLPH," "GEORGE WASHINGTON AND MOUNT VERNON," "WASHINGTON'S ' RULES OF CIVILITY,' " ETC.

TO WHICH IS ADDED A SKETCH OF PAINE
BY WILLIAM COBBETT

(HITHERTO UNPUBLISHED)

VOLUME I.

G. P. PUTNAM'S SONS

NEW YORK   LONDON
27 WEST TWENTY-THIRD STREET   24 BEDFORD STREET, STRAND

The Knickerbocker Press

1892

CONTENTS OF VOLUME I.

INSCRIBED

TO

GEORGE HOADLY

PREFACE.

At Hornsey, England, I saw a small round mahogany table, bearing at its centre the following words : " This Plate is inscribed by Thos. Clio Rickman in Remembrance of his dear friend Thomas Paine, who on this table in the year 1792 wrote several of his invaluable Works."

The works written by Paine in Rickman's house were the second part of " The Rights of Man," and " A Letter to the Addressers." Of these two books vast numbers were circulated, and though the government prosecuted them, they probably contributed largely to make political progress in England evolutionary instead of revolutionary. On this table he set forth constitutional reforms that might be peacefully obtained, and which have been substantially obtained. And here he warned the " Addressers," petitioning the throne for suppression of his works : " It is dangerous in any government to say to a nation, *Thou shalt not read.* This is now done in Spain, and was formerly done under the old government of France ; but it served to procure the downfall of the latter, and is subverting that of the former ; and it will have the same tendency in all countries ; because Thought, by some means or

other, is got abroad in the world, and cannot be restrained, though reading may."

At this table the Quaker chieftain, whom Danton
rallied for hoping to make revolutions with rose-
water, unsheathed his pen and animated his Round
Table of Reformers for a conflict free from the
bloodshed he had witnessed in America, and saw
threatening France.   This little table was the field
chosen for the battle of free speech ; its abundant
ink-spots were the shed blood of hearts transfused
with humanity.   I do not wonder that Rickman
was wont to show the table to his visitors, or that
its present owner, Edward Truelove—a bookseller
who has suffered imprisonment for selling pro-
scribed books,—should regard it with reverence.

The table is what was once called a candle-stand,
and there stood on it, in my vision, Paine's clear,
honest candle, lit from his "inner light," now covered by a bushel of prejudice.   I myself had once
supposed his light an infernal torch ; now I sat at
the ink-spotted candle-stand to write the first page
of this history, for which I can invoke nothing
higher than the justice that inspired what Thomas
Paine here wrote.

The educated ignorance concerning Paine is
astounding.   I once heard an English prelate speak
of "the vulgar atheism of Paine."   Paine founded
the first theistic society in Christendom ; his will
closes with the words, " I die in perfect composure,
and resignation to the will of my Creator, God."
But what can be expected of an English prelate
when an historian like Jared Sparks, an old Unitarian minister, could suggest that a letter written

by Franklin, to persuade some one not to publish a certain attack on religion, was "probably" addressed to Paine. (Franklin's "Writings," vol. x., p. 281.) Paine never wrote a page that Franklin could have so regarded, nor anything in the way of religious controversy until three years after Franklin's death. "The remarks in the above letter," says Sparks, "are strictly applicable to the deistical writings which Paine afterwards published." On the contrary, they are strictly inapplicable. They imply that the writer had denied a "particular providence," which Paine never denied, and it is asked, "If men are so wicked with religion, what would they be without it?" Paine's "deism" differed from Franklin's only in being more fervently religious. No one who had really read Paine could imagine the above question addressed to the author to whom the Bishop of Llandaff wrote : "There is a philosophical sublimity in some of your ideas when speaking of the Creator of the Universe." The reader may observe at work, in this example, the tiny builder, prejudice, which has produced the large formation of Paine mythology. Sparks, having got his notion of Paine's religion at second-hand, becomes unwittingly a weighty authority for those who have a case to make out. The American Tract Society published a tract entitled "Don't Unchain the Tiger," in which it is said : "When an infidel production was submitted—probably by Paine—to Benjamin Franklin, in manuscript, he returned it to the author, with a letter from which the following is extracted : 'I would advise you not to attempt unchaining the Tiger, but to burn

this piece before it is seen by any other person.'"
Thus our Homer of American history nods, and a
tract floats through the world misrepresenting both
Paine and Franklin, whose rebuke is turned from
some anti-religious essay against his own convic-
tions. Having enjoyed the personal friendship of
Mr. Sparks, while at college, and known his charity
to all opinions, I feel certain that he was an uncon-
scious victim of the Paine mythology to which he
added. His own creed was, in essence, little different from Paine's. But how many good, and even
liberal, people will find by the facts disclosed in this
volume that they have been accepting the Paine
mythology and contributing to it ? It is a notable
fact that the most effective distortions of Paine's
character and work have proceeded from unor-
thodox writers—some of whom seem not above
throwing a traditionally hated head to the orthodox
mob. A recent instance is the account given of
Paine in Leslie Stephen's " History of English
Thought in the Eighteenth Century." On its appearance I recognized the old effigy of Paine
elaborately constructed by Oldys and Cheetham,
and while writing a paper on the subject (*Fort-
nightly Review*, March, 1879) discovered that those
libels were the only "biographies" of Paine in the
London Library, which (as I knew) was used by
Mr. Stephen. The result was a serious miscarriage
of historical and literary justice. In his second
edition Mr. Stephen adds that the portrait presented "is drawn by an enemy," but on this Mr.
Robertson pertinently asks why it was allowed to
stand ? ("Thomas Paine : an Investigation," by

John M. Robertson, London, 1888). Mr. Stephen, eminent as an agnostic and editor of a biographical dictionary, is assumed to be competent, and his disparagements of a fellow heretic necessitated by verified facts. His scholarly style has given new lease to vulgar slanders. Some who had discovered their untruth, as uttered by Paine's personal enemies, have taken them back on Mr. Stephen's authority. Even brave O. B. Frothingham, in his high estimate of Paine, introduces one or two of Mr. Stephen's depreciations (Frothingham's " Recollection and Impressions," 1891).

There has been a sad absence of magnanimity among eminent historians and scholars in dealing with Paine. The vignette in Oldys—Paine with his " Rights of Man " preaching to apes ;—the Tract Society's picture of Paine's death-bed—hair on end, grasping a bottle,—might have excited their inquiry. Goethe, seeing Spinoza's face demonized on a tract, was moved to studies of that philosopher which ended in recognition of his greatness. The chivalry of Goethe is indeed almost as rare as his genius, but one might have expected in students of history an historic instinct keen enough to suspect in the real Paine some proportion to his monumental mythology, and the pyramidal cairn of curses covering his grave. What other last-century writer on political and religious issues survives in the hatred and devotion of a time engaged with new problems ? What power is confessed in that writer who was set in the place of a decadent Satan, hostility to him being a sort of sixth point of Calvinism, and fortieth article of the Church ? Large indeed must have been the influence of a man still perennially denounced by sectarians after heretical progress has left him comparatively orthodox, and retained as the figure-head of " Freethought " after his theism has been abandoned by its leaders. " Religion," said Paine, " has two principal enemies, Fanaticism and Infidelity." It was his strange destiny to be made a battle-field between these enemies. In the smoke of the conflict the man has been hidden. In the catalogue of the British Museum Library I counted 327 entries of books by or concerning Thomas Paine, who in most of them is a man-shaped or devil-shaped shuttlecock tossed between fanatical and " infidel " rackets.

Here surely were phenomena enough to attract the historic sense of a scientific age, yet they are counterpart of an historic suppression of the most famous author of his time. The meagre references to Paine by other than controversial writers are perfunctory ; by most historians he is either wronged or ignored. Before me are two histories of " American Slavery " by eminent members of Congress ; neither mentions that Paine was the first political writer who advocated and devised a scheme of emancipation. Here is the latest " Life of Washington " (1889), by another member of Congress, who manages to exclude even the name of the man who, as we shall see, chiefly converted Washington to the cause of independence. And here is a history of the " American Revolution " (1891), by John Fiske, who, while recognizing the effect of " Common Sense," reveals his ignorance of that pamphlet, and of all Paine's works, by describing it as full of scurrilous abuse of the English people,—whom Paine regarded as fellow-sufferers with the Americans under royal despotism.

It may be said for these contemporaries that the task of sifting out the facts about Paine was formidable. The intimidated historians of the last generation, passing by this famous figure, left an historic vacuum, which has been filled with mingled fact and fable to an extent hardly manageable by any not prepared to give some years to the task. Our historians, might, however, have read Paine's works, which are rather historical documents than literary productions. None of them seem to have done this, and the omission appears in many a flaw in their works. The reader of some documents in this volume, left until now to slumber in accessible archives, will get some idea of the cost to historic truth of this long timidity and negligence. But some of the results are more deplorable and irreparable, and one of these must here be disclosed.

In 1802 an English friend of Paine, Redman Yorke, visited him in Paris. In a letter written at the time Yorke states that Paine had for some time been preparing memoirs of his own life, and his correspondence, and showed him two volumes of the same. In a letter of Jan. 25, 1805, to Jefferson, Paine speaks of his wish to publish his works, which will make, with his manuscripts, five octavo volumes of four hundred pages each. Besides which he means to publish " a miscellaneous volume of correspondence, essays, and some pieces of poetry." He had also, he says, prepared historical prefaces,

stating the circumstances under which each work
was written.   All of which confirms Yorke's statement, and shows that Paine had prepared at least
two volumes of autobiographic matter and correspondence.   Paine never carried out the design
mentioned to Jefferson, and his manuscripts passed
by bequest to Madame Bonneville.   This lady, after
Paine's death, published a fragment of Paine's third
part of " The Age of Reason," but it was afterwards
found that she had erased passages that might
offend the orthodox.   Madame Bonneville returned
to her husband in Paris, and the French " Biographical Dictionary" states that in 1829 she, as the
depositary of Paine's papers, began " editing " his
life.   This, which could only have been the autobiography, was never published.   She had become
a Roman Catholic.   On returning (1833) to America, where her son, General Bonneville, also a
Catholic, was in military service, she had personal
as well as religious reasons for suppressing the
memoirs.   She might naturally have feared the
revival of an old scandal concerning her relations
with Paine.   The same motives may have prevented her son from publishing Paine's memoirs
and manuscripts.   Madame Bonneville died at the
house of the General, in St. Louis.   I have a note
from his widow, Mrs. Sue Bonneville, in which
she says : " The papers you speak of regarding
Thomas Paine are all destroyed—at least all which
the General had in his possession.   On his leaving
St. Louis for an indefinite time all his effects—a
handsome library and valuable papers included—
were stored away, and during his absence the store-

house burned down, and all that the General stored away were burned."

There can be little doubt that among these papers burned in St. Louis were the two volumes of Paine's autobiography and correspondence seen by Redman Yorke in 1802. Even a slight acquaintance with Paine's career would enable one to recognize this as a catastrophe. No man was more intimately acquainted with the inside history of the revolutionary movement, or so competent to record it. Franklin had deposited with him his notes and papers concerning the American Revolution. He was the only Girondist who survived the French Revolution who was able to tell their secret history. His personal acquaintance included nearly every great or famous man of his time, in England, America, France. From this witness must have come testimonies, facts, anecdotes, not to be derived from other sources, concerning Franklin, Goldsmith, Ferguson, Rittenhouse, Rush, Fulton, Washington, Jefferson, Monroe, the Adamses, Lees, Morrises, Condorcet, Vergennes, Sièyes, Lafayette, Danton, Genêt, Brissot, Robespierre, Marat, Burke, Erskine, and a hundred others. All this, and probably invaluable letters from these men, have been lost through the timidity of a woman before the theological "boycott" on the memory of a theist, and the indifference of this country to its most important materials of History.

When I undertook the biography of Edmund Randolph I found that the great mass of his correspondence had been similarly destroyed by fire in New Orleans, and probably a like fate will befall

the Madison papers, Monroe papers, and others,
our national neglect of which will appear criminal
to posterity.   After searching through six States to
gather documents concerning Randolph which
should all have been in Washington City, the writer
petitioned the Library Committee of Congress to
initiate some action towards the preservation of our
historical manuscripts.   The Committee promptly
and unanimously approved the proposal, a definite
scheme was reported by the Librarian of Congress,
and—there the matter rests.   As the plan does not
include any device for advancing partisan interests,
it stands a fair chance of remaining in our national
oubliette of intellectual *desiderata.*

In writing the " Life of Paine " I have not been
saved much labor by predecessors in the same field.
They have all been rather controversial pamphlet-
eers than biographers, and I have been unable to
accept any of their statements without verification.
They have been useful, however, in pointing out
regions of inquiry, and several of them—Rickman,
Sherwin, Linton—contain valuable citations from
contemporary papers.   The truest delineation of
Paine is the biographical sketch by his friend Rickman.   The " Life " by Vale, and sketches by Richard Carlile, Blanchard, and others, belong to the
controversial *collectanea* in which Paine's posthu-
mous career is traceable.   The hostile accounts of
Paine, chiefly found in tracts and encyclopædias,
are mere repetitions of those written by George
Chalmers and James Cheetham.

The first of these was published in 1791 under
the title : " The Life of Thomas Pain, Author of

'The Rights of Men,' with a Defence of his Writings. By Francis Oldys, A.M., of the University of Pennsylvania. London. Printed for John Stockdale, Pickadilly." This writer, who begins his vivisection of Paine by accusing him of adding "e" to his name, assumed in his own case an imposing pseudonym. George Chalmers never had any connection with the University of Philadelphia, nor any such degree. Sherwin (1819) states that Chalmers admitted having received £500 from Lord Hawksbury, in whose bureau he was a clerk, for writing the book; but though I can find no denial of this I cannot verify it. In his later editions the author claims that his book had checked the influence of Paine, then in England, and his "Rights of Man," which gave the government such alarm that subsidies were paid several journals to counteract their effect. (See the letter of Freching, cited from the Vansitart Papers, British Museum, by W. H. Smith, in the *Century*, August, 1891.) It is noticeable that Oldys, in his first edition, entitles his work a "Defence" of Paine's writings—a trick which no doubt carried this elaborate libel into the hands of many "Paineites." The third edition has, "With a Review of his Writings." In a later edition we find the vignette of Paine surrounded by apes. Cobbett's biographer, Edward Smith, describes the book as "one of the most horrible collections of abuse which even that venal day produced." The work was indeed so overweighted with venom that it was sinking into oblivion when Cobbett reproduced its libels in America, for which he did penance through many years. My reader

will perceive, in the earlier chapters of this work,
that Chalmers tracked Paine in England with enterprise, but there were few facts that he did not
manage to twist into his strand of slander.

In 1809, not long after Paine's death, James
Cheetham's " Life of Thomas Paine " appeared in
New York.   Cheetham had been a hatter in Manchester, England, and would probably have continued in that respectable occupation had it not
been for Paine.   When Paine visited England and
there published " The Rights of Man " Cheetham
became one of his idolaters, took to political writing, and presently emigrated to America.   He
became editor of *The American Citizen*, in New
York.   The cause of Cheetham's enmity to Paine
was the discovery by the latter that he was betraying the Jeffersonian party while his paper was enjoying its official patronage.   His exposure of the
editor was remorseless ; the editor replied with personal vituperation ; and Paine was about instituting
a suit for libel when he died.   Of Cheetham's inge-
nuity in falsehood one or two specimens may be
given.   During Paine's trial in London, for writing
" The Rights of Man," a hostile witness gave testimony which the judge pronounced "impertinent";
Cheetham prints it "important."   He says that
Madame de Bonneville accompanied Paine on his
return from France in 1802 ; she did not arrive
until a year later.   He says that when Paine was
near his end Monroe wrote asking him to acknowledge a debt for money loaned in Paris, and that
Paine made no reply.   But before me is Monroe's
statement, while President, that for his advances to

Paine "no claim was ever presented on my part, nor is any indemnity now desired." Cheetham's book is one of the most malicious ever written, and nothing in it can be trusted.

Having proposed to myself to write a critical and impartial history of the man and his career, I found the vast Paine literature, however interesting as a shadow measuring him who cast it, containing conventionalized effigies of the man as evolved by friend and foe in their long struggle. But that war has ended among educated people. In the laborious work of searching out the real Paine I have found a general appreciation of its importance, and it will be seen in the following pages that generous assistance has been rendered by English clergymen, by official persons in Europe and America, by persons of all beliefs and no beliefs. In no instance have I been impeded by any prejudice, religious or political. The curators of archives, private collectors, owners of important documents bearing on the subject, have welcomed my effort to bring the truth to light. The mass of material thus accumulated is great, and its compression has been a difficult task. But the interest that led me to the subject has increased at every step; the story has abounded in thrilling episodes and dramatic surprises; and I have proceeded with a growing conviction that the simple facts, dispassionately told, would prove of importance far wider than Paine's personality, and find welcome with all students of history. I have brought to my task a love for it, the studies of some years, and results of personal researches made in Europe and America: qualifications which I count

less than another which I venture to claim—the
sense of responsibility, acquired by a public teacher
of long service, for his words, which, be they truths
or errors, take on life, and work their good or evil
to all generations.

THE LIFE OF THOMAS PAINE.

CHAPTER I.

EARLY INFLUENCES.

THE history here undertaken is that of an English mechanic, of Quaker training, caught in political cyclones of the last century, and set at the centre of its revolutions, in the old world and the new.

In the church register of Euston Parish, near Thetford, England, occurs this entry: " 1734. Joseph Pain and Frances Cocke were married June 20th." These were the parents of Thomas Paine. The present rector of Euston Church, Lord Charles Fitz Roy, tells me that the name is there plainly " Pain," but in the Thetford town-records of that time it is officially entered " Joseph Paine."

Paine and Cocke are distinguished names in the history of Norfolk County. In the sixteenth century Newhall Manor, on the road between Thetford and Norwich, belonged to a Paine family. In 1553 Thomas Paine, Gent., was, by license from Queen Mary, trustee for the Lady Elizabeth, daughter of Henry VIII., by Queen Anne Bullen. In St. Thomas Church, Norwich, stands the monument of Sir Joseph Paine, Knt., the most famous mayor

and benefactor of that city in the seventeenth
century. In St. John the Baptist Church is the
memorial of Justice Francis Cocke (d. 1628).
Whether our later Joseph and Thomas were related to these earlier Paines has not been ascertained, but Mr. E. Chester Waters, of London, an
antiquarian especially learned in family histories,
expressed to me his belief that the Norfolk County
Paines are of one stock. There is equal probability
that John Cocke, Deputy Recorder of Thetford in
1629, pretty certainly ancestor of Thomas Paine's
mother, was related to Richard Cock, of Norwich,
author of " English Law, or a Summary Survey of
the Household of God upon Earth " (London,
1651). The author of " The Rights of Man " may
therefore be a confutation of his own dictum : " An
hereditary governor is as inconsistent as an hereditary author." One Thomas Payne, of the Norfolk
County family, was awarded £20 by the Council of
State (1650) " for his sufferings by printing a book
for the cause of Parliament." Among the seques-
trators of royalist church livings was Charles George
Cock, " student of Christian Law, of the Society of
the Inner Temple, now [1651] resident of Norwich."
In Blomefield's " History of Norfolk County " other
notes may be found suggesting that whatever may
have been our author's genealogy he was spiritually
descended from these old radicals.

At Thetford I explored a manuscript—-" Freeman's Register Book " (1610–1756)—and found
that Joseph Paine (our author's father) was made
a freeman of Thetford April 18, 1737, and Henry
Cock May 16, 1740. The freemen of this borough

were then usually members of trade guilds. Their
privileges amounted to little more than the right of
pasturage on the commons. The appointment did
not imply high position, but popularity and influence. Frances Cocke had no doubt resided in
Euston Parish, where she was married. She was
a member of the Church of England and daughter
of an attorney of Thetford. Her husband was a
Quaker and is said to have been disowned by the
Society of Friends for being married by a priest.
A search made for me by official members of that
Society in Norfolk County failed to discover either
the membership or disownment of any one of the
name. Joseph's father, a farmer, was probably a
Quaker. Had the son (b. 1708) been a Quaker by
conversion he would hardly have defied the rules
of the Society at twenty-six.

Joseph was eleven years younger than his wife.
According to Oldys he was " a reputable citizen
and though poor an honest man," but his wife was
" a woman of sour temper and an eccentric character." Thomas Paine's writings contain several
affectionate allusions to his father, but none to his
mother. " They say best men are moulded out of
faults," and the moulding begins before birth.

Thomas Paine was born January 29, 1736–7, at
Thetford. The house was in Bridge Street (now
White Hart) and has recently made way for a
pretty garden and fountain. I was inclined to
adopt a more picturesque tradition that the birth-
place was in old Heathenman Street, as more
appropriate for a *paien* (no doubt the origin of
Paine's name), who also bore the name of the

doubting disciple. An appeal for allowances might be based on such a conjunction of auspices, but a manuscript of Paine's friend Rickman, just found by Dr. Clair J. Grece, identifies the house beyond question.

Thomas Paine is said by most of his biographers to have never been baptized. This rests solely on a statement by Oldys :

" It arose probably from the tenets of the father, and from the eccentricity of the mother, that our author was never baptized, though he was privately named ; and never received, like true Christians, into the bosom of any church, though he was indeed confirmed by the bishop of Norwich : This last circumstance was owing to the orthodox zeal of Mistress Cocke, his aunt, a woman of such goodness, that though she lived on a small annuity, she imparted much of this little to his mother. . . .

" As he was not baptized, the baptism of Thomas Pain is not entered on the parish books of Thetford. It is a remarkable fact, that the leaves of the two registers of the parishes of St. Cuthbert's and St. Peter's, in Thetford, containing the marriages, births, and burials, from the end of 1733, to the beginning of 1737, have been completely cut out. Thus, a felony has been committed against the public, and an injury done to individuals, by a hand very malicious and wholly unknown. Whether our author, when he resided in Thetford in 1787, looked into these registers for his own birth ; what he saw, or what he did, we will not conjecture. They contain the baptism of his sister Elizabeth, on the 28th of August, 1738."

This is Oldysian. Of course, if there was any mischief Paine did it, albeit against his own interests. But a recent examination shows that there has been no mutilation of the registers. St. Peter's and St. Cuthbert's had at the time one minister. In 1736, just before Paine's birth, the minister

(John Price) died, and his successor (Thomas Vaughan) appears to have entered on his duties in March, 1737. A little before and during this interregnum the registers were neglected. In St. Cuthbert's register is the entry: " Elizabeth, Daughter of Joseph Payne and Frances his wife of this parish, was born Aug't the 29th, 1738, baptized September ye 20, 1738." This (which Oldys has got inaccurately, *suo more*) renders it probable that Thomas Paine was also baptized. Indeed, he would hardly have been confirmed otherwise.

The old historian of Norfolk County, Francis Blomefield, introduces us to Thetford (Sitomagus, Tedford, Theford, " People of the Ford ") with a strain of poetry :

> " No situation but may envy thee,
>   Holding such intimacy with the sea,
>   Many do that, but my delighted muse
>   Says, Neptune's fairest daughter is the Little Ouse."

After reading Blomefield's history of the ancient town, and that of Martin, and after strolling through the quaint streets, I thought some poet should add to this praise for picturesqueness some tribute on Thetford's historic vistas. There is indeed " a beauty buried everywhere," as Browning says.

Evelyn, visiting his friend Lord Arlington at Euston in September, 1677, writes :

" I went to Thetford, the Burrough Towne, where stand the ruines of a religious house ; there is a round mountaine artificially raised, either for some castle or monument, which makes a pretty landscape. As we went and return'd, a tumbler shew'd his extraordinary addresse in the Warren. I also saw the Decoy, much pleas'd with the stratagem."

Evelyn leaves his own figure, his princely friends, and the tumbler in the foreground of "a pretty landscape" visible to the antiquarian all around Thetford, whose roads, fully followed, would lead past the great scenes of English history. In general appearance the town (population under five thousand) conveys the pleasant impression of a fairly composite picture of its eras and generations. There is a continuity between the old Grammar School, occupying the site of the ancient cathedral, and the new Guildhall, with its Mechanics' Institute. The old churches summon their flocks from eccentric streets suggestive of literal sheep-paths. Of the ignorance with which our democratic age sweeps away as cobwebs fine threads woven by the past around the present, Thetford showed few signs, but it is sad to find "Guildhall" effacing "Heathenman" Street, which pointed across a thousand years to the march of the "heathen men" (Danes) of Anglo-Saxon chronicles.

"A. 870. This year the [heathen] army rode across Mercia into East Anglia, and took up their winter quarters in Thetford ; and the same winter King Edmund fought against them, and the Danes got the victory, and slew the king, and subdued all the land, and destroyed all the ministers which they came to. The names of their chiefs who slew the king were Hingwar and Habba."

If old Heathenman Street be followed historically, it would lead to Bury St. Edmunds, where, on the spot of his coronation, the young king "was placed in a goodly shrine, richly adorned with jewels and precious stones," and a royal saint added to the calendar. The blood of St. Edmund reconsecrated Thetford.

"A. 1094. Then at Candlemas the king [William Rufus] went to Hastings, and whilst he waited there for a fair wind he caused the monastery on the field of battle to be consecrated; and he took the staff from Herbert Losange, bishop of Thetford."

The letters of this Bishop Herbert, discovered at Brussels, give him an honorable place in the list of Thetford authors; wherein also occur the names of Richard of Thetford, author of a treatise on preaching, Jeffrey de Rocherio, who began a history of the monarchy, and John Brame, writer and translator of various treatises. The works of these Thetford authors are preserved at Cambridge, England.

Thetford was, in a way, connected with the first newspaper enterprise. Its member of Parliament, Sir Joseph Williamson, edited the *London Gazette*, established by the Crown to support its own policy. The Crown claimed the sole right to issue any journal, and its license was necessary for every book. In 1674 Sir Joseph, being Secretary of State (he bought the office for £5,000), had control of the *Gazette* and of literature. In that year, when Milton died, his treatise on "Christian Doctrine" was brought to Williamson for license. He said he could "countenance nothing of Milton's writings," and the treatise was locked up by this first English editor, to be discovered a hundred and forty-nine years later.

On his way to the Grammar School (founded by bequest of Sir Richard Fulmerston, 1566) Paine might daily read an inscription set in the Fulmerston almshouse wall: "Follow peace and holines with all men without the which no man shall see the Lord." But many memorials would remind him of how Williamson, a poor rector's son, had sold his talent to a political lord and reached power to buy and sell Cabinet offices, while suppressing Milton. Thomas Paine, with more talent than Williamson to dispose of, was born in a time semi-barbaric at its best, and savage at its worst. Having got in the Quaker meeting an old head on his young shoulders, he must bear about a burden against most things around him. The old churches were satanic steeple-houses, and if he strolled over to that in which his parents were married, at Euston, its new splendors were accused by surrounding squalor.

Mr. F. H. Millington of Thetford, who has told Williamson's story,[1] has made for me a search into Paine's time there.

"In Paine's boyhood [says Mr. Millington in a letter I have from him] the town (about 2,000 inhabitants) possessed a corporation with mayor, aldermen, sword-bearers, macemen, recorder. The corporation was a corrupt body, under the dominance of the Duke of Grafton, a prominent member of the Whig government. Both members of Parliament (Hon. C. Fitzroy, and Lord Augustus Fitzroy) were nominees of Grafton. The people had no interest and no power, and I do not think politics were of any account in Paine's childhood. From Paine's 'Rights of Man' (Part ii., p. 108) it is clear that his native town was the model in his mind when he wrote on charters and corporations. The Lent Assizes for the Eastern Circuit were held here, and Paine would be familiar with the procedure and pomp of a court of justice. He would also be familiar with the sight of men and women hung for trivial offences. Thetford was on the main road to London, and was a posting centre. Paine

---

[1] " Sir Joseph Williamson, Knt., A.D. 1630-1701. A Page in the History of Thetford." A very valuable contribution to local history.

would be familiar with the faces and equipages of some of the great Whig nobles in Norfolk. Walpole might pass through on his way to Houghton. The river Ouse was navigable to Lynn, and Paine would probably go on a barge to that flourishing seaport. Bury St. Edmunds was a provincial capital for the nobility and gentry of the district. It was twelve miles from Thetford, and in closest connection with it. The religious life of Thetford would be quiet. The churches were poor, having been robbed at the reformation. The Quakers were the only non-conformists in the town. There is a tradition that Wesley visited the town ; if he did Paine would no doubt be among his hearers. On the whole, I think it easy to trace in Paine's works the influence of his boyhood here. He would see the corrupting influence of the aristocracy, the pomp of law, the evils of the unreformed corporations ; the ruins of great ecclesiastical establishments, much more perfect than now, would bring to his mind what a power the church had been. Being of a mechanical turn of mind no doubt he had often played about the paper-mill which was, and is, worked by water-power."

When Paine was a lad the grand gentlemen who purloined parks and mansions from the Treasury were sending children to the gallows for small thefts instigated by hunger. In his thirteenth year he might have seen under the shadow of Ely Minster, ten miles away, the execution of Amy Hutchinson, aged seventeen, for poisoning her husband. "Her face and hands were smeared with tar, and having a garment daubed with pitch, after a short prayer the executioner strangled her, and twenty minutes after the fire was kindled and burnt half an hour." (*Notes and Queries*, 27 September, 1873.) Against the prevailing savagery a human protest was rarely heard outside the Quaker meeting. Whether disowned or not, Paine's father remained a Quaker, and is so registered at burial ;

and his eminent son has repeatedly mentioned his own training in the principles of that Society.   Remembering the extent to which Paine's Quakerism had influenced his political theories, and instances of their bearing on great events, I found something impressive in the little meeting-house in Cage Lane, Thetford.   This was his more important birth-place.   Its small windows and one door open on the tombless graveyard at the back,—perhaps that they might not be smashed by the mob, or admit the ribaldry of the street.   The interior is hardly large enough to seat fifty people.   Plymouth Brethren have for some years occupied the place, but I was told that the congregation, reduced to four or five, would soon cease to gather there. Adjoining the meeting-house, and in contact with it, stands the ancient gaol, from which may have been derived the name " Cage Lane."   In its front are two iron-grated arches, at one of which was the pillory, at the other the stocks,—the latter remembered by some now living.

On "first day," when his schoolmates went in fine clothes to grand churches, to see gay people, and hear fine music, little Thomas, dressed in drab, crept affrighted past the stocks to his childhood's pillory in the dismal meeting-house.   For him no beauty or mirth, no music but the oaths of the pil-loried, or shrieks of those awaiting the gallows. There could be no silent meeting in Cage Lane. Testimonies of the " Spirit " against inhumanity, delivered beside instruments of legal torture, bred pity in the child, who had a poetic temperament. The earliest glimpses we have of his childhood are

in lines written on a fly caught in a spider's web,
and an epitaph for a crow which he buried in the
garden :

> " Here lies the body of John Crow,
>   Who once was high, but now is low ;
>   Ye brother Crows take warning all,
>   For as you rise, so must you fall."

This was when he was eight years of age. It
seems doubtful whether the child was weeping
or smiling, but the humor, if it be such, is grim,
and did not last long. He had even then already,
as we shall see, gained in the Quaker meeting a feeling that " God was too good " to redeem man by his
son's death, as his Aunt Cocke instructed him, and
a heart so precocious was a sad birthright in the
Thetford of that day. We look in vain for anything that can be described as true boyhood in
Paine. Oldys was informed, no doubt rightly,
that " he was deemed a sharp boy, of unsettled
application ; but he left no performances which
denote juvenile vigour or uncommon attainments."
There are, indeed, various indications that, in one
way and another, Thetford and Quakerism together managed to make the early years of their
famous son miserable. Had there been no Quakerism there had been no Thomas Paine ; his consciousness of this finds full recognition in his
works ; yet he says :

" Though I reverence their philanthropy, I cannot help
smiling at the conceit, that if the taste of a Quaker had been
consulted at the creation, what a silent and drab-coloured
creation it would have been ! Not a flower would have
blossomed its gaieties, nor a bird been permitted to sing."

There is a pathos under his smile at this conceit. Paine wrote it in later life, amid the flowers and birds of his garden, which he loved, but whose gaieties he could never imitate. He with difficulty freed himself from his early addiction to an unfashionable garb; he rarely entered a theatre, and could never enjoy cards.

By the light of the foregoing facts we may appreciate the few casual reminiscences of his school-days found in Paine's writings :

"My parents were not able to give me a shilling, beyond what they gave me in education ; and to do this they distressed themselves.

"My father being of the Quaker profession, it was my good fortune to have an exceeding good moral education, and a tolerable stock of useful learning. Though I went to the grammar school (the same school, Thetford in Norfolk, that the present counsellor Mingay went to, and under the same master), I did not learn Latin, not only because I had no inclination to learn languages, but because of the objection the Quakers have against the books in which the language is taught. But this did not prevent me from being acquainted with the subjects of all the Latin books used in the school. The natural bent of my mind was to science. I had some turn, and I believe some talent, for poetry ; but this I rather repressed than encouraged, as leading too much into the field of imagination.

"I happened, when a schoolboy, to pick up a pleasing natural history of Virginia, and my inclination from that day of seeing the western side of the Atlantic never left me."

Paine does not mention his proficiency in mathematics, for which he was always distinguished. To my own mind his "turn" for poetry possesses much significance in the light of his career. In excluding poets from his "Republic" Plato may have had more reasons than he has assigned. The poetic temperament and power, repressed in the purely literary direction, are apt to break out in glowing visions of ideal society and fiery denunciations of the unlovely world.

Paine was not under the master of Thetford School (Colman), who taught Latin, but under the usher, Rev. William Knowler, who admitted the Quaker lad to some intimacy, and related to him his adventures while serving on a man-of-war. Paine's father had a small farm, but he also carried on a stay-making business in Thetford, and his son was removed from school, at the age of thirteen, to be taught the art and mystery of making stays. To that he stuck for nearly five years. But his father became poorer, his mother probably more discontented, and the boy began to dream over the adventures of Master Knowler on a man-of-war.

CHAPTER II.

EARLY STRUGGLES.

In the middle of the eighteenth century England and France were contending for empire in India and in America. For some service the ship *Terrible*, Captain Death, was fitted out, and Thomas Paine made an effort to sail on her. It seems, however, that he was overtaken by his father on board, and carried home again. " From this adventure I was happily prevented by the affectionate and moral remonstrances of a good father, who from the habits of his life, being of the Quaker profession, looked on me as lost." This privateer lost in an engagement one hundred and seventy-five of its two hundred men. Thomas was then in his seventeenth year. The effect of the paternal remonstrances, unsupported by any congenial outlook at Thetford, soon wore off, and, on the formal declaration of war against France (1756), he was again seized with the longing for heroic adventure, and went to sea on the *King of Prussia*, privateer, Captain Mendez. Of that he soon got enough, but he did not return home.

Of Paine's adventures with the privateer there is no record. Of yet more momentous events of his life for some years there is known nothing beyond

the barest outline.   In his twentieth year he found
work in London (with Mr. Morris, stay-maker,
Hanover Street, Longacre), and there remained
near two years.   These were fruitful years.   " As
soon as I was able I purchased a pair of globes, and
attended the philosophical lectures of Martin and
Ferguson, and became afterwards acquainted with
Dr. Bevis, of the society called the Royal Society,
then living in the Temple, and an excellent astron-
omer."

In 1758 Paine found employment at Dover with
a stay-maker named Grace.   In April, 1759, he repaired to Sandwich, Kent, where he established
himself as a master stay-maker.   There is a tradition at Sandwich that he collected a congregation
in his room in the market-place, and preached to
them " as an independent, or a Methodist."   Here,
at twenty-two, he married Mary Lambert.   She
was an orphan and a waiting-woman to Mrs. Richard Solly, wife of a woollen-draper in Sandwich.
The Rev. Horace Gilder, Rector of St. Peter's,
Sandwich, has kindly referred to the register, and
finds the entry : " Thomas Pain, of the parish of
St. Peters, in the town of Sandwich, in Kent, bache-
lor, and Mary Lambert, of the same parish, spins-
ter, were married in this church, by licence, this
27th day of Sept., 1759, by me William Bunce,
Rector."   Signed " Thomas Pain, Mary Lambert.
In the presence of Thomas Taylor, Maria Solly,
John Joslin."

The young couple began housekeeping on Dol-
phin Key, but Paine's business did not thrive, and
he went to Margate.   There, in 1760, his wife died.

Paine then concluded to abandon the stay-making business. His wife's father had once been an exciseman. Paine resolved to prepare himself for that office, and corresponded with his father on the subject. The project found favor, and Paine, after passing some months of study in London, returned to Thetford in July, 1761. Here, while acting as a supernumerary officer of excise, he continued his studies, and enjoyed the friendship of Mr. Cocksedge, the Recorder of Thetford. On 1 December, 1762, he was appointed to guage brewers' casks at Grantham. On 8 August, 1764, he was set to watch smugglers at Alford.

Thus Thomas Paine, in his twenty-fifth year, was engaged in executing Excise Acts, whose application to America prepared the way for independence. Under pressure of two great hungers—for bread, for science—the young exciseman took little interest in politics. " I had no disposition for what is called politics. It 'presented to my mind no other idea than is contained in the word jockeyship." The excise, though a Whig measure, was odious to the people, and smuggling was regarded as not only venial but clever. Within two years after an excise of £1 per gallon was laid on spirits (1746), twelve thousand persons were convicted for offences against the Act, which then became a dead letter. Paine's post at Alford was a dangerous one. The exciseman who pounced on a party of smugglers got a special reward, but he risked his life. The salary was only fifty pounds, the promotions few, and the excise service had fallen into usages of negligence and corruption to which Paine was the first to call public attention. "After tax, charity, and fitting expenses are deducted, there remains very little more than forty-six pounds; and the expenses of housekeeping in many places cannot be brought under fourteen pounds a year, besides the purchase at first, and the hazard of life, which reduces it to thirty-two pounds per annum, or one shilling and ninepence farthing per day."

It is hardly wonderful that Paine with his globes and scientific books should on one occasion have fallen in with the common practice of excisemen called " stamping,"—that is, setting down surveys of work on his books, at home, without always actually travelling to the traders' premises and examining specimens. These detective rounds were generally offensive to the warehouse people so visited, and the scrutiny had become somewhat formal. For this case of " stamping," frankly confessed, Paine was discharged from office, 27 August, 1765.[1]

---

[1] I am indebted to Mr. G. J. Holyoake for documents that shed full light on an incident which Oldys has carefully left in the half-light congenial to his insinuations. The minute of the Board of Excise, dated 27 August, 1765, is as follows :

" Thomas Paine, officer of Alford (Lincolnshire), Grantham collection, having on July 11th stamped the whole ride, as appears by the specimens not being signed in any part thereof, though proper entry was shown in journal, and the victualler's stocks drawn down in his books as if the same had been surveyed that day, as by William Swallow, Supervisor's letter of 3rd instant, and the collector's report thereon, also by the said Paine's own confession of the 13th instant, ordered to be discharged ; that Robert Peat, dropped malt assistant in Lynn collection, succeed him."

The following is Paine's petition for restoration :

" LONDON, July 3, 1766. Honourable Sirs,—In humble obedience to your honours' letter of discharge hearing date August 29, 1765, I delivered up my commission and since that time have given you no trouble. I confess the

After Paine's dismission he supported himself as a journeyman with Mr. Gudgeon, a stay-maker of Diss, Norfolk, where he is said to have frequently quarrelled with his fellow-workmen. To be cast back on the odious work, to be discharged and penniless at twenty-eight, could hardly soothe the poor man's temper, and I suppose he did not remain long at Diss. He is traceable in 1766 in Lincolnshire, by his casual mention of the date in connection with an incident related in his fragment on " Forgetfulness." He was on a visit at the house of a widow lady in a village of the Lincolnshire fens, and as they were walking in the garden, in the summer evening, they beheld at some distance a white figure moving. He quitted Mrs. E. and pursued the figure, and when he at length reached out his hand, " the idea struck me," he says, " will my hand pass through the air, or shall I feel anything?" It proved to be a love-distracted maiden who, on hearing of the marriage of one she supposed her lover, meant to drown herself in a neighboring pond.

justice of your honours' displeasure and humbly beg to add my thanks for the candour and lenity with which you at that unfortunate time indulged me. And though the nature of the report and my own confession cut off all expectations of enjoying your honours' favour then, yet I humbly hope it has not finally excluded me therefrom, upon which hope I humbly presume to entreat your honours to restore me. The time I enjoyed my former commission was short and unfortunate—an officer only a single year. No complaint of the least dishonesty or intemperance ever appeared against me ; and, if I am so happy as to succeed in this, my humble petition, I will endeavour that my future conduct shall as much engage your honours' approbation as my former has merited your displeasure. I am, your honours' most dutiful humble servant, THOMAS PAINE."

Board's minute : " July 4, 1766. Ordered that he be restored on a proper vacancy."

Mr. B. F. Dun, for thirty-three years an officer of excise, discovered the facts connected with Paine's discharge, and also saw Paine's letter and entry books. In a letter before me he says : " I consider Mr. Paine's restoration as creditable to him as to the then Board of Excise."

That Thomas Paine should sue for an office worth, beyond its expenses, thirty-two pounds, argues not merely penury, but an amazing unconsciousness, in his twenty-ninth year, of his powers. In London, for some months there stood between him and starvation only a salary of twenty-five pounds, given him by a Mr. Noble for teaching English in his academy in Goodman's Fields. This was the year 1766, for though Paine was restored to the excise on July 11th of this year no place was found for him. In January, 1767, he was employed by Mr. Gardiner in his school at Kensington. Rickman and others have assigned to this time Paine's attendance of lectures at the Royal Society, which I have however connected with his twentieth year. He certainly could not have afforded globes during this pauperized year 1766. In reply to Rickman's allusion to the lowly situations he had been in at this time, Paine remarked : " Here I derived considerable information ; indeed I have seldom passed five minutes of my life, however circumstanced, in which I did not acquire some knowledge."

According to Oldys he remained in the school at Kensington but three months. " His desire of preaching now returned on him," says the same author, " but applying to his old master for a certificate of his qualifications, to the bishop of London, Mr. Noble told his former usher, that since he was only an English scholar he could not recommend him as a proper candidate for ordination in the church." It would thus appear that Paine had not parted from his employer in Goodman's Fields in any unpleasant way. Of his relation with his pupils only one trace remains—a letter in which he introduces one of them to General Knox, September 17, 1783: "Old friend, I just take the opportunity of sending my respects to you by Mr. Darby, a gentleman who was formerly a pupil of mine in England."

Oldys says that Paine, "without regular orders," preached in Moorfields and elsewhere in England, "as he was urged by his necessities or directed by his spirit." Although Paine's friendly biographers have omitted this preaching episode, it is too creditable to Paine's standing with the teacher with whom he had served a year for Oldys to have invented it. It is droll to think that the Church of England should ever have had an offer of Thomas Paine's services. The Quakerism in which he had been nurtured had never been formally adopted by him, and it offered no opportunities for the impulse to preach which seems to mark a phase in the life of every active English brain.

On May 15, 1767, Paine was appointed excise officer at Grampound, Cornwall, but "prayed leave to wait another vacancy." On February 19, 1768, he was appointed officer at Lewes, Sussex, whither, after a brief visit to Thetford, he repaired.

Not very unlike the old Norfolk borough in which Paine was born was Lewes, and with even literally an Ouse flowing through it. Here also marched the "Heathen Men," who have left only the legend of a wounded son of Harold nursed into health by a Christian maiden. The ruined castle commands a grander landscape than the height of Thetford, and much the same historic views. Seven centuries before Paine opened his office in Lewes came Harold's son, possibly to take charge of the excise as established by Edward the Confessor, just deceased.

" Paine " was an historic name in Lewes also. In 1688 two French refugees, William and Aaron Paine, came to the ancient town, and found there as much religious persecution as in France. It was directed chiefly against the Quakers. But when Thomas Paine went to dwell there the Quakers and the " powers that be " had reached a *modus vivendi*, and the new exciseman fixed his abode with a venerable Friend, Samuel Ollive, a tobacconist. The house then adjoined a Quaker meeting-house, now a Unitarian chapel. It is a quaint house, always known and described as " the house with the monkey on it." The projecting roof is supported by a female nondescript rather more human than anthropoid. I was politely shown through the house by its occupant, Mr. Champion, and observed in the cellar traces of Samuel Ollive's —afterward Paine's—tobacco mill. The best room upstairs long bore on its wall " Tom Paine's study." The plaster has now flaked off, but the proprietor, Mr. Alfred Hammond, told me that he remembers it there in 1840. Not far from the house is the old mansion of the Shelleys,—still called " The Shelleys,"—ancestors of a poet born with the " Rights of Man," and a child of Paine's revolution. And—such are the moral zones and poles in every English town—here in the graveyard of

Jireh Chapel—is the tomb of William Huntington S. S. [Sinner Saved] bearing this epitaph :

" Here lies the Coalheaver, beloved of God, but abhorred of men : the omniscient Judge, at the grand assize, shall ratify and confirm that to the confusion of many thousands ; for England and its metropolis shall know that there hath been a prophet among them.   W. H : S. S."

While Paine was at Lewes this Hunt *alias* Huntington was a pious tramp in that part of England, well known to the police.   Yet in his rubbish there is one realistic story of tramp-life which incidentally portrays an exciseman of the time.   Huntington (born 1744), one of the eleven children of a day-laborer earning from seven to nine shillings a week in Kent, was sent by some friends to an infant school.

" And here I remember to have heard my mistress reprove me for something wrong, telling me that God Almighty took notice of children's sins.   It stuck to my conscience a great while ; and who this God Almighty could be I could not con-jecture ; and how he could know my sins without asking my mother I could not conceive.   At that time there was a person named Godfrey, an exciseman in the town, a man of a stern and hard-favoured countenance, whom I took notice of for having a stick covered with figures, and an ink-bottle hanging at the button-hole of his coat.   I imagined that man to be employed by God Almighty to take notice, and keep an account of children's sins ; and once I got into the market-house, and watched him very narrowly, and found that he was always in a hurry by his walking so fast ; and I thought he had need to hurry, as he must have a deal to do to find out all the sins of children.   I watched him out of one shop into another, all about the town, and from that time eyed him as a most formidable being, and the greatest enemy I had in all the world."

To the shopkeepers this exciseman was really an adversary and an accuser, and one can well believe that his very physiognomy would be affected by such work, and the chronic consciousness of being unwelcome. We may picture Paine among the producers of Lewes—with but four or five thousand people, then a notorious seat of smugglers—with his stick and ink-bottle ; his face prematurely aged, and gathering the lines and the keen look which mask for casual eyes the fundamental candor and kindliness of his face.

Paine's surveys extended to Brighton ; the brilliant city of our time being then a small fishing-town known as Brighthelmston. It was scarce ten miles distant, and had no magistrates, offenders being taken to Lewes. There was a good deal of religious excitement in the neighborhood about the time Paine went there to reside, owing to the preaching of Rev. George Whitefield, chaplain of Lady Huntingdon, at a chapel built by her ladyship at Brighthelmston. Lady Huntingdon already had a quasi-miraculous fame which in Catholic times would have caused her to be honored as St. Selina. In those days a pious countess was more miraculous than the dream that foretold about Lady Huntingdon's coming. Surrounded by crowds, she had to send for her chaplain, Whitefield, who preached in a field till a chapel was built. At the time when Lady Huntingdon was exhorting the poor villagers of Brighton, two relatives of hers, Governor Shirley of Massachusetts and his aide-de-camp Colonel George Washington, were preparing the way for the great events in which Paine was to bear a part.

When Paine went on his survey he might have observed the Washington motto, possibly a trace of the pious countess, which long remained on a house in Brighton: *Exitus acta probat.* There was an ancient Washington who fought at the battle of Lewes; but probably if our exciseman ever thought of any Washington at all it was of the anomalous Colonel in Virginia founding a colonial association to disuse excisable articles imported from England. But if such transatlantic phenomena, or the preaching of Whitefield in the neighborhood, concerned Paine at all, no trace of their impression is now discoverable. And if there were any protest in him at that time, when the English government had reached its nadir of corruption, it cannot be heard. He appears to have been conventionally patriotic, and was regarded as the Lewes laureate. He wrote an election song for the Whig candidate at New Shoreham, for which the said candidate, (Rumbold by name) paid him three guineas; and he wrote a song on the death of General Wolfe, which, when published some years later, was set to music, and enjoyed popularity in the Anacreontic and other societies. While Britannia mourns for her Wolfe, the sire of the gods sends his messengers to console "the disconsolate dame," assuring her that her hero is not dead but summoned to lead "the armies above" against the proud giants marching against Heaven.

The ballad recalls Paine the *païen*, but the Thetford Quaker is not apparent. And, indeed, there are various indications about this time that some reaction had set in after the preaching phase.

"Such was his enterprise on the water," says Oldys, "and his intrepidity on the ice that he became known by the appellation of *Commodore*." William Carver (MS.) says he was at this time "tall and slim, about five feet eight inches."

At Lewes, where the traditions concerning Paine are strong, I met Miss Rickman, a descendant of Thomas "Clio" Rickman—the name Clio, under which his musical contributions to the Revolution were published, having become part of his name. Rickman was a youth in the Lewes of Paine's time, and afterwards his devoted friend. His enthusiasm was represented in children successively named Paine, Washington, Franklin, Rousseau, Petrarch, Volney. Rickman gives an account of Paine at Lewes :

"In this place he lived several years in habits of intimacy with a very respectable, sensible, and convivial set of acquaintance, who were entertained with his witty sallies and informed by his more serious conversations. In politics he was at this time a Whig, and notorious for that quality which has been defined perseverance in a good cause and obstinacy in a bad one. He was tenacious of his opinions, which were bold, acute, and independent, and which he maintained with ardour, elegance, and argument. At this period, at Lewes, the White Hart evening club was the resort of a social and intelligent circle who, out of fun, seeing that disputes often ran very warm and high, frequently had what they called the 'Headstrong Book.' This was no other than an old Greek Homer which was sent the morning after a debate vehemently maintained, to the most obstinate haranguer in the Club : this book had the following title, as implying that Mr. Paine the best deserved and the most frequently obtained it : 'The Headstrong Book, or Original Book of Obstinacy.' Written by ***** ****, of Lewes, in Sussex, and Revised and Corrected by THOMAS PAINE.

> "' Immortal PAINE, while mighty reasoners jar,
>   We crown thee General of the Headstrong War;
>   Thy logic vanquish'd error, and thy mind
>   No bounds but those of right and truth confined.
>   Thy soul of fire must sure ascend the sky,
>   Immortal PAINE, thy fame can never die;
>   For men like thee their names must ever save
>   From the black edicts of the tyrant grave.'

"My friend Mr. Lee, of Lewes, in communicating this to me in September, 1810, said : ' This was manufactured nearly forty years ago, as applicable to Mr. Paine, and I believe you will allow, however indifferent the manner, that I did not very erroneously anticipate his future celebrity.' "

It was probably to amuse the club at the White Hart, an ancient tavern, that Paine wrote his humorous poems.

On the 26 March, 1771, Paine married Elizabeth, daughter of Samuel Ollive, with whom he had lodged. This respected citizen had died in July, 1769, leaving in Lewes a widow and one daughter in poor circumstances. Paine then took up his abode elsewhere, but in the following year he joined the Ollives in opening a shop, and the tobacco-mill went on as before. His motive was probably compassion, but it brought him into nearer acquaintance with the widow and her daughter. Elizabeth is said to have been pretty, and, being of Quaker parentage, she was no doubt fairly educated. She was ten years younger than Paine, and he was her hero. They were married in St. Michael's Church, Lewes, on the 26th of March, 1771, by Robert Austen, curate, the witnesses being Henry Verrall and Thomas Ollive, the lady's brother.

Oldys is constrained to give Paine's ability recognition. " He had risen by superior energy, more than by greater honesty, to be a chief among the excisemen." They needed a spokesman at that time, being united in an appeal to Parliament to raise their salaries, and a sum of money, raised to prosecute the matter, was confided to Paine. In 1772 he prepared the document, which was printed, but not published until 1793.[1] Concerning the plea for the excisemen it need only be said that it is as clear and complete as any lawyer could make it. There was, of course, no room for originality in the simple task of showing that the ill-paid service must be badly done, but the style is remarkable for simplicity and force.

Paine put much time and pains into this composition, and passed the whole winter of 1772-3 trying to influence members of Parliament and others in favor of his cause. "A rebellion of the excisemen," says Oldys, "who seldom have the populace on their side, was not much feared by their superiors." Paine's pamphlet and two further leaflets of his were printed. The best result of his pamphlet was to secure him an acquaintance with Oliver Goldsmith, to whom he addressed the following letter:

---

[1] The document was revived as a pamphlet, though its subject was no longer of interest, at a time when Paine's political writings were under prosecution, and to afford a vehicle for an "introduction," which gives a graphic account of Paine's services in the United States. On a copy of this London edition (1793) before me, one of a number of Paine's early pamphlets bearing marks of his contemporary English editor, is written with pencil: "With a preface (Qy. J. Barlow)." From this, and some characteristics of the composition, I have no doubt that the vigorous introduction was Barlow's. The production is entitled, "The Case of the Officers of Excise; with remarks on the qualifications of Officers; and of the numerous evils arising to the Revenue, from the insufficiency of the present salary. Humbly addressed to the Hon. and Right Hon. Members of both Houses of Parliament."

"HONORED SIR,—Herewith I present you with the Case of the Officers of Excise. A compliment of this kind from an entire stranger may appear somewhat singular, but the following reasons and information will, I presume, sufficiently apologize. I act myself in the humble station of an officer of excise, though somewhat differently circumstanced to what many of them are, and have been the principal promoter of a plan for applying to Parliament this session for an increase of salary. A petition for this purpose has been circulated through every part of the kingdom, and signed by all the officers therein. A subscription of three shillings per officer is raised, amounting to upwards of £500, for supporting the expenses. The excise officers, in all cities and corporate towns, have obtained letters of recommendation from the electors to the members in their behalf, many or most of whom have promised their support. The enclosed case we have presented to most of the members, and shall to all, before the petition appear in the House. The memorial before you met with so much approbation while in manuscript, that I was advised to print 4000 copies; 3000 of which were subscribed for the officers in general, and the remaining 1000 reserved for presents. Since the delivering them I have received so many letters of thanks and approbation for the performance, that were I not rather singularly modest, I should insensibly become a little vain. The literary fame of Dr. Goldsmith has induced me to present one to him, such as it is. It is my first and only attempt, and even now I should not have undertaken it, had I not been particularly applied to by some of my superiors in office. I have some few questions to trouble Dr. Goldsmith with, and should esteem his company for an hour or two, to partake of a bottle of wine, or any thing else, and apologize for this trouble, as a singular favour conferred on

        "His unknown

             "Humble servant and admirer,

                    "THOMAS PAINE.

"Excise Coffee House,

    "Broad Street, Dec. 21, 1772.

    "P. S. Shall take the liberty of waiting on you in a day or two."[1]

---

[1] Goldsmith responded to Paine's desire for his acquaintance. I think Paine may be identified as the friend to whom Goldsmith, shortly before his

To one who reads Paine's argument, it appears wonderful that a man of such ability should, at the age of thirty-five, have had his horizon filled with such a cause as that of the underpaid excisemen. Unable to get the matter before Parliament, he went back to his tobacco-mill in Lewes, and it seemed to him like the crack of doom when, 8 April, 1774, he was dismissed from the excise. The cause of Paine's second dismission from the excise being ascribed by his first biographer (Oldys) to his dealing in smuggled tobacco, without contradiction by Paine, his admirers have been misled into a kind of apology for him on account of the prevalence of the custom. But I have before me the minutes of the Board concerning Paine, and there is no hint whatever of any such accusation.[1] The order of discharge from Lewes is as follows :

"Friday 8th April 1774. Thomas Pain, Officer of Lewes 4th O. Ride Sussex Collection having quitted his Business, without obtaining the Board's Leave for so doing, and being gone off on Account of the Debts which he hath contracted, as by Letter of the 6th instant from Edward Clifford, Supervisor, and the said Pain having been once before Discharged, Ordered that he be again discharged."

In Paine's absence in London, writing his pleas for the excisemen, laboring with members of Parliament, his tobacco-mill had been still, his grocer-

death, gave the epitaph first printed in Paine's *Pennsylvania Magazine,* January, 1775, beginning,

> " Here Whitefoord reclines, and deny it who can,
> Though he merrily lived he is now a *grave* man."

In giving it Goldsmith said, " It will be of no use to me where I am going."

[1] I am indebted for these records to the Secretary of Inland Revenue, England, and to my friend, Charles Macrae, who obtained them for me.

ies unsold, and his wife and her mother had been supported from the bank of flattering hope. No sooner was it known that the hope of an increased salary for the exciseman had failed than he found himself in danger of arrest for debt. It was on this account that he left Lewes for a time, but it was only that he might take steps to make over all of his possessions to his creditors. This was done. The following placard appeared:

" To be sold by auction, on Thursday the 14th of April, and following day, all the household furniture, stock in trade and other effects of Thomas Pain, grocer and tobacconist, near the West Gate, in Lewes: Also a horse tobacco and snuff mill, with all the utensils for cutting tobacco and grinding off snuff ; and two unopened crates of cream-coloured stone ware."

This sale was announced by one Whitfield, grocer, and if there were other creditors they were no doubt paid by the results, for Paine had no difficulty in returning to Lewes. He once more had to petition the Board, which shortly before had commended his assiduity. Its commissioner, George Lewis Scott, labored in his behalf. In vain. Whether it was because it was a rule that a second discharge should be final, or that his failure to move Parliament had made him a scapegoat for the disappointed excisemen, his petition was rejected. At thirty-seven Paine found himself penniless.

CHAPTER III.

DOMESTIC TROUBLE.

THE break-up of Paine's business at Lewes brought to a head a more serious trouble. On June 4th of the same miserable year, 1774, Paine and his wife formally separated.

The causes of their trouble are .enveloped in mystery. It has been stated by both friendly and hostile biographers that there was from the first no cohabitation, and that concerning the responsibility for this neither of them was ever induced to utter a word. Even his friend Rickman was warned off the subject by Paine, who, in reply to a question as to the reason of the separation, said : " It is nobody's business but my own ; I had cause for it, but I will name it to no one."

William Huntington, in his " Kingdom of Heaven," mentions a usage of some Quakers in his time, "that when a young couple are espoused, they are to be kept apart for a season to mourn "; this being their interpretation of Zech. xii., 12–14. As Huntington was mainly acquainted with this Sussex region, it is not inconceivable that Elizabeth Ollive held some such notion, and that this led to dissension ending in separation. Nor is it inconceivable that Paine himself, finding his excise

office no support, and his shop a failure, resolved
that no offspring should suffer his penury or increase it.   It is all mere guesswork.

Mr. Alfred Hammond, of Lewes, who owns the
property, showed me the documents connected with
it.   After the death of Samuel Ollive in 1769,
Esther, his widow, enjoyed the messuage until her
own death, in 1800, when a division among the
heirs became necessary.   Among the documents is
one which recites some particulars of the separation
between Paine and his wife.

"Soon after the Testator's death, his daughter Elizabeth
married Thos. Pain from whom she afterwards lived separate
under articles dated 4th June 1774, and made between the
said Thos. Pain of the first part, the said Elizabeth of the
2nd part, and the Rev. James Castley, Clerk, of the 3d part.
by which Articles, after reciting (inter alia) that Dissentions
had arisen between the said Thos. Pain and Elizabeth his
wife, and that they had agreed to live separate. And also reciting the Will of the said Saml. Ollive and that the said Thomas
Pain had agreed that the said Elizabeth should have and take
her share of the said Monies of the said House when the
same should become due and payable and that he would give
any Discharge that should then be required to and for the
use of the said Elizabeth : The said Thos. Pain did covenant
to permit the said Elizabeth to live separate from him and
to carry on such Trade and Business as she should think fit,
notwithstanding her coverture and as if she were a Feme.
Sole. And that he would not at any time thereafter claim or
demand the said monies which she should be entitled to at the
time of the sale of the said House in Lewes aforesaid, or any
of the Monies Rings Plate Cloathes Linen Woollen Household
Goods or Stock in Trade which the said Elizabeth should
or might at any time thereafter buy or purchase or which
should be devised or given to her or she should otherwise
acquire and that she should and might enjoy and absolutely

dispose of the same as if she were a Feme. Sole and unmarried. And also that it should and might be lawful for the said Elizabeth to have receive and take to her own separate use and benefit her said share of the Monies for which the said Messuage or Tenement in Lewes should be sold when the same should become due and payable."

Another paper is a Release to Francis Mitchener, October 14, 1800, in which it is recited :

" That the said Elizabeth Pain had ever since lived separate from him the said Thos. Pain, and never had any issue, and the said Thomas Pain had many years quitted this kingdom and resided (if living) in parts beyond the seas, but had not since been heard of by the said Elizabeth Pain, nor was it known for certain whether he was living or dead."

This release is signed by Robert Blackman and wife, and eight others, among these being the three children of Samuel Ollive, who under his will were to " share alike "—Samuel, Thomas, and Elizabeth (Mrs. Paine). The large seals attached to the signatures were fortunately well preserved, for each represents the head of Thomas Paine. By the assistance of Mr. Hammond I am able to present this little likeness of Paine that must have been made when he was about thirty-five, or nearly twenty years earlier than any other portrait of him. The reader must form his own conjecture as to the origin of this seal, its preservation by the wife, and use on this document. At this time, and probably since her separation, Elizabeth Paine would appear to have resided with her brother Thomas, a watchmaker in Cranbrook, Kent. That she and the family did not know Paine's whereabouts in 1800, or whether he were dead or alive, argues that they had not followed his career or the course of public events with much interest. One would be glad to believe that Elizabeth cherished kindly remembrance of the man who, considering his forlorn condition, had certainly shown generosity in the justice with which he renounced all of his rights in the property she had brought him, and whose hand she might naturally have suspected behind the monies anonymously sent her. We will therefore hope that it was from some other member of the family that Oldys obtained,—unless, like his " A. M. of the University of Philadelphia," it was invented,—the letter said to have been written by Paine's mother to his wife.[1] The letter may have been manipulated, but it is not improbable that rumors, "exaggerated by enmity or misstated

---

[1] "THETFORD, NORFOLK, 27th July, 1774. Dear Daughter,—I must beg leave to trouble you with my inquiries concerning my unhappy son and your husband : various are the reports, which I find come originally from the Excise-office. Such as his vile treatment to you, his secreting upwards of 30*l.* intrusted with him to manage the petition for advance of salary ; and that since his discharge, he have petitioned to be restored, which was rejected with scorn. Since which I am told he have left England. To all which I beg you'll be kind enough to answer me by due course of post. —You 'll not be a little surprized at my so strongly desiring to know what 's become of him after I repeat to you his undutiful behavior to the tenderest of parents ; he never asked of us anything, but what was granted, that were in our poor abilities to do ; nay, even distressed ourselves, whose works are given over by old age, to let him have 20*l.* on bond, and every other tender mark a parent could possibly shew a child ; his ingratitude, or rather want of duty, has been such, that he have not wrote to me upwards of two years.—If the above account be true, I am heartily sorry, that a woman whose character and amiableness deserves the greatest respect, love, and esteem, as I have always on enquiry been informed yours did, should be tied for life to the worst of husbands. I am, dear daughter, your affectionate mother,

"F. PAIN.

"P. S. For God's sake, let me have your answer, as I am almost distracted."

by malice," as Oldys confesses, elicited some such outburst from Thetford.[1] The excisemen, angry at the failure to get their case before Parliament, and having fixed on Paine as their scapegoat, all other iniquities were naturally laid on him. Eighteen years later, when the scapegoat who had gone into the American wilderness returned with the renown of having helped to make it a nation, he addressed a letter to Lewes, which was about to hold a meeting to respond to a royal proclamation for suppressing seditious writings. His tone is not that of a man who supposed that Lewes had aught against him on the score of his wife.

"It is now upwards of eighteen years since I was a resident inhabitant of the town of Lewes. My situation among you as an officer of the revenue, for more than six years, enabled me to see into the numerous and various distresses which the weight of taxes even at that time of day occasioned ; and feeling, as I then did, and as it is natural for me to do, for the hard condition of others, it is with pleasure I can declare, and every person then under my survey, and now living, can witness the exceeding candor, and even tenderness, with which that part of the duty that fell to my share was executed. The name of Thomas Paine is not to be found in the records of the Lewes justices, in any one act of contention with, or severity of any kind whatever towards, the persons whom he surveyed, either in the town or in the country; of this Mr. Fuller and Mr. Shelley, who will probably attend the meeting, can, if they please, give full testimony. It is, however, not in their power to contradict it. Having thus indulged myself in recollecting a place where I formerly had, and even now have, many friends, rich and poor, and most probably some enemies,

[1] When Paine had the money he did forward twenty pounds to his parents, and made provision for his mother when she was a widow. As to writing to her, in those unhappy years, he probably thought it better to keep his burdens to himself. He may also have been aware of his mother's severity without knowing her interest in him.

I proceed to the import of my letter. Since my departure from Lewes, fortune or providence has thrown me into a line of action which my first setting out in life could not possibly have suggested to me. Many of you will recollect that, whilst I resided among you, there was not a man more firm and open in supporting the principles of liberty than myself, and I still pursue, and ever will, the same path."

Finally, it should be added that Rickman, a truthful man, who admits Paine's faults, says : "This I can assert, that Mr. Paine always spoke tenderly and respectfully of his wife ; and sent her several times pecuniary aid, without her knowing even whence it came."

While Paine was in London, trying to get before Parliament a measure for the relief of excisemen, he not only enjoyed the friendship of Goldsmith, but that of Franklin. In the Doctor's electrical experiments he took a deep interest ; for Paine was devoted to science, and the extent of his studies is attested by his description of a new electrical machine and other scientific papers, signed " Atlanticus," in the *Pennsylvania Magazine.* The sale of his effects in Lewes paid his debts, but left him almost penniless. He came to London, and how he lived is unknown—that is, physically, for we do find some intimation of his mental condition. In a letter written many years after to John King, a political renegade, Paine says :

"When I first knew you in Ailiffe-street, an obscure part of the City, a child, without fortune or friends, I noticed you ; because I thought I saw in you, young as you was, a bluntness of temper, a boldness of opinion, and an originality of thought, that portended some future good. I was pleased to discuss, with you, under our friend *Oliver's* lime-tree, those political notions, which I have since given the world in my ' Rights of Man.' You used to complain of abuses, as well as me, and write your opinions on them in free terms—What then means this sudden attachment to *Kings ?* "

This " Oliver " was probably the famous Alderman Oliver who was imprisoned in the Tower during the great struggle of the City with the Government, on account of Wilkes. Paine tells us that in early life he cared little for politics, which seemed to him a species of " jockeyship " ; and how apt the term is shown by the betting-book kept at Brooks' Club, in which are recorded the bets of the noblemen and politicians of the time on the outcome of every motion and course of every public man or minister. But the contemptuous word proves that Paine was deeply interested in the issues which the people had joined with the king and his servile ministers. He could never have failed to read with excitement the letters of Junius, whose " brilliant pen," he afterwards wrote, " enraptured without convincing ; and though in the plenitude of its rage it might be said to give elegance to bitterness, yet the policy survived the blast." We may feel sure that he had heard with joy that adroit verdict of the jury at the King's Bench on Woodfall, Junius' printer, which secured liberty of the press until, twenty-two years later, it was reversed by revolutionary panic, in the same court, for Paine himself. Notwithstanding the private immorality of Wilkes, in which his associates were aristocratic, the most honorable political elements in England, and the Independents and Presbyterians, were resolute in defending the rights of his constituents against the authority arrogated by the Commons to exclude him. Burke then stood by Wilkes, as John Bright stood by Bradlaugh at a later day. And while Paine was laboring to carry his excise bill through Parliament he had good opportunity to discover how completely that body's real opinions were overruled by royal dictation. It was at that time that George III., indifferent to his brother's profligacies, would not forgive his marriage with a commoner's sister, and forced on Parliament a Marriage Act which made all marriages in the royal family illegitimate without his consent. The indignant resignation of Fox modified the measure slightly, limiting the King's interference at the twenty-sixth year of the marrying parties, and then giving the veto to Parliament. For this the King turned his wrath on Fox. This was but one of the many instances of those years—all told in Trevelyan's admirable work[1]—which added to Paine's studies of the Wilkes conflicts a lasting lesson in the conservation of despotic forces. The barbaric eras of prerogative had returned under the forms of ministerial government. The Ministry, controlled by the Court, ruled by corruption of commoners.

It was a *régime* almost incredible to us now, when England is of all nations most free from corruption and court influence in politics ; and it was little realized in English colonies before the Revolution. But Franklin was in London to witness it, and Paine was there to grow familiar with the facts. To both of them the systematic in-

---

[1] " The Early History of Charles James Fox," 1880.

humanity and injustice were brought home personally. The discharged and insulted postmaster could sympathize with the dismissed and starving exciseman. Franklin recognized Paine's ability, and believed he would be useful and successful in America. So on this migration Paine decided, and possibly the determination brought his domestic discords to a crisis.

CHAPTER IV.

PAINE left England in October and arrived in America November 30, 1774. He bore a letter of introduction from Dr. Franklin to Richard Bache, his son-in-law, dated September 30, 1774:

"The bearer Mr. Thomas Paine is very well recommended to me as an ingenious worthy young man. He goes to Pennsylvania with a view of settling there. I request you to give him your best advice and countenance, as he is quite a stranger there. If you can put him in a way of obtaining employment as a clerk, or assistant tutor in a school, or assistant surveyor, of all of which I think him very capable, so that he may procure a subsistence at least, till he can make acquaintance and obtain a knowledge of the country, you will do well, and much oblige your affectionate father."

On March 4, 1775, Paine writes Franklin from Philadelphia:

"Your countenancing me has obtained for me many friends and much reputation, for which please accept my sincere thanks. I have been applied to by several gentlemen to instruct their sons on very advantageous terms to myself, and a printer and bookseller here, a man of reputation and property, Robert Aitkin, has lately attempted a magazine, but having little or no turn that way himself, he has applied to me for assistance. He had not above six hundred subscribers when I first assisted him. We have now upwards of fifteen hundred, and daily increasing. I have not entered into terms with him This is only the second number. The first I was not concerned in."

It has been often stated that Paine was befriended by Dr. Rush, but there is no indication of this. Their acquaintance was casual.

" About the year 1773 [says Dr. Rush—the date is an error for 1774] I met him accidentally in Mr. Aitkin's bookstore, and was introduced to him by Mr. Aitkin. We conversed a few minutes, and I left him. Soon afterwards I read a short essay with which I was much pleased, in one of Bradford's papers, against the slavery of the Africans in our country, and which I was informed was written by Mr. Paine. This excited my desire to be better acquainted with him. We met soon afterwards in Mr. Aitkin's bookstore, where I did homage to his principles and pen upon the subject of the enslaved Africans. He told me the essay to which I alluded was the first thing he had ever published in his life. After this Mr. Aitkin employed him as the editor of his Magazine, with a salary of fifty pounds currency a year. This work was well supported by him. His song upon the death of Gen. Wolfe, and his reflections upon the death of Lord Clive, gave it a sudden currency which few works of the kind have since had in our country."

As the anti-slavery essay was printed March 8, 1775, it appears that Paine had been in America more than three months before Rush noticed him.

The first number of the *Pennsylvania Magazine,* or *American Museum,* appeared at the end of January, 1775. Though " not concerned " in it pecuniarily, not yet being editor, his contributions increased the subscription list, and he was at once engaged. For eighteen months Paine edited this magazine, and probably there never was an equal amount of good literary work done on a salary of fifty pounds a year. It was a handsome magazine, with neat vignette—book, plough, anchor, and olive-twined shield,—the motto, *Juvat in sylvis habitare.* The future author of the "Rights of Man" and "Age of Reason" admonishes correspondents that religion and politics are forbidden topics! The first number contains a portrait of Goldsmith and the picture of a new electrical machine. A prefatory note remarks that "the present perplexities of affairs" have "encompassed with difficulties the first number of the magazine, which, like the early snowdrop, comes forth in a barren season, and contents itself with modestly foretelling that choicer flowers are preparing to appear." The opening essay shows a fine literary touch, and occasionally a strangely modern vein of thought. "Our fancies would be highly diverted could we look back and behold a circle of original Indians haranguing on the sublime perfections of the age; yet 't is not impossible but future times may exceed us as much as we have exceeded them."

Here is a forerunner of Macaulay's New Zealander sketching the ruins of St. Paul's. It is followed by a prediction that the coming American magazine will surpass the English, "because we are not exceeded in abilities, have a more extended field for inquiry, and whatever may be our political state, our happiness will always depend upon ourselves." A feature of the magazine was the description, with plates, of recent English inventions not known in the new world—threshing-machine, spinning-machine, etc.,—such papers being by Paine. These attracted the members of the Philosophical Society, founded by Franklin, and Paine was welcomed into their circle by Rittenhouse, Clymer, Rush, Muhlenberg, and other representatives of the scientific and literary metropolis. Many a piece composed for the Headstrong Club at Lewes first saw the light in this magazine,—such as the humorous poems, " The Monk and the Jew," " The Farmer and Short's Dog, Porter " ; also the famous ballad " On the Death of General Wolfe," printed March, 1775, with music. Lewes had not, indeed, lost sight of him, as is shown by a communication in April from Dr. Matthew Wilson, dated from that town, relating to a new kind of fever raging in England.

The reader who has studied Paine's avowed and well-known works finds no difficulty in tracking him beneath the various signatures by which he avoided an appearance of writing most of the articles in the *Pennsylvania Magazine*, though he really did. He is now " Atlanticus," now " Vox Populi," or " Æsop," and oftener affixes no signature. The Thetford Quaker is still here in " Reflections on the Death of Lord Clive " (reprinted as a pamphlet in England), " A New Anecdote of Alexander the Great," and " Cursory Reflections on the Single Combat or Modern Duel." The duel was hardly yet challenged in America when Paine wrote (May, 1775)

" From the peculiar prevalence of this custom in countries where the religious system is established which, of all others, most expressly prohibits the gratification of revenge, with every species of outrage and violence, we too plainly see how little mankind are in reality influenced by the precepts of the religion by which they profess to be guided, and in defence of which they will occasionally risk even their lives."

But with this voice from Thetford meeting-house mingles the testimony of "common sense." In July, 1775, he writes :

" I am thus far a Quaker, that I would gladly agree with all the world to lay aside the use of arms, and settle matters by negotiations ; but, unless the whole world wills, the matter ends, and I take up my musket, and thank heaven he has put it in my power. . . . We live not in a world of angels. The reign of Satan is not ended, neither can we expect to be defended by miracles."

Titles he sees through (May, 1775) :

" The Honourable plunderer of his country, or the Right Honourable murderer of mankind, create such a contrast of ideas as exhibit a monster rather than a man. The lustre of the Star, and the title of My Lord, overawe the superstitious vulgar, and forbid them to enquire into the character of the possessor : Nay more, they are, as it were, bewitched to admire in the great the vices they would honestly condemn in themselves. . . . The reasonable freeman sees through the magic of a title, and examines the man before he approves him. To him the honours of the worthless seem to write their masters' vices in capitals, and their Stars shine to no other end than to read them by. Modesty forbids men separately, or collectively, to assume titles. But as all honours, even that of kings, originated from the public, the public may justly be called the true fountain of honour. And it is with much pleasure I have heard the title ' Honourable ' applied to a body of men, who nobly disregarding private case and interest for public welfare, have justly merited the address of *The Honourable Continental Congress.*"

He publishes (May, 1775), and I think wrote, a poetical protest against cruelty to animals, to whose rights Christendom was then not awakened. His pen is unmistakable in "Reflections on Unhappy Marriages" (June, 1775) : "As extasy abates coolness succeeds, which often makes way for indifference, and that for neglect. Sure of each other by the nuptial bond, they no longer take any pains to be mutually agreeable. Careless if they displease, and yet angry if reproached ; with so little relish for each other's company that anybody else's is more welcome, and more entertaining." It is a more pointed statement of the problem already suggested, in the April magazine, by his well-known fable "Cupid and Hymen," whose controversies are now settled in the Divorce Court.

In his August (1775) number is found the earliest American plea for woman. It is entitled "An Occasional Letter on the Female Sex," and unsigned, but certainly by Paine. His trick of introducing a supposititious address from another person, as in the following extract, appears in many examples.

"Affronted in one country by polygamy, which gives them their rivals for inseparable companions ; inslaved in another by indissoluble ties, which often join the gentle to the rude, and sensibility to brutality : Even in countries where they may be esteemed most happy, constrained in their desires in the disposal of their goods, robbed of freedom of will by the laws, the slaves of opinion, which rules them with absolute sway, and construes the slightest appearances into guilt, surrounded on all sides by judges who are at once their tyrants and seducers, and who after having prepared their faults, punish every lapse with dishonour—nay usurp the right of degrading them on suspicion !—who does not feel for the tender sex ? Yet such I am sorry to say is the lot of woman over the whole earth. Man with regard to them, in all climates and in

all ages, has been either an insensible husband or an oppressor ;
but they have sometimes experienced the cold and deliberate
oppression of pride, and sometimes the violent and terrible
tyranny of jealousy. When they are not beloved they are
nothing ; and when they are they are tormented. They have
almost equal cause to be afraid of indifference and love. Over
three quarters of the globe Nature has placed them between
contempt and misery."

"Even among people where beauty receives the highest
homage we find men who would deprive the sex of every kind
of reputation. 'The most virtuous woman,' says a celebrated
Greek, 'is she who is least talked of.' That morose man,
while he imposes duties on women, would deprive them of the
sweets of public esteem, and in exacting virtues from them
would make it a crime to aspire to honour. If a woman were
to defend the cause of her sex she might address him in the
following manner :

"'How great is your injustice ! If we have an equal right
with you to virtue, why should we not have an equal right to
praise ? The public esteem ought to wait upon merit. Our
duties are different from yours, but they are not less difficult
to fulfil, or of less consequence to society : They are the
foundations of your felicity, and the sweetness of life. We are
wives and mothers. 'T is we who form the union and the
cordiality of families ; 't is we who soften that savage rudeness
which considers everything as due to force, and which would
involve man with man in eternal war. We cultivate in you
that humanity which makes you feel for the misfortunes of
others, and our tears forewarn you of your own danger. Nay,
you cannot be ignorant that we have need of courage not less
than you : More feeble in ourselves, we have perhaps more
trials to encounter. Nature assails us with sorrow, law and
custom press us with constraint, and sensibility and virtue
alarm us by their continual conflict. Sometimes also the name
of citizen demands from us the tribute of fortitude. When
you offer your blood to the state, think that it is ours. In
giving it our sons and our husbands we give it more than ourselves. You can only die on the field of battle, but we have
the misfortune to survive those whom we love the most. Alas !

while your ambitious vanity is unceasingly laboring to cover
the earth with statues, with monuments, and with inscriptions
to eternize, if possible, your names, and give yourselves an
existence when this body is no more, why must we be condemned to live and to die unknown ? Would that the grave
and eternal forgetfulness should be our lot. Be not our tyrants
in all : Permit our names to be sometime pronounced beyond
the narrow circle in which we live : Permit friendship, or at
least love, to inscribe its emblems on the tomb where our
ashes repose ; and deny us not the public esteem which, after
the esteem of one's self, is the sweetest reward of well-
doing.' "

Thus the *Pennsylvania Magazine*, in the time
that Paine edited it, was a seed-bag from which
this sower scattered the seeds of great reforms
ripening with the progress of civilization. Through
the more popular press he sowed also. Events
selected his seeds of American independence, of
republican equality, freedom from royal, ecclesiastical, and hereditary privilege, for a swifter and
more imposing harvest; but the whole circle of
human ideas and principles was recognized by this
lone wayfaring man. The first to urge extension
of the principles of independence to the enslaved
negro ; the first to arraign monarchy, and to point
out the danger of its survival in presidency ; the
first to propose articles of a more thorough nationality to the new-born States ; the first to advocate
international arbitration ; the first to expose the
absurdity and criminality of duelling ; the first to
suggest more rational ideas of marriage and divorce ; the first to advocate national and international copyright ; the first to plead for the
animals ; the first to demand justice for woman :

what brilliants would our modern reformers have
contributed to a coronet for that man's brow, had
he not presently worshipped the God of his fathers
after the way that theologians called heresy!
" Be not righteous overmuch," saith cynical Solomon ; " neither make thyself over-wise : why
shouldest thou destroy thyself ? "

CHAPTER V.

LIBERTY AND EQUALITY.

WITH regard to Paine's earliest publication there has been needless confusion. In his third *Crisis* he says to Lord Howe: "I have likewise an aversion to monarchy, as being too debasing to the dignity of man; but I never troubled others with my notions till very lately, nor ever published a syllable in England in my life." It has been alleged that this is inconsistent with his having written in 1772 "The Case of the Officers of Excise." But this, though printed (by William Lee of Lewes) was not published until 1793. It was a document submitted to Parliament, but never sold. The song on Wolfe, and other poetical pieces, though known to the Headstrong Club in Lewes, were first printed in Philadelphia.[1]

[1] Mr. W. H. Burr maintains that Paine wrote in the English *Crisis* (1775) under the name of "Casca." As Casca's articles bear intrinsic evidence of being written in London—such as his treating as facts General Gage's fictions about Lexington—the theory supposes Paine to have visited England in that year. But besides the facts that Rush had an interview with Paine near the middle of March, and Franklin in October, the accounts of Aitkin, preserved in Philadelphia, show payments to Paine in May, July, and August, 1775. As Mr. Burr's further theory, that Paine wrote the letters of Junius, rests largely on the identification with "Casca," it might be left to fall with disproof of the latter. It is but fair, however, to the labors of a courageous writer, and to the many worthy people who have adopted his views, to point out the impossibilities of their case. An able

In America Wolfe again rises before Paine's imagination. In the *Pennsylvania Journal*, January 4th, appears a brief " Dialogue between General Wolfe and General Gage in a Wood near Boston." Wolfe, from the Elysian Fields, approaches Gage with rebuke for the errand on which he has come to America, and reminds him that he is a citizen as well as a soldier. " If you have any regard for the glory of the British name, and if you prefer the society of Grecian, Roman, and British heroes in the world of spirits to the company of Jeffries, Kirk, and other royal executioners, I conjure you immediately to resign your commission."

Although this " Dialogue " was the first writing

summary of the facts discoverable concerning the personality of Junius, in Macaulay's " Warren Hastings," says : "As to the position, pursuits, and connexions of Junius, the following are the most important facts which can be considered as clearly proved : first, that he was acquainted with the technical forms of the Secretary of State's office ; secondly, that he was intimately acquainted with the business of the War Office ; thirdly, that he, during the year 1770, attended debates in the House of Lords, and took notes of speeches, particularly of the speeches of Lord Chatham ; fourthly, that he bitterly resented the appointment of Mr. Chamier to the place of Deputy Secretary of War ; fifthly, that he was bound by some strong tie to the first Lord Holland."

Now during the period of Junius' letters (Jan. 21, 1769, to Jan. 21, 1772) Paine was occupied with his laborious duties as exciseman at Lewes, and with the tobacco mill from which he vainly tried to extort a living for himself and wife, and her mother. Before that period there was no time at which Paine could have commanded the leisure or opportunities necessary to master the political and official details known to Junius, even had he been interested in them. He declares that he had no interest in politics, which he regarded as a species of " jockeyship." How any one can read a page of Junius and then one of Paine, and suppose them from the same pen appears to me inconceivable. Junius is wrapped up in the affairs of Lord This and Duke That, and a hundred details. I can as easily imagine Paine agitated with the movements of a battle of chessmen. But apart from this, the reader need only refer to the facts of his life before coming to America to acquit him of untruth in saying that he had published nothing in England, and that the cause of America made him an author.

of Paine published, it was not the first written for publication. The cause that first moved his heart and pen was that of the negro slave. Dr. Rush's date of his meeting with Paine, 1773,—a year before his arrival,—is one of a number of errors in his letter, among these being his report that Paine told him the antislavery essay was the first thing he had ever published. Paine no doubt told him it was the first thing he ever wrote and offered for publication; but it was not published until March 8th. Misled by Rush's words, Paine's editors and our historians of the antislavery movement have failed to discover this early manifesto of abolitionism. It is a most remarkable article. Every argument and appeal, moral, religious, military, economic, familiar in our subsequent antislavery struggle, is here found stated with eloquence and clearness. Having pointed out the horrors of the slave trade and of slavery, he combats the argument that the practice was permitted to the Jews. Were such a plea allowed it would justify adoption of other Jewish practices utterly unlawful "under clearer light." The Jews indeed had no permission to enslave those who never injured them, but all such arguments are unsuitable "since the time of reformation came under Gospel light. All distinctions of nations, and privileges of one above others, are ceased. Christians are taught to account all men their neighbours, and love their neighbours as themselves; and do to all men as they would be done by; to do good to all men; and man-stealing is ranked with enormous crimes." Bradford might naturally hesitate some weeks before printing these pointed reproofs. "How just, how suitable to our crime is the punishment with which Providence threatens us? We have enslaved multitudes, and shed much innocent blood, and now are threatened with the same." In the conclusion, a practical scheme is proposed for liberating all except the infirm who need protection, and settling them on frontier lands, where they would be friendly protectors instead of internal foes ready to help any invader who may offer them freedom.

This wonderful article is signed "Justice and Humanity." Thomas Paine's venture in this direction was naturally welcomed by Dr. Rush, who some years before had written a little pamphlet against the slave trade, and deploring slavery, though he had not proposed or devised any plan for immediate emancipation. Paine's paper is as thorough as Garrison himself could have made it. And, indeed, it is remarkable that Garrison, at a time when he shared the common prejudices against Paine, printed at the head of his *Liberator* a motto closely resembling Paine's. The motto of Paine was: "The world is my country, my religion is to do good"; that of the *Liberator* : "Our country is the world, our countrymen are all mankind." Garrison did characteristic justice to Paine when he had outgrown early prejudices against him.[1] On April 12th, thirty-five days after Paine's plea for emancipation, the first American Antislavery Society was formed, in Philadelphia.

[1] It will be seen by the "Life of William Lloyd Garrison," i., p. 219, and iii., p. 145, that Mr. Garrison did not know of Paine's motto ("Rights of Man," i., chap. v.). His review of Paine's works appeared November 21, 1845. The *Liberator* first appeared January 1, 1831.

Although the dialogue between Wolfe and Gage (January 4th) shows that Paine shared the feeling of America, the earlier numbers of his *Pennsylvania Magazine* prove his strong hope for reconciliation. That hope died in the first collision ; after Lexington he knew well that separation was inevitable. A single sentence in the magazine intimates the change. The April number, which appeared soon after the " Lexington massacre," contains a summary of Chatham's speech, in which he said the crown would lose its lustre if " robbed of so principal a jewel as America." Paine adds this footnote : " The principal jewel of the crown actually dropt out at the coronation." There was probably no earlier printed suggestion of independence by any American.[1]

There are three stages in the evolution of the Declaration of Independence. The colonies reached first the resolution of resistance, secondly of separation, and thirdly of republicanism.

In the matter of resistance the distribution of honors has been rather literary than historical. In considering the beginnings of the Revolution our minds fly at once to the Tea-party in Boston harbor, then to Lexington, where seven Massachusetts men fell dead, and seven years of war followed. But two years before the tea was thrown overboard,

---

[1] The *London Chronicle*, of October 25, 1774, printed Major Cartwright's "American Independence the Interest and Glory of Great Britain," and it was reprinted in the *Pennsylvania Journal.* Although it has little relation to the form in which the question presently suggested itself, the article is interesting as an indication that separation was then more talked of in England than in America. Twelve years before the Revolution a pamphlet in favor of separation was written by Josiah Tucker of Bristol, England. Then as now colonists were more loyal than the English at home.

and four years before the Lexington massacre, North Carolinians had encountered British troops, had left two hundred patriots fallen, and seen their leaders hanged for treason. Those earliest martyrs are almost forgotten because, in the first place, North Carolina produced no historians, poets, magazines, to rehearse their story from generation to generation. In the second place, the rebellion which Governor Tryon crushed at Alamance, though against the same oppressions, occurred in 1771, before the colonies had made common cause.

Governmental anachronisms have a tendency to take refuge in colonies. Had Great Britain conceded to Americans the constitutional rights of Englishmen there could have been no revolution. Before the time of George III. British governors had repeatedly revived in America prerogatives extinct in England, but the colonists had generally been successful in their appeals to the home government. Even in 1774 the old statesmen in America had not realized that a king had come who meant to begin in America his mad scheme of governing as well as reigning. When, in September, 1774, the first Continental Congress assembled, its members generally expected to settle the troubles with the " mother country " by petitions to Parliament. There is poetic irony in the fact that the first armed resistance to royal authority in America was by the North Carolina " Regulators." On the frontiers, before official courts were established, some kind of law and order had to be maintained, and they were protected by a volunteer police called " Regulators." In

the forests of Virginia, two hundred years ago, Peter
Lynch was appointed judge by his neighbors because of his wisdom and justice, and his decisions
were enforced by " Regulators." Judge Lynch's
honorable name is now degraded into a precedent
for the cowardly ruffians who hunt down unarmed
negroes, Italians, and Chinamen, and murder them
without trial, or after their acquittal. But such was
not the case with our frontier courts and " Regulators," which were civilized organizations, though
unauthorized. For several years before the Revolution lawful and civilized government in some of
the colonies depended on unauthorized administrations. The authorized powers were the " lynchers," as they would now be called, with traditional
misrepresentation of Peter Lynch. The North
Carolina Regulators of 1771 were defending the
English constitution against a king and a governor
acting as lawlessly as our vile lynchers and " White
Caps." It was remarked, by Paine among others
that after the royal authority was abolished, though
for a long time new governments were not established, " order and harmony were preserved as
inviolate as in any country in Europe." [1]

In the dialogue between Wolfe and Gage, Paine
writes as an Englishman ; he lays no hand on the
constitution, nor considers the sovereign involved
in ministerial iniquities. Apart from his Quaker
sentiments he felt dismay at a conflict which interrupted his lucrative school, and the literary opportunities afforded by his magazine. " For my own
part," he wrote to Franklin, " I thought it very

[1] " The Rights of Man," part ii., chapter i.

hard to have the country set on fire about my ears
almost the moment I got into it." And indeed
there was a general disgust among the patriots
during the year 1775, while as yet no great aim or
idea illumined the smoke of battle. They were
vehemently protesting that they had no wish for
separation from England, just as in the beginning
of our civil war leading Unionists declared that
they would not interfere with slavery. In March,
1775, Franklin maintained the assurance he had
given Lord Chatham in the previous year, that he
had never heard in America an expression in favor
of independence, "from any person drunk or sober."
Paine says that on his arrival he found an obstinate
attachment to Britain; "it was at that time a kind
of treason to speak against it." " Independence
was a doctrine scarce and rare even towards the
conclusion of the year 1775." In May, George
Washington, on his way to Congress, met the Rev.
Jonathan Boucher, in the middle of the Potomac;
while their boats paused, the clergyman warned his
friend that the path on which he was entering might
lead to separation from England. " If you ever
hear of my joining in any such measures," said
Washington, "you have my leave to set me down
for everything wicked."[1] Although Paine, as we
shall see, had no reverence for the crown, and
already foresaw American independence, he abhorred the method of war. In the first number of
his magazine he writes : " The speeches of the different governors pathetically lament the present

<hr>

[1] *Notes and Queries* (Eng.), series 3 and 5. See also in *Lippincott's Magazine*, May, 1889, my paper embodying the correspondence of Washington
and Boucher.

distracted state of affairs. Yet they breathe a spirit of mildness as well as tenderness, and give encouragement to hope that some happy method of accommodation may yet arise."

But on April 19th came the "massacre at Lexington," as it was commonly called. How great a matter is kindled by a small fire! A man whose name remains unknown, forgetful of Captain Parker's order to his minute-men not to fire until fired on, drew his trigger on the English force advancing to Concord ; the gun missed fire, but the little flash was answered by a volley; seven men lay dead. In the blood of those patriots at Lexington the Declaration of Independence was really written. From town-meetings throughout the country burning resolutions were hurled on General Gage in Boston, who had warned Major Pitcairn, commander of the expedition, not to assume the offensive. From one county, Mecklenburg, North Carolina, were sent to Congress twenty resolutions passed by its committee, May 31st, declaring "all laws and commissions confirmed by or derived from the authority of the King and Parliament are anulled and vacated," and that, "whatever person shall hereafter receive a commission from the crown, or attempt to exercise any such commission heretofore received, shall be deemed an enemy to his country." [1]

[1] These resolutions further organized a provisional government to be in force until "the legislative body of Great Britain resign its unjust and arbitrary pretensions with respect to America." In 1819 a number of witnesses stated that so early as May 20th Mecklenburg passed an absolute Declaration of Independence, and it is possible that, on receipt of the tidings from Lexington, some popular meeting at Charlottetown gave vent to its indignation in expressions, or even resolutions, which were tempered by

Many years after the independence of America had been achieved, William Cobbett, on his return to England after a long sojourn in the United States, wrote as follows :

"As my Lord Grenville introduced the name of Burke, suffer me, my Lord, to introduce that of a man who put this Burke to shame, who drove him off the public stage to seek shelter in the pension list, and who is now named fifty million times where the name of the pensioned Burke is mentioned once. The cause of the American colonies was the cause of the English Constitution, which says that no man shall be taxed without his own consent. . . . A little thing sometimes produces a great effect ; an insult offered to a man of great talent and unconquerable perseverance has in many instances produced, in the long run, most tremendous effects ; and it appears to me very clear that some beastly insults, offered to Mr. Paine while he was in the Excise in England, was the real cause of the Revolution in America ; for, though the nature of the cause of America was such as I have before described it ; though the principles were firm in the minds of the people of that country ; still, it was Mr. Paine, and Mr. Paine alone, who brought those principles into action."

In this passage Cobbett was more epigrammatic than exact. Paine, though not fairly treated, as we have seen, in his final dismissal from the excise, was not insulted. But there is more truth in what Cobbett suggests as to Paine's part than he fully realized. Paine's unique service in the work of independence may now be more clearly defined. It

the County Committee eleven days later. The resolutions embodying the supposititious "Declaration," written out (1800) from memory by the alleged secretary of the meeting (Dr. Joseph McKnitt Alexander), are believed by Dr. Welling to be "an honest effort to reproduce, according to the best of his recollection, the facts and declarations contained in the genuine manuscripts of May 31, after that manifesto had been forgotten."— (*North American Review*, April, 1874.) But the testimony is very strong in favor of two sets of resolutions.

was that he raised the Revolution into an evolution.
After the " Lexington massacre" separation was
talked of by many, but had it then occurred America
might have been another kingdom.   The members
of Congress were of the rich conservative "gentry,"
and royalists.   Had he not been a patriot, Peyton
Randolph, our first president, would probably have
borne a title like his father, and Washington would
certainly have been knighted.   Paine was in the position of the abolitionists when the secession war began.   They also held peace principles, and would
have scorned a war for the old slave-holding union,
as Paine would have scorned a separation from England preserving its political institutions.   The war
having begun, and separation become probable,
Paine hastened to connect it with humanity and with
republicanism.   As the abolitionists resolved that
the secession war should sweep slavery out of the
country, Paine made a brave effort that the Revolution should clear away both slavery and monarchy.
It was to be in every respect a new departure for
humanity.   So he anticipated the Declaration of
Independence by more than eight months with one
of his own, which was discovered by Moreau in the
file of the *Pennsylvania Journal,* October 18th.[1]

" A SERIOUS THOUGHT.

" When I reflect on the horrid cruelties exercised by Britain
in the East Indies—How thousands perished by artificial famine—How religion and every manly principle of honor and
honesty were sacrificed to luxury and pride—When I read

[1] Mr. Moreau mentions it as Paine's in his MS. notes in a copy of
Cheetham's book, now owned by the Pennsylvania Historical Society.   No
one familiar with Paine's style at the time can doubt its authorship.

of the wretched natives being blown away, for no other crime than because, sickened with the miserable scene, they refused to fight—When I reflect on these and a thousand instances of similar barbarity, I firmly believe that the Almighty, in compassion to mankind, will curtail the power of Britain.

"And when I reflect on the use she hath made of the discovery of this new world—that the little paltry dignity of earthly kings hath been set up in preference to the great cause of the King of kings—That instead of Christian examples to the Indians, she hath basely tampered with their passions, imposed on their ignorance, and made them the tools of treachery and murder—And when to these and many other melancholy reflections I add this sad remark, that ever since the discovery of America she hath employed herself in the most horrid of all traffics, that of human flesh, unknown to the most savage nations, hath yearly (without provocation and in cold blood) ravaged the hapless shores of Africa, robbing it of its unoffending inhabitants to cultivate her stolen dominions in the West—When I reflect on these, I hesitate not for a moment to believe that the Almighty will finally separate America from Britain. Call it Independancy or what you will, if it is the cause of God and humanity it will go on.

"And when the Almighty shall have blest us, and made us a people *dependent only upon him*, then may our first gratitude be shown by an act of continental legislation, which shall put a stop to the importation of Negroes for sale, soften the hard fate of those already here, and in time procure their freedom.

" HUMANUS."

CHAPTER VI.

"COMMON SENSE."

In furrows ploughed deep by lawless despotism, watered with blood of patriots, the Thetford Quaker sowed his seed—true English seed. Even while he did so he was suspected of being a British spy, and might have been roughly handled in Philadelphia had it not been for Franklin. Possibly this suspicion may have arisen from his having, in the antislavery letter, asked the Americans "to consider with what consistency or decency they complain so loudly of attempts to enslave them, while they hold so many thousands in slavery." Perfectly indifferent to this, Paine devoted the autumn of 1775 to his pamphlet "Common Sense," which with the new year "burst from the press with an effect which has rarely been produced by types and paper in any age or country." So says Dr. Benjamin Rush, and his assertion, often quoted, has as often been confirmed.

Of the paramount influence of Paine's "Common Sense" there can indeed be no question.[1] It reached Washington soon after tidings that Norfolk, Virginia, had been burned (Jan. 1st) by Lord Dunmore,

[1] " This day was published, and is now selling by Robert Bell, in Third Street, [Phil.] price two shillings, ' Common Sense,' addressed to the inhabitants of North America."—*Pennsylvania Journal*, Jan. 10, 1776.

as Falmouth (now Portland), Maine, had been, Oct.
17, 1775, by ships under Admiral Graves. The
General wrote to Joseph Reed, from Cambridge,
Jan. 31st: "A few more of such flaming arguments
as were exhibited at Falmouth and Norfolk, added
to the sound doctrine and unanswerable reasoning
contained in the pamphlet 'Common Sense,' will
not leave numbers at a loss to decide upon the propriety of separation."[1]

Henry Wisner, a New York delegate in Congress,
sent the pamphlet to John McKesson, Secretary of
the Provincial Congress sitting in New York City,
with the following note : "Sir, I have only to ask
the favour of you to read this pamphlet, consulting
Mr. Scott and such of the Committee of Safety as
you think proper, particularly Orange and Ulster,
and let me know their and your opinion of the general spirit of it. I would have wrote a letter on the
subject, but the bearer is waiting." In pursuance
of this General Scott suggested a private meeting,
and McKesson read the pamphlet aloud. New
York, the last State to agree to separation, was
alarmed by the pamphlet, and these leaders at first
thought of answering it, but found themselves without the necessary arguments. Henry Wisner, however, required arguments rather than orders, and
despite the instructions of his State gave New York
the honor of having one name among those who,
on July 4th, voted for independence.[2] Joel Barlow,

---

[1] "The Writings of George Washington." Collected and edited by
Worthington Chauncey Ford, vol. iii., p. 396.

[2] *Mag. Am. Hist.*, July, 1880, p. 62, and Dec., 1888, p. 479. The
Declaration passed on July 4th was not signed until Aug. 2d, the postponement being for the purpose of removing the restrictions placed by New York

a student in Yale College at the beginning of the
Revolution, has borne testimony to the great effect
of Paine's pamphlet, as may be seen in his biography
by Mr. Todd. An original copy of Paine's excise
pamphlet (1792) in my possession contains a note
in pencil, apparently contemporary, suggesting that
the introduction was written by Barlow. In this
introduction—probably by Barlow, certainly by a
competent observer of events in America—it is
said :

"On this celebrated publication ['Common Sense'], which
has received the testimony of praise from the wise and learned
of different nations, we need only remark (for the merit of
every work should be judged by its effect) that it gave spirit
and resolution to the Americans, who were then wavering and
undetermined, to assert their rights, and inspired a decisive
energy into their counsels : we may therefore venture to say,
without fear of contradiction, that the great American cause
owed as much to the pen of Paine as to the sword of Washington." [1]

Edmund Randolph, our first Attorney-General,
who had been on Washington's staff in the beginning of the war, and conducted much of his correspondence, ascribed independence primarily to
George III., but next to " Thomas Paine, an Englishman by birth, and possessing an imagination
which happily combined political topics, poured
forth in a style hitherto unknown on this side of

and Maryland on their delegates. Wisner, the only New York delegate who
had voted for the Declaration, did not return until after the recess. In
Trumbull's picture at the Capitol Thomas Stone, a signer for Maryland, is
left out, and Robert Livingston of New York is included, though he did not
sign it.

[1] And yet—such was the power of theological intimidation—even heretical
Barlow could find no place for Paine in his *Columbiad* (1807).

the Atlantic, from the ease with which it insinuated itself into the hearts of the people who were un-learned, or of the learned." [1]   This is from a devout churchman, writing after Paine's death. Paine's malignant biographer, Cheetham (1809), is con-strained to say of " Common Sense ": " Speaking a language which the colonists had felt but not thought, its popularity, terrible in its consequences to the parent country, was unexampled in the history of the press." [2]

Let it not be supposed that Washington, Frank-lin, Jefferson, Randolph, and the rest, were carried away by a meteor.   Deep answers only unto deep. Paine's ideas went far because they came far.   He was the authentic commoner, representing English freedom in the new world.   There was no dreg in the poverty of his people that he had not tasted, no humiliation in their dependence, no outlook of their hopelessness, he had not known, and with the addition of intellectual hungers which made his old-world despair conscious.   The squalor and ab-jectness of Thetford, its corporation held in the hollow of Grafton's hand, its commoners nomina-ted by him, the innumerable villages equally help-less, the unspeakable corruptions of the government, the repeated and always baffled efforts of the out-raged people for some redress,—these had been brought home to Paine in many ways, had finally driven him to America, where he arrived on the

---

[1] Randolph's " History " (MS.), a possession of the Virginia Historical Society, has been confided to my editorial care for publication.

[2] See also the historians, Ramsay (Rev., i., p. 336, London, 1793), Gordon (Rev., ii., p. 78, New York, 1794), Bryant and Gay (U. S., iii., p. 471, New York, 1879).

hour for which none had been so exactly and thoroughly trained. He had thrown off the old world, and that America had virtually done the same constituted its attraction for him. In the opening essay in his magazine, written within a month of his arrival in the country (Nov. 30, 1774), Paine speaks of America as a " nation," and his pregnant sentences prove how mature the principles of independence had become in his mind long before the outbreak of hostilities.

" America has now outgrown the state of infancy. Her strength and commerce make large advances to manhood ; and science in all its branches has not only blossomed, but even ripened upon the soil. The cottages as it were of yesterday have grown to villages, and the villages to cities ; and while proud antiquity, like a skeleton in rags, parades the streets of other nations, their genius, as if sickened and disgusted with the phantom, comes hither for recovery. . . . America yet inherits a large portion of her first-imported virtue. Degeneracy is here almost a useless word. Those who are conversant with Europe would be tempted to believe that even the air of the Atlantic disagrees with the constitution of foreign vices ; if they survive the voyage they either expire on their arrival, or linger away in an incurable consumption. There is a happy something in the climate of America which disarms them of all their power both of infection and attraction."

In presently raising the standard of republican independence, Paine speaks of separation from England as a foregone conclusion. " I have always considered the independency of this continent as an event which sooner or later must arrive." Great Britain having forced a collision, the very least that America can demand is separation.

" The object contended for ought always to bear some just proportion to the expence. The removal of North, or the

whole detestable junto, is a matter unworthy the millions we
have expended. A temporary stoppage of trade was an inconvenience which would have sufficiently ballanced the repeal of
all the acts complained of, had such repeals been obtained ;
but if the whole Continent must take up arms, if every man
must be a soldier, 't is scarcely worth our while to fight against
a contemptible ministry only. Dearly, dearly do we pay for
the repeal of the acts, if that is all we fight for ; for, in a just
estimation, 't is as great a folly to pay a Bunker-hill price for
law as for land. . . . It would be policy in the king, at
this time, to repeal the acts for the sake of reinstating himself
in the government of the provinces, in order that he may
accomplish by craft and subtlety, in the long run, what he
cannot do by force and violence in the short one. Reconciliation and ruin are nearly related."

Starting with the lowest demand, separation,
Paine shows the justice and necessity of it lying
fundamentally in the nature of monarchy as represented by Great Britain, and the potential republicanism of colonies composed of people from
all countries. The keynote of this is struck in
the introduction. The author withholds his name
" because the object of attention is the Doctrine
itself, not the Man " ; and he affirms, " the cause
of America is in a great measure the cause of all
mankind."

No other pamphlet published during the Revolution is comparable with " Common Sense " for
interest to the reader of to-day, or for value as an
historical document. Therein as in a mirror is beheld the almost incredible England, against which
the colonies contended. And therein is reflected the
moral, even religious, enthusiasm which raised the
struggle above the paltriness of a rebellion against
taxation to a great human movement,—a war for

an idea. The art with which every sentence is feathered for its aim is consummate.

The work was for a time generally attributed to Franklin. It is said the Doctor was reproached by a loyal lady for using in it such an epithet as "the royal brute of Britain." He assured her that he had not written the pamphlet, and would never so dishonor the brute creation.

In his letter to Cheetham (1809) already referred to, Dr. Rush claims to have suggested the work to Paine, who read the sheets to him and also to Dr. Franklin. This letter, however, gives so many indications of an enfeebled memory, that it cannot be accepted against Paine's own assertion, made in the year following the publication of "Common Sense," when Dr. Rush and Dr. Franklin might have denied it.

"In October, 1775, Dr. Franklin proposed giving me such materials as were in his hands towards completing a history of the present transactions, and seemed desirous of having the first volume out the next spring. I had then formed the outlines of 'Common Sense,' and finished nearly the first part; and as I supposed the doctor's design in getting out a history was to open the new year with a new system, I expected to surprise him with a production on that subject much earlier than he thought of; and without informing him of what I was doing, got it ready for the press as fast as I conveniently could, and sent him the first pamphlet that was printed off."

On the other hand, Paine's memory was at fault when he wrote (December 3, 1802) : "In my publications, I follow the rule I began with in 'Common Sense,' that is, to consult nobody, nor to let anybody see what I write till it appears publicly." This was certainly his rule, but in the case of

" Common Sense " he himself mentions (*Penn. Jour.*, April 10, 1776) having shown parts of the MS. to a " very few."   Dr. Rush is correct in his statement that Paine had difficulty in finding "a printer who had boldness enough to publish it," and that he (Rush) mentioned the pamphlet to the Scotch bookseller, Robert Bell.   For Bell says, in a contemporary leaflet : " When the work was at a stand for want of a courageous Typographer, I was then recommended by a gentleman nearly in the following words : ' There is Bell, he is a Republican printer, give it to him, and I will answer for his courage to print it.' "   Dr. Rush probably required some knowledge of the contents of the pamphlet before he made this recommendation.

That Dr. Rush is mistaken in saying the manuscript was submitted to Franklin, and a sentence modified by him, is proved by the fact that on February 19th, more than a month after the pamphlet appeared, Franklin introduced Paine to Gen. Charles Lee with a letter containing the words, " He is the reputed and, I think, the real author of ' Common sense.' "   Franklin could not have thus hesitated had there been in the work anything of his own, or anything he had seen.   Beyond such disclosures to Dr. Rush, and one or two others, as were necessary to secure publication, Paine kept the secret of his authorship as long as he could.   His recent arrival in the country might have impaired the force of his pamphlet.

The authorship of " Common Sense " was guessed by the " Tory " President of the University of Philadelphia, the Rev. William Smith, D.D., who knew pretty well the previous intellectual resources of that city. Writing under the name of " Cato " he spoke of " the foul pages of interested writers, and strangers intermeddling in our affairs." To which " The Forester " (Paine) answers : " A freeman, Cato, is a stranger nowhere,—a slave, everywhere." [1]

The publication of " Common Sense " had been followed by a number of applauding pamphlets, some of them crude or extravagant, from Bell's press. " Cato " was anxious to affiliate these " additional doses " on the author of " Common Sense," who replies :

"Perhaps there never was a pamphlet, since the use of letters were known, about which so little pains were taken, and of which so great a number went off in so short a time. I am certain that I am within compass when I say one hundred and twenty thousand. The book was turned upon the world like an orphan to shift for itself ; no plan was formed to support it, neither hath the author ever published a syllable on the subject from that time till after the appearance of Cato's fourth letter."

This letter of " The Forester " is dated April 8th (printed on the 10th). " Common Sense," published January 10th, had, therefore, in less than three months, gained this sale. In the end probably half a million copies were sold. In reply to " Cato's " sneer about " interested writers," Paine did not announce the fact that he had donated the copyright to the States for the cause of independence. It was sold at two shillings, and the author thus

[1] " The writer of ' Common Sense ' and ' The Forester ' is the same person. His name is Paine, a gentleman about two years ago from England,—a man who, General Lee says, has genius in his eyes."—John Adams to his wife.

gave away a fortune in that pamphlet alone. It never brought him a penny ; he must even have paid for copies himself, as the publisher figured up a debt against him, on account of " Common Sense," for £29 12*s.* 1*d.* Notwithstanding this experience and the popularity he had acquired, Paine also gave to the States the copyright of his *Crisis* (thirteen numbers), was taunted by Tories as a " garreteer," ate his crust contentedly, peace finding him a penniless patriot, who might easily have had fifty thousand pounds in his pocket.

The controversy between " Cato " and " The Forester " was the most important that preceded the Declaration of Independence. The president of the University represented " Toryism " in distress. The "massacre at Lexington " disabled him from justifying the government, which, however, he was not prepared to denounce. He was compelled to assume the tone of an American, while at the same time addressing his appeal " To the People of Pennsylvania," trying to detach its non-resident Quakers and its mercantile interest from sympathy with the general cause. Having a bad case, in view of Lexington, he naturally resorted to abuse of the plaintiff's attorney. He soon found that when it came to Quaker sentiment and dialect, his unknown antagonist was at home.

"Remember, thou hast thrown me the glove, Cato, and either thee or I must tire. I fear not the field of fair debate, but thou hast stepped aside and made it personal. Thou hast tauntingly called me by name ; and if I cease to hunt thee from every lane and lurking hole of mischief, and bring thee not a trembling culprit before the public bar, then brand me with reproach by naming me in the list of your confederates."

" The Forester " declares his respect for the honest and undisguised opponents of independence. "To be nobly wrong is more manly than to be meanly right."   But " Cato " wears the mask of a friend, and shall be proved a foe.

The so-called " Tories " of the American Revolution have never had justice done them.   In another work I have told the story of John Randolph, King's Attorney in Virginia, and there were many other martyrs of loyalty in those days.[1]   Four months after the affair at Lexington, Thomas Jefferson wrote to John Randolph, in London : " Looking with fondness towards a reconciliation with Great Britain, I cannot help hoping you may be able to contribute towards expediting the good work."   This was written on August 25, 1775 ; and if this was the feeling of Jefferson only ten months before the Declaration, how many, of more moderate temper, surrounded " Cato " and " The Forester " in loyal and peace-loving Philadelphia ?   But " Cato " was believed ungenuine.   The Rev. Dr. William Smith, who wrote under that name, a native of Aberdeen with an Oxonian D.D., had been a glowing Whig patriot until June, 1775. But his wife was a daughter of the loyalist, William Moore.   This lady of fashion was distinguished by her contempt for the independents, and her husband, now near fifty, was led into a false position.[2]   He held the highest literary position in

---

[1] "Omitted Chapters of History, Disclosed in the Life and Papers of Edmund Randolph," p. 20.

[2] R. H. Lee, in a letter to his brother (July 5, 1778) says : " We had a magnificent celebration of the anniversary of independence. The Whigs of the city dressed up a woman of the town with the monstrous head-dress of the Tory ladies, and escorted her through the town with a great concourse

Philadelphia, and perhaps felt some jealousy of Paine's fame. He picked out all the mistakes he could find in "Common Sense," and tried in every way to belittle his antagonist. Himself a Scotchman, his wife an Englishwoman, he sneered at Paine for being a foreigner ; having modified his principles to those of the loyalist's daughter, he denounced Paine as an "interested writer." He was out of his element in the controversy he began with personalities. He spoke of the trouble as a lovers' quarrel. Paine answers :

"It was not in the power of France or Spain, or all the other powers in Europe, to have given such a wound, or raised us to such mortal hatred as Britain hath done. We see the same kind of undescribed anger at her conduct, as we would at the sight of an animal devouring its young."

The strongest point of "Cato" was based on the proposed embassy for negotiation, and he demanded reverence for "Ambassadors coming to negotiate a peace." To this "The Forester" replied :

of people. Her head was elegantly and expensively dressed, I suppose about three feet high and proportionate width, with a profusion of curls, etc. The figure was droll, and occasioned much mirth. It has lessened some heads already, and will probably bring the rest within the bounds of reason, for they are monstrous indeed. The Tory wife of Dr. Smith has christened this figure Continella, or the Duchess of Independence, and prayed for a pin from her head by way of relic. The Tory women are very much mortified, notwithstanding this."—"Omitted Chapters of History," p. 40.

"Cato's" brilliant wife had to retire before "Continella" in the following year. The charter of the College of Philadelphia was taken away, and its president retired to an obscure living at Chestertown, Maryland. He had, however, some of the dexterity of the Vicar of Bray ; when the cause he had reviled was nearly won he founded a "Washington" college in Maryland. He was chosen by that diocese for a bishop (1783), but the General Convention refused to recommend him for consecration. In 1789 he managed to regain his place as college president in Philadelphia.

"Cato discovers a gross ignorance of the British Constitution in supposing that these men *can* be empowered to act as Ambassadors. To prevent his future errors, I will set him right. The present war differs from every other, in this instance, viz., that it is not carried on under the prerogative of the crown, as other wars have always been, but under the authority of the whole legislative power united ; and as the barriers which stand in the way of a negotiation are not proclamations, but acts of Parliament, it evidently follows that were even the King of England here in person, he could not ratify the terms or conditions of a reconciliation ; because, in the single character of King, he could not stipulate for the repeal of any acts of Parliament, neither can the Parliament stipulate for him. There is no body of men more jealous of their privileges than the Commons : Because they sell them."

Paine wrote three letters in reply to " Cato," the last of which contained a memorable warning to the people on the eve of the Declaration of Independence : " *Forget not the hapless African.*" That was forgotten, but the summing up made Dr. William Smith an object of detestation. He never ventured into political controversy again, and when he returned from exile to Philadelphia, a penitent patriot, he found his old antagonist, Thomas Paine, honored by a degree from the University of Pennsylvania into which the college had been absorbed.

On May 8th a fourth letter, signed " The Forester," appeared in the same paper (*Pennsylvania Journal*), which I at first suspected of not being from Paine's pen.[1] This was because of a sentence

---

[1] A theft of Paine's usual signature led to his first public identification of himself (Feb. 13, 1779). " As my signature, ' Common Sense,' has been counterfeited, either by Mr. [Silas] Deane, or some of his adherents in Mr. Bradford's paper of Feb. 3, I shall subscribe this with my name, Thomas Paine." He, however, in Almon's *Remembrancer* (vol. viii.) is indexed by name in connection with a letter of the previous year signed " Common Sense."

beginning : " The clergy of the English Church, of which I profess myself a member," etc. There is no need to question the truth of this, for, as we have seen, Paine had been confirmed, and no doubt previously baptized ; nor is there reason to disbelieve the statement of Oldys that he wished to enter holy orders. There was a good deal of rationalism in the American church at that time, and that Paine, with his religious fervor and tendency to inquire, should have maintained his place in that scholarly church is natural. His quakerism was a philosophy, but he could by no means have found any home in its rigid and dogmatic societies in Philadelphia. The casual sentence above quoted was probably inserted for candor, as the letter containing it opens with a censure on the attitude of the Quakers towards the proposal for independence. The occasion was an election of four burgesses to represent Philadelphia in the State Assembly, a body in which Quakers (loyalists) preponderated. Had the independents been elected they must have taken the oath of allegiance to the crown, with which the State was at war. Indeed Paine declares that the " Tories " succeeded in the election because so many patriots were absent for defence of their country. Under these circumstances Paine urges the necessity of a popular convention. The House of Assembly is disqualified from " sitting in its own case."

The extracts given from this letter are of historic interest as reflecting the conflict of opinions in Pennsylvania amid which the Declaration was passed two months later.

"Whoever will take the trouble of attending to the progress and changeability of times and things, and the conduct of mankind thereon, will find that *extraordinary circumstances* do sometimes arise before us, of a species, either so purely natural or so perfectly original, that none but the man of nature can understand them. When precedents fail to assist us, we must return to the first principles of things for information, and *think*, as if we were the *first men* that *thought*. And this is the true reason, that in the present state of affairs, the wise are become foolish, and the foolish wise. I am led to this reflection by not being able to account for the conduct of the Quakers on any other ; for although they do not seem to perceive it themselves, yet it is amazing to hear with what unanswerable ignorance many of that body, wise in other matters, will discourse on the present one. Did they hold places or commissions under the king, were they governors of provinces, or had they any interest apparently distinct from us, the mystery would cease ; but as they have not, their folly is best attributed to that superabundance of *worldly knowledge* which in original matters is too cunning to be wise. Back to the first plain path of nature, friends, and begin anew, for in this business your first footsteps were wrong. You have now travelled to the summit of inconsistency, and that, with such accelerated rapidity as to acquire autumnal ripeness by the first of May. Now your *rotting time comes on.*"

" The Forester " reminds the Quakers of their predecessors who, in 1704, defended the rights of the people against the proprietor. He warns them that the people, though unable to vote, represent a patriotic power tenfold the strength of Toryism, by which they will not submit to be ruled.

" He that is wise will reflect, that the safest asylum, especially in times of general convulsion, when no settled form of government prevails, is *the love of the people.* All property is safe under their protection. Even in countries where the lowest and most licentious of them have risen into outrage, they have never departed from the path of *natural* honor.

Volunteers unto death in defence of the person or fortune of
those who had served or defended them, division of property
never entered the mind of the populace. It is incompatible
with that spirit which impels them into action. An avaricious
mob was never heard of; nay, even a miser, pausing in the
midst of them, and catching their spirit, would from that
instant cease to be covetous."

The Quakers of Pennsylvania.and New Jersey
had held a congress in Philadelphia and issued
(January 20th) " The Ancient Testimony and Principles of the People called Quakers renewed, with respect to the King and Government ; and touching
the Commotions now prevailing in these and other
Parts of America ; addressed to the People in General." Under this lamb-like tract, and its bleat of
texts, was quite discoverable the " Tory " wolf ;
but it was widely circulated and became a danger.
The Quakers of Rhode Island actually made efforts
to smuggle provisions into Boston during the siege.
Paine presently reviewed this testimony in a pamphlet, one extract from which will show that he could
preach a better Quaker sermon than any of them :

"O ye partial ministers of your own acknowledged principles ! If the bearing arms be sinful, the first going to war
must be more so, by all the difference between wilful attack
and unavoidable defence. Wherefore, if ye really preach
from conscience, and mean not to make a political hobby-
horse of your religion, convince the world thereof by pro-
claiming your doctrine to our enemies, for they likewise bear
arms. Give us proof of your sincerity by publishing it at St.
James's, to the commanders in chief at Boston, to the admirals
and captains who are piratically ravaging our coasts, and to all
the murdering miscreants who are acting in authority under
HIM whom ye profess to serve. Had ye the honest soul of
Barclay ye would preach repentance to your king ; ye would

tell the Royal Wretch his sins, and warn him of eternal ruin ; ye would not spend your partial invectives against the injured and insulted only, but, like faithful ministers, cry aloud and spare none."

[1] Paine was not then aware of the extent of the intrigues of leading Quakers with the enemy. The State archives of England and France contain remarkable evidences on this subject. Paul Wentworth, in a report to the English government (1776 or 1777,) mentions the loyalty of Pemberton and the Quakers. Wentworth says that since the publication of "Common Sense" it had become hard to discover the real opinions of leading men. "Mr. Payne," he says, "should not be forgot. He is an Englishman, was schoolmaster in Philadelphia ; must be driven to work ; naturally indolent ; led by His passions." These "passions," chiefly for liberty and humanity, seem to have so driven the indolent man to work that, according to Wentworth, his pamphlet "worked up [the people] to such a high temper as fitted them for the impression of the Declaration, etc." The Quakers, however, held out long, though more covertly. M. Gérard de Rayneval, in a letter from Philadelphia, Sept. 18, 1778, reports to his government : "During the occupation of Philadelphia by the English, proofs were obtained of the services rendered them by the Quakers ; some of these were caught acting as spies, etc." La Luzerne writes (May 4, 1781) : "All the Quakers in Philadelphia who have taken up arms, or voluntarily paid war taxes, have been excommunicated ; these, increasing in number, declare themselves loyal." See for further information on this matter, "New Materials for the History of the American Revolution," etc. By John Durand. New York, 1889.

CHAPTER VII.

UNDER THE BANNER OF INDEPENDENCE.

As in North Carolina had occurred the first armed resistance to British oppressions (1771), and its Mecklenburg County been the first to organize a government independent of the Crown, so was that colony the first to instruct its delegates in Congress to vote for national independence. She was followed in succession by South Carolina,[1] Virginia,[2] Massachusetts, Rhode Island, Connecticut, New Hampshire, Georgia, New Jersey, Delaware, and Pennsylvania. Maryland passed patriotic resolutions, but not sufficiently decisive for its delegates

[1] Colonel Gadsden, having left the Continental Congress to take command in South Carolina, appeared in the provincial Congress at Charleston February 10, 1776. "Col. Gadsden (having brought the first copy of Paine's pamphlet 'Common Sense, etc.,') boldly declared himself . . . for the absolute Independence of America. This last sentiment came like an explosion of thunder on the members" (Rev. John Drayton's *Memoirs, etc.*, p. 172). The sentiment was abhorred, and a member "called the author of 'Common Sense' ———"; but on March 21st the pamphlet was reinforced by tidings of an Act of Parliament (Dec. 21, 1775) for seizure of American ships, and on March 23d South Carolina instructed its delegates at Philadelphia to agree to whatever that Congress should "judge necessary, etc."

[2] A thousand copies of "Common Sense" were at once ordered from Virginia, and many more followed. On April 1st Washington writes to Joseph Reed: "By private letters which I have lately received from Virginia, I find 'Common Sense' is working a wonderful change there in the minds of many men." On June 29th union with England was "totally dissolved" by Virginia.

to act. New York alone forbade its delegates to vote for independence.

Meanwhile, on June 7th, Richard Henry Lee, in behalf of the Virginians, had submitted resolutions of independence ; but as six States hesitated, Congress adjourned the decision until July 1st, appointing, however, (June 11th) a committee to consider the proper form of the probable Declaration— Jefferson, John Adams, Franklin, Roger Sherman, and Robert R. Livingston. But this interval, from June 7th to July 1st, was perilous for independence. News came of the approach of Lord Howe bearing from England the "olive branch." The powerful colonies New York and Pennsylvania were especially anxious to await the proposals for peace. At this juncture Paine issued one of his most effective pamphlets, "A Dialogue between the Ghost of General Montgomery, Just Arrived from the Elysian Fields, and an American Delegate, in a Wood near Philadelphia." Montgomery, the first heroic figure fallen in the war, reproaches the hesitating delegate for willingness to accept pardon from a royal criminal for defending "the rights of humanity." He points out that France only awaits their declaration of independence to come to their aid, and that America "teems with patriots, heroes, and legislators who are impatient to burst forth into light and importance." The most effective part of the pamphlet, however, was a reply to the commercial apprehensions of New York and Pennsylvania. "Your dependance upon the Crown is no advantage, but rather an injury, to the people of Great Britain, as it increases the power and influence of the King. The people are benefited only by your trade, and this they may have after you are independant of the Crown." There is a shrewd prescience of what actually happened shown in this opportune work. Of course the gallant ghost remarks that "monarchy and aristocracy have in all ages been the vehicles of slavery." The allusion to the arming of negroes and Indians against America, and other passages, resemble clauses in one of the paragraphs eliminated from the original Declaration of Independence.

At this time Paine saw much of Jefferson, and there can be little doubt that the anti-slavery clause struck out of the Declaration was written by Paine, or by some one who had Paine's anti-slavery essay before him. In the following passages it will be observed that the antitheses are nearly the same— "infidel and Christian," "heathen and Christian."

<table>
<tr><td>PARAGRAPH STRUCK OUT OF
THE DECLARATION.</td><td>THOMAS PAINE.</td></tr>
<tr><td>" He has waged cruel war against human nature itself, violating its most sacred rights of life and liberty in the persons of a distant people who never offended him, captivating and carrying them into slavery in another hemisphere, or to incur miserable death in their transportation thither. This piratical warfare, the opprobrium of INFIDEL powers, is the warfare of the CHRISTIAN king of Great</td><td>"—these inoffensive people are brought into slavery, by stealing them, tempting kings to sell subjects, which they can have no right to do, and hiring one tribe to war against another, in order to catch prisoners. By such wicked and inhuman ways the English, etc. . . . an hight of outrage that seems left by *Heathen* nations to be practised by pretended *Chris-tians*."</td></tr>
</table>

Britain. Determined to keep open a market where MEN should be bought and sold, he has prostituted his negative for suppressing every legislative attempt to prohibit or restrain this execrable commerce. And that this assemblage of horrors might want no fact of distinguished die, he is now exciting those very people to rise in arms among us, and to purchase that liberty of which he has deprived them by murdering the people on whom he has obtruded them, thus paying off former crimes committed against the LIBERTIES of one people with crimes which he urges them to commit against the LIVES of another."

"—that barbarous and hellish power which has stirred up the Indians and Negroes to destroy us ; the cruelty hath a double guilt—it is dealing brutally by us and treacherously by them."

Thus did Paine try to lay at the corner the stone which the builders rejected, and which afterwards ground their descendants to powder. Jefferson withdrew the clause on the objection of Georgia and South Carolina, which wanted slaves, and of Northerners interested in supplying them. That, however, was not known till all the parties were dead. Paine had no reason to suppose that the Declaration of human freedom and equality, passed July 4th, could fail eventually to include the African slaves. The Declaration embodied every principle he had been asserting, and indeed Cobbett is correct in saying that whoever may have written the Declaration Paine was its author. The world being his country, and America having founded its independence on such universal interests, Paine could not hesitate to become a soldier for mankind.[1] His Quaker principles, always humanized, were not such as would applaud a resistance in which he was not prepared to participate. While the signers of the Declaration of Independence were affixing their names—a procedure which reached from August 2d into November—Paine resigned his *Pennsylvania Magazine*, and marched with his musket to the front. He enlisted in a Pennsylvania division of the Flying Camp of ten thousand men, who were to be sent wherever needed. He was under General Roberdeau, and assigned at first to service at Amboy, afterwards at Bergen. The Flying Camp was enlisted for a brief period, and when that had expired Paine travelled to Fort Lee, on the Hudson, and renewed his enlistment. Fort Lee was under the command of General Nathaniel Greene who, on or about September 19th, appointed Paine

[1] Professor John Fiske (whose "American Revolution" suffers from ignorance of Paine's papers) appreciates the effect of Paine's "Common Sense" but not its cause. He praises the pamphlet highly, but proves that he has only glanced at it by his exception : "The pamphlet is full of scurrilous abuse of the English people ; and resorts to such stupid arguments as the denial of the English origin of the Americans " (i., p. 174). Starting with the principle that the cause of America is "the cause of all mankind," Paine abuses no people, but only their oppressors. As to Paine's argument, it might have appeared less "stupid" to Professor Fiske had he realized that in Paine's mind negroes were the equals of whites. However, Paine does not particularly mention negroes ; his argument was meant to carry its point, and it might have been imprudent for him, in that connection, to have classed the slaves with the Germans, who formed a majority in Pennsylvania, and with the Dutch of New York. In replying to the " Mother-Country " argument it appears to me far from stupid to point out that Europe is our parent country, and that if English descent made men Englishmen, the descendants of William the Conqueror and half the peers of England were Frenchmen, and, if the logic held, should be governed by France.

a Volunteer Aide-de-camp. General Greene in a gossipy letter to his wife (November 2d) says: "Common Sense (Thomas Paine) and Colonel Snarl, or Cornwell, are perpetually wrangling about mathematical problems." On November 20th came the surprise of Fort Lee; the boiling kettles and baking ovens of a dinner to be devoured by the British were abandoned, with three hundred tents, for a retreat made the more miserable by hunger and cold. By November 22d the whole army had retreated to Newark, where Paine began writing his famous first *Crisis*.[1]

He could only write at night; during the day there was constant work for every soldier of the little force surrounding Washington. "I am wearied almost to death with the retrogade motion of things," wrote Washington to his brother (November 9th), "and I solemnly protest that a pecuniary reward of twenty thousand pounds a year would not induce me to undergo what I do; and after all, perhaps to lose my character, as it is impossible, under such a variety of distressing circumstances, to conduct matters agreeably to public expectation." On November 27th he writes from Newark to

---

[1] See Almon's *Remembrancer*, 1777, p. 28, for Paine's graphic journal of this retreat, quoted from the *Pennsylvania Journal*. In reply to those who censured the retreat as pusillanimous, he states that "our army was at one time less than a thousand effective men and never more than 4,000," the pursuers being "8,000 exclusive of their artillery and light horse"; he declares that posterity will call the retreat "glorious—and the names of Washington and Fabius will run paralell to eternity." In the *Pennsylvania Packet* (March 20, 1779) Paine says: "I had begun the first number of the *Crisis* while on the retreat, at Newark, with a design of publishing it in the Jersies, as it was General Washington's intention to have made a stand at Newark, could he have been timely reenforced; instead of which nearly half the army left him at that place, or soon after, their time being out."

General Lee: "It has been more owing to the badness of the weather that the enemy's progress has been checked, than to any resistance we could make." Even while he wrote the enemy drew near, and the next day (November 28th) entered one end of Newark as Washington left the other. At Brunswick he was joined by General Williamson's militia, and on the Delaware by the Philadelphia militia, and could muster five thousand against Howe's whole army. "I tremble for Philadelphia," writes Washington to Lund Washington (December 10th). "Nothing in my opinion, but General Lee's speedy arrival, who has been long expected, though still at a distance (with about three thousand men), can save it." On December 13th Lee was a prisoner, and on the 17th Washington writes to the same relative:

"Your imagination can scarce extend to a situation more distressing than mine. Our only dependence now is upon the speedy enlistment of a new army. If this fails, I think the game will be pretty well up, as from disaffection and want of spirit and fortitude, the inhabitants, instead of resistance, are offering submission and taking protection from Gen. Howe in Jersey."

The day before, he had written to the President of Congress that the situation was critical, and the distresses of his soldiers "extremely great, many of 'em being entirely naked and most so thinly clad as to be unfit for service." On December 18th he writes to his brother:

"You can form no idea of the perplexity of my situation. No man, I believe, ever had a greater choice of difficulties, and less means to extricate himself from them. However, under a full persuasion of the justice of our cause, I cannot entertain an Idea that it will finally sink, tho' it may remain for some time under a cloud."

Under that cloud, by Washington's side, was silently at work the force that lifted it.   Marching by day, listening to the consultations of Washington and his generals, Paine wrote by the camp fires; the winter storms, the Delaware's waves, were mingled with his ink; the half-naked soldiers in their troubled sleep dreaming of their distant homes, the skulking deserter creeping off in the dusk, the pallid face of the heavy-hearted commander, made the awful shadows beneath which was written that leaflet which went to the Philadelphia printer along with Washington's last foreboding letters to his relatives in Virginia.   It was printed on December 19th,[1] and many copies reached the camp above Trenton Falls on the eve of that almost desperate attack on which Washington had resolved.   On the 23d December he wrote to Colonel Joseph Reed:

"Christmas-day, at night, one hour before day, is the time fixed upon for our attempt on Trenton.   For Heaven's sake keep this to yourself, as the discovery of it may prove fatal to us; our numbers, sorry I am to say, being less than I had any conception of; but necessity, dire necessity will, nay must, justify *any* attempt."

America has known some utterances of the lips equivalent to decisive victories in the field,—as some of Patrick Henry's, and the address of President Lincoln at Gettysburg.   But of utterances by

---

[1] The pamphlet was dated December 23rd, but it had appeared on the 19th in the *Pennsylvania Journal.*

the pen none have achieved such vast results as
Paine's " Common Sense " and his first *Crisis.*
Before the battle of Trenton the half-clad, dis-
heartened soldiers of Washington were called
together in groups to listen to that thrilling exhortation. The opening words alone were a victory.

" These are the times that try men's souls. The summer
soldier and the sunshine patriot will, in this crisis, shrink from
the service of his country ; but he that stands it now, deserves
the love and thanks of man and woman. Tyranny, like hell,
is not easily conquered ; yet we have this consolation with us,
that the harder the conflict the more glorious the triumph :
what we obtain too cheap we esteem too lightly ; 't is dearness
only that gives everything its value. Heaven knows how to
put a proper price upon its goods ; and it would be strange
indeed if so celestial an article as Freedom should not be
highly rated."

Not a chord of faith, or love, or hope was left
untouched. The very faults of the composition,
which the dilettanti have picked out, were effective
to men who had seen Paine on the march, and
knew these things were written in sleepless intervals of unwearied labors. He speaks of what Joan
of Arc did in " the fourteenth century," and ex-
claims : " Would that heaven might inspire some
Jersey maid to spirit up her countrymen, and save
her fair fellow sufferers from ravage and ravish-
ment !" Joan was born in 1410, but Paine had no
cyclopædia in his knapsack. The literary musket
reaches its mark. The pamphlet was never surpassed for true eloquence—that is, for the power
that carries its point. With skilful illustration of
lofty principles by significant 'etails, all summed
with simplicity and sympathy, three of the most

miserable weeks ever endured by men were raised into epical dignity.   The wives, daughters, mothers, sisters, seemed stretching out appealing hands against the mythically monstrous Hessians.   The great commander, previously pointed to as "a mind that can even flourish upon care," presently saw his dispirited soldiers beaming with hope, and bounding to the onset,—their watchword : *These are the times that try men's souls !*   Trenton was won, the Hessians captured, and a New Year broke for America on the morrow of that Christmas Day, 1776.[1]

Paine's Trenton musket had hardly cooled, or the pen of his first *Crisis* dried, before he began to write another.   It appeared about four weeks after the battle and is addressed to Lord Howe. The Thetford mechanic has some pride in confronting this English lord who had offered the Americans mercy.   "Your lordship, I find, has now commenced author, and published a Proclamation ; I have published a Crisis."   The rumors of his being a hireling scribe, or gaining wealth by his publications, made it necessary for Paine to speak of himself at the conclusion :

[1] Paine's enemy, Cheetham, durst not, in the face of Washington's expression of his "lively sense of the importance of your [Paine's] works," challenge well known facts, and must needs partly confess them : "The number was read in the camp, to every corporal's guard, and in the army and out of it had more than the intended effect.   The convention of New York, reduced by dispersion, occasioned by alarm, to nine members, was rallied and reanimated.   Militiamen who, already tired of the war, were straggling from the army, returned.   Hope succeeded to despair, cheerfulness to gloom, and firmness to irresolution.   To the confidence which it inspired may be attributed much of the brilliant little affair which in the same month followed at Trenton."   Even Oldys is somewhat impressed by Paine's courage : "The Congress fled.   All were dismayed.   Not so our author."

"What I write is pure nature, and my pen and my soul have ever gone together. My writings I have always given away, receiving only the expense of printing and paper, and sometimes not even that. I never counted either fame or interest, and my manner of life, to those who know it, will justify what I say. My study is to be useful, and if your lordship loves mankind as well as I do, you would, seeing you cannot conquer us, cast about and lend your hand towards accomplishing a peace. Our independence, with God's blessing, we will maintain against all the world ; but as we wish to avoid evil ourselves, we wish not to inflict it on others. I am never over-inquisitive into the secrets of the cabinet, but I have some notion that, if you neglect the present opportunity, it will not be in our power to make a separate peace with you afterwards ; for whatever treaties or alliances we form we shall most faithfully abide by ; wherefore you may be deceived if you think you can make it with us at any time."

Thus the humble author of the *Crisis* offers the noble author of the Proclamation "mercy," on condition of laying down his arms, and going home ; but it must be at once !

If Howe, as is most likely, considered this mere impudence, he presently had reason to take it more seriously. For there were increasing indications that Paine was in the confidence of those who controlled affairs. On January 21st he was appointed by the Council of Safety in Philadelphia secretary to the commission sent by Congress to treat with the Indians at Easton, Pennsylvania. The commissioners, with a thousand dollars' worth of presents, met the Indian chiefs in the German Reformed Church (built 1776), and, as they reported to Congress, "after shaking hands, drinking rum, while the organ played, we proceeded to business."[1]

[1] Condit's "History of Easton," pp. 60, 118.

The report was, no doubt, written by Paine, who for his services was paid £300 by the Pennsylvania Assembly (one of its advances for Congress, afterwards refunded). In a public letter, written in 1807, Paine relates an anecdote concerning this meeting with the Indians.

"The chief of the tribes, who went by the name of King *Last-night*, because his tribe had sold their lands, had seen some English men-of-war in some of the waters of Canada, and was impressed with the power of those great canoes ; but he saw that the English made no progress against us by land. This was enough for an Indian to form an opinion by. He could speak some English, and in conversation with me, alluding to the great canoes, he gave me his idea of the power of a king of England, by the following metaphor. 'The king of England,' said he, 'is like a fish. When he is in the water he can wag his tail ; when he comes on land he lays down on his side.' Now if the English government had but half the sense this Indian had, they would not have sent Duckworth to Constantinople, and Douglas to Norfolk, to lay down on their side."

On April 17th, when Congress transformed the " Committee of Secret Correspondence " into the " Committee of Foreign Affairs," Paine was elected its secretary. His friend, Dr. Franklin, had reached France in December, 1776, where Arthur Lee and Silas Deane were already at work. Lord Howe might, indeed, have done worse than take Paine's advice concerning the " opportunity," which did not return. General Howe did, indeed, presently occupy a fine abode in Philadelphia, but only kept it warm, to be afterwards the executive mansion of President Washington.

CHAPTER VIII.

AFTER their disaster at Trenton, the English forces suspended hostilities for a long time. Paine, maintaining his place on General Greene's staff, complied with the wish of all the generals by wielding his pen during the truce of arms. He sat himself down in Philadelphia, " Second Street, opposite the Quaker meeting,"—as he writes the address. The Quakers regarded him as Antichrist pursuing them into close quarters. Untaught by castigation, the leaders of the Society, and chiefly one John Pemberton, disguised allies of the Howes, had put forth, November 20, 1776, a second and more dangerous " testimony." In it they counsel Friends to refuse obedience to whatever " instructions or ordinances " may be published, not warranted by " that happy constitution under which they and others long enjoyed tranquillity and peace." In his second *Crisis* (January 13, 1777) Paine refers to this document, and a memorial, from " a meeting of a reputable number of the inhabitants of the city of Philadelphia," called attention of the Board of Safety to its treasonable character. The Board, however, not having acted, Paine devoted his next three months to a treatment of that and all other moral and political problems which had been developed by the course of the Revolution, and must be practically dealt with.   In reading this third *Crisis*, one feels in every sentence its writer's increased sense of responsibility. Events had given him the seat of a lawgiver.   His first pamphlet had dictated the Declaration of Independence, his second had largely won its first victory, his third had demonstrated the impossibility of subjugation, and offered England peace on the only possible terms.   The American heart had responded without a dissonant note; he held it in his hand; he knew that what he was writing in that room "opposite the Quaker meeting" were Acts of Congress.   So it proved.   The third *Crisis* was dated April 19, 1777, the second anniversary of the first collision (Lexington).   It was as effective in dealing with the internal enemies of the country as the first had been in checking its avowed foes. It was written in a city still largely, if not preponderantly, "tory," and he deals with them in all their varieties, not arraigning the Friends as a Society. Having carefully shown that independence, from being a natural right, had become a political and moral necessity, and the war one "on which a world is staked," he says that "Tories" endeavoring to insure their property with the enemy should be made to fear still more losing it on the other side.   Paine proposes an "oath or affirmation" renouncing allegiance to the King, pledging support to the United States.   At the same time let a tax of ten, fifteen, or twenty per cent. be levied on all property.   Each who takes the oath may exempt his property by holding himself ready to do what service he can for the cause; they who refuse the oath will be paying a tax on their insurance with the enemy. " It would not only be good policy but strict justice to raise fifty or one hundred thousand pounds, or more, if it is necessary, out of the estates and property of the King of England's votaries, resident in Philadelphia, to be distributed as a reward to those inhabitants of the city and State who should turn out and repulse the enemy should they attempt to march this way."

These words were written at a moment when a vigorous opposition, in and out of Congress, was offered to Washington's Proclamation (Morristown, January 25, 1777,) demanding that an oath of allegiance to the United States should be required of all who had taken such an oath to the King, non-jurors to remove within the enemy's lines, or be treated as enemies. Paine's proposal was partly followed on June 13th, when Pennsylvania exacted an oath of allegiance to the State from all over eighteen years of age.

Paine was really the Secretary of Foreign Affairs. His election had not been without opposition, and, according to John Adams, there was a suggestion that some of his earlier writings had been unfavorable to this country. What the reference was I cannot understand unless it was to his anti-slavery essay, in which he asked Americans with what consistency they could protest against being enslaved while they were enslaving others. That essay, I have long believed, caused a secret, silent, hostility to the author by which he suffered much without suspecting it. But he was an indefatigable secretary. An example of the care with which foreign representatives were kept informed appears in a letter to William Bingham, agent of Congress at Martinique.

"PHILADELPHIA, July 16th, 1777.—SIR,—A very sudden opportunity offers of sending you the News-papers, from which you will collect the situation of our Affairs. The Enemy finding their attempt of marching thro' the Jersies to this City impracticable, have retreated to Staten Island seemingly discontented and dispirited and quite at a loss what step next to pursue. Our Army is now well recruited and formidable. Our Militia in the several States ready at a day's notice to turn out and support the Army when occasion requires; and tho' we cannot, in the course of a Campaign, expect everything in the several Parts of the Continent, to go just as we wish it; yet the general face of our Affairs assures us of final success.

"In the Papers of June 18th & 25 and July 2d you will find Genl. Washington and Arnold's Letters of the Enemy's movement in, and retreat from the Jersies. We are under some apprehensions for Ticonderoga, as we find the Enemy are unexpectedly come into that Quarter. The Congress have several times had it in contemplation to remove the Garrison from that Place—as by Experience we find that Men shut up in Forts are not of so much use as in the field, especially in the highlands where every hill is a natural fortification.

"I am Sir

"Your Obt. Humble Servt.

"THOMAS PAINE.

"Secretry. to the Committee for Foreign Affairs."[1]

After the occupation of Philadelphia by the British (September 26, 1777), Paine had many adventures, as we shall presently see. He seems to have been with Washington at Valley Forge

---

[1] MS., for which I am indebted to Mr. Simon Gratz, Philadelphia.

when the Pennsylvania Assembly and President (Thomas Wharton, Jr.,) confided to him the delicate and arduous task assigned by the following from Timothy Matlack, Secretary of the Assembly:

"LANCASTER, Oct. 10, 1777. SIR,—The Hon'ble house of As'y have proposed and Council have adopted a plan of obtaining more regular and constant intelligence of the proceeding of Gen. Washington's army than has hitherto been had. Everyone agrees that you are the proper person for this purpose, and I am directed by his Exc'y, the pr't, to write to you hereon (the Prs't being engaged in writing to the Gen'l, and the Express in waiting).

"The Assembly have agreed to make you a reasonable compensation for your services in this business, if you think proper to engage in it, which I hope you will ; as it is a duty of importance that there are few, however well disposed, who are capable of doing in a manner that will answer all the intentions of it—perhaps a correspondence of this kind may be the fairest opportunity of giving to Council some important hints that may occur to you on interesting subjects.

"Proper expresses will be engaged in this business. If the expresses which pass from headquarters to Congress can be made use of so much the better ;—of this you must be judge.

"I expect Mr. Rittenhouse will send you a copy of the testimony of the late Y. M. by this opp'y, if time will admit it to be copied—'t is a poor thing.—Yours, &c., T. M." [1]

What with this service, and his correspondence with foreign agents, Paine had his hands pretty full. But at the same time he wrote important letters to leading members of Congress, then in session at York, Pennsylvania.

The subjoined letter sheds fresh light on a somewhat obscure point in our revolutionary history,— the obscurity being due to the evasions of Ameri-

[1] Pa. Arch., 1779, p. 659. Paine at once set to work : p. 693, 694.

can historians on an episode of which we have little reason to be proud. An article of Burgoyne's capitulation (October 17th) was as follows :

"A free passage to be granted to the army under General Burgoyne to Great Britain, upon condition of not serving again in North America during the present contest: and the port of Boston to be assigned for entry of transports to receive the troops whenever General Howe shall so order."

A letter was written by Paine to Hon. Richard Henry Lee, dated at "Headquarters, fourteen miles from Philadelphia," October 30th, 1777.

"I wrote you last Tuesday 21st Inst., including a Copy of the King's speech, since which nothing material has happened at Camp. Genl. McDougal was sent last Wednesday night 22d. to attack a Party of the Enemy who lay over the Schuylkill at Grey's Ferry where they have a Bridge. Genls. Greene & Sullivan went down to make a diversion below German Town at the same Time. I was with this last Party, but as the Enemy withdrew their Detachment We had only our Labor for our Pains.

"No Particulars of the Northern Affair have yet come to head Qrs., the want of which has caused much Speculation. A copy, said to be the Articles of Capitulation was recd. 3 or 4 days ago, but they rather appear to be some proposals made by Burgoyne, than the Capitulation itself. By those Articles it appears to me that Burgoyne has capitulated upon Terms, which we have a right to doubt the full performance of, Vizt., 'That the Offrs. and Men shall be Transported to England and not serve in or against North America during the present War '— or words to this effect.

"I remark, that this Capitulation, if true, has the air of a National treaty ; it is binding, not only on Burgoyne as a *General*, but on England as a *Nation ;* because the Troops are to be subject to the conditions of the Treaty after they return to England and are out of his Command. It regards England and America as Separate Sovereign States, and puts them on an equal footing by staking the faith and honor of the former for the performance of a Contract entered into with the latter.

"What in the Capitulation is stiled the '*Present War*' England affects to call a '*Rebellion*,' and while she holds this Idea and denies any knowledge of America as a Separate Sovereign Power, she will not conceive herself bound by any Capitulation or Treaty entered into by her Generals which is to bind her as a *Nation*, and more especially in those Cases where both Pride and present Advantage tempt her to a Violation. She will deny Burgoyne's Right and Authority for making such a Treaty, and will, very possibly, show her insult by first censuring him for entering into it, and then immediately sending the Troops back.

"I think we ought to be exceedingly cautious how we trust her with the power of abusing our Credulity. We have no authority for believing she will perform that part of the Contract which subjects her not to send the Troops to America during the War. The insolent Answer given to the Commissrs. by Ld. Stormont, '*that the King's Ambassadors recd. no Letters from Rebels but when they came to crave Mercy*,' sufficiently instructs us not to entrust them with the power of insulting Treaties of Capitulation.

"Query, Whether it wd. not be proper to detain the Troops at Boston & direct the Commissioners at Paris to present the Treaty of Capitulation to the English Court thro' the hands of Ld. Stormont, to know whether it be the intention of that Court to abide strictly by the Conditions and Obligations thereof, and if no assurance be obtained to keep the Troops until they can be exchanged here.

"Tho' we have no immediate knowledge of any alliance formed by our Commissioners with France or Spain, yet we have no assurance there is not, and our immediate release of those prisoners, by sending them to England, may operate to the injury of such Allied Powers, and be perhaps directly contrary to some contract subsisting between us and them prior to the Capitulation. I think we ought to know this first.—Query, ought we not (knowing the infidelity they have already acted) to suspect they will evade the Treaty by putting back into New York under pretence of distress.—I would not trust them an inch farther than I could see them in the present state of things.

"The Army was to have marched yesterday about 2 or 3 Miles but the weather has been so exceedingly bad for three days past as to prevent any kind of movement, the waters are so much out and the rivulets so high there is no passing from one part of ye Camp to another.

"I wish the Northern Army was down here. I am apt to think that nothing materially offensive will take place on our part at present. Some Means must be taken to fill up the Army this winter. I look upon the recruiting service at an end and that some other plan must be adopted. Suppose the Service be by draft—and that those who are not drawn should contribute a Dollar or two Dollars a Man to him on whom the lot falls.—something of this kind would proportion the Burthen, and those who are drawn would have something either to encourage them to go, or to provide a substitute with— After closing this Letter I shall go again to Fort Mifflin ; all was safe there on the 27th, but from some preparations of the Enemy they expect another attack somewhere.

"The enclosed return of provision and Stores is taken from an account signed by Burgoyne and sent to Ld. George Germain. I have not time to Copy the whole. Burgoyne closes his Letter as follows, ' By a written account found in the Commissary's House at Ticonderoga Six thousand odd hundred Persons were fed from the Magazine the day before the evacuation.'

"I am Dear Sir, Yr. Affectionate Hble. Servt.

"T. PAINE.

"Respectful Compts. to Friends.

"If the Congress has the Capitulation and Particulars of ye Surrender, they do an exceeding wrong thing by not publishing ym. because they subject the whole Affair to Suspicion." [1]

Had this proposal of Paine, with regard to Burgoyne's capitulation, been followed at once, a blot

---

[1] I am indebted for this letter to Dr. John S. H. Fogg of Boston. It bears the superscription : " Honbl. Richd. Henry Lee Esq. (in Congress) York Town. Forwarded by yr humble Servt. T. Matlack, Nov. 1, 1777." Endorsed in handwriting of Lee : " Oct : 1777. Mr. Paine, Author of ' Common Sense.' "

on the history of our Revolution might have been prevented. The time required to march the prisoners to Boston and prepare the transports would have given England opportunity to ratify the articles of capitulation. Washington, with characteristic inability to see injustice in anything advantageous to America, desired Congress to delay in every possible way the return of the prisoners to England, "since the most virtuous adhesion to the articles would not prevent their replacing in garrison an equal number of soldiers who might be sent against us." The troops were therefore delayed on one pretext and another until Burgoyne declared that "the publick faith is broke." Congress seized on this remark to resolve that the embarkation should be suspended until an "explicit ratification of the Convention of Saratoga shall be properly ratified by the Court of Great Britain." This resolution, passed January 8, 1778, was not communicated to Burgoyne until February 4th. If any one should have suffered because of a remark made in a moment of irritation it should have been Burgoyne himself ; but he was presently allowed to proceed to England, while his troops were retained,—a confession that Burgoyne's casual complaint was a mere pretext for further delay. It may be added that the English government behaved to its surrendered soldiers worse than Congress. The question of ratifying the Saratoga Convention was involved in a partisan conflict in Parliament, the suffering prisoners in America were forgotten, and they were not released until the peace,—five years after they had marched "with the honours of war," under a pledge of departure conceded by Gen. Gates in reply to a declaration that unless conceded they would "to a man proceed to any act of desperation sooner than submit."

Concerning this ugly business there is a significant silence in Paine's public writings. He would not have failed to discuss the matter in his *Crisis* had he felt that anything honorable to the American name or cause could be made out of it.[1]

In his letter to Hon. R. H. Lee (October 30, 1777) Paine mentions that he is about leaving the head-quarters near Philadelphia for Fort Mifflin. Mr. Asa Bird Gardener, of New York, who has closely studied Paine's military career, writes me some account of it.

"Major-Gen. Greene was charged with the defence of the Delaware, and part of Brig.-Gen. Varnum's brigade was placed in garrison at Fort Mercer, Red Bank, and at Fort Mifflin, Mud Island. A bloody and unsuccessful assault was made by Count Donop and 1,200 Hessians on Fort Mercer, defended by the 1st and 2d Reg'ts. R. I. Continental Inf'y. The entire British fleet was then brought up opposite Fort Mifflin, and the most furious cannonade, and most desperate but finally unsuccessful defence of the place was made. The entire works were demolished, and most of the garrison killed and wounded. Major-Gen. Greene being anxious for the garrison and desirous of knowing its ability to resist sent Mr. Paine to ascertain. He accordingly went to Fort Mercer, and from thence, on Nov. 9 (1777) went with Col. Christopher Greene, commanding Fort Mercer, in an open boat to Fort Mifflin, during the cannonade, and were there when the enemy opened with two-gun batteries and a mortar battery. This *very* gallant act

---

[1] Professor Fiske ("Am. Revolution," i., p. 341) has a ferocious attack on Congress for breaking faith in this matter, but no doubt he has by this time read, in Ford's "Writings of Washington," (vol. vi.) the letters which bring his attack on the great commander's own haloed head.

shows what a fearless man Mr. Paine was, and entitles him to the same credit for service in the Revolution as any Continental could claim."

The succession of mistakes, surprises, panics, which occasioned the defeats before Philadelphia and ended in the occupation of that city by the British general, seriously affected the reputation of Washington.   Though Paine believed that Washington's generalship had been at fault (as Washington himself probably did[1]), he could utter nothing that might injure the great cause.   He mistrusted the singleness of purpose of Washington's opponents, and knew that the commander-in-chief was as devoted as himself to the American cause, and would never surrender it whatever should befall. While, therefore, the intrigues were going on at Yorktown, Pennsylvania, whither Congress had retreated, and Washington with his ill-fed and ill-clad army were suffering at Valley Forge, Paine was writing his fifth *Crisis*, which had the most happy effect.   It was dated at Lancaster, March 21, 1778.   Before that time (February 19th) General Gates had made his peace with Washington, and the intrigue was breaking up, but gloom and dissatisfaction remained.   The contrast between the luxurious " Tories" surrounding Howe in Philadelphia, and Washington's wretched five thousand at Valley Forge, was demoralizing the country.   The first part of this *Crisis*, addressed "to General Sir William Howe," pointed wrangling patriots to the common enemy ; the second, addressed " to the

[1] See his letter to the President of Congress.   Ford's " Writings of Washington," vol. vi., p. 82.

inhabitants of America," sounded a note of courage, and gave good reasons for it. Never was aid more artistic than that Paine's pen now gave Washington. The allusions to him are incidental, there is no accent of advocacy. While mentioning "the unabated fortitude of a Washington," he lays a laurel on the brow of Gates, on that of Herkimer, and even on the defeated. While belittling all that Howe had gained, telling him that in reaching Philadelphia, he "mistook a trap for a conquest," he reunites Washington and Gates, *in the public mind,* by showing the manœuvres of the one near Philadelphia part of the other's victory at Saratoga. It is easy for modern eulogists of Washington to see this, but when Paine said it,—apparently aiming only to humiliate Howe,—the sentence was a sunbeam parting a black cloud. Coming from a member of Greene's staff, from an author whose daring at Fort Mifflin had made him doubly a hero; from the military correspondent of the Pennsylvania Council, and the Secretary of the Congressional Committee of Foreign Affairs,—Paine's optimistic view of the situation had immense effect. He hints his official knowledge that Britain's "reduced strength and exhausted coffers in a three years' war with America hath given a powerful superiority to France and Spain," and advises Americans to leave wrangling to the enemy. "We never had so small an army to fight against, nor so fair an opportunity of final success as *now.*"

This fifth *Crisis* was written mainly at Lancaster, Pa., at the house of William Henry, Jr., where he several times found shelter while dividing his time between Washington's head-quarters and York.[1] Every number of the *Crisis* was thus written with full information from both the military and political leaders. This *Crisis* was finished and printed at York, and there Paine begins No. VI. The " stone house on the banks of the Cadorus," at York, is still pointed out by a trustworthy tradition as that to which he bore the chest of congressional papers with which he had fled to Trenton, when Howe entered Philadelphia.[2] It is a pleasant abode in a picturesque country, and no doubt Paine would have been glad to remain there in repose. But whoever slept on his watch during the Revolution Paine did not. The fifth *Crisis* printed, he goes to forward the crisis he will publish next. In April he is again at Lancaster, and on the 11th writes thence to his friend Henry Laurens, President of Congress.[3]

" LANCASTER, April 11th, 1778. Sir,—I take the liberty of mentioning an affair to you which I think deserves the attention of Congress. The persons who came from Philadelphia some time ago with, or in company with, a flag from the Enemy, and were taken up and committed to Lancaster Jail for attempting to put off counterfeit Contl. money, were yesterday brought to Tryal and are likely to escape by means of an artful and partial Construction of an Act of this State for punishing such offences. The Act makes it felony to counterfeit the money *emitted* by Congress, or to circulate such counterfeits knowing them to be so. The offenders' Council

---

[1] This I learn by a note from Mr. Henry's descendant, John W. Jordan. At this time Paine laid before Henry his scheme for steam-navigation.

[2] The house is marked " B. by J. B. Cookis in the year 1761." It is probable that Congress deemed it prudent to keep important documents a little way from the edifice in the centre of the town where it met, a building which no longer stands.

[3] I am indebted to Mr. Simon Gratz, of Philadelphia, for this and several other letters of Paine to Laurens.

explained the word 'emitted' to have only a retrospect
meaning by supplying the Idea of '*which have been*' 'emitted
by Congress.' Therefore say they the Act cannot be applied to any money emitted after the date of the Act. I
believe the words 'emitted by Congress' means only, and
should be understood, to distinguish Continental Money from
other Money, and not one Time from another Time. It has,
as I conceive, no referrence to any Particular Time, but only to
the particular authority which distinguishes Money so emitted
from Money emitted by the State. It is meant only as a discription of the Money, and not of the Time of striking it, but
includes the Idea of all Time as inseparable from the Continuance of the authority of Congress. But be this as it may ; the
offence is Continental and the consequences of the same extent. I can have no Idea of any particular State pardoning
an offence against all, or even their letting an offender slip
legally who is accountable to all and every State alike for his
crime. The place where he commits it is the least circumstance of it. It is a mere accident and has nothing or very
little to do with the crime itself. I write this hoping the Information will point out the necessity of the Congress supporting their emissions by claiming every offender in this line
where the present deficiency of the Law or the Partial Interpretation of it operates to the Injustice and Injury of the
whole Continent.

"I beg leave to trouble you with another hint. Congress I
learn has something to propose thro' the Commissrs. on the
Cartel respecting the admission and stability of the Continental
Currency. As Forgery is a Sin against all men alike, and reprobated by all civil nations, Query, would it not be right to
require of General Howe the Persons of Smithers and others
in Philadelphia suspected of this crime ; and if He, or any
other Commander, continues to conceal or protect them in
such practices, that, in such case, the Congress will consider
the crime as the Act of the Commander-in-Chief. Howe
affects not to know the Congress—he ought to be made to
know them ; and the apprehension of Personal Consequences
may have some effect on his Conduct. I am, Dear Sir,
            "Your obt. and humble Servt.,
                        " T. PAINE.

"Since writing the foregoing the Prisoners have had their Tryal, the one is acquitted and the other convicted only of a Fraud ; for as the law now stands, or rather as it is explained, the counterfeiting—or circulating counterfeits—is only a fraud. I do not believe it was the intention of the Act to make it so, and I think it misapplied Lenity in the Court to suffer such an Explanation, because it has a tendency to invite and encourage a Species of Treason, the most prejudicial to us of any or all the other kinds.   I am aware how very difficult it is to make a law so very perfect at first as not to be subject to false or perplexed conclusions.   There never was but one Act (said a Member of the House of Commons) which a man might not creep out of, *i. e.* the Act which obliges a man to be buried in woollen.   T. P."

The active author and secretary had remained in Philadelphia two days after Howe had crossed the Schuylkill, namely, until September 21st.   The events of that time, and of the winter, are related in a letter to Franklin, in Paris, which is of too much historical importance for any part of it to be omitted.   It is dated Yorktown, May 16, 1778.

"Your favor of Oct. 7th did not come to me till March.   I was at Camp when Capt. Folger, arrived with the Blank Packet. The private Letters were, I believe, all safe.   Mr. Laurens forwarded yours to York Town where I afterwards recd. it.

"The last winter has been rather barren of military events, but for your amusement I send you a little history how I have passed away part of the time.

"The 11th of Sepr. last I was preparing Dispatches for you when the report of cannon at Brandywine interrupted my proceeding.   The event of that day you have doubtless been informed of, which, excepting the Enemy keeping the ground, may be deemed a drawn battle.   Genl. Washington collected his Army at Chester, and the Enemy's not moving towards him next day must be attributed to the disability they sustained and the burthen of their wounded.   On the 16th of the same month, the two Armies were drawn up in order of battle near the White horse on the Lancaster road, when a most violent and incessant storm of rain prevented an action. Our Army sustained a heavy loss in their Ammunition, the Cartouch Boxes, especially as they were not of the most seasoned leather, being no proof agst. the almost incredible fury of the weather, which obliged Genl. Washn. to draw his Army up into the country till those injuries could be repaired, and a new supply of ammunition procured. The Enemy in the mean time kept on the West Side of Schuylkill. On Fryday the 19th about one in the morning the first alarm of their crossing was given, and the confusion, as you may suppose, was very great. It was a beautiful still moonlight morning and the streets as full of men women and children as on a market day. On the eveng. before I was fully persuaded that unless something was done the City would be lost ; and under that anxiety I went to Col. Bayard, speaker of the house of Assembly, and represented, as I very particularly knew it, the situation we were in, and the probability of saving the City if proper efforts were made for that purpose. I reasoned thus—Genl. Washn. was about 30 Miles up the Schuylkill with an Army properly collected waiting for Ammunition, besides which, a reinforcement of 1500 men were marching from the Norfh River to join him ; and if only an appearance of defence be made in the City by throwing up works at the heads of streets, it will make the Enemy very suspicious how they throw themselves between the City and Genl. Washington, and between two Rivers, which must have been the case ; for notwithstanding the knowledge which military gentlemen are supposed to have, I observe they move exceedingly cautiously on new ground, are exceedingly suspicious of Villages and Towns, and more perplexed at seemingly little things which they cannot clearly understand than at great ones which they are fully acquainted with. And I think it very probable that Genl. Howe would have mistaken our necessity for a deep laid scheme and not have ventured himself in the middle of it. But admitting that he had, he must either have brought his whole Army down, or a part of it. If the whole, Gen. W. would have followed him, perhaps the same day, in two or three days at most, and our assistance in the City would have been material. If only a part of it, we should have been a match for them, and Gen. W. superior to those which remained above. The chief thing was, whether the cityzens would turn out to defend the City. My proposal to Cols. Bayard and Bradford was to call them together the next morning, make them fully acquainted with the situation and the means and prospect of preserving themselves, and that the City had better voluntarily assess itself 50,000 for its defence than suffer an Enemy to come into it. Cols. Bayard and Bradford were in my opinion, and as Genl. Mifflin was then in town, I next went to him, acquainted him with our design, and mentioned likewise that if two or three thousand men could be mustered up whether we might depend on him to command them, for without some one to lead, nothing could be done. He declined that part, not being then very well, but promised what assistance he could.—A few hours after this the alarm happened. I went directly to Genl. Mifflin but he had sett off, and nothing was done. I cannot help being of opinion that the City might have been saved, but perhaps it is better otherwise.

"I staid in the City till Sunday [Sep. 21st], having sent my Chest and everything belonging to the foreign Committee to Trenton in a Shallop. The Enemy did not cross the river till the Wednesday following. Hearing on the Sunday that Genl. Washn. had moved to Swederford I set off for that place but learning on the road that it was a mistake and that he was six or seven miles above that place, I crossed over to Southfield and the next Morning to Trenton, to see after my Chest. On the Wednesday Morning I intended returning to Philadelphia, but was informed at Bristol of the Enemy's crossing the Schuylkill. At this place I met Col. Kirkbride of Pennsburg Manor, who invited me home with him. On Fryday the 26th a Party of the Enemy about 1500 took possession of the City, and the same day an account arrived that Col. Brown had taken 300 of the Enemy at the old french lines at Ticonderoga and destroyed all their Water Craft, being about 200 boats of different kinds.

"On the 29th Sept. I sett off for Camp without well knowing where to find it, every day occasioning some movement. I kept pretty high up the country, and being unwilling to ask questions, not knowing what company I might be in, I was three days before I fell in with it. The Army had moved about three

miles lower down that morning. The next day they made a
movement about the same distance, to the 21 Mile Stone on the
Skippach Road—Head Quarters at John Wince's. On the 3d
Octr. in the morning they began to fortify the Camp, as a deception ; and about 9 at Night marched for German Town.
The Number of Continental Troops was between 8 and 9000,
besides Militia, the rest remaining as Guards for the security of
Camp. Genl. Greene, whose Quarters I was at, desired me to
remain there till Morning. I set off for German Town about 5
next morning. The Skirmishing with the Pickets began soon
after. I met no person for several miles riding, which I concluded to be a good sign ; after this I met a man on horseback
who told me he was going to hasten on a supply of ammunition, that the Enemy were broken and retreating fast, which
was true. I saw several country people with arms in their
hands running cross a field towards German Town, within about
five or six miles, at which I met several of the wounded on
waggons, horseback, and on foot. I passed Genl. Nash on a
litter made of poles, but did not know him. I felt unwilling to
ask questions lest the information should not be agreeable, and
kept on. About two miles after this I passed a promiscuous
crowd of wounded and otherwise who were halted at a house
to refresh. Col: Biddle D.Q.N.G. was among them, who called
after me, that if I went farther on that road I should be taken,
for that the firing which I heard ahead was the Enemy's. I
never could, and cannot now learn, and I believe no man can
inform truly the cause of that day's miscarriage.

"The retreat was as extraordinary. Nobody hurried themselves. Every one marched his own pace. The Enemy kept
a civil distance behind, sending every now and then a Shot
after us, and receiving the same from us. That part of the
Army which I was with collected and formed on the Hill on
the side of the road near White Marsh Church ; the Enemy
came within three quarters of a mile and halted. The orders
on Retreat were to assemble that night on the back of Perkiominy Creek, about 7 miles above Camp, which had orders to
move. The Army had marched the preceding night 14 miles
and having full 20 to march back were exceedingly fatigued.
They appeared to me to be only sensible of a disappointment,
not a defeat, and to be more displeased at their retreating from

German Town, than anxious to get to their rendezvous. I was so lucky that night to get to a little house about 4 miles wide of Perkiominy, towards which place in the morning I heard a considerable firing, which distressed me exceedingly, knowing that our army was much harassed and not collected. However, I soon relieved myself by going to see. They were discharging their pieces, wch. tho' necessary, prevented several Parties going till next day. I breakfasted next morning at Genl. W. Quarters, who was at the same loss with every other to account for the accidents of the day. I remember his expressing his Surprise, by saying, that at the time he supposed every thing secure, and was about giving orders for the Army to proceed down to Philadelphia ; that he most unexpectedly saw a Part (I think of the Artillery) hastily retreating. This partial Retreat was, I believe, misunderstood, and soon followed by others. The fog was frequently very thick, the Troops young and unused to breaking and rallying, and our men rendered suspicious to each other, many of them being in Red. A new Army once disordered is difficult to manage, the attempt dangerous. To this may be added a prudence in not putting matters to too hazardous a tryal the first time. Men must be taught *regular* fighting by practice and degrees, and tho' the expedition failed, it had this good effect—that they seemed to feel themselves more important *after* it than *before*, as it was the first general attack they had ever made.

"I have not related the affair at Mr Chew's house German Town, as I was not there, but have seen it since. It certainly afforded the Enemy time to rally—yet the matter was difficult. To have pressed on and left 500 Men in ye rear, might by a change of circumstances been ruinous. To attack them was loss of time, as the house is a strong stone building, proof against any 12 pounder. Genl. Washington sent a flag, thinking it would procure their surrender and expedite his march to Philadelphia ; it was refused, and circumstances changed almost directly after.

" I staid in Camp two days after the Germantown action, and lest any ill impression should get among the Garrisons at Mud Island and Red Bank, and the Vessels and Gallies stationed there, I crossed over to the Jersies at Trenton and went down to those places. I laid the first night on board the Champion Continental Galley, who was stationed off the mouth of

Schuylkill. The Enemy threw up a two Gun Battery on the point of the river's mouth opposite the Pest House. The next morning was a thick fog, and as soon as it cleared away, and we became visible to each other, they opened on the Galley, who returned the fire. The Commodore made a signal to bring the Galley under the Jersey shore, as she was not a match for the Battery, nor the Battery a sufficient Object for the Galley. One Shot went thro' the fore sail, wch. was all. At noon I went with Col. [Christopher] Greene, who commanded at Red Bank, over to fort Mifflin (Mud Island). The Enemy opened that day 2 two-gun Batteries, and a Mortar Battery, on the fort. They threw about 30 Shells into it that afternoon, without doing any damage ; the ground being damp and spongy, not above five or six burst ; not a man was killed or wounded. I came away in the evening, laid on board the Galley, and the next day came to Col. Kirkbride's [Bordentown N. J.] ; staid a few days, and came again to Camp. An Expedition was on foot the evening I got there in which I went as Aid de Camp to Genl. Greene, having a Volunteer Commission for that purpose. The Occasion was—a Party of the Enemy, about 1500, lay over the Schuylkill at Grey's ferry. Genl. McDougall with his Division was sent to attack them ; and Sullivan & Greene with their Divisions were to favor the enterprise by a feint on the City, down the Germantown road. They set off about nine at night, and halted at day break, between German Town and the City, the advanced Party at the three Miles Run. As I knew the ground I went with two light horse to discover the Enemy's Picket, but the dress of the light horse being white made them, I thought, too visible, as it was then twilight ; on which I left them with my horse, and went on foot, till I distinctly saw the Picket at Mr. Dickerson's place,—which is the nearest I have been to Philadelphia since Sepr., except once at Coopers ferry, as I went to the forts. Genl. Sullivan was at Dr. Redman's house, and McDougall's beginning the attack was to be the Signal for moving down to the City. But the Enemy either on the approach of McDougall, or on information of it, called in their Party, and the Expedition was frustrated.

" A Cannonade, by far the most furious I ever heard, began down the river, soon after daylight, the first Gun of which we supposed to be the Signal ; but was soon undeceived, there being no small Arms.   After waiting two hours beyond the time, we marched back, the cannon was then less frequent ; but on the road between German town and White marsh we were stuned with a report as loud as a peal from a hundred Cannon at once ; and turning round I saw a thick smoke rising like a pillar, and spreading from the top like a tree.   This was the blowing up of the Augusta.   I did not hear the explosion of the Berlin.

" After this I returned to Col. Kirkbride's where I staid about a fortnight, and set off again to Camp.   The day after I got there Genls. Greene, Wayne, and Cadwallader, with a Party of light horse, were ordered on a reconnoitering Party towards the forts.   We were out four days and nights without meeting with any thing material.   An East Indiaman, whom the Enemy had cut down so as to draw but little water, came up, without guns, while we were on foot on Carpenter's Island, going to Province Island.   Her Guns were brought up in the evening in a flat, she got in the rear of the Fort, where few or no Guns could bear upon her, and the next morning, played on it incessantly.   The night following the fort was evacuated.   The obstruction the Enemy met with from those forts, and the *Chevaux de frise* was extraordinary, and had it not been that the Western Channel, deepened by the current, being somewhat obstructed by the *Chevaux de frise* in the main river, which enabled them to bring up the light Indiaman Battery, it is a doubt whether they would have succeeded at last.   By that assistance they reduced the fort, and got sufficient command of the river to move some of the late sunk *Chevaux de frise.*   Soon after this the fort on Red Bank, (which had bravely repulsed the Enemy a little time before) was avacuated, the Gallies ordered up to Bristol, and the Capts. of such other armed Vessels as *thought* they could not pass on the Eastward side of Wind mill Island, very precipitately set them on fire.   As I judged from this event that the Enemy would winter in Philadelphia, I began to think of preparing for York Town, which however I was willing to delay, hoping that the ice would afford opportunity for new Manœuvres.   But the season passed very barrenly away.   I staid at Col. Kirkbride's till the latter end of Janay.   Commodore Haslewood, who commanded the remains of the fleet at Trenton, acquainted me with a scheme of his for burning the Enemy's Shipping, which was by sending a charged boat across the river from Cooper's ferry, by means of a Rocket fixt in its stern. Considering the width of the river, the tide, and the variety of accidents that might change its direction, I thought the project trifling and insufficient; and proposed to him, that if he would get a boat properly choyed, and take a Batteau in tow, sufficient to bring three or four persons off, that I would make one with him and two other persons who might be relied on to go down on that business. One of the Company, Capn. Blewer of Philadelphia, seconded the proposal, but the Commodore, and, what I was more surprized at, Col. Bradford, declined it. The burning of part of the Delaware fleet, the precipitate retreat of the rest, the little service rendered by them and the great expence they were at, make the only national blot in the proceedings of the last Campaign. I felt a strong anxiety for them to recover their credit, wch., among others, was one motive for my proposal. After this I came to camp, and from thence to York Town, and published the Crisis No. 5, To Genl. Howe. I have began No. 6, which I intend to address to Ld. North.

"I was not at Camp when Genl. Howe marched out on the 20th of Decr. towards White marsh. It was a most contemptible affair, the threatenings and seeming fury he sate out with, and haste and Terror the Army retreated with, make it laughable. I have seen several persons from Philadelphia who assure me that their coming back was a mere uproar, and plainly indicated their apprehensions of a pursuit. Genl. Howe, in his Letter to Ld. Go. Germain, dated Dec. 13th, represented Genl. Washington's Camp as a strongly fortified place. There was not, Sir, a work thrown up in it till Genl. Howe marched out, and then only here and there a breast work. It was a temporary Station. Besides which, our men begin to think Works in the field of little use.

"Genl. Washington keeps his Station at the Valley forge. I was there when the Army first began to build huts; they appeared to me like a family of Beavers; every one busy; some carrying Logs, others Mud, and the rest fastening them together. The whole was raised in a few days, and is a curious collection of buildings in the true rustic order.

"As to Politics, I think we are now safely landed. The apprehension which Britain must be under from her neighbours must effectually prevent her sending reinforcements, could she procure them. She dare not, I think, in the *present* situation of affairs trust her troops so far from home.

"No Commissrs. are yet arrived. I think fighting is nearly over, for Britain, mad, wicked, and foolish, has done her utmost. The only part for her now to act is frugality, and the only way for her to get out of debt is to lessen her Government expenses. Two Millions a year is a sufficient allowance, and as much as she ought to expend exclusive of the interest of her Debt. The Affairs of England are approaching either to ruin or redemption. If the latter, she may bless the resistance of America.

"For my own part, I thought it very hard to have the Country set on fire about my Ears almost the moment I got into it ; and among other pleasures I feel in having uniformly done my duty, I feel that of not having discredited your friendship and patronage.

"I live in hopes of seeing and advising with you respecting the History of the American Revolution, as soon as a turn of Affairs make it safe for me to take a passage to Europe. Please to accept my thanks for the Pamphlets, which Mr. Temple Franklin informs me he has sent. They are not yet come to hand. Mr. & Mrs. Bache are at Mainheim, near Lancaster ; I heard they were well a few days ago. I laid two nights at Mr. Duffield's, in the winter. Miss Nancy Clifton was there, who said the Enemy had destroyed or sold a great quantity of your furniture. Mr. Duffield has since been taken by them and carried into the City, but is now at his own house. I just now hear they have burnt Col. Kirkbride's, Mr. Borden's, and some other houses at Borden Town. Governor Johnstone (House of Commons) has wrote to Mr. Robt. Morriss informing him of Commissioners coming from England. The letter is printed in the Newspapers without signature, and is dated Febry. 5th, by which you will know it.[1]

---

[1] The arrival of the Commissioners caused Paine to address his *Crisis VI.* to them instead of to Lord North, as he tells Franklin is his intention. The above letter was no doubt written in the old stone house at York.

"Please, Sir, to accept this, rough and incorrect as it is, as I have [not] time to copy it fair, which was my design when I began it ; besides which, paper is most exceedingly scarce.

"I am, Dear Sir, your Obliged and Affectionate humble Servt.,

"T. PAINE.

"The Honble. BENJ. FRANKLIN, Esqr."

Paine's prophecy at the close of his fifth *Crisis* (March, 1778), that England, reduced by her war with America, was in peril from France, was speedily confirmed. The treaty between France and America (February 6th) was followed by a war-cloud in Europe, which made the Americans sanguine that their own struggle was approaching an end. It was generally expected that Philadelphia would be evacuated. On this subject Paine wrote the following letter to Washington :

"York Town, June 5th, 1778.—Sir,—As a general opinion prevails that the Enemy will quit Philadelphia, I take the Liberty of transmitting you my reasons why it is probable they will not. In your difficult and distinguished Situation every hint may be useful.

"I put the immediate cause of their evacuation, to be a declaration of War in Europe made by them or against them : in which case, their Army would be wanted for other Service, and likewise because their present situation would be too un-safe, being subject to be blocked up by France and attacked by you and her jointly.

"Britain will avoid a War with France if she can ; which according to my arrangement of Politics she may easily do— She must see the necessity of acknowledging, sometime or other, the Independance of America ; if she is wise enough to make that acknowledgment *now*, she of consequence admits the Right of France to the quiet enjoyment of her Treaty, and therefore no War can take place upon the Ground of having concluded a Treaty with revolted British Subjects.

"This being admitted, their apprehension of being doubly attacked, or of being wanted elsewhere, cease of consequence ; and they will then endeavor to hold all they can, that they may have something to restore, in lieu of something else which they will demand ; as I know of no Instance where conquered Plans were surrendered up prior to, but only in consequence of a Treaty of Peace.

"You will observe, Sir, that my reasoning is founded on the supposition of their being reasonable Beings, which if they are not, then they are not within the compass of my System. I am, Sir, with every wish for your happiness, Your Affectionate and Obt. humble Servant,

"THOS. PAINE.

"His Excellency, GENL. WASHINGTON, Valley Forge."

Shortly after this letter to Washington tidings came that a French fleet, under Count d'Estaing, had appeared on the coast, and was about to blockade the Delaware. The British apparently in panic, really by order from England, left Philadelphia, June 18th. This seeming flight was a great encouragement. Congress was soon comfortably seated in Philadelphia, where Paine had the pleasure of addressing his next *Crisis* to the British Peace Commissioners.

In Philadelphia Congress was still surrounded by a hostile population ; Paine had still to plead that there should be no peace without republican independence. Even so late as November 24, 1778, the French Minister (Gérard) writes to his government : " Scarcely one quarter of the ordinary inhabitants of Philadelphia now here favour the cause (of independence). Commercial and family ties, together with an aversion to popular government, seem to account for this. The same feeling exists in New York and Boston, which is not the case in the rural districts." While Franklin was offered in Paris the bribe of a peerage, and the like for several revolutionary leaders, similar efforts were made in America to subdue the " rebellion " by craft. For that purpose had come the Earl of Carlisle, Sir George Johnstone, and William Eden. Paine omits the name of Johnstone, America's friend. Referring to the invitation of the Peace Commissioners, that America should join them against France, he says : " Unless you were capable of such conduct yourselves, you would never have supposed such a character in us." He reminds the commissioners, who had threatened that America must be laid waste so as to be useless to France, that increased wants of America must make her a more valuable purchaser in France. Paine includes Sir H. Clinton with the commissioners, and suspects the truth that he had brought orders, received from England, overruling an intention of the peace envoys to burn Philadelphia if their terms were rejected. He says he has written a *Crisis* for the English people because there was a convenient conveyance ; " for the Commissioners—*poor Commissioners !*—having proclaimed that '*yet forty days and Nineveh shall be overthrown*,' have waited out the date, and, discontented with their God, are returning to their gourd. And all the harm I wish them is that it may not wither about their ears, and that they may not make their exit in the belly of a whale."

CHAPTER IX.

FRENCH AID, AND THE PAINE–DEANE CONTROVERSY.

In Bell's addenda to "Common Sense," which contained Paine's Address to the Quakers (also letters by others), appeared a little poem which I believe his, and the expression of his creed.

"THE AMERICAN PATRIOT'S PRAYER.

" Parent of all, omnipotent
   In heaven, and earth below,
Through all creation's bounds unspent,
   Whose streams of goodness flow,

" Teach me to know from whence I rose,
   And unto what designed ;
No private aims let me propose,
   Since link'd with human kind.

" But chief to hear my country's voice,
   May all my thoughts incline ;
'T is reason's law, 't is virtue's choice,
   'T is nature's call and thine.

" Me from fair freedom's sacred cause
   Let nothing e'er divide ;
Grandeur, nor gold, nor vain applause,
   Nor friendship false misguide.

> " Let me not faction's partial hate
>   Pursue to this Land's woe ;
> Nor grasp the thunder of the state
>   To wound a private foe.
>
> " If, for the right to wish the wrong
>   My country shall combine,
> Single to serve th' erroneous throng,
>   Spight of themselves, be mine."

Every sacrifice contemplated in this self-dedication had to be made.   Paine had held back nothing from the cause.   He gave America the copyrights of his eighteen pamphlets.   While they were selling by thousands, at two or three shillings each, he had to apologize to a friend for not sending his boots, on the ground that he must borrow the money to pay for them !   He had given up the magazine so suited to his literary and scientific tastes, had dismissed his lucrative school in Philadelphia, taken a musket on his Quaker shoulders, shared the privations of the retreat to the Delaware, braved bullets at Trenton and bombs at Fort Mifflin.   But now he was to give up more.   He was

> " Single to serve th' erroneous throng,
>   Spight of themselves,"

and thereby lose applause and friendship.   An ex-Congressman, sent to procure aid in France, having, as Paine believed, attempted a fraud on the scanty funds of this country, he published his reasons for so believing.   In doing so he alarmed the French Ambassador in America, and incurred the hostility of a large party in Congress ; the result being his resignation of the secretaryship of its Foreign Affairs Committee.

It has been traditionally asserted that, in this controversy, Paine violated his oath of office. Such is not the fact. His official oath, which was prepared for Paine himself—the first secretary of a new committee,—was framed so as to leave him large freedom as a public writer.

"That the said secretary, previous to his entering on his office, take an oath, to be administered by the president, well and faithfully to execute the trust reposed in him, according to his best skill and judgment ; and to disclose no matter, the knowledge of which shall be acquired in consequence of his office, *that he shall be directed to keep secret.*"

Not only was there no such direction of secrecy in this case, but Congress did not know the facts revealed by Paine. Compelled by a complaint of the French Minister to disown Paine's publication, Congress refused to vote that it was " an abuse of office," or to discharge him. The facts should be judged on their merits, and without prejudice. I have searched and sifted many manuscripts in European and American archives to get at the truth of this strange chapter in our revolutionary history, concerning which there is even yet an unsettled controversy.[1] The reader who desires

---

[1] "Beaumarchais et son Temps," par M. De Lomenie, Paris, 1856. "Histoire de la Participation de la France à l'Établissement des Etats Unis d'Amérique," par M. Doniol, Paris. "Beaumarchais and ' The Lost Million,' " by Charles J. Stillé (privately printed in Philadelphia). " New Materials for the History of the American Revolution," by John Durand, New York, 1889. *Magazine of American History*, vol. ii., p. 663. " Life and Times of Benjamin Franklin," by James Parton, New York, 1864. "Papers in Relation to the Case of Silas Deane," Philadelphia, printed for the Seventy-six Society, 1855.

to explore the subject will find an ample literature concerning it, but with confusing omissions, partly due to a neglect of Paine's papers.

The suggestion of French aid to America was first made in May, 1775, by Dubourg, and a scheme was submitted by Beaumarchais to the King. This was first brought to light in November, 1878, in the *Magazine of American History*, where it is said : "It is without date, but must have been written after the arrival of the American Commissioners in Paris." This is an error. A letter of December 7, 1775, from Beaumarchais proves that the undated one had been answered. Moreover, on June 10, 1776, a month before Deane had reached Paris, and six months before Franklin's arrival, the million for America had been paid to Beaumarchais and re-ceipted. It was Deane's ruin that he appeared as if taking credit for, and bringing within the scope of his negotiations, money paid before his arrival. It was the ruin of Beaumarchais that he deceived Deane about that million.

In 1763 France had suffered by her struggle with England humiliations and territorial losses far heavier than those suffered by her last war with Germany. With the revolt of the English colonies in America the hour of French revenge struck. Louis XVI. did not care much about it, but his minister Vergennes did. Inspired by him, Beau-marchais, adventurer and playwright, consulted Arthur Lee, secret agent of Congress in London, and it was arranged that Beaumarchais should write a series of letters to the King, to be previously revised by Vergennes. The letters are such as might be expected from the pen that wrote " The Marriage of Figaro." He paints before the King the scene of France driven out of America and India ; he describes America as advancing to engage the conqueror of France with a force which a little help would make sufficient to render England helpless beside her European foes—France and Spain. Learning through Vergennes that the King was mindful of his treaty with England, Beaumarchais made a proposal that the aid should be rendered as if by a commercial house, without knowledge of the government. This, the most important document of the case, suppressed until 1878, was unknown to any of the writers who have discussed this question, except Durand and Stillé, the latter alone having recognized its bearing on the question of Beaumarchais' good faith. Beaumarchais tells the King that his " succor " is not to end the war in America, but " to continue and feed it to the great damage of the English " ; that " to sacrifice a million to put England to the expense of a hundred millions, is exactly the same as if you advance a million to gain ninety-nine." Half of the million (livres) is to be sent to America in gold, and half in powder. So far from this aid being gratuitous, the powder is to be taken from French magazines at " four to six sols per pound," and sent to America " on the basis of twenty sols per pound." " The constant view of the affair in which the mass of Congress ought to be kept is the certainty that your Majesty is not willing to enter in any way into the affair, but that a company is very generously about to turn over a certain sum to the prudent management of a faithful agent to give successive aid to the Americans by the shortest and the surest means of return in tobacco."

How much of this scheme actually reached the King, and was approved by him, is doubtful. He still hesitated, and another appeal was made (February 29, 1776) embodying one from Arthur Lee, who says: "We offer to France, in return for her secret assistance, a secret treaty of commerce, by which she will secure for a certain number of years after peace is declared all the advantages with which we have enriched England for the past century, with, additionally, a guarantee of her possessions according to our forces." Nothing is said by Arthur Lee about other payments. The Queen had now become interested in the gallant Americans, and the King was brought over to the scheme in April. On May 2, 1776, Vergennes submits to the King the order for a million livres which he is to sign ; also a letter, to be written by the hand of the Minister's son, aged fifteen, to Beaumarchais, who, he says, will employ M. Montandoin (the name was really Montieu) to transmit to the Americans "such funds as your Majesty chooses to appropriate for their benefit." There are various indications that the pecuniary advantages, in the way of "sols" and tobacco, were not set before the King, and that he yielded to considerations of state policy.

After receiving the million (June 10th) Beaumarchais wrote to Arthur Lee in London (June 12, 1776): "The difficulties I have found in my negotiations with the Minister have *determined me to form a company* which will enable the munitions

and powder to be transmitted sooner to *your friend*
on condition of his returning tobacco to Cape
Francis."

To Arthur Lee, whom he had met at the table
of Lord Mayor John Wilkes, Beaumarchais had
emphasized the "generous" side of his scheme.
Tobacco was indeed to be sent, chiefly to give a
commercial color to the transaction for the King's
concealment, but there appeared no reason to do
more with Lee, who had no power of contract,
than impress him with the magnanimity and friendship of the French government. This Lee was to
report to the Secret Committee of Congress, which
would thus be prepared to agree to any arrangement of Beaumarchais' agent, without any suspicion that it might be called on to pay twenty sols a
pound for powder that had cost from four to six.
Lee did report it, sending a special messenger
(Story) to announce to Congress the glad tidings
of French aid, and much too gushingly its quasi-
gratuitous character.

A month later Silas Deane, belated since March
5th by wind and wave, reached Paris, and about
July 17, 1776, by advice of Vergennes, had his first
interview with Beaumarchais. Had Beaumarchais
known that an agent, empowered by Congress to
purchase munitions, was on his way to France, he
would have had nothing to do with Lee ; now
he could only repudiate him, and persuade Deane
to disregard him. Arthur Lee informed Deane
that Beaumarchais had told him that he had received two hundred thousand pounds sterling of
the French administration for the use of Congress,
but Deane believed Beaumarchais, who " constantly

and positively denied having said any such thing."
It had been better for Deane if he had believed
Lee.[1]   It turned out in the end that Beaumarchais
had received the sum Lee named, and the French
government—more anxious for treaty concessions
from America than for Beaumarchais' pocket—
assured the American Commissioners that the million was a royal gift.

This claim to generosity, however, or rather the
source of it, was a secret of the negotiation.   In
October, 1777, the commissioners wrote to Congress a letter which, being intercepted, reached
that body only in duplicate, March, 1778, saying
they had received assurances " that no repayment
will ever be required from us for what has already
been given us either in money or military stores."
One of these commissioners was Silas Deane himself (the others Franklin and Lee).   But meanwhile Beaumarchais had claimed of Congress, by
an agent (De Francy) sent to America, payment
of his bill, which included the million which his
government declared had been a gift.   This com-
plication caused Congress to recall Deane for
explanations.

Deane arrived in America in July, 1778.   There
were suspicious circumstances around him.   He
had left his papers in Paris ; he had borrowed

---

[1] M. Doniol and Mr. Durand are entirely mistaken in supposing that Lee
was "substantially a traitor."   That he wrote to Lord Shelburne that " if
England wanted to prevent closer ties between France and the United States
she must not delay," proves indeed the reverse.   He wanted recognition of
the independence of his country, and peace, and was as willing to get it
from England as from France.   He was no doubt well aware that French
subsidies were meant, as Beaumarchais reminded the King, to continue the
war in America, not to end it.   Arthur Lee had his faults, but lack of
patriotism was not among them.

money of Beaumarchais for personal expenses, and
the despatch he had signed in October, saying the
million was a gift, had been intercepted, other
papers in the same package having duly arrived.
Thus appearances were against Deane. The following statement, in Paine's handwriting, was no
doubt prepared for submission to Congress, and
probably was read during one of its secret discussions of the matter. It is headed " Explanatory
Circumstances."

" 1st. The lost dispatches are dated Oct. 6th and Oct. 7th.
They were sent by a private hand—that is, they were not sent
by the post. Capt. Folger had the charge of them. They were
all under one cover containing five separate Packets ; three of
the Packets were on commercial matters only—one of these was
to Mr. R[obert] Morris, Chairman of the Commercial Committee, one to Mr. Hancock (private concerns), another to Barnaby
Deane, S. Deane's brother. Of the other two Packets, one of
them was to the Secret Committee, then stiled the Committee
for foreign Affairs, the other was to Richard H. Lee—these two
last Packets had nothing in them but blank white French Paper.

" 2d. In Sept'r preceding the date of the dispatches Mr. B[eau-
marchais] sent Mr. Francis [De Francy] to Congress to press
payment to the amount mentioned in the official Letter of Oct. 6.
Mr. F[rancy] brought a letter signed only by S. Deane—the Capt.
of the vessel (Landais) brought another letter from Deane ; both
of these letters were to enforce Mr. B[eaumarchais'] demand.
Mr. F[rancy] arrived with his letters and demand. The official
despatches (if I may so say) arrived blank. Congress therefore
had no authoritative information to act by. About this time
Mr. D[eane] was recalled and arrived in America in Count
D'Estaing's fleet. He gave out that he had left his accounts in
France.

" With the Treaty of Alliance come over the Duplicates of
the lost Despatches. They come into my office not having
been seen by Congress ; and as they contain an injunction not
to be conceded by [to ?] Congress, I kept them secret in the office

because at that time the foreign Committee were dispersed and new members not appointed.

"On the 5th of Dec. 1778, Mr. D[eane] published an inflamatory piece against Congress. As I saw it had an exceeding ill effect out of doors I made some remarks upon it—with a view of preventing people running mad. This piece was replied to by a piece under the Signature of Plain Truth—in which it was stated, that Mr. D[eane] though a stranger in France and to the Language, and without money, had by himself procured 30,000 stand of Arms, 30,000 suits of Cloathing, and more than 200 pieces of Brass Cannon. I replied that these supplies were in a train of Execution before he was sent to France. That Mr. Deane's private letters and his official despatches jointly with the other two Commissioners contradicted each other.

"At this time I found Deane had made a large party in Congress—and that a motion had been made but not decided upon for dismissing me from the foreign office, with a kind of censure."

Deane was heard by Congress twice (August 9 and 21, 1778) but made a bad impression, and a third hearing was refused. In wrath he appealed in the press "to the free and virtuous Citizens of America," (December 5, 1778) against the injustice of Congress. This Paine answered in the *Pennsylvania Packet* of December 15, 1779. His motives are told in the following letter addressed to the Hon. Henry Laurens:

"PHILADELPHIA, Dec. 15th, 1778.—DEAR SIR.—In this morning's paper is a piece addressed to Mr. Deane, in which your name is mentioned. My intention in relating the circumstances with wch. it is connected is to prevent the Enemy drawing any unjust conclusions from an accidental division in the House on matters no ways political. You will please to observe that I have been exceedingly careful to preserve the honor of Congress in the minds of the people who have been so exceedingly fretted by Mr. Deane's address—and this will appear the more necessary when I inform you that a proposal has been made for calling a Town Meeting to demand justice for Mr. Deane. I have been applied to smoothly and roughly not to publish this piece. Mr. Deane has likewise been with the Printer. I am, &c."

To Paine, who had given his all to the American cause, nothing could appear more natural than that France and her King should do the same with pure disinterestedness. Here were Lafayette and other Frenchmen at Washington's side. However, the one thing he was certain of was that Deane had no claim to be credited with the French subsidies. Had Henry Laurens been President of Congress it would have been easy to act on that body through him; but he had resigned, and the new president, John Jay, was a prominent member of the Deane party. So Paine resolved to defeat what he considered a fraud on the country at whatever cost. In the course of the controversy he wrote (January 2, 1779):

"If Mr. Deane or any other gentleman will procure an order from Congress to inspect an account in my office, or any of Mr. Deane's friends in Congress will take the trouble of coming themselves, I will give him or them my attendance, and shew them in handwriting which Mr. Deane is well acquainted with, that the supplies he so pompously plumes himself upon were promised and engaged, and that as a present, before he ever arrived in France; and the part that fell to Mr. Deane was only to see it done, and how he has performed that service the public are acquainted with."

Although Paine here gave the purport of the commissioners' letter, showing plainly that Deane had nothing to do with obtaining the supplies, he is not so certain that they were gratuitous, and adds, in the same letter (January 2d):   "The supplies here alluded to are those which were sent from France in the Amphitrite, Seine, and Mercury, about two years ago.   They had at first the appearance of a present, but whether so or on credit the service was a great and a friendly one."   To transfer the debt to the French government would secure such a long credit that the American cause would not suffer. Perhaps no official notice might have been taken of this, but in another letter (January 5th) Paine wrote : "Those who are now her [America's] allies, pre-faced that alliance by an early and generous friend-ship ; yet that we might not attribute too much to human or auxiliary aid, so unfortunate were these supplies that only one ship out of three arrived ; the Mercury and Seine fell into the hands of the enemy."

It was this last paragraph that constituted Paine's indiscretion.   Unless we can suppose him for once capable of a rôle so Machiavellian as the forcing of France's hand, by revealing the connec-tion between the King and the subsidies of Beau-marchais, we can only praise him for a too-impulsive and self-forgetting patriotism.   It was of course necessary for the French Minister (Gérard) to complain, and for Congress to soothe him by voting the fiction that his most Christian Majesty " did not preface his alliance with any supplies whatever sent to America."   But in order to do this, Paine had somehow to be dealt with.   A serio-comical performance took place in Congress. The members knew perfectly well that Paine had documents to prove every word he had printed; but as they did not yet know these documents officially, and were required by their ally's minister to deny Paine's statement, they were in great fear that Paine, if summoned, might reveal them. As the articles were only signed " Common Sense," it was necessary that the Secretary should acknowledge himself their author, and Congress, in dread of discovering its own secrets, contrived that he should be allowed to utter at the bar only one word.

Congress received M. Gérard's complaint on January 5th, and on the 6th, to which action thereon had been adjourned, the following memorial from Paine.

" HONORABLE SIRS.—Understanding that exceptions have been taken at some parts of my conduct, which exceptions as I am unacquainted with I cannot reply to : I therefore humbly beg leave to submit every part of my conduct public and private, so far as relate to public measures, to the judgment of this Honble. House, to be by them approved or censured as they shall judge proper—at the same time reserving to myself that conscious satisfaction of having ever intended well and to the best of my abilities executed those intentions.

" The Honble. Congress in April, 1777, were pleased, not only unsolicited on my part, but wholly unknown to me, to appoint me unanimously Secretary to the Committee for foreign affairs, which mode of appointment I conceive to be the most honorable that can take place. The salary they were pleased to affix to it was 70 dollars per month. It has remained at the same rate ever since, and is not at this time equal to the most moderate expences I can live at ; yet I have never complained, and always conceiving it my duty to bear a share of the inconveniences of the country, have ever cheerfully submitted to them. This being my situation, I am at this time conscious of no error, unless the cheapness of my services, and the generosity with which I have endeavored to do good in other respects, can be imputed to me as a crime, by such individuals as may have acted otherwise.

"As my appointment was honorable, therefore whenever it shall appear to Congress that I have not fulfilled their expectations, I shall, tho' with concern at any misapprehension that might lead to such an opinion, surrender up the books and papers intrusted to my care.

"Were my appointment an office of profit it might become me to resign it, but as it is otherwise I conceive that such a step in me might imply a dissatisfaction on account of the smallness of the pay. Therefore I think it my duty to wait the orders of this Honble. House, at the same time begging leave to assure them that whatever may be their determination respecting me, my disposition to serve in so honorable a cause, and in any character in which I can best do it, will suffer no alteration. I am, with profound respect, your Honors' dutiful and obt. hble. Servant,

"THOMAS PAINE."

On the same day Paine was summoned before Congress (sitting always with closed doors), and asked by its president (Jay) if he wrote the articles. He replied "Yes," and was instantly ordered to withdraw. On the following day Paine, having discovered that Deane's party were resolved that he should have no opportunity to reveal any fact in Congress, submitted a second memorial.

"Honorable Sirs.—From the manner in which I was called before the House yesterday, I have reason to suspect an unfavorable disposition in them towards some parts in my late publications. What the parts are against which they object, or what those objections are, are wholly unknown to me. If any gentleman has presented any Memorial to this House which contains any charge against me, or any-ways alludes in a censurable manner to my character or interest, so as to become the ground of any such charge, I request, as a servant under your authority,

9

an attested copy of that charge, and in my present character as a freeman of this country, I demand it.   I attended at the bar of this House yesterday as their servant, tho' the warrant did not express my official station, which I conceive it ought to have done, otherwise it could not have been compulsive unless backed by a magistrate.   My hopes were that I should be made acquainted with the charge, and admitted to my defence, which I am all times ready to make either in writing or personally.

"I cannot in duty to my character as a freeman submit to be censured unheard.   I have evidence which I presume will justify me.   And I entreat this House to consider how great their reproach will be should it be told that they passed a sentence upon me without hearing me, and that a copy of the charge against me was refused to me ; and likewise how much that reproach will be aggravated should I afterwards prove the censure of this House to be a libel, grounded upon a mistake which they refused fully to inquire into.

"I make my application to the heart of every gentleman in this House, that, before he decides on a point that may affect my reputation, he will duly consider his own.   Did I court popular praise I should not send this letter.   My wish is that by thus stating my situation to the House, they may not commit an act they cannot justify.

"I have obtained fame, honor, and credit in this country. I am proud of these honors.   And as they cannot be taken from me by any unjust censure grounded on a concealed charge, therefore it will become my duty afterwards to do justice to myself.   I have no favor to ask more than to be candidly and honorably dealt by ; and such being my right I ought to have no doubt but this House will proceed accordingly.   Should Congress be disposed to hear me, I have to request that they will give me sufficient time to prepare."

It was, of course, a foregone conclusion that the story of what had occurred in France must not be told.   M. Gérard had identified himself with the interests of Beaumarchais, as well as with those of his government, and was using the privileges of the alliance to cover that speculator's demand.   Paine, therefore, pleaded in vain.   Indeed, the foregoing memorial seems to have been suppressed, as it is not referred to in the journal of the House for that day (January 7th).   On the day following his resignation was presented in the following letter :

" Honorable Sirs.—Finding by the Journals of this House, of yesterday, that I am not to be heard, and having in my letter of the same day, prior to that resolution, declared that I could not 'in duty to my character as a freeman submit to be censured unheard,' therefore, consistent with that declaration, and to maintain that Right, I think it my duty to resign the office of Secretary to the Committee for foreign Affairs, and I do hereby resign the same.   The Papers and documents in my charge I shall faithfully deliver up to the Committee, either on honor or oath, as they or this House shall direct.

" Considering myself now no longer a servant of Congress, I conceive it convenient that I should declare what have been the motives of my conduct.   On the appearance of Mr. Deane's Address to the Public of the 5 of Dec, in which he said ' The ears of the Representatives were shut against him,' the honor and justice of this House were impeached and its reputation sunk to the lowest ebb in the opinion of the People.   The expressions of suspicion and degradation which have been uttered in my hearing and are too indecent to be related in this letter, first induced me to set the Public right ; but so grounded were they, almost without exception, in their ill opinion of this House, that instead of succeeding as I wished in my first address, I fell under the same reproach and was frequently told that I was defending Congress in their bad designs.   This obliged me to go farther into the matters, and I have now reason to believe that my endeavours have been and will be effectual.

" My wish and my intentions in all my late publications were to preserve the public from error and imposition, to support as far as laid in my power the just authority of the Representatives of the People, and to cordiallize and cement the Union that has so happily taken place between this country and France.

"I have betrayed no Trust because I have constantly employed that Trust to the public good. I have revealed no secrets because I have told nothing that was, or I conceive ought to be a secret. I have convicted Mr. Deane of error, and in so doing I hope I have done my duty.

"It is to the interest of the Alliance that the People should know that before America had any agent in Europe the 'public-spirited gentlemen' in that quarter of the world were her warm friends. And I hope this Honorable House will receive it from me as a farther testimony of my affection to that Alliance, and of my attention to the duty of my office, that I mention, that the duplicates of the Dispatches of Oct. 6 and 7, 1777, from the *Commissioners*, the originals of which are in the Enemy's possession, seem to require on *that account* a reconsideration.

"His Excellency, the Minister of France, is well acquainted with the liberality of my sentiments, and I have had the pleasure of receiving repeated testimonies of his esteem for me. I am concerned that he should in any instance misconceive me. I beg likewise to have it understood that my appeal to this Honorable House for a hearing yesterday was as a *matter of Right* in the character of a Freeman, which Right I ought to yield up to no Power whatever. I return my utmost thanks to the Honorable Members of this House who endeavored to support me in that Right, so sacred to themselves and to their constituents ; and I have the pleasure of saying and reflecting that as I came into office an honest man, I go out of it with the same character."

This letter also was suppressed, and the same fate was secured by Mr. Jay for several other letters written by Paine to Congress. On March 30, 1779, he quotes a letter of the commissioners of November 30, 1777, saying that the supplies from France were "the effects of private benevolence." On April 21st he reminds Congress that "they began their hard treatment of me while I was defending their injured and insulted honor, and which I cannot account for on any other ground than supposing that a private unwarrantable connection was formed between Mr. Deane and certain Members of this Honorable House." On April 23d he again addresses the " Honorable Sirs " :

" On inquiring yesterday of Mr. Thomson, your Secretary, I find that no answer is given to any of my letters. I am unable to account for the seeming inattention of Congress in collecting information at this particular time, from whatever quarter it may come ; and this wonder is the more increased when I recollect that a private offer was made to me, about three months ago, amounting in money to £700 a year ; yet however polite the proposal might be, or however friendly it might be designed, I thought it my duty to decline it ; as it was accompanied with a condition which I conceived had a tendency to prevent the information I have since given, and shall yet give to the Country on Public Affairs.

" I have repeatedly wrote to Congress respecting Mr. Deane's dark incendiary conduct, and offered every information in my power. The opportunities I have had of knowing the state of foreign affairs is greater than that of many gentlemen of this House, and I want no other knowledge to declare that I look on Mr. Deane to be, what Mr. Carmichael calls him, a rascal."

The offer of money came from M. Gérard. This clever diplomatist perceived in all Paine's letters his genuine love of France, and esteem for the King who had so generously allied himself with the Americans in their struggle for independence. Since M. Gérard's arrival Paine had been on friendly terms with him. I have explored the State Archives of France for M. Gérard's versions of these affairs, and find them more diplomatic than exact. Immediately on the appearance of Paine's first attack on Deane, the Minister appears to have visited Paine. He reports to Vergennes, January 10th,

that he had been at much pains to convince Paine
of his error in saying that the supplies furnished by
Beaumarchais had been " promised as a gift " ; but
he had not retracted, and he (Gérard) then thought
it necessary to refer what he wrote to Congress.
" Congress, however, did not wait for this to show
me its indignation."   The journals of Congress do
not, however, reveal any reference to the matter
previous to M. Gérard's memorial of January 5th.
In his next letter M. Gérard asserts that Congress
had dismissed Paine, whereas Paine resigned, and
a motion for his dismission was lost.   This letter
is dated January 17th.

"When I had denounced to Congress the assertions of
M. Payne, I did not conceal from myself the bad effects that
might result to a head puffed up by the success of his political
writings, and the importance he affected. I foresaw the loss
of his office, and feared that, separated from the support which
has restrained him, he would seek only to avenge himself with
his characteristic impetuosity and impudence. All means of
restraining him would be impossible, considering the enthusiasm
here for the license of the press, and in the absence of any
laws to repress audacity even against foreign powers. The
only remedy, my lord, I could imagine to prevent these inconveniences, and even to profit by the circumstances, was to have
Payne offered a salary in the King's name, in place of that he
had lost. He called to thank me, and I stipulated that he
should publish nothing on political affairs, nor about Congress,
without advising with me, and should employ his pen mainly in
impressing on the people favorable sentiments towards France
and the Alliance, of the kind fittest to foster hatred and defi-
ance towards England. He appeared to accept the task with
pleasure. I promised him a thousand dollars per annum, to
begin from the time of his dismission by Congress. He has
already begun his functions in declaring in the Gazette that the
affair of the military effects has no reference to the Court and

is not a political matter. You know too well the prodigious effects produced by the writings of this famous personage among the people of the States to cause me any fear of your disapproval of my resolution."

M. Gérard adds that he has also employed Dr. Cooper, an intimate friend of Dr. Franklin. On May 29th he informs Vergennes that the Paine arrangement did not work.

"A piece in a Gazette of the third by M. Payne, under his usual title of Common Sense proves his loss of it. In it he declares that he is the only honest man thus far employed in American affairs, and demands that the nation shall give him the title and authority of Censor-general, especially to purify and reform Congress. This bit of folly shows what he is capable of. He gives me marks of friendship, but that does not contribute to the success of my exhortations."

In another despatch of the same date M. Gérard writes :

"I have had the honor to acquaint you with the project I had formed to engage Sir Payne [le Sr. Payne] to insert in the public papers paragraphs relative to the Alliance, calculated to encourage the high idea formed by the people of the king, and its confidence in his friendship ; but this writer having tarnished his reputation and being sold to the opposition, I have found another."

He goes on to say that he has purchased two eminent gentlemen, who write under the names " Honest Politician " and " Americanus."

M. Gérard, in his statements concerning his relations with Paine, depended on the unfamiliarity of Vergennes with the Philadelphia journals. In these Paine had promptly made known the overtures made to him.

"Had I been disposed to make money I undoubtedly had many opportunities for it. The single pamphlet 'Common Sense' would at that time of day have produced a tolerable fortune, had I only taken the same profits from the publication which all writers have ever done ; because the sale was the most rapid and extensive of anything that was ever published in this country, or perhaps in any other. Instead of which I reduced the price so low, that instead of getting, I stand £39, 11, o out of pocket on Mr. Bradford's books, exclusive of my time and trouble ; and I have acted the same disinterested part by every publication I have made.

"At the time the dispute arose respecting Mr. Deane's affairs, I had a conference with Mr. Gérard at his own request, and some matters on that subject were freely talked over, which it is here necessary to mention. This was on the 2d of January. On the evening of the same day, or the next, Mr. Gérard through the medium of another gentleman made me a very genteel and profitable offer. My answer to the offer was precisely in these words : 'Any service I can render to either of the countries in alliance, or to both, I ever have done and shall readily do, and Mr. Gérard's *esteem* will be the only compensation I shall desire.'"

Paine never received a cent of M. Gérard's money, but he became convinced that the French government might be compromised by his allusion to its early generosity to America, and on January 26th wrote that the letter to which he had alluded had not mentioned "the King of France by any name or title nor yet the nation of France." This was all that the French Minister could get out of Paine, and it was willingly given. The more complaisant "Honest Politician" and "Americanus," however, duly fulfilled the tasks for which they had been employed by the French Ambassador. This will be seen by reference to their letters in the *Pennsylvania Gazette* of June 23d. In June and July Paine entered on a controversy with " Americanus " on the terms upon which America should insist, in any treaty of peace.   He intimates his suspicion that " Americanus " is a hireling.

It should be mentioned that the English archives prove that in Paris Deane and Gérard had long been intimate, and often closeted with Vergennes. (See the reports of Wentworth and others in Stevens' *Fac-Similes*.)   Deane and Gérard came over together, on one of d'Estaing's ships.   According to the English information Gérard was pecuniarily interested in the supplies sent to America, and if so had private reasons for resisting Paine's theory of their gratuitous character.

CHAPTER X.

A STORY BY GOUVERNEUR MORRIS.

THE Paine-Deane incident had a number of curious sequels, some of which are related in a characteristic letter of Gouverneur Morris to John Randolph, which has not, I believe, hitherto been printed. Gouverneur Morris had much to do with the whole affair; he was a member of Congress during the controversy, and he was the Minister in France who, fifteen years later, brought to light the receipt for the King's million livres charged by Beaumarchais against this country.

" WASHINGTON, Jany. 20, 1812.

" It would give me pleasure to communicate the information you ask, but I can only speak from memory respecting matters, some of which were transacted long ago and did not command my special attention. But it is probable that the material facts can be established by documents in the Secretary of State's office.

" It will, I believe, appear from the correspondence between Mr. Arthur Lee and the Secret and Commercial Committee, that early in our dispute with Great Britain the French Court made through him a tender of military supplies, and employed as their agent for that purpose M. Beaumarchais, who, having little property and but slender standing in society, might (if needful) be disavowed, imprisoned, and punished for presuming to use the King's name on such an occasion. In the course of our Revolutionary War, large supplies were sent by M.

Beaumarchais under the name of Roderique Hortalez and Co., a supposed mercantile name. But the operations were impeded by complaints of the British Ambassador, Lord Stormont, which obliged the French Court to make frequent denials, protestations, seizure of goods and detention of ships. Every step of this kind bound them more strongly to prevent a disclosure of facts.

"After the Congress returned to Philadelphia, M. de Francy, agent of M. Beaumarchais, applied to Congress for payment. This application was supported on the ground of justice by many who were not in the secret, for the Congress had then so much good sense as not to trust itself with its own secrets. There happened unluckily at that time a feud between Mr. Lee and Mr. Deane. The latter favored (in appearance at least) M. Beaumarchais' claim. Paine, who was clerk to the Secret and Commercial Committee, took part in the dispute, wrote pieces for the Gazettes, and at length, to overwhelm Deane and those who defended him with confusion, published a declaration of the facts confidentially communicated to the Committee by Mr. Lee, and signed this declaration as American Secretary for Foreign Affairs.[1] The French Minister, M. Gérard, immediately made a formal complaint of that publication, and an equally formal denial of what it contained. The Congress was therefore obliged to believe, or at least to act as if they believed, that Paine had told a scandalous falsehood. He was in consequence dismissed, which indeed he deserved for his impudence if for nothing else.[2]

"Beaumarchais and his agent had already received from the Committee tobacco and perhaps other articles of produce on account of his demand ; what and how much will of course be found from investigating the files of the Treasury. But he wanted and finally obtained a larger and more effectual payment. Bills were drawn in his favor on Dr. Franklin, our Minister in France, at long sight, for about one hundred thousand pounds sterling. This was done in the persuasion that the Doctor would, when they were presented, communicate the fact

---

[1] Error. Paine signed " Common Sense," and in one instance " Thomas Paine."

[2] Paine resigned. Several motions for his dismissal were lost.

to Comte de Vergennes, from whom he would afterwards be obliged to solicit the means of payment. It was hoped that the French Court would then interfere and either lay hold of the bills or compel M. Beaumarchais to refund the money, so that no real deduction would on that account be afterwards made from the loans or subsidies to us. The death of all who were privy to it has spread an impenetrable veil over what passed on this occasion between M. Beaumarchais and his employer, but the bills were regularly paid, and we were thereby deprived in a critical moment of the resources which so large a sum would have supplied. When this happened, M. de la Luzerne, then Minister of France at Philadelphia, expressed himself with so much freedom and so much indignation respecting M. Beaumarchais and his claim, that there was reason to believe nothing more would have been heard of it. In that persuasion, perhaps, Dr. Franklin, when he came to settle our national accounts with M. de Vergennes, was less solicitous about a considerable item than he otherwise might have been. He acknowledged as a free gift to the United States the receipt on a certain day of one million livres, for which no evidence was produced. He asked indeed for a voucher to establish the payment, but the Count replied that it was immaterial whether we had received the money or not, seeing that we were not called on for repayment. With this reassuring the old gentleman seems to have been satisfied, and the account was settled accordingly. Perhaps the facts may have been communicated to him under the seal of secrecy, and if so he showed firmness in that he had shared in the plunder with Deane and Beaumarchais.

" Things remained in that state till after the late king of France was dethroned. The Minister of the United States at Paris [1] was then directed to enquire what had become of the million livres. The correspondence will of course be found in the office of the Secretary of State. It seems that he had the good fortune to obtain copies of M. Beaumarchais' receipt for a million, bearing date on the day when the gift was said to have been made, so that no reasonable doubt could exist as to the identity of the sum.[2]

[1] Gouverneur Morris himself.

[2] This was the receipt dated June 10, 1776, on which the King had marked " Bon," and was obtained by Morris in 1794.

"So much, my dear Sir, for what memory can command. You will, I think, find papers containing a more accurate statement in the New York "Evening Post," about the time when Mr. Rodney's opinion was made public. At least I recollect having seen in that gazette some facts with which I had not been previously acquainted, or which I had forgotten. A gentleman from Connecticut, who was on the Committee of Claims last year, can I believe give you the papers. I remember also to have been told by a respectable young gentleman, son of the late Mr. Richard Henry Lee, that important evidence on this subject, secured from his uncle Arthur, was in his possession, and I believe it may be obtained from Mr. Carroll of Annapolis, or his son-in-law Mr. Harper of Baltimore. [1]

"The Hon'le Mr. JOHN RANDOLPH, of Roanoke."

Beaumarchais, barely escaping the guillotine, died in poverty in Holland. He bequeathed his claim to his daughter who (1835) was paid 800,000 francs, but the million which he had received from the King and then charged on the United States, was never paid. Silas Deane suffered a worse fate. His claims for commissions and services in France remained unpaid, and after his return to France he occupied himself with writing to his brother Simeon and others the intercepted letters printed by Rivington in 1782. In these letters he urges submission to England. Franklin took the charitable view that his head had been turned by his misfortunes. He went over to England, where he became the friend of Benedict Arnold, and died in poverty in 1789. In recent years his heirs were paid $35,000 by Congress. But his character and his performances in France, during the Revolution, remain an enigma.

[1] The documents referred to are no doubt among the Lee Papers preserved at the University of Virginia, which I have examined.

The determination with which Paine, to his cost, withstood Deane, may seem at first glance quixotic. His attack was animated by a belief that the supplies sent from France were a covert gift, and, at any rate, that the demand for instant payment to agents was fraudulent. Evidence having been supplied, by the publication of Beaumarchais' notes to Arthur Lee, under pseudonym of " Mary Johnston," that returns in tobacco were expected, this, if not a mercantile mask, was still a matter of credit, and very different from payments demanded by Beaumarchais and Deane from the scanty treasury of the struggling colonies.[1] But there was something more behind the vehemence of Paine's letters.   This he intimated, but his revelation

---

[1] In one of Deane's intercepted letters (May 20, 1781) there is an indication that he had found more truth in what Paine had said about the gratuitous supplies than Beaumarchais had led him to believe. " The first plan of the French government evidently was to assist us just so far as might be absolutely necessary to prevent an accommodation, and to give this assistance with so much secresy as to avoid any rupture with Great Britain.   On this plan succors were first permitted to be sent out to us by private individuals, and only on condition of future payment, but afterward we were thought to be such cheap and effectual instruments of mischief to the British nation that more direct and gratuitous aids were furnished us."   But now M. Doniol has brought to light the *Réflexions* and *Considérations* of the French Minister, Count de Vergennes, which led to his employment of Beaumarchais, which contain such propositions as these : " It is essential that France shall at present direct its care towards this end : she must nourish the courage and perseverance of the insurgents by flattering their hope of effectual assistance when circumstances permit." " It will be expedient to give the insurgents secret aid in munitions and money ; utility suggests this small sacrifice." " Should France and Spain give succors, they should seek compensation only in the political object they have at heart, reserving to themselves subsequent decision, after the events and according to the situations." " It would be neither for the king's dignity or interest to bargain with the insurgents." It is certain that Beaumarchais was required to impress these sentiments on Arthur Lee, who continued to take them seriously, and made Paine take them so, after Beaumarchais was taking only his own interests seriously.

seems to have received no attention at the time. He says (January 5th): "In speaking of Mr. Deane's contracts with foreign officers, I concealed, out of pity to him, a circumstance that must have sufficiently shown the necessity of recalling him, and either his want of judgment or the danger of trusting him with discretionary power. It is no less than that of his throwing out a proposal, in one of his foreign letters, for contracting with a German prince to command the American army." This personage, who was " to supersede General Washington," he afterwards declares to be Prince Ferdinand. It is known that Count de Broglie had engaged Kalb and Deane to propose him as generalissimo of America, but the evidence of this other proposal has disappeared with other papers missing from Deane's diplomatic correspondence. I find, however, that ex-provost Stillé, who has studied the proceedings of Beaumarchais thoroughly, has derived from another source an impression that he (Beaumarchais) made an earlier proposition of the same kind concerning Prince Ferdinand. It would be unsafe to affirm that Deane did more than report the proposals made to him, but his silence concerning this particular charge of his antagonist, while denying every other categorically, is suspicious. At that early period Washington had not loomed up in the eye of the world. The French and Germans appear to have thought of the Americans and their commander as we might think of rebellious red men and their painted chief. There is nothing in Deane's letters from Europe to suggest that he did not share their delusion, or that he appreciated the necessity of independence.   Paine, who conducted the foreign correspondence, knew that the secrets of the American office in Paris were open to Lord Stormont, who stopped large supplies prepared for America, and suspected Deane of treachery.   It now appears that one of Deane's assistants, George Lupton, was an English "informer."   (Steven's *Facsimiles*, vii., No. 696.)   Deane had midnight meetings in the Place Vendome with an English " Unknown " (now known as the informer Paul Wentworth) to whom he suggested that the troubles might be ended by England's forming a " federal union " with America. All of which shows Deane perilously unfit for his mission, but one is glad to find him appearing no worse in Wentworth's confidental portraiture (January 4, 1778) of the American officials :

" Dr. Franklin is taciturn, deliberate, and cautious ; Mr. Deane is vain, desultory, and subtle ; Mr. Arthur Lee, suspicious and indolent ; Alderman Lee, peevish and ignorant ; Mr. Izzard, costive and dogmatical—all of these insidious, and Edwards vibrating between hope and fear, interest and attachment."

CHAPTER XI.

CAUSE, COUNTRY, SELF.

WHATEVER might be thought of Paine's course in the Deane-Beaumarchais affair, there could be no doubt that the country was saved from a questionable payment unjustly pressed at a time when it must have crippled the Revolution, for which the French subsidies were given. Congress was relieved, and he who relieved it was the sufferer. From the most important congressional secretaryship he was reduced to a clerkship in Owen Biddle's law office.

Paine's patriotic interest in public affairs did not abate. In the summer of 1779 he wrote able articles in favor of maintaining our right to the Newfoundland fisheries in any treaty of peace that might be made with England. Congress was secretly considering what instructions should be sent to its representatives in Europe, in case negotiations should arise, and the subject was discussed by " Americanus " in a letter to the *Pennsylvania Gazette*, June 23d. This writer argued that the fisheries should not be mentioned in such negotiations ; England would stickle at the claim, and our ally, France, should not be called on to guarantee a right which should be left to the determination of natural laws. This position Paine combated ; he maintained that independence was not a change of ministry, but a real thing ; it should mean prosperity as well as political liberty. Our ally would be aggrieved by a concession to Great Britain of any means of making our alliance useful. " There are but two natural sources of wealth—the Earth and the Ocean,—and to lose the right to either is, in our situation, to put up the other for sale." The fisheries are needed, "*first*, as an Employment. *Secondly*, as producing national Supply and Commerce, and a means of national wealth. *Thirdly*, as a Nursery for Seamen." Should Great Britain be in such straits as to ask for peace, that would be the right opportunity to settle the matter. " To leave the Fisheries wholly out, on any pretence whatever, is to sow the seeds of another war." (*Pennsylvania Gazette*, June 30th, July 14th, 21st.)

The prospects of peace seemed now sufficiently fair for Paine to give the attention which nobody else did to his own dismal situation. His scruples about making money out of the national cause were eccentric. The manuscript diary of Rickman, just found by Dr. Clair Grece, contains this note :

" Franklin, on returning to America from France, where he had been conducting great commercial and other concerns of great import and benefit to the States of America, on having his accounts looked over by the Committee appointed to do so, there was a deficit of £100,000. He was asked how this happened. ' I was taught,' said he very gravely, ' when a boy to read the scriptures and to attend to them, and it is there said : muzzle not the ox that treadeth out his master's grain.' No further inquiry was ever made or mention of the deficient £100,000, which, it is presumed, he devoted to some good and great purpose to serve the people,—his own aim through life."

Rickman, who named a son after Franklin, puts a more charitable construction on the irregularities of the Doctor's accounts than Gouverneur Morris (p. 140). The anecdote may not be exact, but it was generally rumored, in congressional circles, that Franklin had by no means been muzzled. Nor does it appear to have been considered a serious matter. The standard of political ethics being thus lowered, it is easy to understand that Paine gave more offence by his Diogenes-lantern than if he had quietly taken his share of the grain he trod out. The security of independence and the pressure of poverty rendered it unnecessary to adhere to his quixotic Quaker repugnance to the sale of his inspirations, and he now desired to collect these into marketable shape. His plans are stated in a letter to Henry Laurens.

"PHILADELPHIA, Sepr. 14th, 1779.—DEAR SIR,—It was my intention to have communicated to you the substance of this letter last Sunday had I not been prevented by a return of my fever ; perhaps finding myself unwell, and feeling, as well as apprehending, inconveniences, have produced in me some thoughts for myself as well as for others. I need not repeat to you the part I have acted or the principle I have acted upon ; and perhaps America would feel the less obligation to me, did she know, that it was neither the place nor the people but the Cause itself that irresistibly engaged me in its support ; for I should have acted the same part in any other Country could the same circumstances have arisen there which have happened here. I have often been obliged to form this distinction to myself by way of smoothing over some disagreeable ingratitudes, which, you well know, have been shewn to me from a certain quarter.

" I find myself so curiously circumstanced that I have both too many friends and too few, the generality of them thinking that from the public part I have so long acted I cannot have less than a mine to draw from—What they have had from me they have got for nothing, and they consequently suppose I must be able to afford it. I know but one kind of life I am fit for, and that is a thinking one, and, of course, a writing one—but I have confined myself so much of late, taken so little exercise, and lived so very sparingly, that unless I alter my way of life it will alter me. I think I have a right to ride a horse of my own, but I cannot now even afford to hire one, which is a situation I never was in before, and I begin to know that a sedentary life cannot be supported without jolting exercise. Having said thus much, which, in truth, is but loss of time to tell to you who so well know how I am situated, I take the liberty of communicating to you my design of doing some degree of justice to myself, but even this is accompanied with some present difficulties, but it is the easiest, and, I believe, the most useful and reputable of any I can think of. I intend this winter to collect all my Publications, beginning with Common Sense and ending with the fisheries, and publishing them in two volumes Octavo, with notes. I have no doubt of a large subscription. The principal difficulty will be to get Paper and I can think of no way more practicable than to desire Arthur Lee to send over a quantity from France in the Confederacy if she goes there, and settling for it with his brother. After that work is compleated, I intend prosecuting a history of the Revolution by means of a subscription—but this undertaking will be attended with such an amazing expense, and will take such a length of Time, that unless the States individually give some assistance therein, scarcely any man could afford to go through it. Some kind of an history might be easily executed made up of daily events and triffling matters which would lose their Importance in a few years. But a proper history cannot even be began unless the secrets of the other side of the water can be obtained, for the first part is so interwoven with the Politics of England, that, that which will be the last to get at must be the first to begin with—and this single instance is sufficient to show that no history can take place of some time. My design, if I undertake it, is to comprise it in three quarto volumes and to publish one each year from the time of beginning, and to make an abridgment afterwards in an easy agreeable language for a school book.

All the histories of ancient wars that are used for this purpose, promotes no Moral Reflection, but like the beggars opera renders the villain pleasing in the hero. Another thing that will prolong the completion of an history is the want of Plates which only can be done in Europe, for that part of a history which is intended to convey discription of places or persons will ever be imperfect without them. I have now, Sir, acquainted you with my design, and unwilling, as you know I am, to make use of a friend while I can possibly avoid it, I am really obliged to say that I should now be glad to consult with two or three on some matters that regard my situation till such time as I can bring the first of those subscriptions to bear, or set them on foot, which cannot well be until I can get the paper ; for should I [be] disappointed of that, with the subscriptions in my hand, I might be reflected upon, and the reason, tho' a true one, would be subject to other explanations.

" Here lies the difficulty I alluded to in the beginning of this letter, and I would rather wish to borrow something of a friend or two in the interim than run the risk I have mentioned, because should I be disappointed by the Paper being taken or not arriving in time, the reason being understood by them beforehand will not injure me, but in the other case it would, and in the mean Time I can be preparing for publication. I have hitherto kept all my private matters a secret, but as I know your friendship and you a great deal of my situation, I can with more ease communicate them to you than to another.

" P. S. If you are not engaged to-morrow evening I should be glad to spend part of it with you—if you are, I shall wait your opportunity." [1]

It was a cruel circumstance of Paine's poverty that he was compelled to call attention not only to that but to his services, and to appraise the value of his own pen. He had to deal with hard men, on whom reserve was wasted. On September 28th

---

[1] I am indebted to Mr. Simon Gratz of Philadelphia for a copy of this letter.

he reminded the Excutive Council of Pennsylvania of his needs and his uncompensated services, which, he declared, he could not afford to continue without support. The Council realized the importance of Paine's pen to its patriotic measures, but was afraid of offending the French Minister. Its president, Joseph Reed, on the following day (September 29th) wrote to that Minister intimating that they would like to employ Paine if he (the minister) had no objection. On October 11th Gérard replies with a somewhat equivocal letter, in which he declares that Paine had agreed to terms he had offered through M. de Mirales, but had not fulfilled them. "I willingly," he says, "leave M. Payne to enjoy whatever advantages he promises himself by his denial of his acceptance of the offers of M. de Mirales and myself. I would even add, Sir, that if you feel able to direct his pen in a way useful to the public welfare—which will perhaps not be difficult to your zeal, talents, and superior lights,—I will be the first to applaud the success of an attempt in which I have failed."[1] On the same date Paine, not having received any reply to his previous letter, again wrote to the Council.

"HONBLE. SIRS.—Some few days ago I presented a letter to this Honble. Board stating the inconveniences which I lay under from an attention to public interest in preference to my own, to which I have recd. no reply. It is to me a matter of great concern to find in the government of this State, that which appears to be a disposition in them to neglect their friends and to throw discouragements in the way of genius and Letters.

"At the particular request of the Gentleman who presides

[1] " Life and Correspondence of Joseph Reed." By his grandson. 1847.

at this board, I took up the defence of the Constitution, at a
time when he declared to me that unless he could be assisted
he must give it up and quit the state ; as matters then
pressed too heavy upon him, and the opposition was gaining
ground ; yet this Board has since suffered me to combat with
all the inconveniences incurred by that service, without any
attention to my interest or my situation. For the sake of not
dishonoring a cause, good in itself, I have hitherto been silent
on these matters, but I cannot help expressing to this board
the concern I feel on this occasion, and the ill effect which
such discouraging examples will have on those who might
otherwise be disposed to act as I have done.

" Having said this much, which is but a little part of which
I am sensible, I have a request to make which if complied
with will enable me to overcome the difficulties alluded to and
to withdraw from a service in which I have experienced nothing
but misfortune and neglect. I have an opportunity of import-
ing a quantity of printing paper from France, and intend
collecting my several pieces, beginning with Common Sense,
into two Volumes, and publishing them by Subscription, with
notes ; but as I cannot think of beginning the Subscription
until the paper arrive, and as the undertaking, exclusive of the
paper, will be attended with more expense than I, who have
saved money both in the Service of the Continent and the
State, can bear, I should be glad to be assisted with the loan
of fifteen hundred pounds for which I will give bond payable
within a year. If this should not be complied with, I request
that the services I have rendered may be taken into consideration and such compensation made me therefor as they shall
appear to deserve.

" I am, Honble. Sirs, your obt. and humble servt.,

"THOMAS PAINE."

The constitution which Paine, in the above letter,
speaks of defending was that of 1776, which he had
assisted Dr. Franklin, James Cannon and others in
framing for Pennsylvania. It was a fairly republican constitution, and by its enfranchisement of the
people generally reduced the power enjoyed by the

rich and reactionary under the colonial government.
In Stillé's biography of John Dickinson the continued conflicts concerning this constitution are
described.   In 1805, when a constitutional convention was proposed in Pennsylvania, Paine pointed
out the superiority of its constitution of 1776, which
"was conformable to the Declaration of Independence and the Declaration of Rights, which the
present constitution [framed in 1790] is not."[1]
The constitution of 1776, and Paine's exposure of
the services rendered to the enemy by Quakers,
cleared the Pennsylvania Assembly of the members
of that society who had been supreme.   This process had gone on.   The oath of allegiance to the
State, proposed by Paine in 1777, and adopted, had
been followed in 1778 (April 1st) by one imposing
renunciation of all allegiance to George III., his
heirs and successors, to be taken by all trustees,
provosts, professors, and masters.   This was particularly aimed at the nest of "Tories" in the
University of Philadelphia, whose head was the
famous Dr. William Smith.   This provost, and all
members of the University except three trustees,
took the oath, but the influence of those who had
been opposed to independence remained the same.
In 1779 the Assembly got rid of the provost
(Smith), and this was done by the act of Novem-

---

[1] Paine forgot the curious inconsistency in this constitution of 1776,
between the opening Declaration of Rights in securing religious freedom
and equality to all who "acknowledge the being of a God," and the oath
provided for all legislators, requiring belief in future rewards and punish-
ments, and in the divine inspiration of the Old and New Testaments.   This
deistical oath, however, was probably considered a victory of latitudiarian-
ism, for the members of the convention had taken a rigid trinitarian oath on
admission to their seats.

ber which took away the charter of the University.[1]
It was while this agitation was going on, and the
Philadelphia "Tories" saw the heads of their chief-
tains falling beneath Paine's pen, that his own
official head had been thrown to them by his own
act. The sullen spite of the "Tories" did not fail
to manifest itself. In conjunction with Deane's
defeated friends, they managed to give Paine many
a personal humiliation. This was, indeed, easy
enough, since Paine, though willing to fight for his
cause, was a non-resistant in his own behalf. It
may have been about this time that an incident
occurred which was remembered with gusto by the
aged John Joseph Henry after the "Age of Reason"
had added horns and cloven feet to his early hero.
Mr. Mease, Clothier-General, gave a dinner party,
and a company of his guests, on their way home,
excited by wine, met Paine. One of them remarking, "There comes 'Common Sense,'" Matthew
Slough said, "Damn him, I shall common-sense
him," and thereupon tripped Paine into the gutter.[2]

But patriotic America was with Paine, and
missed his pen ; for no *Crisis* had appeared for
nearly a year. Consequently on November 2, 1779,
the Pennsylvania Assembly elected him its Clerk.

[1] See "A Memoir of the Rev. William Smith, D.D.," by Charles J.
Stillé, Philadelphia, 1869. Provost Stillé, in this useful historical pamphlet,
states all that can be said in favor of Dr. Smith, but does not refer to his
controversy with Paine.

[2] This incident is related in the interest of religion in Mr. Henry's
"Account of Arnold's Campaign against Quebec." The book repeats the
old charge of drunkenness against Paine, but the untrustworthiness of the
writer's memory is shown in his saying that his father grieved when Paine's
true character appeared, evidently meaning his "infidelity." His father
died in 1786, when no suspicion either of Paine's habits or orthodoxy had
been heard.

On the same day there was introduced into that Assembly an act for the abolition of slavery in the State, which then contained six thousand negro slaves. The body of this very moderate measure was prepared by George Bryan, but the much admired preamble has been attributed by tradition to the pen of Paine.[1] That this tradition is correct is now easily proved by a comparison of its sentiments and phraseology with the antislavery writings of Paine presented in previous pages of this work. The author, who alone seems to have been thinking of the negroes and their rights during that revolutionary epoch, thus had some reward in writing the first proclamation of emancipation in America. The act passed March 1, 1780. The Preamble is as follows :

"I. When we contemplate our abhorrence of that condition, to which the arms and tyranny of Great Britain were exerted to reduce us, when we look back on the variety of dangers to which we have been exposed, and how miraculously our wants in many instances have been supplied, and our deliverances wrought, when even hope and human fortitude have become unequal to the conflict, we are unavoidably led to a serious and grateful sense of the manifold blessings, which we have undeservedly received from the hand of that Being, from whom every good and perfect gift cometh. Impressed with these ideas, we conceive that is is our duty, and we rejoice that it is in our power, to extend a portion of that freedom to others, which hath been extended to us, and release from that state of thraldom, to which we ourselves were tyrannically doomed, and from which we have now every prospect of being delivered. It is not for us to enquire why, in the creation of mankind, the inhabitants of the several parts of the

---

[1] " Life and Correspondence of Joseph Reed," ii., p. 177; *North American Review*, vol. lvii., No. cxx.

earth were distinguished by a difference in feature or complexion.
It is sufficient to know that all are the work of the Almighty
Hand. We find in the distribution of the human species, that
the most fertile as well as the most barren parts of the earth
are inhabited by men of complexions different from ours, and
from each other ; from whence we may reasonably as well as
religiously infer, that He, who placed them in their various
situations, hath extended equally his care and protection to
all, and that it becometh not us to counteract his mercies.
We esteem it a peculiar blessing granted to us, that we are
enabled this day to add one more step to universal civilization, by removing, as much as possible, the sorrows of those,
who have lived in undeserved bondage, and from which, by
the assumed authority of the Kings of Great Britain, no
effectual, legal relief could be obtained. Weaned, by a long
course of experience, from those narrow prejudices and par-
tialities we had imbibed, we find our hearts enlarged with
kindness and benevolence towards men of all conditions and
nations ; and we conceive ourselves at this particular period
particularly called upon by the blessings which we have received, to manifest the sincerity of our profession, and to give
a substantial proof of our gratitude.

"II. And whereas the condition of those persons, who have
heretofore been denominated Negro and Mulatto slaves, has
been attended with circumstances, which not only deprived
them of the common blessings that they were by nature entitled to, but has cast them into the deepest afflictions, by an
unnatural separation and sale of husband and wife from each
other and from their children, an injury, the greatness of
which can only be conceived by supposing that we were in the
same unhappy case. In justice, therefore, to persons so un-
happily circumstanced, and who, having no prospect before
them whereon they may rest their sorrows and their hopes,
have no reasonable inducement to render their service to
society, which they otherwise might, and also in grateful commemoration of our own happy deliverance from that state of
unconditional submission to which we were doomed by the
tyranny of Britain.

"III. *Be it enacted,* &c."

The New Year, 1780, found Washington amid much distress at Morristown. Besides the published letters which attest this I have found an extract from one which seems to have escaped the attention of Washington's editors.[1] It was written at Morristown, January 5th.

"It gives me extreme Pain that I should still be holding up to Congress our wants on the score of Provision, when I am convinced that they are doing all that they can for our relief. Duty and necessity, however, constrain me to it. The inclosed copies of Letters from Mr. Flint, the Assistant Commissary, and from Gen. Irvine, who commands at present our advanced troops, contain a just Representation of our situation. To add to our Difficulties I very much fear that the late violent snow storm has so blocked up the Roads, that it will be some days before the scanty supplies in this quarter can be brought to camp. The troops, both officers and men, have borne their Distress, with a patience scarcely to be conceived. Many of the latter have been four or five days without meat entirely and short of Bread, and none but very scanty Supplies—Some for their preservation have been compelled to maraud and rob from the Inhabitants, and I have it not in my power to punish or reprove the practice. If our condition should not undergo a very speedy and considerable change for the better, it will be difficult to point out all the consequences that may ensue. About forty of the Cattle mentioned by Mr. Flint got in last night."

The times that tried men's souls had come again. The enemy, having discovered the sufferings of the soldiers at Morristown, circulated leaflets inviting them to share the pleasures of New York. Nor were they entirely unsuccessful. On May 28th was penned the gloomiest letter Washington ever

---

[1] It is in the Ward Collection at Lafayette College, Easton, Pa., copied by a (probably) contemporary hand.

wrote.   It was addressed to Reed, President of Pennsylvania, and the Clerk (Paine) read it to the Assembly.   " I assure you," said the Commander's letter, " every idea you can form of our distresses will fall short of the reality.   There is such a combination of circumstances to exhaust the patience of the soldiery that it begins at length to be worn out, and we see in every line of the army the most serious features of mutiny and sedition."   There was throughout the long letter a tone of desperation which moved the Assembly profoundly.   At the close there was a despairing silence, amid which a member arose and said, " We may as well give up first as last."   The treasury was nearly empty, but enough remained to pay Paine his salary, and he headed a subscription of relief with $500.[1]   The money was enclosed to Mr. M'Clenaghan, with a vigorous letter which that gentleman read to a meeting held in a coffee-house the same evening. Robert Morris and M'Clenaghan subscribed £200 each, hard money.   The subscription, dated June 8th, spread like wildfire, and resulted in the raising of £300,000, which established a bank that supplied the army through the campaign, and was incorporated by Congress on December 21st.

Paine, by his timely suggestion of a subscription, and his " mite," as he called it, proved that he could meet a crisis as well as write one.   He had written a cheery *Crisis* in March, had helped to make good its hopefulness in May, and was

---

[1] The salary was drawn on June 7th, and amounted to $1,699.   For particulars concerning Paine's connection with the Assembly I am indebted to Dr. William H. Egle, State Librarian of Pennsylvania.

straightway busy on another. This was probably begun on the morning when M'Clenaghan came to him with a description of the happy effect and result produced by his letter and subscription on the gentlemen met at the coffee-house. This *Crisis* (June 9, 1780) declares that the reported fate of Charleston, like the misfortunes of 1776, had revived the same spirit ; that such piecemeal work was not conquering the continent ; that France was at their side ; that an association had been formed for supplies, and hard-money bounties. In a postscript he adds : " Charleston is gone, and I believe for the want of a sufficient supply of provisions. The man that does not now feel for the honor of the best and noblest cause that ever a country engaged in, and exert himself accordingly, is no longer worthy of a peaceable residence among a people determined to be free."

Meanwhile, on " Sunday Morning, June 4th," Paine wrote to President Reed a private letter :

" SIR,—I trouble you with a few thoughts on the present state of affairs. Every difficulty we are now in arises from an empty treasury and an exhausted credit. These removed and the prospect were brighter. While the war was carried on by emissions at the pleasure of Congress, any body of men might conduct public business, and the poor were of equal use in government with the rich. But when the means must be drawn from the country the case becomes altered, and unless the wealthier part throw in their aid, public measures must go heavily on.

" The people of America understand *rights* better than *politics*. They have a clear idea of their object, but are greatly deficient in comprehending the means. In the first place, they do not distinguish between sinking the debt, and raising the current expenses. They want to have the war carried on, the Lord knows how.

"It is always dangerous to spread an alarm of danger unless the prospect of success be held out with it, and that not only as probable, but naturally essential. These things premised, I beg leave to mention, that suppose you were to send for some of the richer inhabitants of the City, and state to them the situation of the army and the treasury, not as arising so much from defect in the departments of government as from a neglect in the country generally, in not contributing the necessary support in time. If they have any spirit, any foresight of their own interest or danger, they will promote a subscription either of money or articles, and appoint a committee from among themselves to solicit the same in the several Counties ; and one State setting the example, the rest, I presume, will follow. Suppose it was likewise proposed to them to deposit their plate to be coined for the pay of the Army, crediting the government for the value, by weight.

"If measures of this kind could be promoted by the richer of the Whigs, it would justify your calling upon the other part to furnish their proportion without ceremony, and these two measures carried, would make a draft or call for personal service the more palatable and easy.

"I began to write this yesterday. This morning, it appears clear to me that Charleston is in the hands of the enemy, and the garrison prisoners of war. Something must be done, and that something, to give it popularity, must begin with men of property. Every care ought now to be taken to keep goods from rising. The rising of goods will have a most ruinous ill effect in every light in which it can be viewed.

"The army must be reunited, and that by the most expeditious possible means. Drafts should first be countenanced by subscriptions, and if men would but reason rightly, they would see that there are some thousands in this State who had better subscribe thirty, forty, or fifty guineas apiece than run the risk of having to settle with the enemy. Property is always the object of a conqueror, wherever he can find it. A rich man, says King James, makes a bonny traitor ; and it cannot be supposed that Britain will not reimburse herself by the wealth of others, could she once get the power of doing it. We must at least recruit eight or ten thousand men in this State, who had better raise a man apiece, though it should cost them a thousand pounds apiece, than not have a sufficient force, were it only for safety sake. Eight or ten thousand men, added to what we have now got, with the force that may arrive, would enable us to make a stroke at New York, to recover the loss of Charleston—but the measure must be expeditious.

" I suggest another thought. Suppose every man, working a plantation, who has not taken the oath of allegiance, in Philadelphia County, Bucks, Chester, Lancaster, Northampton, and Berks, were, by the new power vested in the Council, called immediately upon for taxes in kind at a certain value. Horses and wagons to be appraised. This would not only give immediate relief, but popularity to the new power. I would remark of taxes in kind, that they are hard-money taxes, and could they be established on the non-jurors, would relieve us in the articles of supplies.

" But whatever is necessary or proper to be done, must be done immediately. We must rise vigorously upon the evil, or it will rise upon us. A show of spirit will grow into real spirit, but the Country must not be suffered to ponder over their loss for a day. The circumstance of the present hour will justify any means from which good may arise. We want rousing.

" On the loss of Charleston I would remark—the expectation of a foreign force arriving will embarrass them whether to go or to stay ; and in either case, what will they do with their prisoners ? If they return, they will be but as they were as to dominion ; if they continue, they will leave New York an attackable post. They can make no new movements for a considerable time. They may pursue their object to the Southward in detachments, but then in every main point they will naturally be at a stand ; and we ought immediately to lay hold of the vacancy.

" I am, Sir, your obedient humble servant,

"Thomas Paine."

If Paine had lost any popularity in consequence of his indirect censure by Congress, a year before, it had been more than regained by his action in

heading the subscription, and the inspiriting effect
of his pamphlets of March and June, 1780. The
University of the State of Pennsylvania, as it was
now styled, celebrated the Fourth of July by con-
ferring on him the degree of Master of Arts.[1]
Among the trustees who voted to confer on him
this honor were some who had two years before
refused to take the American oath of allegiance.

In the autumn appeared Paine's *Crisis Extraordinary.* It would appear by a payment made to
him personally, that in order to make his works
cheap he had been compelled to take his publications into his own hands.[2] The sum of $360 paid
for ten dozen copies of this pamphlet was really at
the rate of five cents per copy. It is a forcible
reminder of the depreciation of the Continental
currency. At one period Paine says he paid $300
for a pair of woollen stockings.

Although the financial emergency had been tided
over by patriotic sacrifices, it had disclosed a chaos.

---

[1] Mr. Burk, Secretary of the University of Pennsylvania, sends me some
interesting particulars. The proposal to confer the degree on Paine was
unanimously agreed to by the trustees present, who were the Hon. Joseph
Reed, President of the Province ; Mr. Moore, Vice-President ; Mr. Sproat
(Presbyterian minister), Mr. White (the Bishop), Mr. Helmuth, Mr. Wei-
borg (minister of the German Calvinist Church), Mr. Farmer (Roman Catholic Rector of St. Mary's), Dr. Bond, Dr. Hutchkinson, Mr. Muhlenberg
(Lutheran minister). There were seven other recipients of the honor on
that day, all eminent ministers of religion ; and M.D. was conferred on
David Ramsay, a prisoner with the enemy.

[2] " In Council. Philadelphia, October 10th, 1780. SIR,—Pay to Thomas
Paine Esquire, or his order, the amount of three hundred and sixty dollars
Continental money in State money, at sixty to one, amount of his account
for 10 dozen of the Crisis Extraordinary. WM. MOORE, Vice President.—
To DAVID RITTENHOUSE Esquire, Treasurer."

" SIR,—Please to pay the within to Mr. Willm. Harris, and you will oblige
yr. obt. Hble. Sert., *Thos. Paine.*—DAVID RITTENHOUSE ESQ."

" Rcd. in full, H. WM. HARRIS." [Harris printed the pamphlet].

11

Congress, so far from being able to contend with Virginia on a point of sovereignty, was without power to levy taxes. "One State," writes Washington (May 31st) "will comply with a requisition of Congress; another neglects to do it; a third executes it by halves; and all differ either in the manner, the matter, or so much in point of time, that we are always working up hill, and ever shall be; and, while such a system as the present one or rather want of one prevails, we shall ever be unable to apply our strength or resources to any advantage." In the letter of May 28th, to the President of Pennsylvania, which led to the subscription headed by Paine, Washington pointed out that the resources of New York and Jersey were exhausted, that Virginia could spare nothing from the threatened South, and Pennsylvania was their chief dependence. "The crisis, in every point of view, is extraordinary." This sentence of Washington probably gave Paine his title, *Crisis Extraordinary*. It is in every sense a masterly production. By a careful estimate he shows that the war and the several governments cost two millions sterling annually. The population being 3,000,000, the amount would average 13*s.* 4*d.* per head. In England the taxation was £2 per head. With independence a peace establishment in America would cost 5*s.* per head; with the loss of it Americans would have to pay the £2 per head like other English subjects. Of the needed annual two millions, Pennsylvania's quota would be an eighth, or £250,000; that is, a shilling per month to her 375,000 inhabitants,—which subjugation would increase to three-and-threepence per month. He points out that the Pennsylvanians were then paying only £64,280 per annum, instead of their real quota of £250,000, leaving a deficiency of £185,-720, and consequently a distressed army. After showing that with peace and free trade all losses and ravages would be speedily redressed, Paine proposes that half of Pennsylvania's quota, and £60,000 over, shall be raised by a tax of 7s. per head. With this sixty thousand (interest on six millions) a million can be annually borrowed. He recommends a war-tax on landed property, houses, imports, prize goods, and liquors. " It would be an addition to the pleasures of society to know that, when the health of the army goes round, a few drops from every glass become theirs."

On December 30, 1780, Dunlap advertised Paine's pamphlet " Public Good." Under a charter given the Virginia Company in 1609 the State of Virginia claimed that its southern boundary extended to the Pacific ; and that its northern boundary, starting four hundred miles above, on the Atlantic coast, stretched due northwest. To this Paine replies that the charter was given to a London company extinct for one hundred and fifty years, during which the State had never acted under that charter. Only the heirs of that company's members could claim anything under its extinct charter. Further, the State unwarrantably assumed that the northwestern line was to extend from the northern point of its Atlantic base ; whereas there was more reason to suppose that it was to extend from the southern point, and meet a due west line from the northern point, thus forming a triangular territory of forty-five thousand square miles. Moreover, the charter of 1609 said the lines should stretch " from sea to sea." Paine shows by apt quotations that the western sea was supposed to be a short distance from the Atlantic, and that the northwestern boundary claimed by Virginia would never reach the said sea, "but would form a spiral line of infinite windings round the globe, and after passing over the northern parts of America and the frozen ocean, and then into the northern parts of Asia, would, when eternity should end, and not before, terminate in the north pole." Such a territory is nondescript, and a charter that describes nothing gives nothing. It may be remarked here that though the Attorney-General of Virginia, Edmund Randolph, had to vindicate his State's claim, he used a similar argument in defeating Lord Fairfax's claim to lands in Virginia which had not been discovered when his grant was issued.[1] All this, however, was mere fencing preliminary to the real issue. The western lands, on the extinction of the Virginia companies, had reverted to the Crown, and the point in which the State was really interested was its succession to the sovereignty of the Crown over all that territory. It was an early cropping up of the question of State sovereignty. By royal proclamation of 1763 the province of Virginia was defined so as not to extend beyond heads of rivers emptying in the Atlantic. Paine contended that to the sovereignty

---

[1] " Omitted Chapters of History Disclosed in the Life and Papers of Edmund Randolph," pp. 47, 60.

of the Crown over all territories beyond limits of the thirteen provinces the United States had succeeded. This early assertion of the federal doctrine, enforced with great historical and legal learning, alienated from Paine some of his best Southern friends. The controversy did not end until some years later. After the peace, a proposal in the Virginia Legislature to present Paine with something for his services, was lost on account of this pamphlet.[1]

The students of history will soon be enriched by a " Life of Patrick Henry," by his grandson, William Wirt Henry, and a " Life of George Mason," by his descendant, Miss Rowland. In these works by competent hands important contributions will be made (as I have reason to know) to, right knowledge of the subject dealt with by Paine in his " Public Good." It can here only be touched on ; but in passing I may say that Virginia

[1] Of course this issue of State *v.* National sovereignty was adjourned to the future battle-field, where indeed it was not settled. Congress accepted Virginia's concession of the territory in question (March 1, 1784), without conceding that it was a donation ; it accepted some of Virginia's conditions, but refused others, which the State surrendered. A motion that this acceptance did not imply endorsement of Virginia's claim was lost, but the contrary was not affirmed. The issue was therefore settled only in Paine's pamphlet, which remains a document of paramount historical interest.

There was, of course, a rumor that Paine's pamphlet was a piece of paid advocacy. I remarked among the Lee MSS., at the University of Virginia, an unsigned scrap of paper saying he had been promised twelve thousand acres of western land. Such a promise could only have been made by the old Indiana, or Vandalia, Company, which was trying to revive its defeated claim for lands conveyed by the Indians in compensation for property they had destroyed. Their agent, Samuel Wharton, may have employed Paine's pen for some kind of work. But there is no faintest trace of advocacy in Paine's " Public Good." He simply maintains that the territories belong to the United States, and should be sold to pay the public debt,—a principle as fatal to the claim of a Company as to that of a State.

had good ground for resisting even the semblance
of an assertion of sovereignty by a Congress representing only a military treaty between the colonies;
and that Paine's doctrine confesses itself too ideal-
istic and premature by the plea, with which his
pamphlet closes, for the summoning of a " continental convention, for the purpose of forming a
continental constitution, defining and describing
the powers and authority of Congress."

CHAPTER XII.

A JOURNEY TO FRANCE.

THE suggestion of Franklin to Paine, in October, 1775, that he should write a history of the events that led up to the conflict, had never been forgotten by either. From Franklin he had gathered important facts and materials concerning the time antedating his arrival in America, and he had been a careful chronicler of the progress of the Revolution. He was now eager to begin this work. At the close of the first year of his office as Clerk of the Assembly, which left him with means of support for a time, he wrote to the Speaker (November 3, 1780) setting forth his intention of collecting materials for a history of the Revolution, and saying that he could not fulfil the duties of Clerk if re-elected.[1]

---

[1] Dr. Egle informs me that the following payments to Paine appear in the Treasurer's account : 1779, November 27, £450. 1780, February 14. For public service at a treaty held at Easton in 1777, £300. February 14. Pay as clerk, £582. 10. 0. March 18. On account as clerk, £187. 10. 0. March 27, " for his services " (probably those mentioned on p. 94), £2,355. 7. 6. June 7, " for 60 days attendance and extra expenses," £1,699. 1. 6. (This was all paper money, and of much less value than it seems. The last payment was drawn on the occasion of his subscription of the $500, apparently hard money, in response to Washington's appeal.) In March, 1780, a Fee Act was passed regulating the payment of officers of the State in accordance with the price of wheat ; but this was ineffectual to preserve the State paper from depreciation. In June, 1780, a list of lawyers and State officers willing to take paper money of the March issue as gold and silver was published, and in it appears " Thomas Paine, clerk to the General Assembly."

This and another letter (September 14, 1780), addressed to the Hon. John Bayard, Speaker of the late Assembly, were read, and ordered to lie on the table. Paine's office would appear to have ended early in November ; the next three months were devoted to preparations for his history.

But events determined that Paine should make more history than he was able to chronicle. Soon after his *Crisis Extraordinary* (dated October 6, 1780) had appeared, Congress issued its estimate of eight million dollars (a million less than Paine's) as the amount to be raised. It was plain that the money could not be got in the country, and France must be called on for help. Paine drew up a letter to Vergennes, informing him that a paper dollar was worth only a cent, that it seemed almost impossible to continue the war, and asking that France should supply America with a million sterling per annum, as subsidy or loan. This letter was shown to M. Marbois, Secretary of the French Legation, who spoke discouragingly. But the Hon. Ralph Izard showed the letter to some members of Congress, whose consultation led to the appointment of Col. John Laurens to visit France. It was thought that Laurens, one of Washington's aids, would be able to explain the military situation. He was reluctant, but agreed to go if Paine would accompany him.

It so happened that Paine had for some months had a dream of crossing the Atlantic, with what purpose is shown in the following confidential letter (September 9, 1780), probably· to Gen. Nathaniel Greene.

"Sir,—Last spring I mentioned to you a wish I had to take a passage for Europe, and endeavour to go privately to England. You pointed out several difficulties in the way, respecting my own safety, which occasioned me to defer the matter at that time, in order not only to weigh it more seriously, but to submit to the government of subsequent circumstances. I have frequently and carefully thought of it since, and were I now to give an opinion on it as a measure to which I was not a party, it would be this :—that as the press in that country is free and open, could a person possessed of a knowledge of America, and capable of fixing it in the minds of the people of England, go suddenly from this country to that, and keep himself concealed, he might, were he to manage his knowledge rightly, produce a more general disposition for peace than by any method I can suppose. I see my way so clearly before me in this opinion, that I must be more mistaken than I ever yet was on any political measure, if it fail of its end. I take it for granted that the whole country, ministry, minority, and all, are tired of the war ; but the difficulty is how to get rid of it, or how they are to come down from the high ground they have taken, and accommodate their feelings to a treaty for peace. Such a change must be the effect either of necessity or choice. I think it will take, at least, three or four more campaigns to produce the former, and they are too wrong in their opinions of America to act from the latter. I imagine that next spring will begin with a new Parliament, which is so material a crisis in the politics of that country, that it ought to be attended to by this ; for, should it start wrong, we may look forward to six or seven years more of war. The influence of the press rightly managed is important ; but we can derive no service in this line, because there is no person in England who knows enough of America to treat the subject properly. It was in a great measure owing to my bringing a knowledge of England with me to America, that I was enabled to enter deeper into politics, and with more success, than other people ; and whoever takes the matter up in England must in like manner be possessed of a knowledge of America. I do not suppose that the acknowledgment of Independence is at this time a more unpopular doctrine in England than the declaration of it was in America immediately before the publication of the pamphlet 'Common Sense,' and the ground appears as open for the one now as it did for the other then.

"The manner in which I would bring such a publication out would be under the cover of an Englishman who had made the tour of America *incog*. This will afford me all the foundation I wish for and enable me to place matters before them in a light in which they have never yet viewed them. I observe that Mr. Rose in his speech on Governor Pownall's bill, printed in Bradford's last paper, says that 'to form an opinion on the propriety of yielding independence to America requires an accurate knowledge of the state of that country, the temper of the people, the resources of their Government,' &c. Now there is no other method to give this information a national currency but this,—the channel of the press, which I have ever considered the tongue of the world, and which governs the sentiments of mankind more than anything else that ever did or can exist.

"The simple point I mean to aim at is, to make the acknowledgment of Independence a popular subject, and that not by exposing and attacking their errors, but by stating its advantages and apologising for their errors, by way of accomodating the measure to their pride. The present parties in that country will never bring one another to reason. They are heated with all the passion of opposition, and to rout the ministry, or to support them, makes their capital point. Were the same channel open to the ministry in this country which is open to us in that, they would stick at no expense to improve the opportunity. Men who are used to government know the weight and worth of the press, when in hands which can use it to advantage. Perhaps with me a little degree of literary pride is connected with principle ; for, as I had a considerable share in promoting the declaration of Independence in this country, I likewise wish to be a means of promoting the acknowledgment of it in that ; and were I not persuaded that the measure I have proposed would be productive of much essential service, I would not hazard my own safety, as I have everything to apprehend should I fall into their hands ; but, could I escape in safety, till I could get out a publication in England, my apprehensions would be over, because the manner in which I mean to treat the subject would procure me protection.

"Having said thus much on the matter, I take the liberty of hinting to you a mode by which the expense may be defrayed without any new charge. Drop a delegate in Congress at the next election, and apply the pay to defray what I have proposed ; and the point then will be, whether you can possibly put any man into Congress who could render as much service in that station as in the one I have pointed out. When you have perused this, I should be glad of some conversation upon it, and will wait on you for that purpose at any hour you may appoint. I have changed my lodgings, and am now in Front Street opposite the Coffee House, next door to Aitkin's bookstore.

　　　　"I am, Sir, your ob't humble servant,

　　　　　　　　"THOMAS PAINE."

The invitation of Colonel Laurens was eagerly accepted by Paine, who hoped that after their business was transacted in France he might fulfil his plan of a literary descent on England. They sailed from Boston early in February, 1781, and arrived at L'Orient in March.

Young Laurens came' near ruining the scheme by an imprudent advocacy, of which Vergennes complained, while ascribing it to his inexperience. According to Lamartine, the King "loaded Paine with favors." The gift of six millions was "confided into the hands of Franklin and Paine." The author now revealed to Laurens, and no doubt to Franklin, his plan for going to England, but was dissuaded from it. From Brest, May 28th, he writes to Franklin in Paris :

"I have just a moment to spare to bid you farewell. We go on board in an hour or two, with a fair wind and everything ready. I understand that you have expressed a desire to withdraw from business, and I beg leave to assure you that every wish of mine, so far as it can be attended with any service, will be employed to make your resignation, should it be accepted, attended with every possible mark of honor which your long services and high character in life justly merit." [1]

They sailed from Brest on the French frigate *Resolve* June 1st, reaching Boston August 25th, with 2,500,000 livres in silver, and in convoy a ship laden with clothing and military stores.

The glad tidings had long before reached Washington, then at New Windsor. On May 14, 1781, the General writes to Philip Schuyler:

"I have been exceedingly distressed by the repeated accounts I have received of the sufferings of the troops on the frontier, and the terrible consequences which must ensue unless they were speedily supplied. What gave a particular poignancy to the sting I felt on the occasion was my inability to afford relief."

On May 26th his diary notes a letter from Laurens reporting the relief coming from France. The information was confided by Washington only to his diary, lest it should forestall efforts of self-help. Of course Washington knew that the starting of convoys from France could not escape English vigilance, and that their arrival was uncertain; so he passed near three months in preparations, reconnoitrings, discussions. By menacing the British in New York he made them draw away some of the forces of Cornwallis from Virginia, where he meant to strike; but his delay in march-

---

[1] He confides to Franklin a letter to be forwarded to Bury St. Edmunds, the region of his birth. Perhaps he had already been corresponding with some one there about his projected visit. Ten years later the *Bury Post* vigorously supported Paine and his "Rights of Man."

ing south brought on him complaints from Governor Jefferson, Richard Henry Lee, and others, who did not know the secret of that delay. Washington meant to carry to Virginia an army well clad, with hard money in their pockets, and this he did. The arrival of the French supplies at Boston, August 25th, was quickly heralded, and while sixteen ox-teams were carrying them to Philadelphia, Washington was there getting, on their credit, all the money and supplies he wanted for the campaign that resulted in the surrender of Cornwallis.

For this great service Paine never received any payment or acknowledgment. The plan of obtaining aid from France was conceived by him, and mainly executed by him. It was at a great risk that he went on this expedition ; had he been captured he could have hoped for little mercy from the British. Laurens, who had nearly upset the business, got the glory and the pay ; Paine, who had given up his clerkship of the Assembly, run the greater danger, and done the real work, got nothing. But it was a rôle he was used to. The young Colonel hastened to resume his place in Washington's family, but seems to have given little attention to Paine's needs, while asking attention to his own. So it would appear by the following friendly letter of Paine, addressed to " Col. Laurens, Head Quarters, Virginia :

" PHILADELPHIA, Oct. 4, 1781.—DEAR SIR,—I received your favor (by the post,) dated Sep. 9th, Head of Elk, respecting a mislaid letter. A gentleman who saw you at that place about the same time told me he had likewise a letter from you to me which he had lost, and that you mentioned something to him respecting baggage. This left me in a difficulty to judge whether after writing to me by post, you had not found the letter you wrote about, and took that opportunity to inform me about it. However, I have wrote to Gen. Heath in case the trunk should be there, and inclosed in it a letter to Blodget in case it should not. I have yet heard nothing from either. I have preferred forwarding the trunk, in case it can be done in a reasonable time, to the opening it, and if it cannot, then to open it agreeably to your directions, tho' I have no idea of its being there.

" I went for your boots, the next day after you left town, but they were not done, and I directed the man to bring them to me as soon as finished, but have since seen nothing of him, neither do wish him to bring them just now, as I must be obliged to borrow the money to pay for them ; but I imagine somebody else has taken them off his hands. I expect Col. Morgan in town on Saturday, who has some money of mine in his hands, and then I shall renew my application to the bootmaker.

" I wish you had thought of me a little before you went away, and at least endeavored to put matters in a train that I might not have to reexperience what has already past. The gentleman who conveys this to you, Mr. Burke, is an assistant judge of South Carolina, and one to whose friendship I am much indebted. He lodged some time in the house with me.

" I enclose you the paper of this morning, by which you will see that Gillam had not sailed (or at least I conclude so) on the 4th of July, as Major Jackson was deputy toast master, or Burgos-master, or something, at an entertainment on that day. As soon as I can learn anything concerning Gillam I will inform you of it.

" I am with every wish for your happiness and success, &c.

" Please to present my Compts. and best wishes to the General. I have wrote to the Marquis and put all my politics into his letter. A paper with Rivington's account of the action is enclosed in the Marquis' letter." [1]

It will be seen by the following letter to Franklin's nephew that Paine was now on good terms

---

[1] The original is in Mr. W. F. Havermeyer's collection.

with the Congressmen who had opposed him in the
Deane matter. The letter (in the Historical Society
of Pennsylvania) is addressed to " Mr. Jonathan
Williams, Merchant, Nantz," per " Brig Betsey."

" PHILADELPHIA, NOV. 26, 1781.—DEAR SIR,—Since my
arrival I have received a letter from you dated Passy May 18,
and directed to me at Brest. I intended writing to you by
Mr. Baseley who is consul at L'Orient but neglected it till it
was too late.—Mem : I desired Baseley to mention to you
that Mr. Butler of S: Carolina is surprised at Capt Rob——n's
drawing on him for money ; this Mr. Butler mentioned to me,
and as a friend I communicate it to you.—I sent you Col.
Laurens's draft on Madam Babut (I think that is her name)
at Nantz for 12 I.' d'ors for the expence of the Journey but
have never learned if you received it.

" Your former friend Silas Deane has run his last length.
In france he is reprobating America, and in America (by letters) he is reprobating france, and advising her to abandon
her alliance, relinquish her independence, and once more
become subject to Britain. A number of letters, signed Silas
Deane, have been published in the New York papers to this
effect : they are believed, by those who formerly were his
friends, to be genuine ; Mr. Robt. Morris assured me that he
had been totally deceived in Deane, but that he now looked
upon him to be a bad man, and his reputation totally ruined.
Gouverneur Morris hopped round upon one leg, swore they
had all been duped, himself among the rest, complimented
me on my quick sight,—and by Gods says he nothing carries
a man through the world like honesty :—and my old friend
Duer ' Sometimes a sloven and sometimes a Beau,' says,
Deane is a damned artful rascal. However Duer has fairly
cleared himself. He received a letter from him a considerable
time before the appearance of these in the New York papers
—which was so contrary to what he expected to receive, and
of such a traitorous cast, that he communicated it to Mr.
Luzerne the Minister.

" Lord Cornwallis with 7247 officers and men are nabbed
nicely in the Cheasepeake, which I presume you have heard

already, otherwise I should send you the particulars. I think the enemy can hardly hold out another campaign. General Greene has performed wonders to the southward, and our affairs in all quarters have a good appearance. The french Ministry have hit on the right scheme, that of bringing their force and ours to act in conjunction against the enemy.

" The Marquis de la fayette is on the point of setting out for france, but as I am now safely on this side the water again, I believe I shall postpone my second journey to france a little longer.—Lest Doctr. Franklin should not have heard of Deane I wish you would write to him, and if anything new transpires in the meantime and the Marquis do not set off too soon, I shall write by him.

" Remember me to Mr. & Mrs. Johnstone, Dr. Pierce, Mr. Watson & Ceasey and Mr. Wilt. Make my best wishes to Mrs. Williams, Mrs. Alexander, and all the good girls at St. Germain.

" I am your friend &c.

" THOMAS PAINE.

" P. S. Mind, I 'll write no more till I hear from you. The French fleet is sailed from the Cheasepeake, and the British fleet from New York—and since writing the above, a vessel is come up the Delaware, which informs that he was chased by two french frigates to the southward of Cheasepeake, which on their coming up acquainted him that the french fleet was a head in chase of a fleet which they supposed to be the British.

" N. B. The french fleet sailed the 4th of this month, and the british much about the same time—both to the southward."

CHAPTER XIII

THE MUZZLED OX TREADING OUT THE GRAIN.

WHILE Washington and Lafayette were in Virginia, preparing for their grapple with Cornwallis, Philadelphia was in apprehension of an attack by Sir Henry Clinton, for which it was not prepared. It appeared necessary to raise for defence a body of men, but the money was wanting. Paine (September 20th) proposed to Robert Morris the plan of "empowering the tenant to pay into the Treasury one quarter's rent, to be applied as above [*i. e.*, the safety of Philadelphia], and in case it should not be necessary to use the money when collected, the sums so paid to be considered a part of the customary taxes." This drastic measure would probably have been adopted had not the cloud cleared away. The winter was presently made glorious summer by the sun of Yorktown.

Washington was received with enthusiasm by Congress on November 28th. In the general feasting and joy Paine participated, but with an aching heart. He was an unrivalled literary lion ; he had to appear on festive occasions ; and he was without means. Having given his all,—copyrights, secretaryship, clerkship,—to secure the independence of a nation, he found himself in a state of dependence.   He fairly pointed the moral of Solomon's fable : By his wisdom he had saved the besieged land, yet none remembered that poor man, so far as his needs were concerned.   If in his confidential letter to Washington, given below, Paine seems egotistical, it should be borne in mind that his estimate of his services falls short of their appreciation by the national leaders.   It should not have been left to Paine to call attention to his sacrifices for his country's cause, and the want in which it had left him.   He knew also that plain speaking was necessary with Washington.

> "Second Street, opposite the Quaker Meeting-house, Nov. 30th, 1781.

"Sir,—As soon as I can suppose you to be a little at leisure from business and visits, I shall, with much pleasure, wait on you, to pay you my respects and congratulate you on the success you have most deservedly been blest with.

"I hope nothing in the perusal of this letter will add a care to the many that employ your mind ; but as there is a satisfaction in speaking where one can be conceived and understood, I divulge to you the secret of my own situation ; because I would wish to tell it to somebody, and as I do not want to make it public, I may not have a fairer opportunity.

"It is seven years, *this day*, since I arrived in America, and tho' I consider them as the most honorary time of my life, they have nevertheless been the most inconvenient and even distressing.   From an anxiety to support, as far as laid in my power, the reputation of the Cause of America, as well as the Cause itself, I declined the customary profits which authors are entitled to, and I have always continued to do so ; yet I never thought (if I thought at all on the matter,) but that as I dealt generously and honorably by America, she would deal the same by me.   But I have experienced the contrary—and it gives me much concern, not only on account of the inconvenience it has occasioned to me, but because it unpleasantly lessens my opinion of the character of a country which once appeared so fair, and it hurts my mind to see her so cold and inattentive to matters which affect her reputation.

" Almost every body knows, not only in this country but in Europe, that I have been of service to her, and as far as the interest of the heart could carry a man I have shared with her in the worst of her fortunes, yet so confined has been my private circumstances that for one summer I was obliged to hire myself as a common clerk to Owen Biddle of this city for my support : but this and many others of the like nature I have always endeavored to conceal, because to expose them would only serve to entail on her the reproach of being ungrateful, and might start an ill opinion of her honor and generosity in other countries, especially as there are pens enough abroad to spread and aggravate it.

" Unfortunately for me, I knew the situation of Silas Deane when no other person knew it, and with an honesty, for which I ought to have been thanked, endeavored to prevent his fraud taking place. He has himself proved my opinion right, and the warmest of his advocates now very candidly acknowledge their deception.

" While it was every body's fate to suffer I chearfully suffered with them, but tho' the object of the country is now nearly established and her circumstances rising into prosperity, I feel myself left in a very unpleasant situation. Yet I am totally at a loss what to attribute it to ; for wherever I go I find respect, and every body I meet treats me with friendship ; all join in censuring the neglect and throwing blame on each other, so that their civility disarms me as much as their conduct distresses me. But in this situation I cannot go on, and as I have no inclination to differ with the Country or to tell the story of her neglect, it is my design to get to Europe, either to France or Holland. I have literary fame, and I am sure I cannot experience worse fortune than I have here. Besides a person who understood the affairs of America, and was capable and disposed to do her a kindness, might render her considerable service in Europe, where her situation is but imperfectly understood and much misrepresented by the publications which have appeared on that side the water, and tho' she has not behaved to me with any proportionate return of friendship, my wish for her prosperity is no ways abated, and I shall be very happy to see her character as fair as her cause.

"Yet after all there is something peculiarly hard that the country which ought to have been to me a home has scarcely afforded me an asylum.

"In thus speaking to your Excellency, I know I disclose myself to one who can sympathize with me, for I have often cast a thought at your difficult situation to smooth over the unpleasantness of my own.

"I have began some remarks on the Abbe Raynal's 'History of the Revolution.' In several places he is mistaken, and in others injudicious and sometimes cynical. I believe I shall publish it in America, but my principal view is to republish it in Europe both in French and English.

"Please, Sir, to make my respectful compts. to your Lady, and accept to yourself the best wishes of,

"Your obedt. humble servant,

"THOMAS PAINE.[1]

"His Excellency General WASHINGTON."

Paine's determination to make no money by his early pamphlets arose partly from his religious and Quaker sentiments. He could not have entered into any war that did not appear to him sacred, and in such a cause his "testimony" could not be that of a "hireling." His "Common Sense," his first *Crisis*, were inspirations, and during all the time of danger his pen was consecrated to the cause. He had, however, strict and definite ideas of copyright, and was the first to call attention of the country to its necessity, and even to international justice in literary property. In the chaotic condition of such matters his own sacrifices for the national benefit had been to some extent defeated by the rapacity of his first publisher, Bell, who pocketed much of

[1] I am indebted to Mr. Simon Gratz of Philadelphia for a copy of this letter.

what Paine had intended for the nation. After he had left Bell for Bradford, the former not only published another edition of "Common Sense," but with "large additions," as if from Paine's pen. When the perils of the cause seemed past Paine still desired to continue his literary record clear of any possible charge of payment, but he believed that the country would appreciate this sensitiveness, and, while everybody was claiming something for services, would take care that he did not starve. In this he was mistaken. In that very winter, after he had ventured across the Atlantic and helped to obtain the six million livres, he suffered want. Washington appears to have been the first to consider his case. In the diary of Robert Morris, Superintendent of Finance, there is an entry of January 26, 1782, in which he mentions that Washington had twice expressed to him a desire that some provision should be made for Paine.[1] Morris sent for Paine and, in the course of a long conversation, expressed a wish that the author's pen should continue its services to the country ; adding that though he had no position to offer him something might turn up. In February Morris mentions further interviews with Paine, in which his assistant, Gouverneur Morris, united ; they expressed their high appreciation of his services to the country, and their desire to have the aid of his pen in promoting measures necessary to draw out the resources of the country for the completion of its purpose. They strongly disclaimed any private or partial ends, or a wish to bind his pen to any par-

---

[1] Sparks' "Diplomatic Correspondence," xii., p. 95.

ticular plans. They proposed that he should be paid eight hundred dollars per annum from some national fund. Paine having consented, Robert Morris wrote to Robert R. Livingston on the subject, and the result was a meeting of these two with Washington, at which the following was framed :

" PHILADELPHIA, Feb. 10, 1782.—The subscribers, taking into consideration the important situation of affairs at the present moment, and the propriety and even necessity of informing the people and rousing them into action ; considering also the abilities of Mr. Thomas Paine as a writer, and that he has been of considerable utility to the common cause by several of his publications : They are agreed that it will be much for the interest of the United States that Mr. Paine be engaged in their service for the purpose above mentioned. They are therefore agreed that Mr. Paine be offered a salary of $800 per annum, and that the same be paid him by the Secretary of Foreign Affairs. The salary to commence from this day, and to be paid by the Secretary of Foreign Affairs out of monies to be allowed by the Superintendent of Finance for secret services. The subscribers being of opinion that a salary publicly and avowedly given for the above purpose would injure the effect of Mr. Paine's publications, and subject him to injurious personal reflections.

" ROBT. MORRIS.
" ROBT. LIVINGSTON.
" GO. WASHINGTON."

Before this joint note was written, Paine's pen had been resumed. March 5th is the date of an extended pamphlet, that must long have been in hand. It is introduced by some comments on the King's speech, which concludes with a quotation of Smollett's fearful description of the massacres and rapine which followed the defeat of the Stuarts at Culloden in 1746. This, a memory from Paine's boyhood at Thetford, was an effective comment on the King's expression of his desire "to restore the public tranquillity," though poor George III., who was born in the same year as Paine, would hardly have countenanced such vengeance. He then deals —no doubt after consultation with Robert Morris, Superintendent of Finance—with the whole subject of finance and taxation, in the course of which he sounds a brave note for a more perfect union of the States, which must be the foundation-stone of their independence. As Paine was the first to raise the flag of republican independence he was the first to raise that of a Union which, above the States, should inherit the supremacy wrested from the Crown. These passages bear witness by their nicety to the writer's consciousness that he was touching a sensitive subject. The States were jealous of their "sovereignty," and he could only delicately intimate the necessity of surrendering it. But he manages to say that "each state (with a small *s*) is to the United States what each individual is to the state he lives in. And it is on this grand point, this movement upon one centre, that our existence as a nation, our happiness as a people, and our safety as individuals, depend." He also strikes the federal keynote by saying: "The United States will become heir to an extensive quantity of vacant land "—the doctrine of national inheritance which cost him dear.

Before the Declaration, Paine minted the phrases "Free and Independent States of America," and "The Glorious Union." In his second *Crisis*, dated January 13, 1777, he says to Lord Howe: " '*The*

United States *of* America ' will sound as pompously in the world or in history as 'the kingdom of Great Britain.'"

The friendliness of Robert Morris to the author is creditable to him. In the Deane controversy, Paine had censured him and other members of Congress for utilizing that agent of the United States to transact their commercial business in Europe. Morris frankly stated the facts, and, though his letter showed irritation, he realized that Paine was no respecter of persons where the American cause was concerned.[1] In 1782 the Revolution required nicest steering. With the port in sight, the people were prone to forget that it is on the coast that dangerous rocks are to be found. Since the surrender of Cornwallis they were over-confident, and therein likely to play into the hands of the enemy, which had lost confidence in its power to conquer the States by arms. England was now making efforts to detach America and France from each other by large inducements. In France Paine was shown by Franklin and Vergennes the overtures that had been made, and told the secret history of the offers of mediation from Russia and Austria. With these delicate matters he resolved to deal, but before using the documents in his possession consulted Washington and Morris. This, I suppose, was the matter alluded to in a note of March 17, 1782, to Washington, then in Philadelphia :

"You will do me a great deal of pleasure if you can make it convenient to yourself to spend a part of an evening at my apartments, and eat a few oysters or a crust of bread and

---

[1] Almon's *Remembrancer* 1778–9, p. 382.

cheese ; for besides the favour you will do me, I want much to consult with you on a matter of public business, tho' of a secret nature, which I have already mentioned to Mr. Morris, whom I likewise intend to ask, as soon as yourself shall please to mention the evening when."

A similar note was written to Robert Morris four days before. No doubt after due consultation the next *Crisis*, dated May 22, 1782, appeared. It dealt with the duties of the alliance :

" General Conway," he says, " who made the motion in the British parliament for discontinuing *offensive* war in America, is a gentleman of an amiable character. We have no personal quarrel with him. But he feels not as we feel ; he is not in our situation, and that alone without any other explanation is enough. The British parliament suppose they have many friends in America, and that, when all chance of conquest is over, they will be able to draw her from her alliance with France. Now if I have any conception of the human heart, they will fail in this more than in anything that they have yet tried. This part of the business is not a question of policy only, but of honor and honesty."

Paine's next production was a public letter to Sir Guy Carleton, commanding in New York, concerning a matter which gave Washington much anxiety. On April 12th Captain Huddy had been hanged by a band of " refugees," who had sallied from New York into New Jersey (April 12th). The crime was traced to one Captain Lippencott, and, after full consultation with his officers, Washington demanded the murderer. Satisfaction not being given, Washington and his generals determined on retaliation, and Colonel Hazen, who had prisoners under guard at Lancaster, was directed to have an officer of Captain Huddy's rank chosen by lot to suffer death. Hazen included the officers who had capitulated with Cornwallis, though they were expressly relieved from liability to reprisals (Article 14). The lot fell upon one of these, young Captain Asgill (May 27th). It sufficiently proves the formidable character of the excitement Huddy's death had caused in the army that Washington did not at once send Asgill back. The fact that he was one of the capitulation officers was not known outside the military circle. Of this circumstance Paine seems ignorant when he wrote his letter to Sir Guy Carleton, in which he expresses profound sympathy with Captain Huddy, and warns Carleton that by giving sanctuary to the murderer he becomes the real executioner of the innocent youth. Washington was resolved to hang this innocent man, and, distressing as the confession is, no general appears to have warned him of the wrong he was about to commit.[1] But Paine, with well-weighed

[1] Historians have evaded this ugly business. I am indebted to the family of General Lincoln, then Secretary of War, for the following letter addressed to him by Washington, June 5, 1782 : "Col. Hazen's sending me an officer under the capitulation of Yorktown for the purpose of retaliation has distressed me exceedingly. Be so good as to give me your opinion of the propriety of doing this upon Captain Asgill, if we should be driven to it for want of an unconditional prisoner. Presuming that this matter has been a subject of much conversation, pray with your own let me know the opinions of the most sensible of those with whom you have conversed. Congress by their resolve has unanimously approved of my determination to retaliate. The army have advised it, and the country look for it. But how far is it justifiable upon an officer under the faith of a capitulation, if none other can be had is the question ? Hazen's sending Captain Asgill on for this purpose makes the matter more distressing, as the whole business will have the appearance of a farce, if some person is not sacrificed to the mains of poor Huddy ; which will be the case if an unconditional prisoner cannot be found, and Asgill escapes. I write you in exceeding great haste ; but beg your sentiments may be transmitted as soon as possible (by express), as I may be forced to a decision in the course of a few days.—I am most sincerely and affectionately, D'r Sir, yr. obed't,

" G. WASHINGTON."

words, gently withstood the commander, prudently
ignoring the legal point, if aware of it.

"For my own part, I am fully persuaded that a suspension
of his fate, still holding it *in terrorem*, will operate on a greater
quantity of their passions and vices, and restrain them more,·
than his execution would do. However, the change of measures which seems now to be taking place, gives somewhat of a
new cast to former designs; and if the case, without the
execution, can be so managed as to answer all the purposes of
the last, it will look much better hereafter, when the sensa-
tions that now provoke, and the circumstances which would
justify his exit shall be forgotten."

This was written on September 7th, and on the
30th Washington, writing to a member of Congress, for the first time intimates a desire that
Asgill shall be released by that body.

In October came from Vergennes a letter, inspired by Marie Antoinette, to whom Lady Asgill
had appealed, in which he reminds Washington
that the Captain is a prisoner whom the King's
arms contributed to surrender into his hands.
That he had a right, therefore, to intercede for his
life. This letter (of July 29, 1782) was laid before
Congress, which at once set Asgill at liberty.
Washington was relieved, and wrote the Captain
a handsome congratulation.

Although Paine could never find the interval of
leisure necessary to write consecutively his "History of the Revolution," it is to a large extent
distributed through his writings. From these and
his letters a true history of that seven years can be
gathered, apart from the details of battles; and
even as regards these his contributions are of high

importance, notably as regards the retreat across
the Delaware, the affairs at Trenton and Princeton, and the skirmishes near Philadelphia following the British occupation of that city. The latter are vividly described in his letter to Franklin
(p. 104), and the former in his review of the Abbé
Raynal.

In his letter to Washington, of November 30,
1781, Paine mentioned that he had begun "some
remarks" on the Abbé's work "On the Revolution
of the English Colonies in North America." It
was published early in September, 1782. The
chief interest of the pamphlet, apart from the passages concerning the military events of 1776, lies
in its reflections of events in the nine months during which the paper lingered on his table. In
those months he wrote four numbers of the *Crisis*,
one of urgent importance on the financial situation.
The review of the Abbé's history was evidently
written at intervals. As a literary production it is
artistic. With the courtliness of one engaged in
"an affair of honor," he shakes the Abbé's hand,
sympathizes with his misfortune in having his
manuscript stolen, and thus denied opportunity to
revise the errors for which he must be called to
account. His main reason for challenging the
historian is an allegation that the Revolution originated in the question "whether the mother country
had, or had not, a right to lay, directly or indi-
rectly, a slight tax upon the colonies." The
quantity of the tax had nothing to do with it.
The tax on tea was a British experiment to test its
declaratory Act affirming the right of Parliament

"to bind America in all cases whatever," and that claim was resisted in the first stage of its execution. Secondly, the Abbé suffers for having described the affair at Trenton as accidental. Paine's answer is an admirable piece of history. Thirdly, the Abbé suggests that the Americans would probably have accommodated their differences with England when commissioners visited them in April, 1778, but for their alliance with France. Paine affirms that Congress had rejected the English proposals (afterwards brought by the commissioners) on April 22d, eleven days before news arrived of the French alliance.[1] The Abbé is metaphysically punished for assuming that a French monarchy in aiding defenders of liberty could have no such motive as "the happiness of mankind." Not having access to the archives of France, Paine was able to endow Vergennes with the enthusiasm of Lafayette, and to see in the alliance a new dawning era of international affection. All such alliances are republican. The Abbé is leniently dealt with for his clear plagiarisms from Paine, and then left for a lecture to England. That country is advised to form friendship with France and Spain ; to

[1] Here Paine is more acute than exact. On June 3, 1778, the English Commissioners sent Congress the resolutions for negotiation adopted by Parliament, February 17th. Congress answered that on April 22d it had published its sentiments on these acts. But these sentiments had admitted a willingness to negotiate if Great Britain should "as a preliminary thereto, either withdraw their fleets and armies, or else, in positive and express terms, acknowledge the independence of the said States." But in referring the commissioners (June 6th) to its manifesto of April 22d, the Congress essentially modified the conditions: it would treat only as an independent nation, and with "sacred regard" to its treaties. On June 17th Congress returned the English Commissioners their proposal (sent on the 9th) unconsidered, because of its insults to their ally.

expand its mind beyond its island, and improve its manners.   This is the refrain of a previous passage.

" If we take a review of what part Britain has acted we shall find everything which should make a nation blush.   The most vulgar abuse, accompanied by that species of haughtiness which distinguishes the hero of a mob from the character of a gentleman ; it was equally as much from her manners as her injustice that she lost the colonies.   By the latter she provoked their principle, by the former she wore out their temper ; and it ought to be held out as an example to the world, to show how necessary it is to conduct the business of government with civility."

The close of this essay, written with peace in the air, contains some friendly advice to England.   She is especially warned to abandon Canada, which, after loss of the thirteen colonies, will be a constant charge.   Canada can never be populous, and of all that is done for it " Britain will sustain the expense, and America reap the advantage."

In a letter dated " Bordentown, September 7, 1782," Paine says to Washington :

" I have the honour of presenting you with fifty copies of my Letter to the Abbé Raynal, for the use of the army, and to repeat to you my acknowledgments for your friendship.

" I fully believe we have seen our worst days over.   The spirit of the war, on the part of the enemy, is certainly on the decline full as much as we think.   I draw this opinion not only from the present promising appearance of things, and the difficulties we know the British Cabinet is in ; but I add to it the peculiar effect which certain periods of time have, more or less, on all men.   The British have accustomed themselves to think of *seven years* in a manner different to other portions of time.   They acquire this partly by habit, by reason, by religion, and by superstition.   They serve seven years' apprenticeship—they elect their parliament for seven years—they punish by seven years' transportation, or the duplicate or triplicate of that term—they let their leases in the same manner, and they read that Jacob served seven years for one wife, and after that seven years for another ; and the same term likewise extinguishes all obligations (in certain cases) of debt, or matrimony : and thus this particular period of time, by a variety of concurrences, has obtained an influence on their mind. They have now had seven years of war, and are no farther on the Continent than when they began. The superstitious and populous part will therefore conclude that *it is not to be*, and the rational part of them will think they have tried an unsuccessful and expensive experiment long enough, and that it is in vain to try it any longer, and by these two joining in the same eventual opinion the obstinate part among them will be beaten out, unless, consistent with their former sagacity, they get over the matter at once by passing a new declaratory Act *to bind Time in all cases whatsoever*, or declare him a rebel."

The rest of this letter is the cautious and respectful warning against the proposed execution of Captain Asgill, quoted elsewhere. Washington's answer is cheerful, and its complimentary close exceptionally cordial.

Head-Quarters, Verplank's Point, 18 September, 1782. —Sir,—I have the pleasure to acknowledge your favor, informing me of your proposal to present me with fifty copies of your last publication for the amusement of the army. For this intention you have my sincere thanks, not only on my own account, but for the pleasure, which I doubt not the gentlemen of the army will receive from the perusal of your pamphlets. Your observations on the *period of seven years*, as it applies itself to and affects British minds, are ingenious, and I wish it may not fail of its effects in the present instance. The measures and the policy of the enemy are at present in great perplexity and embarrassment—but I have my fears, whether their necessities (which are the only operating motives with them) are yet arrived to that point, which must drive them unavoidably into what they will esteem disagreeable and dishonorable terms of peace,—such, for instance, as an absolute, unequivocal admission of American Independence, upon the terms on which she can accept it. For this reason, added to the obstinacy of the King, and the probable consonant principles of some of the principal ministers, I have not so full a confidence in the success of the present negociation for peace as some gentlemen entertain. Should events prove my jealousies to be ill founded, I shall make myself happy under the mistake, consoling myself .with the idea of having erred on the safest side, and enjoying with as much satisfaction as any of my countrymen the pleasing issue of our severe contest.

" The case of Captain Asgill has indeed been spun out to a great length—but, with you, I hope that its termination will not be unfavourable to this country.

" I am, sir, with great esteem and regard,
" Your most obedient servant,
" G. WASHINGTON."

A copy of the answer to the Abbé Raynal was sent by Paine to Lord Shelburne, and with it in manuscript his newest *Crisis*, dated October 29, 1782. This was suggested by his lordship's speech of July 10th, in which he was reported to have said : " The independence of America would be the ruin of England." " Was America then," asks Paine, " the giant of empire, and England only her dwarf in waiting ? Is the case so strangely altered, that those who once thought we could not live without them are now brought to declare that they cannot exist without us ? "

Paine's prediction that it would be a seven years' war was nearly true. There was indeed a dismal eighth year, the army not being able to disband until the enemy had entirely left the country,—a year when peace seemed to " break out " like another war. The army, no longer uplifted by ardors of conflict with a foreign foe, became conscious of its hunger, its nakedness, and the prospect of returning in rags to pauperized homes. They saw all the civil officers of the country paid, while those who had defended them were unpaid ; and the only explanations that could be offered—the inability of Congress, and incoherence of the States—formed a new peril. The only hope of meeting an emergency fast becoming acute, was the unanimous adoption by the States of the proposal of Congress for a five-per-cent. duty on imported articles, the money to be applied to the payment of interest on loans to be made in Holland. Several of the States had been dilatory in their consent, but Rhode Island absolutely refused, and Paine undertook to reason with that State. In the *Providence Gazette*, December 21st, appeared the following note, dated "Philadelphia, November 27, 1782 " :

" Sir,—Inclosed I send you a Philadelphia paper of this day's date, and desire you to insert the piece signed 'A Friend to Rhode Island and the Union.' I am concerned that Rhode Island should make it necessary to address a piece to her, on a subject which the rest of the States are agreed in. —Yours &c. Thomas Paine."

The insertion of Paine's letter led to a fierce controversy, the immediate subject of which is hardly of sufficient importance to detain us long.[1]

[1] It may be traced through the *Providence Gazette* of December 21, 28 (1782), January 4, 11, 18, 25, February 1 (1783) ; also in the *Newport Mercury*. Paine writes under the signature of " A Friend to Rhode Island and the Union." I am indebted to Professor Jamieson of Brown University for assistance in this investigation.

Yet this controversy, which presently carried Paine to Providence, where he wrote and published six letters, raised into general discussion the essential principles of Union. Rhode Island's jealousy of its " sovereignty "—in the inverse ratio of its size,—made it the last to enter a Union which gave it equal legislative power with the greatest States; it need not be wondered then that at this earlier period, when sovereignty and self-interest combined, our pioneer of nationality had to undergo some martyrdom. " What," he asked, " would the sovereignity of any individual state be, if left to itself to contend with a foreign power? It is on our united sovereignty that our greatness and safety, and the security of our foreign commerce, rest. This united sovereignty then must be something more than a name, and requires to be as completely organized for the line it is to act in as that of any individual state, and, if anything, more so, because more depends on it." He received abuse, and such ridicule as this (February 1st) :

"In the Name of Common Sense, Amen, I, Thomas Paine, having according to appointment, proceeded with all convenient speed to answer the objections to the five per cent, by endeavouring to cover the design and blind the subject, before I left Philadelphia, and having proceeded to a *convenient* place of action in the State of Rhode Island, and there republished my first letter," etc.

In the same paper with this appeared a letter of self-defence from Paine, who speaks of the personal civility extended to him in Rhode Island, but of proposals to stop his publications. He quotes a letter of friendship from Colonel Laurens, who gave

him his war-horse, and an equally cordial one from
General Nathaniel Greene, Rhode Island's darling
hero, declaring that he should be rewarded for his
public services.

This visit to Rhode Island was the last work
which Paine did in pursuance of his engagement,
which ended with the resignation of Morris in
January. Probably Paine received under it one
year's salary, $800—certainly no more. I think
that during the time he kept his usual signature,
"Common Sense," sacred to his individual "testimonies."

On his return to Philadelphia Paine wrote a
memorial to Chancellor Livingston, Secretary for
Foreign Affairs, Robert Morris, Minister of Finance,
and his assistant Gouverneur Morris, urging the
necessity of adding "a Continental Legislature to
Congress, to be elected by the several States." Robert Morris invited the Chancellor and a number of
eminent men to meet Paine at dinner, where his
plea for a stronger union was discussed and approved. This was probably the earliest of a series
of consultations preliminary to the constitutional
Convention.

The newspaper combat in Rhode Island, which
excited general attention, and the continued postponement of all prospect of paying the soldiers, had
a formidable effect on the army. The anti-republican elements of the country, after efforts to seduce
Washington, attempted to act without him. In
confronting the incendiary efforts of certain officers
at Newburg to turn the army of liberty into muti-
neers against it, Washington is seen winning his

noblest victory after the revolution had ended. He not only subdued the reactionary intrigues, but the supineness of the country, which had left its soldiers in a condition that played into the intriguers' hands.

On April 18th Washington formally announced the cessation of hostilities. On April 19th—eighth anniversary of the collision at Lexington—Paine printed the little pamphlet entitled "Thoughts on Peace and the Probable Advantages Thereof," included in his works as the last *Crisis*. It opens with the words : " The times that tried men's souls are over—and the greatest and completest revolution the world ever knew, gloriously and happily accomplished." He again, as in his first pamphlet, pleads for a supreme nationality, absorbing all cherished sovereignties. This is Paine's " farewell address."

" It was the cause of America that made me an author. The force with which it struck my mind, and the dangerous condition in which the country was in, by courting an impossible and an unnatural reconciliation with those who were determined to reduce her, instead of striking out into the only line that could save her, a Declaration of Independence, made it impossible for me, feeling as I did, to be silent ; and if, in the course of more than seven years, I have rendered her any service, I have likewise added something to the reputation of literature, by freely and disinterestedly employing it in the great cause of mankind. . . . But as the scenes of war are closed, and every man preparing for home and happier times, I therefore take leave of the subject. I have most sincerely followed it from beginning to end, and through all its turns and windings ; and whatever country I may hereafter be in, I shall always feel an honest pride at the part I have taken and acted, and a gratitude to nature and providence for putting it in my power to be of some use to mankind."

CHAPTER XIV.

GREAT WASHINGTON AND POOR PAINE.

THE world held no other man so great and so happy as Washington, in September, 1783,—the month of final peace. Congress, then sitting at Princeton, had invited him to consult with them on the arrangements necessary for a time of peace, and prepared a mansion for him at Rocky Hill. For a time the General gave himself up to hilarity, as ambassadors of congratulation gathered from every part of the world. A glimpse of the festivities is given by David Howell of Rhode Island in a letter to Governor Greene.

"The President, with all the present members, chaplains, and great officers of Congress, had the honor of dining at the General's table last Friday. The tables were spread under a marquise or tent taken from the British. The repast was elegant, but the General's company crowned the whole. As I had the good fortune to be seated facing the General, I had the pleasure of hearing all his conversation. The President of Congress was seated on his right, and the Minister of France on his left. I observed with much pleasure that the General's front was uncommonly open and pleasant; the contracted, pensive phiz betokening deep thought and much care, which I noticed at Prospect Hill in 1775, is done away, and a pleasant smile and sparkling vivacity of wit and humor succeeds. On the President observing that in the present situation of our affairs he believed that Mr. [Robert] Morris had his hands full, the General replied at the same instant, 'he wished he had his pockets full too.' On Mr. Peters observing that the man who made these cups (for we drank wine out of silver cups) was turned a Quaker preacher, the General replied that 'he wished he had turned a Quaker preacher before he made the cups.' You must also hear the French Minister's remark on the General's humor—'You tink de penitence wou'd have been good for de cups.' Congress has ordered an Egyptian statue of General Washington, to be erected at the place where they may establish their permanent residence. No honors short of those which the Deity vindicates to himself can be too great for Gen. Washington."

At this time Paine sat in his little home in Bordentown, living on his crust. He had put most of his savings in this house (on two tenths of an acre) so as to be near his friend Col. Joseph Kirkbride. The Colonel was also of Quaker origin, and a hearty sympathizer with Paine's principles. They had together helped to frame the democratic constitution of Pennsylvania (1776), had fought side by side, and both had scientific tastes. Since the burning of his house, Bellevue (Bucks), Colonel Kirkbride had moved to Bordentown, N. J., and lived at Hill Top, now part of a female college. A part of Paine's house also stands. At Bordentown also resided Mr. Hall, who had much mechanical skill, and whom he had found eager to help him in constructing models of his inventions. To such things he now meant to devote himself, but before settling down permanently he longed to see his aged parents and revisit his English friends. For this, however, he had not means. Robert Morris advised Paine to call the attention of Congress to various unremunerated services. His secretaryship of the Foreign Affairs Committee, terminated by an admitted injustice to him, had been burdensome and virtually unpaid; its nominal $70 per month was really about $15. His perilous journey to France, with young Laurens, after the millions that wrought wonders, had not brought him even a paper dollar. Paine, therefore, on June 7th, wrote to Elias Boudinot, President of Congress, stating that though for his services he had "neither sought, received, nor stipulated any honors, advantages, or emoluments," he thought Congress should inquire into them. The letter had some effect, but meanwhile Paine passed three months of poverty and gloom, and had no part in the festivities at Princeton.

One day a ray from that festive splendor shone in his humble abode. The great Commander had not forgotten his unwearied fellow-soldier, and wrote him a letter worthy to be engraved on the tombs of both.

"ROCKY HILL, Sept. 10, 1783.

" DEAR SIR,

" I have learned since I have been at this place, that you are at Bordentown. Whether for the sake of retirement or economy, I know not. Be it for either, for both, or whatever it may, if you will come to this place, and partake with me, I shall be exceedingly happy to see you.

" Your presence may remind Congress of your past services to this country; and if it is in my power to impress them, command my best services with freedom, as they will be rendered cheerfully by one who entertains a lively sense of the importance of your works, and who, with much pleasure, subscribes himself,

" Your sincere friend,

"G. WASHINGTON."

The following was Paine's reply :

"BORDEN TOWN, Sept. 21.—SIR,—I am made exceedingly happy by the receipt of your friendly letter of the 10th. instant, which is this moment come to hand ; and the young gentleman that brought it, a son of Col. Geo. Morgan, waits while I write this. It had been sent to Philadelphia, and on my not being there, was returned, agreeable to directions on the outside, to Col. Morgan at Princetown, who forwarded it to this place.

"I most sincerely thank you for your good wishes and friendship to me, and the kind invitation you have honored me with, which I shall with much pleasure accept.

"On the resignation of Mr. Livingston in the winter and likewise of Mr. R. Morris, at [the same] time it was judged proper to discontinue the matter which took place when you were in Philadelphia.[1] It was at the same time a pleasure to me to find both these gentlemen (to whom I was before that time but little known) so warmly disposed to assist in rendering my situation permanent, and Mr. Livingston's letter to me, in answer to one of mine to him, which I enclose, will serve to show that his friendship to me is in concurrence with yours.

"By the advice of Mr. Morris I presented a letter to Congress expressing a request that they would be pleased to direct me to lay before them an account of what my services, such as they were, and situation, had been during the course of the war. This letter was referred to a committee, and their report is now before Congress, and contains, as I am informed, a recommendation that I be appointed historiographer to the continent.[2] I have desired some members that the further consideration of it be postponed, until I can state to the committee some matters which I wish them to be acquainted with, both with regard to myself and the appointment. And as it was my intention, so I am now encouraged by your friendship to take your confidential advice upon it before I present it. For though I never was at a loss in writing on public matters, I feel exceedingly so in what respects myself.

---

[1] See page 182.
[2] This had been Washington's suggestion.

"I am hurt by the neglect of the collective ostensible body of America, in a way which it is probable they do not perceive my feelings. It has an effect in putting either my reputation or their generosity at stake; for it cannot fail of suggesting that either I (notwithstanding the appearance of service) have been undeserving their regard or that they are remiss towards me. Their silence is to me something like condemnation, and their neglect must be justified by my loss of reputation, or my reputation supported at their injury; either of which is alike painful to me. But as I have ever been dumb on everything which might touch national honor so I mean ever to continue so.

"Wishing you, Sir, the happy enjoyment of peace and every public and private felicity I remain &c.

"THOMAS PAINE.

"Col. Kirkbride at whose house I am, desires me to present you his respectful compliments."

Paine had a happy visit at Washington's headquarters, where he met old revolutionary comrades, among them Humphreys, Lincoln, and Cobb. He saw Washington set the river on fire on Guy Fawkes Day with a roll of cartridge-paper. When American art is more mature we may have a picture of war making way for science, illustrated by the night-scene of Washington and Paine on a scow, using their cartridge-paper to fire the gas released from the river-bed by soldiers with poles![1]

There was a small party in Congress which looked with sullen jealousy on Washington's friendliness with Paine. The States, since the conclusion of the war, were already withdrawing into their several shells of "sovereignty," while

---

[1] See Paine's essay on "The Cause of the Yellow Fever." These experiments on the river at Rocky Hill were followed by others in Philadelphia, with Rittenhouse.

Paine was arguing with everybody that there could be no sovereignty but that of the United States,—and even that was merely the supremacy of Law. The arguments in favor of the tax imposed by Congress, which he had used in Rhode Island, were repeated in his last *Crisis* (April 19th), and it must have been under Washington's roof at Rocky Hill that he wrote his letter "To the People of America" (dated December 9th), in which a high national doctrine was advocated. This was elicited by Lord Sheffield's pamphlet, "Observations on the Commerce of the United States," which had been followed by a prohibition of commerce with the West Indies in American bottoms. Lord Sheffield had said : "It will be a long time before the American States can be brought to act as a nation ; neither are they to be feared by us as such." Paine calls the attention of Rhode Island to this, and says : "America is now sovereign and independent, and ought to conduct her affairs in a regular style of character." She has a perfect right of commercial retaliation.

"But it is only by acting in union that the usurpations of foreign nations on the freedom of trade can be counteracted, and security extended to the commerce of America. And when we view a flag, which to the eye is beautiful, and to contemplate its rise and origin inspires a sensation of sublime delight, our national honor must unite with our interest to prevent injury to the one or insult to the other."

Noble as these sentiments now appear, they then excited alarm in certain Congressmen, and it required all Washington's influence to secure any favorable action in Paine's case. In 1784, however, New York presented Paine with "two hundred and seventy-seven acres, more or less, which became forfeited to and vested in the People of this State by the conviction of Frederick Devoe." [1]

With such cheerful prospects, national and personal, Paine rose into song, as appears by the following letter ("New York, April 28th") to Washington :

"DEAR SIR,—As I hope to have in a few days the honor and happiness of seeing you well at Philadelphia, I shall not trouble you with a long letter.

"It was my intention to have followed you on to Philadelphia, but when I recollected the friendship you had shewn to me, and the pains you had taken to promote my interests, and knew likewise the untoward disposition of two or three Members of Congress, I felt an exceeding unwillingness that your friendship to me should be put to further tryals, or that you should experience the mortification of having your wishes disappointed, especially by one to whom delegation is his daily bread.

"While I was pondering on these matters, Mr. Duane and some other friends of yours and mine, who were persuaded that nothing would take place in Congress (as a single man when only nine states were present could stop the whole), proposed a new line which is to leave it to the States individually ; and a unanimous resolution has passed the senate of this State, which is generally expressive of their opinion and friendship. What they have proposed is worth at least a thousand guineas, and other States will act as they see proper. If I do but get enough to carry me decently thro' the world and independently thro' the History of the Revolution, I neither wish nor care for more ; and that the States may very easily do if they are

[1] The indenture, made June 16, 1784, is in the Register's Office of Westchester County, Vol. T. of Grantees, p. 163. The confiscated estate of the loyalist Devoe is the well-known one at New Rochelle on which Paine's monument stands. I am indebted for investigations at White Plains, and documents relating to the estate, to my friend George Hoadly, and Mr. B. Davis Washburn.

disposed to it. The State of Pennsylvania might have done it alone.

"I present you with a new song for the Cincinnati ; and beg to offer you a remark on that subject.[1] The intention of the name appears to me either to be lost or not understood. For it is material to the future freedom of the country that the example of the late army retiring to private life, on the principles of Cincinnatus, should be commemorated, that in future ages it may be imitated. Whether every part of the institution is perfectly consistent with a republic is another question, but the precedent ought not to be lost.

"I have not yet heard of any objection in the Assembly of this State, to the resolution of the Senate, and I am in hopes there will be none made. Should the method succeed, I shall stand perfectly clear of Congress, which will be an agreeable circumstance to me ; because whatever I may then say on the necessity of strengthening the union, and enlarging its powers, will come from me with a much better grace than if Congress had made the acknowledgment themselves.

"If you have a convenient opportunity I should be much obliged to you to mention this subject to Mr. President Dickinson. I have two reasons for it, the one is my own interest and circumstances, the other is on account of the State, for what with their parties and contentions, they have acted to me with a churlish selfishness, which I wish to conceal unless they force it from me.

"As I see by the papers you are settling a tract of land, I enclose you a letter I received from England on the subject of settlements. I think lands might be disposed of in that country to advantage. I am, dear Sir, &c."

The estate at New Rochelle had a handsome house on it (once a patrimonial mansion of the

---

[1] Paine wrote four patriotic American songs : " Hail, Great Republic of the World" (tune " Rule Britannia ") ; " To Columbia, who Gladly Reclined at her Ease"; "Ye Sons of Columbia, who Bravely have Fought,"—both of the latter being for the tune of " Anacreon in Heaven " ; and " Liberty Tree" (tune " Gods of the Greeks"), beginning, " In a chariot of light, from the regions of Day," etc.

Jays), and Paine received distinguished welcome when he went to take possession. This he reciprocated, but he did not remain long at New Rochelle.[1] Bordentown had become his home; he had found there a congenial circle of friends,— proved such during his poverty. He was not, indeed, entirely relieved of poverty by the New York *honorarium*, but he had expectation that the other States would follow the example. In a letter to Jefferson also Paine explained his reason for desiring that the States, rather than Congress, should remunerate him. That Washington appreciated this motive appears by letters to Richard Henry Lee and James Madison.

"Mount Vernon, 12 June.—Unsollicited by, and unknown to Mr. Paine, I take the liberty of hinting the services and the distressed (for so I think it may be called) situation of that Gentleman.

"That his Common Sense, and many of his Crisis, were well timed and had a happy effect upon the public mind, none, I believe, who will recur to the epocha's at which they were published will deny.—That his services hitherto have passed of [f] unnoticed is obvious to all;—and that he is chagreened and necessitous I will undertake to aver.—Does not common justice then point to some compensation?

"He is not in circumstances to refuse the bounty of the

1 " An old lady, now a boarding-house keeper in Cedar Street, remembers when a girl visiting Mr. Paine when he took possession of his house and farm at New Rochelle, and gave a village fête on the occasion ; she then only knew him as ' Common Sense,' and supposed that was his name. On that day he had something to say to everybody, and young as she was she received a portion of his attention ; while he sat in the shade, and assisted in the labor of the feast, by cutting or breaking sugar to be used in some agreeable liquids by his guests. Mr. Paine was then, if not handsome, a fine agreeable looking man."—*Vale, 1841.* The original house was accidentally destroyed by fire, while Paine was in the French Convention. The present house was, however, occupied by him after his return to America.

public. New York, not the least distressed nor most able State in the Union, has set the example. He prefers the benevolence of the States individually to an allowance from Congress, for reasons which are conclusive in his own mind, and such as I think may be approved by others. His views are moderate, a decent independency is, I believe, the height of his ambition, and if you view his services in the American cause in the same important light that I do, I am sure you will have pleasure in obtaining it for him.—I am with esteem and regard, Dr. sir, yr. most obdt. servt.,

" GEORGE WASHINGTON." [1]

" MOUNT VERNON, June 12.—DEAR SIR,—Can nothing be done in our Assembly for poor Paine? Must the merits and services of *Common Sense* continue to glide down the stream of time, unrewarded by this country?

" His writings certainly have had a powerful effect on the public mind,—ought they not then to meet an adequate return? He is poor! he is chagreened! and almost if not altogether in despair of relief.

" New York, it is true, not the least distressed nor best able State in the Union, has done something for him. This kind of provision he prefers to an allowance from Congress, he has reasons for it, which to him are conclusive, and such, I think, as would have weight with others. His views are moderate—a decent independency is, I believe, all he aims at. Should he not obtain this? If you think so I am sure you will not only move the matter but give it your support. For me it only remains to feel for his situation and to assure you of the sincere esteem and regard with which I have the honor to be, D Sir,

" Yr. Most Obedt. Humble Servt.,

" G. WASHINGTON. [2]

" JAMES MADISON, Esq."

A similar letter was written to Patrick Henry and perhaps to others. A bill introduced into the

---

[1] I found this letter (to Lee) among the Franklin MSS. in the Philosophical Society, Philadelphia.

[2] I am indebted for this letter to Mr. Frederick McGuire, of Washington.

Virginia Legislature (June 28th) to give Paine a tract of land, being lost on the third reading, Madison (June 30th) offered a "bill for selling the public land in the county of Northampton, called the Secretary's land, and applying part of the money arising therefrom to the purchase of a tract to be vested in Thomas Payne and his heirs." The result is described by Madison (July 2d) to Washington :

"The easy reception it found, induced the friends of the measure to add the other moiety to the proposition, which would have raised the market value of the donation to about four thousand pounds, or upwards, though it would not probably have commanded a rent of more than one hundred pounds per annum. In this form the bill passed through two readings. The third reading proved that the tide had suddenly changed, for the bill was thrown out by a large majority. An attempt was next made to sell the land in question, and apply two thousand pounds of the money to the purchase of a farm for Mr. Paine. This was lost by a single voice. Whether a greater disposition to reward patriotic and distinguished exertions of genius will be found on any succeeding occasion, is not for me to predetermine. Should it finally appear that the merits of the man, whose writings have so much contributed to enforce and foster the spirit of independence in the people of America, are unable to inspire them with a just beneficence, the world, it is to be feared, will give us as little credit for our policy as for gratitude in this particular."

R. H. Lee—unfortunately not present, because of illness—writes Washington (July 22d) :

"I have been told that it miscarried from its being observed that he had shown enmity to this State by having written a pamphlet injurious to our claim of Western Territory. It has ever appeared to me that this pamphlet was the consequence of Mr. Paine's being himself imposed upon, and that it was rather the fault of the place than the man."[1]

So the news came that Virginia had snubbed Paine, at the moment of voting a statue to Washington. But his powerful friend did not relax his efforts, and he consulted honest John Dickinson, President of Pennsylvania. Under date of November 27th, the following was written by Paine to General Irwin, Vice-President of Pennsylvania:

"The President has made me acquainted with a Conversation which General Washington had with him at their last interview respecting myself, and he is desirous that I should communicate to you his wishes, which are, that as he stands engaged on the General's request to recommend to the Assembly, so far as lies in his power, their taking into consideration the part I have acted during the war, that you would join your assistance with him in the measure.—Having thus, Sir, opened the matter to you in general terms, I will take an opportunity at some time convenient to yourself to state it to you more fully, as there are many parts in it that are not publicly known. —I shall have the pleasure of seeing you at the President's to-day to dine and in the mean time I am etc."

On December 6th the Council sent this message to the General Assembly of Pennsylvania:

"GENTLEMEN : The President having reported in Council a conversation between General Washington and himself respecting Mr. Thomas Paine, we have thereby been induced to take the services and situation of that gentleman at this time into our particular consideration.

[1] "Arthur Lee was most responsible for the failure of the measure, for he was active in cultivating a prejudice against Paine. This was somewhat ungracious, as Paine had befriended Lee in his controversy with Deane."— Ford's "Writings of Washington," x., p. 395. Had there been any belief at this time that Paine had been paid for writing the pamphlet objected to, "Public Good," it would no doubt have been mentioned.

" Arriving in America just before the war broke out, he commenced his residence here, and became a citizen of this Commonwealth by taking the oath of allegiance at a very early period. So important were his services during the late contest, that those persons whose own merits in the course of it have been the most distinguished concur with a highly honorable unanimity in entertaining sentiments of esteem for him, and interesting themselves in his deserts. It is unnecessary for us to enlarge on this subject. If the General Assembly shall be pleased to appoint a Committee, they will receive information that we doubt not will in every respect prove satisfactory.

" We confide that you will, then, feel the attention of Pennsylvania is drawn towards Mr. Paine by motives equally grateful to the human heart, and reputable to the Republic ; and that you will join with us in the opinion that a suitable acknowledgment of his eminent services, and a proper provision for the continuance of them in an independent manner, should be made on the part of this State."

Pennsylvania promptly voted to Paine £500,— a snug little fortune in those days.

Paine thus had a happy New Year. Only two States had acted, but they had made him independent. Meanwhile Congress also was willing to remunerate him, but he had put difficulties in the way. He desired, as we have seen, to be independent of that body, and wished it only to pay its debts to him ; but one of these—his underpaid secretaryship—would involve overhauling the Paine-Deane case again. Perhaps that was what Paine desired ; had the matter been passed on again the implied censures of Paine on the journal of Congress would have been reversed. When therefore a gratuity was spoken of Paine interfered, and wrote to Congress, now sitting in New

York, asking leave to submit his accounts. This letter was referred to a committee (Gerry, Pettit, King).

"Mr. Gerry,' says Paine, came to me and said that the Committee had consulted on the subject, and they intended to bring in a handsome report, but that they thought it best not to take any notice of your letter, or make any reference to Deane's affair, or your salary. They will indemnify you without it. The case is, there are some motions on the journals of Congress for censuring you, with respect to Deane's affair, which cannot now be recalled, because they have been printed. Therefore [we] will bring in a report that will supersede them without mentioning the purport of your letter."

On the committee's report Congress resolved (August 26th) :

" That the early, unsolicited, and continued labors of Mr. Thomas Paine, in explaining and enforcing the principles of the late revolution by ingenious and timely publications upon the nature of liberty, and civil government, have been well received by the citizens of these States, and merit the approbation of Congress ; and that in consideration of these services, and the benefits produced thereby, Mr. Paine is entitled to a liberal gratification from the United States."

This of course was not what Paine wished, and he again (September 27th) urged settlement of his accounts. But, on October 3d, Congress ordered the Treasurer to pay Paine $3,000, " for the considerations mentioned in the resolution of the 26th of August last." " It was," Paine maintained to the last, " an indemnity to me for some injustice done me, for Congress had acted dishonorably by me." The Committee had proposed $6,000, but the author's enemies had managed to reduce it. The sum paid was too small to cover Paine's journey to France with Laurens, which was never repaid.

The services of Thomas Paine to the American cause cannot, at this distance of time, be estimated by any records of them, nor by his printed works. They are best measured in the value set on them by the great leaders most cognizant of them,—by Washington, Franklin, Jefferson, Adams, Madison, Robert Morris, Chancellor Livingston, R. H. Lee, Colonel Laurens, General Greene, Dickinson. Had there been anything dishonorable or mercenary in Paine's career, these are the men who would have known it; but their letters are searched in vain for even the faintest hint of anything disparaging to his patriotic self-devotion during those eight weary years. Their letters, however, already quoted in these pages, and others omitted, show plainly that they believed that all the States owed Paine large "returns (as Madison wrote to Washington) of gratitude for voluntary services," and that these services were not merely literary. Such was the verdict of the men most competent to pass judgment on the author, the soldier, the secretary. It can never be reversed.

To the radical of to-day, however, Paine will seem to have fared pretty well for a free lance; and he could now beat all his lances into bridge iron, without sparing any for the wolf that had haunted his door.

CHAPTER XV.

PONTIFICAL AND POLITICAL INVENTIONS.

PAINE was the literary lion in New York—where Congress sat in 1785—and was especially intimate with the Nicholsons, whose house was the social *salon* of leading republicans.[1] One may easily read between the lines of the following note to Franklin that the writer is having "a good time" in New York, where it was written September 23d :

"MY DEAR SIR,—It gives me exceeding great pleasure to have the opportunity of congratulating you on your return home, and to a land of Peace ; and to express to you my heartfelt wishes that the remainder of your days may be to you a time of happy ease and rest. Should Fate prolong my life to the extent of yours, it would give me the greatest felicity to have the evening scene some resemblance of what you now enjoy.

"In making you this address I have an additional pleasure in reflecting, that, so far as I have hitherto gone, I am not conscious of any circumstance in my conduct that should give

---

[1] "Commodore Nicholson was an active republican politician in the city of New York, and his house was a headquarters for the men of his way of thinking. The young ladies' letters are full of allusions to the New York society of that day, and to calls from Aaron Burr, the Livingstons, the Clintons, and many others. . . . An other man still more famous in some respects was a frequent visitor at their house. It is now almost forgotten that Thomas Paine, down to the time of his departure for Europe in 1787, was a fashionable member of society, admired and courted as the greatest literary genius of his day. . . . Here is a little autograph, found among the papers of Mrs. Gallatin [*née* Nicholson] ; its address is to : ' Miss Hannah N., at the Lord knows where.—You Mistress Hannah if you don't come home, I 'll come and fetch you. T. PAINE.' "—Adams' "Life of Gallatin."

you one repentant thought for being my patron and introducer
to America.

"It would give me great pleasure to make a journey to
Philadelphia on purpose to see you, but an interesting affair I
have with Congress makes my absence at this time improper.

"If you have time to let me know how your health is,
I shall be much obliged to you.

"I am, dear Sir, with the sincerest affection and respect,

"Your obedient, humble servant,

"Thomas Paine.

"The Hon'ble Benjamin Franklin, Esquire.

"My address is Messrs. Lawrence and Morris, Merchants."

To this came the following reply, dated Philadelphia, September 24th:

"Dear Sir,—I have just received your friendly congratulations on my return to America, for which, as well as your kind
wishes for my welfare, I beg you to accept my most thankful
acknowledgments. Ben is also very sensible of your polite-
ness, and desires his respects may be presented.

"I was sorry on my arrival to find you had left this city.
Your present arduous undertaking, I easily conceive, demands
retirement, and tho' we shall reap the fruits of it, I cannot help
regretting the want of your abilities here where in the present
moment they might, I think, be successfully employed. Parties still run very high—Common Sense would unite them. It
is to be hoped therefore it has not abandoned us forever."[1]

[1] The remainder of the letter (MS. Philosoph. Soc., Philadelphia) seems
to be in the writing of William Temple Franklin, to whom probably Paine
had enclosed a note: "Mr. Williams whom you inquire after accompanied
us to America, and is now here. We left Mrs. Wms. and her sisters well at
St. Ger's, but they proposed shortly returning to England to live with their
uncle, Mr. J. Alexander, who has entirely settled his affairs with Mr. Walpole and the Bank. Mr. Wm. Alex'r I suppose you know is in Virginia
fulfilling his tobacco contract with the Farmer Gen'l. The Marquis la
Fayette we saw a few days before we left Passy—he was well and on the
point of setting off on an excursion into Germany, and a visit to the Emperor
K. of Prussia.—I purpose shortly being at New York, where I will with
pleasure give you any further information you may wish, and shall be very
happy to cultivate the acquaintance and friendship of Mr. Paine, for whose
character I have a sincere regard and of whose services I, as an American,
have a grateful sense"

The "arduous undertaking" to which Franklin refers was of course the iron bridge. But it will be seen by our next letter that Paine had another invention to lay before Franklin, to whom he hastened after receiving his $3,000 from Congress :

"Dec. 31, 1785.—DEAR SIR,—I send you the Candles I have been making ;—In a little time afer they are lighted the smoke and flame separate, the one issuing from one end of the Candle, and the other from the other end. I supposed this to be because a quantity of air enters into the Candle between the Tallow and the flame, and in its passage downwards takes the smoke with it ; for if you allow a quantity of air up the Candle, the current will be changed, and the smoke reascends, and in passing this the flame makes a small flash and a little noise.

"But to express the Idea I mean, of the smoke descending more clearly it is this,—that the air enters the Candle in the very place where the melted tallow is getting into the state of flame, and takes it down before the change is completed—for there appears to me to be two kinds of smoke, humid matter which never can be flame, and enflameable matter which would be flame if some accident did not prevent the change being completed—and this I suppose to be the case with the descending smoke of the Candle.

"As you can compare the Candle with the Lamp, you will have an opportunity of ascertaining the cause—why it will do in the one and not in the other. When the edge of the enflamed part of the wick is close with the edge of the Tin of the Lamp no counter current of air can enter—but as this contact does not take place in the Candle a counter current enters and prevents the effect [?] in the candles which illuminates the Lamp. For the passing of the air thro' the Lamp does not, I imagine, burn the smoke, but burns up all the oil into flame, or by its rapidity prevents any part of the oil flying off in the state of half-flame which is smoke.

"I do not, my Dear Sir, offer these reasons to you but to myself, for I have often observed that by lending words for my thoughts I understand my thoughts the better. Thoughts are a kind of mental smoke, which require words to illuminate them.

"I am affectionately your Obt. & Hble. servant,

"THOMAS PAINE.

"I hope to be well enough tomorrow to wait on you."

Paine had now to lay aside his iron arch and bridge a financial flood. A party had arisen in Philadelphia, determined to destroy the "Bank of North America." Paine had confidence in this bank, and no one knew its history better, for it had grown out of the subscription he headed (May, 1780) with $500 for the relief of Washington's suffering army. It had been incorporated by Congress, and ultimately by Pennsylvania, April 1, 1782. Investments and deposits by and in the Bank had become very large, and to repeal its charter was to violate a contract. The attack was in the interest of paper money, of which there was a large issue. The repeal had to be submitted to popular suffrage, and even Cheetham admits that Paine's pamphlet "probably averted the act of despotism." The pamphlet was entitled, "Dissertations on Government, the Affairs of the Bank, and Paper Money" (54 pages 8vo). It was written and printed, Paine says in his preface (dated February 18, 1786), "during the short recess of the Assembly." This was between December 22d and February 26th.

The first fourteen pages of the work are devoted to a consideration of general principles. Englishmen who receive their constitutional instruction from Walter Bagehot and Albert Dicey will find in this introduction by Paine the foundation of their

Republic. In discussing "sovereignty" he points
out that the term, when applied to a people, has
a different meaning from the arbitrariness it signi-
fies in a monarchy. " Despotism may be more
effectually acted by many over a few, than by one
over all." " A republic is a sovereignty of justice,
in contradistinction to a sovereignty of will." The
distinct powers of the legislature are stated—those
of legislation and those of agency. " All laws are
acts, but all acts are not laws." Laws are for
every individual ; they may be altered. Acts of
agency or negotiation are deeds and contracts.

" The greatness of one party cannot give it a superiority or
advantage over the other. The state or its representative, the
assembly, has no more power over an act of this kind, after
it has passed, than if the state was a private person. It is the
glory of a republic to have it so, because it secures the individual from becoming the prey of power, and prevents might
from overcoming right. If any difference or dispute arise
between the state and the individuals with whom the agree-
ment is made respecting the contract, or the meaning or extent of any of the matters contained in the act, which may
affect the property or interest of either, such difference or
dispute must be judged of and decided upon by the laws of the
land, in a court of justice and trial by jury ; that is, by the
laws of the land already in being at the time such act and
contract was made."

" That this is justice," adds Paine, " that it is the
true principle of republican government, no man
will be so hardy as to deny." So, indeed, it seemed
in those days. In the next year those principles
were embodied in the Constitution ; and in 1792,
when a State pleaded its sovereign right to repudiate a contract ("Chisholm *vs.* Georgia ") the

Supreme Court affirmed every contention of Paine's pamphlet, using his ideas and sometimes his very phrases.

Our first Attorney-General (Edmund Randolph, of Virginia) eloquently maintained that the inferiority of one party, or dignity of the other, could not affect the balances of justice. Individuals could not be left the victims of States. So it was decided. Justice Wilson remarked that the term sovereignty is unknown to the Constitution : "The term 'sovereign' has for its correlative, 'subject.'" A State contracting as a merchant cannot, when asked to fulfil its contract, take refuge in its "sovereignty." "The rights of individuals," said Justice Cushing, "and the justice due to them are as dear and precious as those of States. Indeed the latter are founded on the former ; and the great end and object of them must be to secure and support the rights of individuals, or else vain is government."[1] But the decline of republicanism set in ; the shameful Eleventh Amendment was adopted ; Chisholm was defrauded of his victory by a retrospective action of this amendment ; and America stands to-day as the only nation professing civilization, which shields repudiation under " State sovereignty."

In the strength of these principles Paine was able to overwhelm the whole brood of heresies,— State privilege, legal tender, repudiation, retrospective laws. His arguments are too modern to need repetition here ; in fineness and force they

---

[1] See " Omitted Chapters of History Disclosed in the Life and Papers of Edmund Randolph," Chap. XVIII., for a full history of this subject.

are like the ribs of his bridge: as to-day commerce travels on Paine's iron span, so on his argumentative arch it passes over freshets endangering honest money.

For a like reason it is unnecessary to give here all the details of his bridge sent by Paine to his correspondents. Of this invention more is said in further chapters, but the subjoined letters are appropriate at this point. The first two were written at Bordentown, where Paine settled himself in the spring.

To Franklin, undated.—" I send you the two essays I mentioned. As the standing or not standing of such an arch is not governed by opinions, therefore opinions one way or the other will not alter the fact. The opinions of its standing will not make it stand, the opinions of its falling will not make it fall ; but I shall be exceedingly obliged to you to bestow a few thoughts on the subject and to communicate to me any difficulties or doubtfulness that may occur to you, because it will be of use to me to know them. As you have not the model to look at I enclose a sketch of a rib, except that the blocks which separate the bars are not represented."

To Franklin, June 6th.—" The gentleman, Mr. Hall, who presents you with this letter, has the care of two models for a bridge, one of wood, the other of cast iron, which I have the pleasure of submitting to you, as well for the purpose of showing my respect to you, as my patron in this country, as for the sake of having your opinion and judgment thereon. —The European method of bridge architecture, by piers and arches, is not adapted to many of the rivers in America on account of the ice in the winter. The construction of those I have the honor of presenting to you is designed to obviate the difficulty by leaving the whole passage of the river clear of the incumbrance of piers. . . My first design in the wooden model was for a bridge over the Harlem River, for my good friend General Morris of Morrisania . . but I cannot help thinking that it might be carried across the Schuylkill. . . . Mr. Hall, who has been with me at Borden Town, and has done the chief share of the working part, for we have done the whole ourselves, will inform you of any circumstance relating to it which does not depend on the mathematical construction. Mr. Hall will undertake to see the models brought safe from the stage boat to you ; they are too large to be admitted into the house, but will stand very well in the garden. Should there be a vessel going round to New York within about a week after my arrival in Philadelphia I shall take that convenience for sending them there, at which place I hope to be in about a fortnight."

Address and date not given ; written in Philadelphia, probably in June.—" Honorable Sir,—I have sent to His Excellency, the President [Franklin] two models for a Bridge, the one of wood the other of cast-iron bars, to be erected over rivers, without piers. As I shall in a few days go to New York, and take them with me, I do myself the honor of presenting an invitation to Council to take a view of them before they are removed. If it is convenient to Council to see and examine their construction to-day, at the usual time of their adjournment, I will attend at the President's at half after twelve o'clock, or any other day or hour Council may please to appoint." [1]

To the Hon. Thomas Fitzsimmons ; addressed "To be left at the Bank, Philadelphia." Written at Bordentown, November 19th.—" I write you a few loose thoughts as they occur to me. Next to the gaining a majority is that of keeping it. This, at least (in my opinion), will not be best accomplished by doing or attempting a great deal of business, but by doing no more than is absolutely necessary to be done, acting moderately and giving no offence. It is with the whole as it is with the members individually, and we always see at every new election that it is more difficult to turn out an old member against whom no direct complaint can be made than it is to put in a new one though a better man. I am sure it will be best

[1] This and the two letters preceding are among the Franklin MSS. in the Philosophical Society, Philadelphia.

not to touch any part of the plan of finance this year. If it falls short, as most probably it will, it would be (I speak for myself) best to reduce the interest that the whole body of those who are stiled public creditors may share it equally as far as it will go. If any thing can be saved from the Civil List expences it ought not to be finally mortgaged to make up the deficiency ; it may be applied to bring the creditors to a balance for the present year. There is more to be said respecting this debt than has yet been said. The matter has never been taken up but by those who were interested in the matter. The public has been deficient and the claimants exorbitant— neglect on one side and grediness on the other. That which is truly Justice may be always advocated. But I could no more think of paying six per cent Interest in real money, in perpetuity, for a debt a great part of which is quondam than I could think of not paying at all. Six per cent on any part of the debt, even to the original holders is ten or twelve per cent, and to the speculators twenty or thirty or more. It is better that the matter rest until it is fuller investigated and better understood, for in its present state it will be hazardous to touch upon.

"I have not heard a word of news from Philadelphia since I came to this place. I wrote a line to Mr. Francis and desired him to give me a little account of matters but he does not, perhaps, think it very necessary now.

"I see by the papers that the subject of the Bank is likely to be renewed. I should like to know when it will come on, as I have some thought of coming down at that time, if I can.

"I see by the papers that the Agricultural Society have presented a petition to the house respecting building a Bridge over the Schuylkill—on a model prepared for that purpose. In this I think they are too hasty. I have already constructed a model of a Bridge of Cast Iron, consisting of one arch. I am now making another of wrought Iron of one arch, but on a different Plan. I expect to finish it in about three weeks and shall send it first to Philadelphia. I have no opinion of any Bridge over the Schuylkill that is to be erected on piers— the sinking of piers will sink more money than they have any Idea of and will not stand when done. But there is another point they have not taken into their consideration ; which is, that the sinking three piers in the middle of the river, large and powerful enough to resist the ice, will cause such an alteration in the bed and channel of the river that there is no saying what course it may take, or whether it will not force a new channel somewhere else." [1]

To George Clymer, Esquire, "to be left at the Bank, Philadelphia." Written at Bordentown, November 19th.— "I observe by the minutes that the Agricultural Society have presented a petition to the house for an act of incorporation for the purpose of erecting a bridge over the Schuylkill on a model in their possession. I hope this business will not be gone into too hastily. A Bridge on piers will never answer for that river, they may sink money but they never will sink piers that will stand. But admitting that the piers do stand—they will cause such an alteration in the Bed and channel of the river, as will most probable alter its course either to divide the channel, and require two bridges or cause it to force a new channel in some other part. It is a matter of more hazard than they are aware of the altering by obstructions the bed and channel of a River ; the water must go somewhere—the force of the freshets and the Ice is very great now but will be much greater then.

"I am finishing as fast as I can my new model of an Iron Bridge of one arch which if it answers, as I have no doubt but it will, the whole difficulty of erecting Bridges over that river, or others of like circumstances, will be removed, and the expense not greater, (and I believe not so great) as the sum mentioned by Mr. Morris in the house, and I am sure will stand four times as long or as much longer as Iron is more durable than wood. I mention these circumstances to you that you may be informed of them—and not let the matter proceed so far as to put the Agricultural Society in a difficult situation at last.

"The giving a Society the exclusive right to build a bridge, unless the plan is prepared before hand, will prevent a bridge being built ; because those who might afterwards pro-

---

[1] I am indebted for this letter to Mr. Simon Gratz of Philadelphia.

duce models preferable to their own, will not present them to
any such body of men, and they can have no right to take
other peoples labours or inventions to compleat their own
undertakings by.

"I have not heard any news since I came to this place. I
wish you would give me a line and let me know how matters
are going on.—The Stage Boat comes to Borden Town every
Wednesday and Sunday from the Crooked Billet Wharf."[1]

At the close of the war Paine was eager to visit
England. He speaks of it in his letter of June 7,
1783, to Elias Boudinot, already referred to—but
he had not the means. The measures for his re-
muneration had delayed him two and a half years,
and it now became imperative that he should put
in a fair way of success his invention of the bridge.
The models made a good impression on Franklin
and the Council, and a committee was appointed
to investigate it. Early in the year following the
Pennsylvania Assembly appointed another committee. But meanwhile Paine's correspondence with
his parents determined him to visit them at once,
and look after the interests of his invention upon
his return.[2] He no doubt also thought, and it may
have been suggested by Franklin, that the success
of his bridge would be assured in America and
England if it should receive approval of the engineers in France. In March, 1787, he is in Philadelphia, consulting committees, and on the 31st writes
to Franklin of his prospects and plans :

"I mentioned in one of my essays my design of going
this spring to Europe.—I intend landing in france and from

---

[1] For this letter I am indebted to Mr. Charles Roberts, of Philadelphia.

[2] It is known that he received an affectionate letter from his father, now in
his 78th year, but it has not been found, and was probably burned with the
Bonneville papers in St. Louis.

thence England,—and that I should take the model with me. The time I had fixed with myself was May, but understanding (since I saw you yesterday) that no french packet sails that month, I must either take the April packet or wait till June. As I can get ready by the April packet I intend not omitting the opportunity. My Father and Mother are yet living, whom I am very anxious to see, and have informed them of my coming over the ensuing summer.

"I propose going from hence by the stage on Wednesday for New York, and shall be glad to be favoured with the care of any letters of yours to France or England. My stay in Paris, when with Col. Laurens, was so short that I do not feel myself introduced there, for I was in no house but at Passy, and the Hotel Col. Laurens was at. As I have taken a part in the Revolution and politics of this country, and am not an unknown character in the political world, I conceive it would be proper on my going to Paris, that I should pay my respects to Count Vergennes, to whom I am personally unknown ; and I shall be very glad of a letter from you to him affording me that opportunity, or rendering my waiting on him easy to me ; for it so often happens that men live to forfeit the reputation at one time they gained at another, that it is prudent not to presume too much on one's self. The Marquis La Fayette I am the most known to of any gentleman in France. Should he be absent from Paris there are none I am much acquainted with. I am on exceeding good terms with Mr. Jefferson which will necessarily be the first place I go to. As I had the honor of your introduction to America it will add to my happiness to have the same friendship continued to me on the present occasion.

" Respecting the model, I shall be obliged to you for a letter to some of the Commissioners in that department. I shall be glad to hear their opinion of it. If they will undertake the experiment of two Ribs, it will decide the matter and promote the work here,—but this need not be mentioned. The Assembly have appointed another Committee, consisting of Mr. Morris, Mr. Clymer, Mr. Fitzsimons, Mr. Wheeler, Mr. Robinson, to confer with me on the undertaking. The matter therefore will remain suspended till my return next winter. It is worth waiting this event, because if a single arch to that extent will answer, all difficulties in that river, or others of the same condition, are overcome at once.

"I will do myself the pleasure of waiting on you to-morrow."

During the time when Paine was perfecting his bridge, and consulting the scientific committees, the country was absorbed with preparations for forming a national Constitution and Union. When the States were nominating and electing delegates to the Convention of 1787, no one seems to have suggested Paine for a seat in it, nor does he appear to have aspired to one. The reasons are not far to seek. Paine was altogether too inventive for the kind of work contemplated by the colonial politicians. He had shown in all his writings, especially in his " Dissertations on Government," that he would build a constitution as he built his bridge : it must be mathematical, founded and shaped in impregnable principles, means adopted and adapted strictly for an ideal national purpose. His iron span did not consider whether there might be large interests invested in piers, or superstitions in favor of oak ; as little did his anti-slavery essays consider the investments in slavery, or his " Public Good " the jealous sovereignty of States. A recent writer says that Paine's " Common Sense " was " just what the moment demanded," and that it " may be briefly described as a plea for independence and a continental government."[1] In setting the nation at once to a discussion of the principles of such government, he led it to assume the principle of

---

[1] " The Development of Constitutional Liberty in the English Colonies of America," by Eben Greenough Scott, 1890.

independence ; over the old English piers on their quicksands, which some would rebuild, he threw his republican arch, on which the people passed from shore to shore. He and Franklin did the like in framing the Pennsylvania constitution of 1776, by which the chasm of " Toryism " was spanned. Every pamphlet of Paine was of the nature of an invention, by which principles of liberty and equality were framed in constructions adapted to emergencies of a republic. But when the emergencies were past, the old contrivances regained their familiar attractions, and these were enhanced by independence. Privilege, so odious in Lords, was not so bad when inherited by democracy ; individual sovereignty, unsuited to King George, might be a fine thing for President George ; and if England had a House of Peers, why should we not make one out of a peerage of States ? " Our experience in republicanism," wrote Paine, " is yet so slender, that it is much to be doubted whether all our public laws and acts are consistent with, or can be justified on, the principles of a republican government." But the more he talked in this way, or reminded the nation of the " Declaration of Independence " and the " Bill of Rights," the more did he close the doors of the Constitutional Convention against himself.

In those days there used to meet in Franklin's library a " Society for Political Inquiries." It had forty-two members, among them Washington, James Wilson, Robert Morris, Gouverneur Morris, Clymer, Rush, Bingham, Bradford, Hare, Rawle, and Paine. A memorandum of Rawle says : " Paine

never opened his mouth, but he furnished one of
the few essays which the members of the Society
were expected to produce. It was a well written
dissertation on the inexpediency of incorporating
towns."[1]   That in such company, and at such a
time, Paine should be silent, or discuss corporations,
suggests political solitude. Franklin, indeed, agreed
with him, but was too old to struggle against the
reaction in favor of the bicameral and other English
institutions.

M. Chanut (" Nouv. Biog. Générale ") says that
Paine's bridge was not erected on the Schuylkill
because of " the imperfect state of iron manufacture
in America." Something of the same kind might
be said of the state of political architecture.
And so it was, that while the Convention was
assembling in Independence Hall, he who first
raised the standard of Independence, and before
the Declaration proposed a Charter of the " United
Colonies of America," was far out at sea on his
way to rejoin his comrades in the old world, whose
hearts and burdens he had represented in the new.

[1] " Memoir of Penn. Hist. Soc., 1840." The gist of Paine's paper (read
Apr. 20, 1787) is no doubt contained in " The Rights of Man," Part II., Ch. 5.

The printed Rules of the Society (founded February 9, 1787) are in the
Philosophical Society, Philadelphia. The preamble, plainly Paine's, says :
" Important as these inquiries are to all, to the inhabitants of these republics
they are objects of peculiar magnitude and necessity. Accustomed to
look up to those nations, from whom we have derived our origin, for our
laws, our opinions, and our manners, we have retained with undistinguishing
reverence their errors, with their improvements ; have blended with our
public institutions the policy of dissimilar countries ; and have grafted on
our infant commonwealth the manners of ancient and corrupted monarchies.
In having effected a separate government, we have as yet effected but a
partial independence. The revolution can only be said to be compleat,
when we shall have freed ourselves, no less from the influence of foreign
prejudices than from the fetters of foreign power."

CHAPTER XVI.

RETURNING TO THE OLD HOME.

EVEN now one can hardly repress regret that Paine did not remain in his beloved Bordentown. There he was the honored man ; his striking figure, decorated with the noblest associations, was regarded with pride ; when he rode the lanes on his horse Button, the folk had a pleasant word with him ; the best homes prized his intimacy, and the young ladies would sometimes greet the old gentleman with a kiss. From all this he was drawn by the tender letter of a father he was never to see again. He sailed in April for a year's absence ; he remained away fifteen,—if such years may be reckoned by calendar.

The French packet from New York had a swift voyage, and early in the summer Paine was receiving honors in Paris. Franklin had given him letters of introduction, but he hardly needed them.[1] He was already a hero of the progressives, who had relished his artistic dissection of the Abbé Raynal's disparagement of the American Revolution. Among those who greeted him was Auberteuil, whose

[1] " This letter goes by Mr. Paine, one of our principal writers at the Revolution, being the author of 'Common Sense,' a pamphlet that had prodigious effects."—*Franklin to M. de Veillard.*

history of the American Revolution Paine had corrected, an early copy having been sent him (1783) by Franklin for that purpose.   But Paine's main object in France was to secure a verdict from the Academy of Sciences, the supreme authority, on his bridge, a model of which he carried with him.   The Academy received him with the honors due to an M.A. of the University of Pennsylvania, a member of the Philosophical Society, and a friend of Franklin.   It appointed M. Leroy, M. Bossou, and M. Borda a committee to report on his bridge. On August 18th he writes to Jefferson, then Minister in Paris :

"I am much obliged to you for the book you are so kind to send me.   The second part of your letter, concerning taking my picture, I must feel as an honor done to me, not as a favour asked of me—but in this, as in other matters, I am at the disposal of your friendship.

"The committee have among themselves finally agreed on their report ; I saw this morning it will be read in the Academy on Wednesday.   The report goes pretty fully to support the principles of the construction, with their reasons for that opinion."

On August 15th, a cheery letter had gone to George Clymer in Philadelphia, in which he says :

"This comes by Mr. Derby, of Massachusetts, who leaves Paris to-day to take shipping at L' [Orient] for Boston.   The enclosed for Dr. Franklin is from his friend Mr. Le Roy, of the Academy of Sciences, respecting the bridge, and the causes that have delayed the completing report.   An arch of 4 or 5 hundred feet is such an unprecedented thing, and will so much attract notice in the northern part of Europe, that the Academy is cautious in what manner to express their final opinion.   It is, I find, their custom to give reasons for their opinion, and this embarrasses them more than the opinion itself. That the model is strong, and that a bridge constructed on the same principles will also be strong, they appear to be well agreed in, but to what particular causes to assign the strength they are not agreed in. The Committee was directed by the Academy to examine all the models and plans for iron bridges that had been proposed in France, and they unanimously gave the preference to our own, as being the simplest, strongest, and lightest. They have likewise agreed on some material points." [1]

Dr. Robinet says that on this visit (1787) Paine, who had long known the "soul of the people," came into relation with eminent men of all groups, philosophical and political,—Condorcet, Achille Duchâtelet, Cardinal De Brienne, and, he believes, also Danton, who, like the English republican, was a freemason.[2] This intercourse, adds the same author, enabled him to print in England his remarkable prophecy concerning the change going on in the French mind. Dr. Robinet quotes from a pamphlet presently noticed, partly written in Paris during this summer. Although it was Paine's grievous destiny soon to be once more a revolutionary figure, it is certain that he had returned to Europe as an apostle of peace and good-will. While the engineers were considering his daring scheme of an iron arch of five hundred feet, he was devising with the Cardinal Minister, De Brienne, a

---

[1] For this letter I am indebted to Mr. Curtis Guild, of Boston. The letter goes on to describe, with drawings, the famous bridge at Schaffhausen, built by Grubenmann, an uneducated carpenter, the model being shown Paine by the King's architect, Perronet. The Academy's committee presently made its report, which was even more favorable than Paine had anticipated.

[2] "Danton Emigré," p. 7. Paine wrote a brief archæological treatise on freemasonry, but I have not met with the statement that he was a freemason except in Dr. Robinet's volume,—certainly high authority.

bridge of friendship across the Channel. He drew up a paper in this sense, on which the Minister wrote and signed his approval. The bridge-model approved by the Academy he sent to Sir Joseph Banks, President of the Royal Society ; the proposal for friendship between France and England, approved by the Cardinal Minister, he carried by his own hand to Edmund Burke.

On his arrival in London Paine gave to the printer a manuscript on which he had been engaged, and straightway went to Thetford.[1] His father had died the year before.[2] His mother, now in her ninety-first year, he found in the comfort his remittances had supplied. The house, with its large garden, stands in Guildhall (then Heathenman) Street. I was politely shown through it by its present occupant, Mr. Brett. Mr. Stephen Oldman, Sr., who went to school in the house, told me that it was identified by " old Jack Whistler," a barber, as the place where he went to shave Paine, in 1787. At this time Paine settled on his mother an allowance of nine shillings per week, which in the Thetford of that period was ample for her comfort. During this autumn with his mother he rarely left her side. As she lived to be ninety-four it may be that he sat beside her in the Quaker

---

[1] The exact time of his arrival in England is doubtful. Oldys says : " He arrived at the White Bear, Picadilly, on the 3d of September, 1787, just thirteen years after his departure for Philadelphia." Writing in 1803 Paine also says it was in September. But his " Rubicon " pamphlet is dated " York Street, St. James's Square, 20th August, 1787." Possibly the manuscript was dated in Paris and forwarded to the London printer with the address at which he wished to find proof on his arrival.

[2] St. Cuthbert's Register : " Burials, 1786. Joseph Payne (a Quaker) aged 78 years. November 14th."

meeting-house, to which she had become attached in her latter years.

Eloquent and pathetic must have been the silence around the gray man when, after so many tempests, he sat once more in the little meeting-house where his childhood was nurtured. From this, his spiritual cradle, he had borne away a beautiful theory, in ignorance of the contrasted actuality. Theoretically the Society of Friends is a theocracy; the Spirit alone rules and directs, effacing all distinctions of rank or sex. As a matter of fact, one old Quaker, or the clerk of a meeting, often over-rules the "inner lights" of hundreds. Of the practical working of Quaker government Paine had no experience; he had nothing to check his ideal formed in boyhood. His whole political system is explicable only by his theocratic Quakerism. His first essay, the plea for negro emancipation, was brought from Thetford meeting-house. His "Common Sense," a new-world scripture, is a "testimony" against the proud who raised their paltry dignities above the divine presence in the lowliest. "But where, say some, is the King of America? I 'll tell you, friend, he reigns above." Paine's love of his adopted country was not mere patriotism; he beheld in it the land of promise for all mankind, seen from afar while on his Thetford Pisgah. Therefore he made so much of the various races in America.

"The mere independence of America, were it to have been followed by a system of government modelled after the corrupt system of the English government, would not have interested me with the unabated ardour that it did. It was to bring forward and establish the representative system of government that was the leading principle with me."

So he spake to Congress, and to its president he said that he would have done the same for any country as for America. The religious basis of his political system has a droll illustration in an anecdote of his early life told by himself. While bowling with friends at Lewes, Mr. Verril remarked that Frederick of Prussia "was the best fellow in the world for a king ; he had so much of the devil in him." It struck Paine that "if it were necessary for a king to have so much of the devil in him, kings might very beneficially be dispensed with." From this time he seems to have developed a theory of human rights based on theocracy ; and so genuinely that in America, while the Bible was still to him the word of God, he solemnly proposed, in the beginning of the Revolution, that a crown should be publicly laid on that book, to signify to the world that "in America the Law is King."

While in America the States were discussing the Constitution proposed by the Convention, Paine sat in the silent meeting at Thetford dreaming of the Parliament of Man, and federation of the world. In America the dawn of the new nation was a splendor, but it paled the ideals that had shone through the night of struggle. The principles of the Declaration, which would have freed every slave,—representation proportionate to population, so essential to equality, the sovereignty of justice instead of majorities or of States,—had become "glittering generalities." The first to affirm the principles of the Declaration, Paine awaited the unsummoned Convention that would not compromise any of them away. For politicians these lofty ideas might be extinguished by the rising of a national sun ; but in Paine there remained the deep Quaker well where the stars shone on through the garish day.[1]

Seated in the Quaker meeting-house beside his mother, and beside his father's fresh grave, Paine revises the past while revising the proofs of his pamphlet. The glamor of war, even of the American Revolution, fades ; the shudder with which he saw in childhood soldiers reeking from the massacres of Culloden and Inverness returns ; he begins his new career in the old world with a "testimony" against war. [2]

"When we consider, for the feelings of Nature cannot be dismissed, the calamities of war and the miseries it inflicts upon the human species, the thousands and tens of thousands of every age and sex who are rendered wretched by the event, surely there is something in the heart of man that calls upon him to think ! Surely there is some tender chord, tuned by the hand of the Creator, that still struggles to emit in the hearing of the soul a note of sorrowing sympathy. Let it then be heard, and let man learn to feel that the true greatness of a nation is founded on principles of humanity. . . . War involves in its progress such a train of unforeseen and unsupposed circumstances, such a combination of foreign matters, that no human wisdom can calculate the end. It has but one thing certain, and that is to increase taxes. . . . I defend the cause of the poor, of the manufacturer, of the tradesman,

[1] " In wells where truth in secret lay

He saw the midnight stars by day."—W. D. Howells.

[2] " Prospects on the Rubicon ; or, An Investigation into the Causes and Consequences of the Politics to be Agitated at the Meeting of Parliament." London, 1787. Pp. 68.

of the farmer, and of all those on whom the real burthen of taxes fall—but above all, I defend the cause of humanity."

So little did Paine contemplate or desire revolution in England or France. His exhortation to young Pitt is to avoid war with Holland, to be friendly with France, to shun alliances involving aid in war, and to build up the wealth and liberties of England by uniting the people with the throne. He has discovered that this healthy change is going on in France. The French people are allying " the Majesty of the Sovereign with the Majesty of the Nation." " Of all alliances this is infinitely the strongest and the safest to be trusted to, because the interest so formed and operating against external enemies can never be divided." Freedom doubles the value of the subject to the government. When the desire of freedom becomes universal among the people, then, " and not before, is the important moment for the most effectual consolidation of national strength and greatness." The government must not be frightened by disturbances incidental to beneficent changes. " The creation we enjoy arose out of a chaos." [1]

[1] The pamphlet was reprinted in London in 1793 under the title : " Prospects on the War, and Paper Currency. The second edition, corrected." Advertisement (June 20th) : " This pamphlet was written by Mr. Paine in the year 1787, on one of Mr. Pitt's armaments, namely, that against Holland. His object was to prevent the people of England from being seduced into a war, by stating clearly to them the consequences which would inevitably befall the credit of this country should such a calamity take place. The minister has at length, however, succeeded in his great project, after three expensive armaments within the space of seven years ; and the event has proved how well founded were the predictions of Mr. Paine. The person who has authority to bring forward this pamphlet in its present shape, thinks his doing so a duty which he owes both to Mr. P—— and the people of England, in order that the latter may judge what credit is due to (what a great judge calls) THE WILD THEORIES OF MR. PAINE."

Paine had seen a good deal of Jefferson in Paris, and no doubt their conversation often related to struggles in the Constitutional Convention at Philadelphia. Jefferson wished the Constitution to include a Declaration of Rights, and wrote Paine some comments on the argument of James Wilson (afterward of the Supreme Court), maintaining that such a Declaration was unnecessary in a government without any powers not definitely granted, and that such a Declaration might be construed to imply some degree of power over the matters it defined. Wilson's speeches, powerfully analyzing the principles of liberty and federation, were delivered on October 6th and November 24th, and it will appear by the subjoined paper that they were more in accord with Paine's than with Jefferson's principles. The manuscript, which is among Jefferson's papers, bears no date, but was no doubt written at Thetford early in the year 1788.

"After I got home, being alone and wanting amusement, I sat down to explain to myself (for there is such a thing) my ideas of national and civil rights, and the distinction between them. I send them to you to see how nearly we agree.

"Suppose twenty persons, strangers to each other, to meet in a country not before inhabited. Each would be a Sovereign in his own natural right. His will would be his law, but his power, in many cases, inadequate to his right; and the consequence would be that each might be exposed, not only to each other, but to the other nineteen. It would then occur to them that their condition would be much improved, if a way could be devised to exchange that quantity of danger into so much protection; so that each individual should possess the strength of the whole number. As all their rights in the first case are natural rights, and the exercise of those rights supported only by their own natural individual power, they would begin by distinguishing between those rights they could individually exercise, fully and perfectly, and those they could not. Of the first kind are the rights of thinking, speaking, forming and giving opinions, and perhaps are those which can be fully exercised by the individual without the aid of exterior assistance ; or in other words, rights of personal competency. Of the second kind are those of personal protection, of acquiring and possessing property, in the exercise of which the individual natural power is less than the natural right.

"Having drawn this line they agree to retain individually the first class of Rights, or those of personal competency ; and to detach from their personal possession the second class, or those of defective power, and to accept in lieu thereof a right to the whole power produced by a condensation of all the parts. These I conceive to be civil rights, or rights of compact, and are distinguishable from natural rights because in the one we act wholly in our own person, in the other we agree not to do so, but act under the guarantee of society.

"It therefore follows that the more of those imperfect natural rights or rights of imperfect power we give up, and thus exchange, the more security we possess ; and as the word liberty is often mistakenly put for security, Mr. Wilson has confused his argument by confounding the terms. But it does not follow that the more natural rights of *every kind* we assign the more security we possess, because if we resign those of the first class we may suffer much by the exchange ; for where the right and the power are equal with each other in the individual, naturally, they ought to rest there.

"Mr. Wilson must have some allusion to this distinction, or his position would be subject to the inference you draw from it.

"I consider the individual sovereignty of the States retained under the act of confederation to be of the second class of right. It becomes dangerous because it is defective in the power necessary to support it. It answers the pride and purpose of a few men in each State, but the State collectively is injured by it."

The paper just quoted may be of importance to those students of Yale College who shall compete for the Ten Eyck prize of 1892, on the interesting subject, " Thomas Paine : Deism and Democracy in the Days of the American Revolution." There was no nearer approach to democracy, in Paine's theory, than that of this paper sent to Jefferson. The Constitutional Convention represented to him the contracting People, all the individuals being parties to a Compact whereby every majority pledges itself to protect the minority in matters not essential to the security of all. In representative government thus limited by compact he recognized the guaranty of individual freedom and influence by which the mass could be steadily enlightened. Royall Tyler considered some of his views on these subjects " whimsical paradoxes " ; but they are not so "unaccountable" as he supposed. Tyler's portraiture of Paine in London, though somewhat adapted to prejudices anent " The Age of Reason," is graphic, and Paine's anti-democratic paradox wittily described.

"I met this interesting personage at the lodgings of the son of a late patriotic American governour [Trumbull]. . . He was dressed in a snuff-coloured coat, olive velvet vest, drab breeches, coarse hose. His shoe buckles of the size of a half dollar. A bob tailed wig covered that head which worked such mickle woe to courts and kings. If I should attempt to describe it, it would be in the same stile and principle with which the veteran soldier bepraiseth an old standard : the more tattered, the more glorious. It is probable that this was the same identical wig under the shadow of whose curls he wrote Common Sense, in America, many years before. He was a spare man, rather under size ; subject to the extreme of low, and highly exhilirating spirits ; often sat reserved in company ; seldom mingled in common chit chat : But when a man of sense and elocution was present, and the company numerous, he delighted in advancing the most unaccountable, and often the most whimsical paradoxes ; which he defended in his own plausible manner. If encouraged by success, or the applause of the company, his countenance was animated with an expression of feature which, on ordinary occasions one would look for in vain, in a man so much celebrated for acuteness of thought ; but if interrupted by extraneous observation, by the inattention of his auditory, or in an irritable moment, even by the accidental fall of the poker, he would retire into himself, and no persuasion could induce him to proceed upon the most favourite topic. . . . I heard Thomas Paine once assert in the presence of Mr. Wolcott, better known, in this country, by the facetious name of Peter Pindar, that the minority, in all deliberative bodies, ought, in all cases, to govern the majority. Peter smiled. You must grant me, said *Un*common Sense, that the proportion of men of sense, to the ignorant among mankind, is at least as twenty, thirty, or even forty-nine, to an hundred. The majority of mankind are consequently most prone to errour ; and if we atchieve the right, the minority ought in all cases to govern. Peter continued to smile archly." [1]

In the end this theory was put to a vote of the company present, and all arose with Paine except Peter Pindar, who thereupon said, " I am the wise minority who ought, in all cases, to govern your ignorant majority."

[1] " The Algerine Captive," 1797. (Paine's shoe-buckles in the National Museum, Washington, are of the fashionable kind.)

CHAPTER XVII.

THE influence of Paine's Quaker training has been traced in his constructive politics, but its repressive side had more perhaps to do with his career. "I had some turn," he said, "and I believe some talent, for poetry; but this I rather repressed than encouraged." It is your half-repressed poets that kindle revolutions. History might be different had Paine not been taught fear of music and poetry. He must have epical commonwealths. The American Republic having temporarily filled his ideal horizon in the political direction, the disguised Muse turned his eye upon the possibilities of nature. Morally utilitarian, he yet rarely writes about physics without betraying the poetic passion for nature of a suppressed Wordsworth. Nature is his Aphrodite and his Madonna.

"Bred up in antediluvian notions, she has not yet acquired the European taste of receiving visitors in her dressing-room ; she locks and bolts up her private recesses with extraordinary care, as if not only resolved to preserve her hoards but conceal her age, and hide the remains of a face that was young and lovely in the days of Adam."

Defining for Jefferson the distinction between attraction and cohesion, he says :

"I recollect a scene at one of the theatres which very well explains the difference. A condemned lady wishes to see her child and the child its mother : that is Attraction. They were admitted to meet, but when ordered to part threw their arms around each other and fastened their persons together : this is Cohesion."

All the atoms or molecules are little mothers and daughters and lovers clasping each other ; it is an interlocking of figures ; "and if our eyes were good enough we should see how it was done." He has a transcendental perception of unity in things dissimilar. On his walks to Challiot he passes trees and fountains, and writes a little essay, with figures, explaining to his friend that the tree is also a fountain, and that by measuring diameters of trunks and tubes, or branches, the quantity of timber thrown up by sap-fountains might be known. Some of his casual speculations he calls " conceits." They are the exuberance of a scientific imagination inspired by philanthropy and naturalistic religion. The "inner light" of man corresponds to an "inner spirit" of nature. The human mind dimmed by ignorance, perverted by passion, turns the very gifts of nature to thorns, amid which her divine beauty sleeps until awakened by the kiss of science.

It would be difficult to find anything in the literature of mechanical invention more naïvely picturesque than this Quaker, passed through furnaces of two revolutions, trying to humanize gunpowder. Here is a substance with maximum of power and minimum of bulk and weight.

"When I consider the wisdom of nature I must think that she endowed matter with this extraordinary property for other purposes than that of destruction. Poisons are capable of other uses than that of killing. If the power which an ounce of gunpowder contains could be detailed out as steam or water can be it would be a most commodious natural power."

Having failed to convert revolutions to Quakerism, Paine tries to soften the heart of gunpowder itself, and insists that its explosiveness may be restrained and detailed like strokes on a boy's top to obtain continual motion. The sleeping top, the chastened repose of perfect motion, like the quiet of the spinning worlds, is the Quaker inventor's ideal, and he begs the President of the United States to try the effect of the smallest pistol made—the size of a quill—on a wheel with peripheral cups to receive the discharges.[1]

"The biographers of Paine," wrote his friend, Joel Barlow, "should not forget his mathematical acquirements and his mechanical genius." But it would require a staff of specialists, and a large volume, to deal with Paine's scientific studies and contrivances—with his planing machine, his new crane, his smokeless candle, his wheel of concentric rim, his scheme for using gunpowder as a motor, above all his iron bridge. As for the bridge, Paine feels that it is a sort of American revolution carried into mechanics ; his eagle cannot help spreading a little in the wondering eyes of the Old World. "Great scenes inspire great ideas," he writes to Sir George Staunton.

"The natural mightiness of America expands the mind, and it partakes of the greatness it contemplates. Even the war,

---

[1] I am reluctantly compelled to give only the main ideas of several theses of this kind by Paine, found among Jefferson's papers. The portion of the "Jefferson Papers" at Washington written by Paine would fill a good volume.

with all its evils, had some advantages. It energized invention and lessened the catalogue of impossibilities. At the conclusion of it every man returned to his home to repair the ravages it had occasioned, and to think of war no more. As one amongst thousands who had borne a share in that memorable revolution, I returned with them to the re-enjoyment of quiet life, and, that I might not be idle, undertook to construct a single arch for this river [Schuylkill]. Our beloved General had engaged in rendering another river, the Potowmac, navigable. The quantity of iron I had allowed in my plan for this arch was five hundred and twenty tons, to be distributed into thirteen ribs, in commemoration of the Thirteen United States."

It is amusing after this to find Paine, in his patent, declaring his special license from " His Most Excellent Majesty King George the Third."[1] Had poor George been in his right senses, or ever heard of the invention, he might have suspected some connection between this insurrection of the iron age and the American " rebellion." However, Paine is successful in keeping America out of his specification, albeit a poetic touch appears.

" The idea and construction of this arch is taken from the figure of a spider's circular web, of which it resembles a section, and from a conviction that when nature empowered this insect to make a web she also instructed her in the strongest mechanical method of constructing it. Another idea, taken from nature in the construction of this arch, is that of increas-

[1] " No. 1667. Specification of Thomas Paine. Constructing Arches, Vaulted Roofs, and Ceilings." The specification, dated August 26, 1788, declares his invention to be " on principles new and different to anything hitherto practised." The patents for England, Scotland, and Ireland were granted in September. An iron arch of one hundred feet was designed by Pritchard and erected by Darby at Coalbrook Dale, Shropshire, in 1779, but it did not anticipate the invention of Paine, as may be seen by the article on " Iron Bridges" in the Encyclopædia Britannica, which also well remarks that Paine's " daring in engineering does full justice to the fervour of his political career."

ing the strength of matter by dividing and combining it, and thereby causing it to act over a larger space than it would occupy in a solid state, as is seen in the quills of birds, bones of animals, reeds, canes, &c. The curved bars of the arch are composed of pieces of any length joined together to the whole extent of the arch, and take curvature by bending."

Paine and his bridge came to England at a fortunate moment. Blackfriars Bridge had just given way, and two over the Tyne, one built by Smeaton, had collapsed by reason of quicksands under their piers. And similarly Pitt's policy was collapsing through the treacherous quicksands on which it was based. Paper money and a " sinking fund " at home, and foreign alliances that disregarded the really controlling interests of nations, Paine saw as piers set in the Channel.[1] He at once took his place in England as a sort of institution. While the engineers beheld with admiration his iron arch clearing the treacherous river-beds, statesmen saw with delight his prospective bridges spanning the political " Rubicon." Nothing could be more felicitous than the title of his inaugural pamphlet, " Prospects on the Rubicon." It remembered an expression in Parliament at the beginning of the war on America. " ' The Rubicon is passed,' was once given as a reason for prosecuting the most expensive war that England ever knew. Sore with the event, and groaning beneath a galling yoke of taxes, she has again been led ministerially on to the shore of the same delusive and fatal river." The bridge-builder

[1] It is droll to find even Paine's iron bridge resting somewhat on a "paper" pier. " Perhaps," he writes Jefferson, " the excess of paper currency, and the wish to find objects for realizing it, is one of the motives for promoting the plan of the Bridge."

stretches his shining arches to France, Holland, Germany,—free commerce and friendship with all peoples, but no leagues with the sinking piers called thrones.

At Rotherham, in Yorkshire, where Messrs. Walker fitted up a workshop for Paine, he was visited by famous engineers and political personages. There and in London he was "lionized," as Franklin had been in Paris. We find him now passing a week with Edmund Burke, now at the country-seat of the Duke of Portland, or enjoying the hospitalities of Lord Fitzwilliam at Wentworth House. He is entertained and consulted on public affairs by Fox, Lord Lansdowne, Sir George Staunton, Sir Joseph Banks ; and many an effort is made to enlist his pen. Lord Lansdowne, it appears, had a notion of Paine's powers of political engineering so sublime that he thought he might bridge the Atlantic, and re-connect England and America ! All of this may be gathered from the Jefferson papers, as we shall presently see ; but it should be remarked here that Paine's head was not turned by his association with the gentry and aristocracy. The impression he made on these eminent gentlemen was largely due to his freedom from airs. They found him in his workshop, hammer in hand, proud only of free America and of his beautiful arch.

Professor Peter Lesley of Philadelphia tells me that when visiting in early life the works at Rotherham, Paine's workshop and the very tools he used were pointed out. They were preserved with care. He conversed with an aged and intelligent workman who had worked under Paine as a lad. Professor Lesley, who had shared some of the prejudice against Paine, was impressed by the earnest words of this old man. Mr. Paine, he said, was the most honest man, and the best man he ever knew. After he had been there a little time everybody looked up to him, the Walkers and their workmen. He knew the people for miles round, and went into their homes; his benevolence, his friendliness, his knowledge, made him beloved by all, rich and poor. His memory had always lasted there.

In truth Paine, who had represented the heart of England, in America, was now representing the heart of America to England. America was working by his hand, looking through his eyes, and silently publishing to the people from whom he sprung what the new nation could make out of a starving English staymaker. He was a living Declaration of Independence. The Americans in London—the artists West and Trumbull, the Alexanders (Franklin's connections), and others—were fond of him as a friend and proud of him as a countryman.

The subjoined letter to Benjamin West (afterwards P. R. A.) shows Paine's pleasant relations with that artist and with Trumbull. It is dated March 8, 1789.

"I have informed James of the matter which you and I talked of on Saturday, and he is much rejoiced at an opportunity of shewing his gratitude to you for the permission you indulged him with in attending Mr. Trumbull at your rooms. As I have known his parents upwards of twenty years, and the manners and habits he has been educated in, and the disposition he is of, I can with confidence to myself undertake to vouch for the faithful discharge of any trust you may repose in him ; and as he is a youth of quick discernment and a great deal of silent observation he cannot be easily imposed upon, or turned aside from his attention, by any contrivance of workmen. I will put him in a way of keeping a diary of every day's work he sees done, and of any observations he may make, proper for you to be informed of, which he can send once or twice a week to you at Windsor ; and any directions you may have to give him in your absence can be conveyed through Mr. Trumbull, or what other method you please, so that James is certified they come from you.

"James has made a tender of his service to Mr. Trumbull, if it should be of any use, when his picture is to be exhibited ; but that will probably not be till nearly the time the impressions will be struck off. James need not entirely omit his drawing while he is attending the plates. Some employment will, in general, fix a person to a place better than having only to stand still and look on. I suppose they strike off about three impressions in an hour, and as James is master of a watch he will find their average of works,—and also how fast they can work when they have a mind to make haste,—and he can easily number each impression, which will be a double check on any being carried off. I intend visiting him pretty often, while he is on duty, which will be an additional satisfaction to yourself for the trust you commit to him."[1]

This chapter may well close with a letter from Paine in London (January 6, 1789) to his young friend "Kitty Nicholson,"—known at the Bordentown school, and in New York,—on the occasion of her marriage with Colonel Few.[2] Let those who would know the real Thomas Paine read this letter!

---

[1] I have not been able to find anything more of Paine's *protégé* James, whose parents were known to him before his departure for American. I am indebted to Mr. W. E. Benjamin for the letter.

[2] To a representative of this family I am indebted for the letter. Concerning the Nicholsons, see page 212.

"I sincerely thank you for your very friendly and welcome letter. I was in the country when it arrived and did not receive it soon enough to answer it by the return of the vessel.

"I very affectionately congratulate Mr. and Mrs. Few on their happy marriage, and every branch of the families allied by that connection ; and I request my fair correspondent to present me to her partner, and to say, for me, that he has obtained one of the highest Prizes on the wheel. Besides the pleasure which your letter gives me to hear you are all happy and well, it relieves me from a sensation not easy to be dismissed ; and if you will excuse a few dull thoughts for obtruding themselves into a congratulatory letter I will tell you what it is. When I see my female friends drop off by matrimony I am sensible of something that affects me like a loss in spite of all the appearances of joy. I cannot help mixing the sincere compliment of regret with that of congratulation. It appears as if I had outlived or lost a friend. It seems to me as if the original was no more, and that which she is changed to forsakes the circle and forgets the scenes of former society. Felicities are cares superior to those she formerly cared for, create to her a new landscape of Life that excludes the little friendships of the past. It is not every lady's mind that is sufficiently capacious to prevent those greater objects crowding out the less, or that can spare a thought to former friendships after she has given her hand and heart to the man who loves her. But the sentiment your letter contains has prevented these dull Ideas from mixing with the congratulation I present you, and is so congenial with the enlarged opinion I have always formed of you, that at the time I read your letter with pleasure I read it with pride, because it convinces me that I have some judgment in that most difficult science—a Lady's mind. Most sincerely do I wish you all the good that Heaven can bless you with, and as you have in your own family an example of domestic happiness you are already in the knowledge of obtaining it. That no condition we can enjoy is an exemption from care—that some shade will mingle itself with the brightest sunshine of Life—that even our affections may become the instruments of our sorrows—that the sweet felicities of home depend on good temper as well as on good sense, and that there is always something to forgive even in the nearest and dearest of our friends,—are truths which, tho' too obvious to be told, ought never to be forgotten ; and I know you will not esteem my friendship the less for impressing them upon you.

" Though I appear a sort of wanderer, the married state has not a sincerer friend than I am. It is the harbour of human life, and is, with respect to the things of this world, what the next world is to this. It is home ; and that one word conveys more than any other word can express. For a few years we may glide along the tide of youthful single life and be wonderfully delighted ; but it is a tide that flows but once, and what is still worse, it ebbs faster than it flows, and leaves many a hapless voyager aground. I am one, you see that have experienced the fate, I am describing.[1] I have lost my tide ; it passed by while every thought of my heart was on the wing for the salvation of my dear America, and I have now as contentedly as I can, made myself a little bower of willows on the shore that has the solitary resemblance of a home. Should I always continue the tenant of this home, I hope my female acquaintance will ever remember that it contains not the churlish enemy of their sex, not the inaccessible cold hearted mortal, nor the capricious tempered oddity, but one of the best and most affectionate of their friends.

" I did not forget the Dunstable hat, but it was not on wear here when I arrived. That I am a negligent correspondent I freely confess, and I always reproach myself for it. You mention only one letter, but I wrote twice ; once by Dr. Derby, and another time by the Chevalier St. Triss—by whom I also

---

[1] Paine's marriage and separation from his wife had been kept a secret in America, where the " Tories " would have used it to break the influence of his patriotic writings. It may be stated here, in addition to what is said on p. 32, that, in the absence of any divorce law in England, a separation under the Common Law was generally held as pronouncing the marriage a nullity *ab initio.* According to Chalmers Paine was dissatisfied with articles of separation drawn up by an attorney, Josias Smith, May 24, 1774, and insisted on new ones, to which the clergyman was a party. The " common lawyers " regarded the marriage as completely annulled, and Paine thus free to marry again. However, he evidently never thought of doing so, and that his relations with ladies were as chaste as affectionate appears in this letter to Mrs. Few, and in his correspondence generally.

wrote to Gen. Morris, Col. Kirkbride, and several friends in Philadelphia, but have received no answers. I had one letter from Gen. Morris last winter, which is all I have received from New York till the arrival of yours.

" I thank you for the details of news you give. Kiss Molly Field for me and wish her joy,—and all the good girls of Borden Town. How is my favorite Sally Morris, my boy Joe, and my horse Button ? pray let me know. Polly and Nancy Rogers,—are they married ? or do they intend to build bowers as I have done ? If they do, I wish they would twist their green willows somewhere near to mine.

" I am very much engaged here about my Bridge—There is one building of my Construction at Messers. Walker's Iron Works in Yorkshire, and I have direction of it. I am lately come from thence and shall return again in two or three weeks.

" As to news on this side the water, the king is mad, and there is great bustle about appointing a Regent. As it happens, I am in pretty close intimacy with the heads of the opposition—the Duke of Portland, Mr. Fox and Mr. Burke. I have sent your letter to Mrs. Burke as a specimen of the accomplishments of the American Ladies. I sent it to Miss Alexander, a lady you have heard me speak of, and I asked her to give me a few of her thoughts how to answer it. She told me to write as I felt, and I have followed her advice.

" I very kindly thank you for your friendly invitation to Georgia and if I am ever within a thousand miles of you, I will come and see you ; though it be but for a day.

" You touch me on a very tender part when you say my friends on your side the water 'cannot be reconciled to the idea of my resigning my adopted America, even for my native England.' They are right. Though I am in as elegant style of acquaintance here as any American that ever came over, my heart and myself are 3000 miles apart ; and I had rather see my horse Button in his own stable, or eating the grass of Bordentown or Morrisania, than see all the pomp and show of Europe.

" A thousand years hence (for I must indulge in a few thoughts) perhaps in less, America may be what England now is ! The innocence of her character that won the hearts of all nations in her favor may sound like a romance, and her inimitable virtue as if it had never been.   The ruins of that liberty which thousands bled for, or suffered to obtain, may just furnish materials for a village tale or extort a sigh from rustic sensibility, while the fashionable of that day, enveloped in dissipation, shall deride the principle and deny the fact.

"When we contemplate the fall of Empires and the extinction of nations of the ancient world, we see but little to excite our regret than the mouldering ruins of pompous palaces, magnificent monuments, lofty pyramids, and walls and towers of the most costly workmanship.   But when the Empire of America shall fall, the subject for contemplative sorrow will be infinitely greater than crumbling brass or marble can inspire. It will not then be said, here stood a temple of vast antiquity, —here rose a Babel of invisible height, or there a palace of sumptuous extravagance ; but here, ah painful thought ! the noblest work of human wisdom, the grandest scene of human glory, the fair cause of freedom rose and fell !

"Read this and then ask if I forget America—But I 'll not be dull if I can help it, so I leave off, and close my letter to-morrow, which is the day the mail is made up for America.

"January 7th.   I have heard this morning with extreme concern of the death of our worthy friend Capt. Read.   Mrs. Read lives in a house of mine at Bordentown, and you will much oblige me by telling her how much I am affected by her loss ; and to mention to her, with that delicacy which such an offer and her situation require, and which no one knows better how to convey than yourself, that the two years' rent which is due I request her to accept of, and to consider herself at home till she hears further from me.

"This is the severest winter I ever knew in England ; the frost has continued upwards of five weeks, and is still likely to continue.   All the vessels from America have been kept off by contrary winds.   The ' Polly ' and the ' Pigeon ' from Philadelphia and the ' Eagle ' from Charleston are just got in.

"If you should leave New York before I arrive (which I hope will not be the case) and should pass through Philadelphia, I wish you would do me the favor to present my compliments to Mrs. Powell, the lady whom I wanted an opportunity to introduce you to when you were in Philadelphia, but was prevented by your being at a house where I did not visit.

" There is a Quaker favorite of mine at New York, formerly
Miss Watson of Philadelphia ; she is now married to Dr.
Lawrence, and is an acquaintance of Mrs. Oswald : be so
kind as to make her a visit for me. You will like her conversation. She has a little of the Quaker primness—but of the
pleasing kind—about her.

" I am always distressed at closing a letter, because it seems
like taking leave of my friends after a parting conversation.—
Captain Nicholson, Mrs. Nicholson, Hannah, Fanny, James,
and the little ones, and you my dear Kitty, and your partner for
life—God bless you all ! and send me safe back to my much
loved America !

" THOMAS PAINE—æt. 52.
" or if you better like it
" ' Common Sense.'

" This comes by the packet which sails from Falmouth, 300
miles from London ; but by the first vessel from London to
New York I will send you some magazines. In the meantime
be so kind as to write to me by the first opportunity. Remember me to the family at Morrisania, and all my friends
at New York and Bordentown. Desire Gen. Morris to take
another guinea of Mr. Constable, who has some money of
mine in his hands, and give it to my boy Joe. Tell Sally to
take care of ' Button.' Then direct for me at Mr. Peter
Whiteside's London. When you are at Charleston remember me to my dear old friend Mrs. Lawrence, Col. and Mrs.
L. Morris, and Col. Washington ; and at Georgia, to Col.
Walton. Adieu."

CHAPTER XVIII.

A NOTE of Paine to Jefferson, dated February 19, 1788, shows him in that city consulting with Lafayette about his bridge, and preparing a memorial for the government. The visit was no doubt meant to secure a patent, and also arrange for the erection of the bridge. This appears to be his last meeting with Jefferson in Europe. He must have returned soon to England, where a letter of June 15th reports to Jefferson large progress in his patent, and other arrangements. Paine's letters were by no means confined to his personal affairs. In one of his letters Jefferson says : " I have great confidence in your communications, and since Mr. Adams' departure I am in need of authentic information from that country." Jefferson subscribes his letters—" I am with great and sincere attachment, dear Sir, your affectionate friend and servant," —and Paine responded with wonted fidelity. For more than a year the United States government was supplied by Paine, mainly through Jefferson, with information concerning affairs in England. It will be seen by some of the subjoined extracts that Paine was recognized by English statesmen as a sort of American Minister, and that the information he transmits is rarely, if ever, erroneous. All of this would appear more clearly could space be here given to the entire letters. The omissions are chiefly of items of news now without interest, or of technical details concerning the bridge. It is only just to remind the reader, before introducing the quotations, that these letters were confidential, and to a very intimate friend, being thus not liable to any charge of egotism from the public, for whose eye they were not intended.

"London, Broad Street Buildings, No. 13. Sept. 9, 1788.—That I am a bad correspondent is so general a complaint against me, that I must expect the same accusation from you—But hear me first—When there is no matter to write upon, a letter is not worth the trouble of receiving and reading and while any thing which is to·be the subject of a letter, is in suspence, it is difficult to write and perhaps best to let it alone —'least said is soonest mended,' and nothing said requires no mending.

" The model has the good fortune of preserving in England the reputation which it received from the Academy of Sciences. It is a favourite hobby horse with all who have seen it ; and every one who has talked with me on the subject advised me to endeavour to obtain a Patent, as it is only by that means that I can secure to myself the direction and management. For this purpose I went, in company with Mr Whiteside to the office which is an appendage to Lord Sydney's—told them who I was, and made an affidavit that the construction was my own Invention. This was the only step I took in the business. Last Wednesday I received a Patent for England, the next day a Patent for Scotland, and I am to have one for Ireland.

" As I had already the opinion of the scientific Judges both in France and England on the Model, it was also necessary that I should have that of the practical Iron men who must finally be the executors of the work. There are several capital Iron Works in this country, the principal of which are those in Shropshire, Yorkshire, and Scotland. It was my intention to have communicated with Mr. Wilkinson, who is one of the proprietors of the Shropshire Iron Works, and concerned in those in France, but his departure for Sweden before I had possession of the patents prevented me. The Iron Works in Yorkshire belonging to the Walkers near to Sheffield are the most eminent in England in point of establishment and property. The proprietors are reputed to be worth two hundred thousand pounds and consequently capable of giving energy to any great undertaking. A friend of theirs who had seen the model wrote to them on the subject, and two of them came to London last Fryday to see it and talk with me on the business. Their opinion is very decided that it can be executed either in wrought or cast Iron, and I am to go down to their Works next week to erect an experiment arch. This is the point I am now got to, and until now I had nothing to inform you of. If I succeed in erecting the arch all reasoning and opinion will be at an end, and, as this will soon be known, I shall not return to France till that time ; and until then I wish every thing to remain respecting my Bridge over the Seine, in the state I left matters in when I came from France. With respect to the Patents in England it is my intention to dispose of them as soon as I have established the certainty of the construction.

" Besides the ill success of Black friars Bridge, two Bridges built successively on the same spot, the last by Mr Smeaton, at Hexham, over the Tyne in Northumberland, have fallen down, occasioned by quicksands under the bed of the river. If therefore arches can be extended in the proportion the model promises, the construction in certain situations, without regard to cheapness or dearness, will be valuable in all countries. . . . As to English news or Politics, there is little more than what the public papers contain. The assembling the States General, and the reappointment of Mr. Neckar, make considerable impression here. They overawe a great deal of the English habitual rashness, and check that triumph of presumption which they indulged themselves in with respect to what they called the deranged and almost ruinous condition of the finances of France. They acknowledge unreservedly that the natural resources of France are greater than those of England, but they plume themselves on the superiority of the means necessary to bring national resources forth. But the two circumstances above mentioned serve very well to lower this exaltation.

"Some time ago I spent a week at Mr. Burke's, and the Duke of Portland's in Buckinghamshire. You will recollect that the Duke was the member during the time of the coalition —he is now in the opposition, and I find the opposition as much warped in some respects as to Continental Politics as the Ministry.—What the extent of the Treaty with Russia is, Mr. B[urke] says that he and all the opposition are totally unacquainted with ; and they speak of it not as a very wise measure, but rather tending to involve England in unnecessary continental disputes. The preference of the opposition is to a connection with Prussia if it could have been obtained. Sir George Staunton tells me that the interference with respect to Holland last year met with considerable opposition from part of the Cabinet. Mr. Pitt was against it at first, but it was a favourite measure with the King, and that the opposition at that crisis contrived to have it known to him that they were disposed to support his measures. This together with the notification of the 16th of September gave Mr. Pitt cause and pretence for changing his ground.

" The Marquis of Landsdown is unconnected either with the Ministry or the opposition. His politics is distinct from both. This plan is a sort of armed neutrality which has many advocates. In conversation with me he reprobated the conduct of the Ministry towards France last year as operating to '*cut the throat of confidence*' (this was his expression) between France and England at a time when there was a fair opportunity of improving it.

" The enmity of this country against Russia is as bitter as it ever was against America, and is carried to every pitch of abuse and vulgarity. What I hear in conversations exceeds what may be seen in the news-papers. They are sour and mortified at every success she acquires, and voraciously believe and rejoice in the most improbable accounts and rumours to the contrary. You may mention this to Mr. Simelin on any terms you please for you cannot exceed the fact.

" There are those who amuse themselves here in the hopes of managing Spain. The notification which the Marquis del Campo made last year to the British Cabinet, is perhaps the only secret kept in this country. Mr. B[urke] tells me that the oppo-sition knows nothing of it. They all very freely admit that if the Combined fleets had had thirty or forty thousand land forces, when they came up the channel last war, there was nothing in England to oppose their landing, and that such a measure would have been fatal to their resources, by at least a tempo-rary destruction of national credit. This is the point on which this country is most impressible. Wars carried on at a dis-tance, they care but little about, and seem always disposed to enter into them. It is bringing the matter home to them that makes them fear and feel, for their weakest part is at home. This I take to be the reason of the attention they are paying to Spain ; for while France and Spain make a common cause and *start* together, they may easily overawe this country.

"I intended sending this letter by Mr. Parker, but he goes by the way of Holland, and as I do not chuse to send it by the English Post, I shall desire Mr. Bartholemy to forward it to you.

"Remember me with much affection to the Marquis de la Fayette. This letter will serve for two letters. Whether I am in London or the country any letter to me at Mr White-side's, Merchant, No. 13 Broad Street Buildings, will come safe. My compliments to Mr. Short."

"LONDON, September 15.—I have not heard of Mr. [Lewis] Littlepage since I left Paris,—if you have, I shall be glad to know it. As he dined sometimes at Mr. Neckar's, he under-took to describe the Bridge to him. Mr. Neckar very readily conceived it. If you have an opportunity of seeing Mr. Neckar, and see it convenient to renew the subject, you might mention that I am going forward with an experiment arch.— Mr. Le Couteulx desired me to examine the construction of the Albion Steam Mills erected by Bolton and Watt. I have not yet written to him because I had nothing certain to write about. I have talked with Mr. Rumsey, who is here, upon this matter, and who appears to me to be master of that sub-ject, and who has procured a model of the Mill, which is worked originally from the steam. . . . When you see Mr. Le Roy please to present my compliments. I hope to realize the opinion of the Academy on the Model, in which case I shall give the Academy the proper information. We have no certain accounts here of the arrangement of the new Ministry. The papers mention Count St. Preist for Foreign Affairs. When you see him please to present my compliments. . . . Please to present my compliments to M. and Madame De Corney."

"LONDON, December 16.—That the King is insane is now old news. He yet continues in the same state, and the Parliament are on the business of appointing a Regent. The Dukes of York and Gloucester have both made speeches in the house of Peers. An embarrassing question, whether the Prince of Wales has a right in himself by succession during the incapacity of his father, or whether the right must derive to him thro' Parliament, has been agitated in both Houses. [Illegible] and the speeches of York and Gloucester of avoiding the question. This day is fixt for bringing the matter on in the house of Commons. A change of Ministry is expected, and I believe determined on. The Duke of Portland and his friends will in all probability come in. I shall be exceedingly glad to hear from you, and to know if you have received my letters, and also when you intend setting off for America, or whether you intend to visit England before you go. In case of change of Ministry here there are certain matters I shall be glad to see you upon. Remember me to the Marquis de la Fayette. We hear good things from France, and I sincerely wish them all well and happy. Remember me to Mr. Short and Mr. Mazzei.[1]"

"LONDON, Jan. 15, 1789.—My last letter requested to know if you had any thoughts of coming to England before you sailed to America. There will certainly be a change of ministry, and probably some change of measures, and it might not be inconvenient if you could know before your sailing, for the information of the new Congress, what measures the new Ministry here intended to pursue or adopt with respect to commercial arrangements with America. I am in some in-

---

[1] Mazzei was a scientific Italian who settled in Virginia with a Tuscan colony before the Revolution, in which he took up arms and was captured by the British. His colony had been under the patronage of Jefferson, to whose fortunes he was always devoted, though the publication of Jefferson's famous letter to him, reflecting on Washington's administration, caused his patron much trouble.

timacy with Mr. Burke, and after the new ministry are formed he has proposed to introduce me to them. The Duke of Portland, at whose seat in the country I was a few days last summer, will be at the head of the Treasury, and Mr. Fox Secretary for Foreign Affairs. The King continues, I believe, as mad as ever. It appears that he has amassed several millions of money, great part of which is in foreign funds. He had made a Will, while he had his senses, and devised it among his children, but a second Will has been produced, made since he was niad, dated the 25th of Oct., in which he gives his property to the Queen. This will probably produce much dispute, as it is attended with many suspicious circumstances. It came out in the examination of the physicians, that one of them, Dr. Warrens, on being asked the particular time of his observing the King's insanity, said the twenty-second of October, and some influence has been exerted to induce him to retract that declaration, or to say that the insanity was not so much as to prevent him making a Will, which he has refused to do."

" LONDON, February 16.—Your favour of the 23d December continued to the —— of Janry. came safe to hand,—for which I thank you. I begin this without knowing of any opportunity of conveyance, and shall follow the method of your letter by writing on till an opportunity offers.

" I thank you for the many and judicious observations about my bridge. I am exactly in your Ideas as you will perceive by the following account.—I went to the Iron Works the latter end of Octr. My intention at the time of writing to you was to construct an experiment arch of 250 feet, but in the first place, the season was too far advanced to work out of doors and an arch of that extent could not be worked within doors, and *nextly*, there was a prospect of a real Bridge being wanted on the spot of 90 feet extent. The person who appeared disposed to erect a Bridge is Mr. Foljambe nephew to the late Sir George Saville, and member in the last Parliament for Yorkshire. He lives about three miles from the works, and the River Don runs in front of his house, over which there is an old ill constructed Bridge which he wants to remove. These circumstances determined me to begin an arch of 90 feet with an elevation of 5 feet. This extent I could manage within doors by working half the arch at a time. . . . A great part of our time, as you will naturally suppose was taken up in preparations, but after we began to work we went on rapidly, and that without any mistake, or anything to alter or amend. The foreman of the works is a Relation to the Proprietors, an excellent mechanic and who fell into all my Ideas with great ease and penetration. I staid at the works till one half the Rib, 45 feet, was compleated and framed horizontally together and came up to London at the meeting of Parliament on the 4th of December. The foreman, whom, as I told him, I should appoint ' President of the Board of Works, in my absence " wrote me word that he has got the other half together with much less trouble than the first. He is now preparing for erecting and I for returning.

" February 26.—A few days ago I received a letter from Mr. Foljambe in which he says : 'I saw the Rib of your Bridge. In point of elegance and beauty, it far exceeded my expectations and is certainly beyond any thing I ever saw.'— My model and myself had many visitors while I was at the works. A few days after I got there, Lord Fitz-William, heir to the Marquis of Rockingham, came with Mr. Burke. The former gave the workmen five guineas and invited me to Wentworth House, a few miles distant from the works, where I went, and staid a few days.

" This Bridge I expect will bring forth something greater, but in the meantime I feel like a Bird from its nest and wishing most anxiously to return. Therefore, as soon as I can bring any thing to bear, I shall dispose of the contract and bid adieu. I can very truly say that my mind is not at home.

" I am very much rejoiced at the account you give me of the state of affairs in France. I feel exceedingly interested in the happiness of that nation. They are now got or getting into the right way, and the present reign will be more Immortalized in France than any that ever preceded it. They have all died away, forgotten in the common mass of things, but this will be to France like an Anno Mundi, or an Anno Domini. The happiness of doing good and the Pride of doing great things unite themselves in this business. But as there are two kinds of Pride—the little and the great, the privileged orders will in some degree be governed by this Division.

Those of little pride (I mean little-minded pride) will be schismatical, and those of the great pride will be orthodox, with respect to the States General. Interest will likewise have some share, and could this operate freely it would arrange itself on the orthodox side. To enrich a Nation is to enrich the individuals which compose it. To enrich the farmer is to enrich the farm—and consequently the Landlord ;—for whatever the farmer is, the farm will be. The richer the subject, the richer the revenue, because the consumption from which Taxes are raised is in proportion to the abilities of people to consume ; therefore the most effectual method to raise both the revenue and the rental of a country is to raise the condition of the people,—or that order known in france by the Tiers Etat. But I ought to ask pardon for entering into reasonings in a letter to you, and only do it because I like the subject.

" I observe in all the companies I go into the impression which the present circumstances of France has upon this Country. *An internal Alliance* in France [between Throne and People] is an alliance which England never dreamed of, and which she most dreads. Whether she will be better or worse tempered afterwards I cannot judge of, but I believe she will be more cautious in giving offence. She is likewise impressed with an Idea that a negotiation is on foot between the King [Louis XVI.] and the Emperor for adding Austrian Flanders to France. This appears to me such a probable thing, and may be rendered so conducive to the interest and good of all the parties concerned, that I am inclined to give it credit and wish it success. I hope then to see the Scheld opened, for it is a sin to refuse the bounties of nature. On these matters I shall be glad of your opinion. I think the States General of Holland could not be in earnest when they applied to France for the payment of the quota to the Emperor. All things considered to request it was meanness, and to expect it absurdity. I am more inclined to think they made it an opportunity to find how they stood with France. Absalom (I think it was) set fire to his brother's field of corn to bring on a conversation.

" March 12.—With respect to Political matters here, the truth is, the people are fools. They have no discernment into principles and consequences. Had Mr. Pitt proposed a National Convention, at the time of the King's insanity, he had done right; but instead of this he has absorbed the right of the Nation into a right of Parliament,—one house of which (the Peers) is hereditary in its own right, and over which the people have no controul (not so much as they have over their King;) and the other elective by only a small part of the Nation. Therefore he has lessened instead of increased the rights of the people; but as they have not sense enough to see it, they have been huzzaing him. There can be no fixed principles of government, or anything like a constitution in a country where the Government can alter itself, or one part of it supply the other.

"Whether a man that has been so compleatly mad as not to be managed but by force and the mad shirt can ever be confided in afterwards as a reasonable man, is a matter I have very little opinion of. Such a circumstance, in my estimation, if mentioned, ought to be a perpetual disqualification.

"The Emperor I am told has entered a caveat against the Elector of Hanover (not the electoral vote) for King of the Romans. John Bull, however, is not so mad as he was, and a message has been manufactured for him to Parliament in which there is nothing particular. The Treaty with Prussia is not yet before Parliament but is to be.

"Had the Regency gone on and the new administration been formed I should have been able to communicate some matters of business to you, both with respect to America and France; as an interview for that purpose was agreed upon and to take place as soon as the persons who were to fill the offices should succeed. I am the more confidential with those persons, as they are distinguished by the name of the Blue & Buff,—a dress taken up during the American War, and is the undress uniform of General Washington with Lapels which they still wear.¹ But, at any rate, I do not think it is worth while for Congress to appoint any Minister to this Court. The greater distance Congress observes on this point the better. It will be all money thrown away to go to any ex-

---

¹ On this Blue and Buff Society, Canning wrote some satirical verses. He also described " French philanthropy " as " Condorcet filtered through the dregs of Paine."

pence about it—at least during the present reign. I know the nation well, and the line of acquaintance I am in enables me to judge better than any other American can judge—especially at a distance. If Congress should have any business to state to the Government here, it can be easily done thro' their Minister at Paris—but the seldomer the better.

" I believe I am not so much in the good graces of the Marquis of Landsdowne as I used to be—I do not answer his purpose. He was always talking of a sort of reconnection of England and America, and my coldness and reserve on this subject checked communication."

" LONDON, April 10.—The King continues in his amended state, but Dr. Willis, his son, and attendants, are yet about his person. He has not been to Parliament nor made any public appearance, but he has fixed the 23d April for a public thanksgiving, and he is to go in great Parade to offer up his Devotions at St. Paul's on that day. Those about him have endeavoured to dissuade him from this ostentatious pilgrimage, most probably from an apprehension of some effect it may have upon him, but he persists. . . . The acts for regulating the trade with America are to be continued as last year. A paper from the Privy Council respecting the American fly is before Parliament. I had some conversation with Sir Joseph Banks upon this subject, as he was the person whom the Privy Council referred to. I told him that the Hessian fly attacked only the green plant, and did not exist in the dry grain. He said that with respect to the Hessian fly, they had no apprehension, but it was the weevil they alluded to. I told him the weevil had always more or less been in the wheat countries of America, and that if the prohibition was on that account it was as necessary fifty or sixty years ago, as now ; that I believe it was only a political manœuvre of the Ministry to please the landed interest, as a balance for prohibiting the exportation of wool to please the manufacturing interest. He did not reply, and as we are on very sociable terms I went farther by saying— The English ought not to complain of the non-payment of Debts from America while they prohibit the means of payment.

" I suggest to you a thought on this subject. The debts due before the war, ought to be distinguished from the debts contracted since, and all and every mode of payment and remittance under which they *have been discharged at the time they were contracted* ought to accompany those Debts, so long as any of them shall continue unpaid ; because the circumstances of payment became united with the debt, and cannot be separated by subsequent acts of one side only. If this was taken up in America, and insisted on as a right co-eval with and inseparable from those Debts, it would force some of the restrictions here to give way.

"You speak very truly of this country when you say ' that they are slumbering under a half reformation of Politics and religion, and cannot be excited by any thing they hear or see to question the remains of prejudice.' Their ignorance on some matters, is unfathomable, for instance the Bank of England discount Bills at 5 p cent, but a proposal is talked of for discounting at 4½ ; and the reason given is the vast quantity of money, and that money of the good houses discounts at 4½ ; from this they deduce the great ability and credit of the nation. Whereas the contrary is the case. This money is all in paper, and the quantity is greater than the object to circulate it upon, and therefore shows that the market is glutted, and consequently the ability for farther paper excretions is lessened.—If a war should ever break out, between the countries again, this is the spot where it ought to be prosecuted, they neither feel nor care for any thing at a distance, but are frightened and spiritless at every thing which happens at home. The Combined fleet coming up the Channel, Paul Jones, and the Mob of 1738, are the dreadful eras of this country. But for national puffing none equals them. The addresses which have been presented are stuffed with nonsense of this kind. One of them published in the *London Gazette* and presented by a Sir William Appleby begins thus,— ' Britain, the Queen of Isles, the pride of Nations, the Arbitress of Europe, perhaps of the world.' . . . On the receipt of your last, I went to Sir Joseph Banks to inform him of your having heard from Ledyard, from Grand Cairo, but found he had a letter from him of the same date. Sir Joseph is one of the society for promoting that undertaking. He has an high opinion of Ledyard, and thinks him the only man fitted for such an exploration. As you may probably hear of Ledyard by accounts that may not reach here, Sir Joseph will be obliged to you to communicate to him any matters respecting him that may come to you (Sir Joseph Banks, Bart., Soho Square).   .   .   .

"While writing this I am informed that the Minister has had a conference with some of the American creditors, and proposed to them to assume the debts and give them ten shillings on the pound—the conjecture is that he means, when the new Congress is established, to demand the payment. If you are writing to General Washington, it may not be amiss to mention this—and if I hear farther on the matter I will inform you.[1] But, as being a money matter it cannot come forward but thro' Parliament, there will be notice given of the business. This would be a proper time to show that the British Acts since the Peace militate against the payment by narrowing the means by which those debts might have been paid when they were contracted, and which ought to be considered as constituant parts of the contract."

"June 17.—I received your last to the 21st May. I am just now informed of Messrs. Parker and Cutting setting off to-morrow morning for Paris by whom this will be delivered to you. Nothing new is showing here. The trial of Hastings, and the Examination of evidence before the house of Commons into the Slave Trade still continue.

"I wrote Sir Joseph Banks an account of my Experiment Arch. In his answer he informs me of its being read before the Royal Society who expressed 'great satisfaction at the Communication.' 'I expect' says Sir Joseph 'many improvements from your Countrymen who think with vigor, and are in a great measure free from those shackles of Theory which are imposed on the minds of our people before they are capable of exerting their mental faculties to advantage.' In the close of his letter he says : 'We have lost poor Ledyard. He had agreed with certain Moors to conduct him to Sennar. The time for their departure was arrived when he found himself ill, and took a large dose of Emetic Tartar, burst a blood-vessel in the operation, which carried him off in three days. We sincerely lament his loss, as the papers we have received from him are full of those emana-

---

[1] This and other parts of Paine's correspondence were forwarded to Washington.

tions of spirit, which taught you to construct a Bridge without any reference to the means used by your predecessors in that art.' I have wrote to the Walkers and proposed to them to manufacture me a compleat Bridge and erect it in London, and afterwards put it up to sale. I do this by way of bringing forward a Bridge over the Thames—which appears to me the most advantageous of all objects. For, if only a fifth of the persons, at a half penny each, pass over a new Bridge as now pass over the old ones the tolls will pay 25 per Cent besides what will arise from carriage and horses. Mrs. Williams tells me that her letters from America mention Dr. Franklin as being exceedingly ill. I have been to see the Cotton Mills,—the Potteries—the Steel furnaces—Tin plate manufacture—White lead manufacture. All those things might be easily carried on in America. I saw a few days ago part of a hand bill of what was called a geometrical wheelbarrow,—but cannot find where it is to be seen. The Idea is one of those that needed only to be thought of,—for it is very easy to conceive that if a wheelbarrow, as it is called, be driven round a piece of land,—a sheet of paper may be placed in it—so as to receive by the tracings of a Pencil, regulated by a little Mechanism—the figure and content of the land—and that neither Theodolite nor chain are necessary."

"ROTHERHAM, YORKSHIRE, July 13.—The Walkers are to find all the materials, and fit and frame them ready for erecting, put them on board a vessel & send them to London. I am to undertake all expense from that time & to compleat the erecting. We intend first to exhibit it and afterwards put it up to sale, or dispose of it by private contract, and after paying the expences of each party the remainder to be equally divided—one half theirs, the other mine. My principal object in this plan is to open the way for a Bridge over the Thames. . . . I shall now have occasion to draw upon some funds I have in America. I have one thousand Dollars stock in the Bank at Philadelphia, and two years interest due upon it last April, £180 in the hands of General Morris ; £40 with Mr. Constable of New York ; a house at Borden Town, and a farm at New Rochelle. The stock and interest in the Bank, which Mr. Willing manages for me, is the easiest negotiated, and full sufficient for what I shall want. On this fund

I have drawn fifteen guineas payable to Mr. Trumbull, tho' I shall not want the money longer than till the Exhibition and sale of the Bridge. I had rather draw than ask to borrow of any body here. If you go to America this year I shall be very glad if you can manage this matter for me, by giving me credit for two hundred pounds, on London, and receiving that amount of Mr. Willing. I am not acquainted with the method of negotiating money matters, but if you can accommodate me in this, and will direct me how the transfer is to be made, I shall be much obliged to you. Please direct to me under cover to Mr. Trumbull. I have some thoughts of coming over to France for two or three weeks, as I shall have little to do here until the Bridge is ready for erecting.

"September 15.—When I left Paris I was to return with the Model, but I could now bring over a compleat Bridge. Tho' I have a slender opinion of myself for executive business, I think, upon the whole that I have managed this matter tolerable well. With no money to spare for such an undertaking I am the sole Patentee here, and connected with one of the first and best established houses in the Nation. But absent from America I feel a craving desire to return and I can scarcely forbear weeping at the thoughts of your going and my staying behind.

"Accept my dear Sir, my most hearty thanks for your many services and friendship. Remember me with an overflowing affection to my dear America—the people and the place. Be so kind to shake hands with them for me, and tell our beloved General Washington, and my old friend Dr. Franklin how much I long to see them. I wish you would spend a day with General Morris of Morrisania, and present my best wishes to all the family.—But I find myself wandering into a melancholy subject that will be tiresome to read,—so wishing you a prosperous passage, and a happy meeting with all your friends and mine, I remain yours affectionately, etc.

"I shall be very glad to hear from you when you arrive. If you direct for me to the care of Mr. Benjamin Vaughn it will find me.—Please present my friendship to Captain Nicholson and family of New York, and to Mr. and Mrs. Few.

"September 18.—I this moment receive yours of ye 13 int. which being Post Night, affords me the welcome opportunity of acknowledging it. I wrote you on the 15th by post—but I was so full of the thoughts of America and my American friends that I forgot France.

"The people of this Country speak very differently on the affairs of France. The mass of them, so far as I can collect, say that France is a much freer Country than England. The Peers, the Bishops, &c. say the National Assembly has gone too far. There are yet in this country, very considerable remains of the feudal System which people did not see till the revolution in france placed it before their eyes. While the multitude here could be terrified with the cry and apprehension of Arbitrary power, wooden shoes, popery, and such like stuff, they thought themselves by comparison an extraordinary free people ; but this bugbear now loses its force, and they appear to me to be turning their eyes towards the Aristocrats of their own Nation. This is a new mode of conquering, and I think it will have its effect.

"I am looking out for a place to erect my Bridge, within some of the Squares would be very convenient. I had thought of Soho Square, where Sir Joseph Banks lives, but he is now in Lincolnshire. I expect it will be ready for erecting and in London by the latter end of October. Whether I shall then sell it in England or bring it over to Paris, and re-erect it there, I have not determined in my mind. In order to bring any kind of a contract forward for the Seine, it is necessary it should be seen, and, as œconomy will now be a principle in the Government, it will have a better chance than before.

"If you should pass thro' Borden Town in Jersey, which is not out of your way from Philadelphia to New York, I shall be glad you would enquire out my particular friend Col. Kirkbride. You will be very much pleased with him. His house is my home when in that part of the Country—and it was there that I made the Model of my Bridge."

CHAPTER XIX.

THE KEY OF THE BASTILLE.

In June, 1777, the Emperor Joseph II. visited his sister, the Queen of France, and passed a day at Nantes. The Count de Menou, commandant of the place, pointed out in the harbor, among the flags raised in his honor, one bearing thirteen stars. The Emperor turned away his eyes, saying : " I cannot look on that ; my own profession is to be royalist."

Weber, foster-brother of Marie Antoinette, who reports the Emperor's remark, recognized the fate of France in those thirteen stars. That republic, he says, was formed by the subjects of a King, aided by another King. These French armies, mingling their flags with those of America, learned a new language. Those warriors, the flower of their age, went out Frenchmen and returned Americans. They returned to a court, but decorated with republican emblems and showing the scars of Liberty. Lafayette, it is said, had in his study a large *carton*, splendidly framed, in two columns : on one was inscribed the American Declaration of Independence ; the other was blank, awaiting the like Declaration of France.[1]

[1] " Mémoires concernant Marie-Antoinette," pp. 34-79.

The year 1789 found France afflicted with a sort of famine, its finances in disorder; while the people, their eyes directed to the new world by the French comrades of Washington, beheld that great chieftain inaugurated as president of a prosperous republic. The first pamphlet of Thomas Paine, expurgated in translation of anti-monarchism, had been widely circulated, and John Adams (1779) found himself welcomed in France as the supposed author of "Common Sense." The lion's skin dropped from Paine's disgusted enemy, and when, ten years later, the lion himself became known in Paris, he was hailed with enthusiasm. This was in the autumn of 1789, when Paine witnessed the scenes that ushered in the "crowned republic," from which he hoped so much. Jefferson had sailed in September, and Paine was recognized by Lafayette and other leaders as the representative of the United States. To him Lafayette gave for presentation to Washington the Key of the destroyed Bastille, ever since visible at Mount Vernon,—symbol of the fact that, in Paine's words, "the principles of America opened the Bastille."

But now an American enemy of Paine's principles more inveterate than Adams found himself similarly eclipsed in Paris by the famous author. Early in 1789 Gouverneur Morris came upon the stage of events in Europe. He was entrusted by the President with a financial mission which, being secret, swelled him to importance in the imagination of courtiers. At Jefferson's request Gouverneur Morris posed to Houdon for the bust of

Washington ; and when, to Morris' joy, Jefferson departed, he posed politically as Washington to the eyes of Europe. He was scandalized that Jefferson should retain recollections of the Declaration of Independence strong enough to desire for France "a downright republican form of government"; and how it happened that under Jefferson's secretaryship of state this man, whom even Hamilton pronounced "an exotic" in a republic, was presently appointed Minister to France, is a mystery remaining to be solved.

Morris had a "high old time" in Europe. Intimacy with Washington secured him influence with Lafayette, and the fine ladies of Paris, seeking official favors for relatives and lovers, welcomed him to the boudoirs, baths, and bedrooms to which his diary now introduces the public.

It was but natural that such a man, just as he had been relieved of the overlaying Jefferson, should try to brush Paine aside. On January 26, 1790, he enters in his diary :

"To-day, at half-past three, I go to M. de Lafayette's. He tells me that he wishes to have a meeting of Mr. Short, Mr. Paine, and myself, to consider their judiciary, because his place imposes on him the necessity of being right. I tell him that Paine can do him no good, for that, although he has an excellent pen to write, he has but an indifferent head to think."

Eight years before, Gouverneur Morris had joined Robert Morris in appealing to the author to enlighten the nation on the subject of finance and the direction of the war. He had also confessed to Paine that he had been duped by Silas Deane, who, by the way, was now justifying all that Paine had said of him by hawking his secret letter-books in

London.   Now, in Paris, Morris discovers that Paine has but an indifferent head to think.[1]

Gouverneur Morris was a fascinating man. His diary and letters, always entertaining, reveal the secret of his success in twisting the Constitution and Jefferson and Washington around his fingers in several important junctures. To Paine also he was irresistible. His cordial manners disarm suspicion, and we presently find the author pouring into the ear of his secret detractor what state secrets he learns in London.

On March 17, 1790, Paine left Paris to see after his Bridge in Yorkshire, now near completion. On the day before, he writes to a friend in Philadelphia how prosperously everything is going on in France, where Lafayette is acting the part of a Washington ; how the political reformation is sure to influence England ; and how he longs for America.

"I wish most anxiously to see my much loved America. It is the country from whence all reformation must originally spring. I despair of seeing an abolition of the infernal traffic in negroes. We must push that matter further on your side of the water. I wish that a few well-instructed could be sent among their brethren in bondage ; for until they are able to take their own part nothing will be done."[2]

---

[1] "Diary and Letters of Gouverneur Morris." Edited by Anne Cary Morris. i., p. 286.

[2] One cannot help wondering how, in this matter, Paine got along with his friend Jefferson, who, at the very time of his enthusiasm for the French Revolution, had a slave in his house at Challiot. Paine was not of the philanthropic type portrayed in the "Biglow Papers" :

"I du believe in Freedom's cause
    Ez fur away ez Payris is ;
I love to see her stick her claws
    In them infarnal Phayrisees.
It 's well enough agin a king
    To dror resolves and triggers,
But libbaty 's a kind 'o thing
    That don't agree with niggers."

On his arrival in London he has the happiness
of meeting his old friend General Morris of Morrisania, and his wife. Gouverneur is presently over
there, to see his brother ; and in the intervals of danc-
ing attendance at the opera on titled ladies—among
them Lady Dunmore, whose husband desolated the
Virginia coast,—he gets Paine's confidences.[1] Poor
Paine was an easy victim of any show of personal
kindness, especially when it seemed like the magnanimity of a political opponent.

The historic sense may recognize a picturesque
incident in the selection by Lafayette of Thomas
Paine to convey the Key of the Bastille to Washington. In the series of intellectual and moral
movements which culminated in the French Revolution, the Bastille was especially the prison of
Paine's forerunners, the writers, and the place
where their books were burned. " The gates of
the Bastille," says Rocquain, "were opened wide
for abbés, savants, brilliant intellects, professors of
the University and doctors of the Sorbonne, all
accused of writing or reciting verses against the
King, casting reflections on the Government, or
publishing books in favor of Deism, and contrary
to good morals. Diderot was one of the first
arrested, and it was during his detention that he
conceived the plan of his ' Encyclopedia.' "[2]

The coming Key was announced to Washington
with the following letters :

---

[1] " Diary," etc., i., pp. 339, 341.

[2] " L'Esprit revolutionaire avant la Revolution." A good service has
just been done by Miss Hunting in translating and condensing the admirable historical treatise of M. Félix Rocquain on " The Revolutionary Spirit
Preceding the Revolution," for which Professor Huxley has written a preface.

"LONDON, May 1, 1790.—Sir,—Our very good friend the Marquis de la Fayette has entrusted to my care the Key of the Bastille, and a drawing, handsomely framed, representing the demolition of that detestable prison, as a present to your Excellency, of which his letter will more particularly inform. I feel myself happy in being the person thro' whom the Marquis has conveyed this early trophy of the Spoils of despotism, and the first ripe fruits of American principles transplanted into Europe, to his great master and patron. When he mentioned to me the present he intended you, my heart leaped with joy. It is something so truly in character that no remarks can illustrate it, and is more happily expressive of his remembrance of his American friends than any letters can convey. That the principles of America opened the Bastille is not to be doubted, and therefore the Key comes to the right place.

"I beg leave to suggest to your Excellency the propriety of congratulating the King and Queen of France (for they have been our friends,) and the National Assembly, on the happy example they are giving to Europe. You will see by the King's speech, which I enclose, that he prides himself on being at the head of the Revolution ; and I am certain that such a congratulation will be well received and have a good effect.

"I should rejoice to be the direct bearer of the Marquis's present to your Excellency, but I doubt I shall not be able to see my much loved America till next Spring. I shall therefore send it by some *American* vessel to New York. I have permitted no drawing to be taken here, tho' it has been often requested, as I think there is a propriety that it should first be presented. B[ut] Mr. West wishes Mr. Trumbull to make a painting of the presentation of the Key to you.

"I returned from France to London about five weeks ago, and I am engaged to return to Paris when the Constitution shall be proclaimed, and to carry the American flag in the procession. I have not the least doubt of the final and compleat success of the French Revolution. Little Ebbings and Flowings, for and against, the natural companions of revolutions, sometimes appear ; but the full current of it, is, in my opinion, as fixed as the Gulph Stream.

"I have manufactured a Bridge (a single arch) of one hundred and ten feet span, and five feet high from the cord of the arch.   It is now on board a vessel coming from Yorkshire to London, where it is to be erected.   I see nothing yet to disappoint my hopes of its being advantageous to me.   It is this only which keeps me [in] Europe, and happy shall I be when I shall have it in my power to return to America.   I have not heard of Mr. Jefferson since he sailed, except of his arrival. As I have always indulged the belief of having many friends in America, or rather no enemies, I have [*mutilated*] to mention but my affectionate [*mutilated*] and am Sir with the greatest respect, &c.

"If any of my friends are disposed to favor me with a letter it will come to hand by addressing it to the care of Benjamin Vaughn Esq., Jeffries Square, London."

"LONDON, May 31, 1790.—SIR,—By Mr. James Morris, who sailed in the May Packet, I transmitted you a letter from the Marquis de la Fayette, at the same time informing you that the Marquis had entrusted to my charge the Key of the Bastille, and a drawing of that prison, as a present to your Excellency.   Mr. J. Rutledge, jun'r, had intended coming in the ship 'Marquis de la Fayette,' and I had chosen that opportunity for the purpose of transmitting the present ; but, the ship not sailing at the time appointed, Mr. Rutledge takes his passage on the Packet, and I have committed to his care that trophie of Liberty which I know it will give you pleasure to receive. The french Revolution is not only compleat but triumphant, and the envious despotism of this nation is compelled to own the magnanimity with which it has been conducted.

"The political hemisphere is again clouded by a dispute between England and Spain, the circumstances of which you will hear before this letter can arrive.   A Messenger was sent from hence the 6th inst. to Madrid with very peremptory demands, and to wait there only forty-eight hours.   His return has been expected for two or three days past.   I was this morning at the Marquis del Campo's but nothing is yet arrived. Mr. Rutledge sets off at four o'clock this afternoon, but should any news arrive before the making up the mail on Wednesday June 2, I will forward it to you under cover.

"The views of this Court as well as of the Nation, so far as they extend to South America, are not for the purpose of freedom, but conquest.   They already talk of sending some of the young branches to reign over them, and to pay off their national debt with the produce of their Mines. The Bondage of those countries will, as far as I can perceive, be prolonged by what this Court has in contemplation.

"My Bridge is arrived and I have engaged a place to erect it in. A little time will determine its fate, but I yet see no cause to doubt of its success, tho' it is very probable that a War, should it break out, will as in all new things prevent its progress so far as regards profits.

"In the partition in the Box, which contains the Key of the Bastille, I have put up half a dozen Razors, manufactured from Cast-steel made at the Works where the Bridge was constructed, which I request you to accept as a little token from a very grateful heart.

"I received about a week ago a letter from Mr. G. Clymer. It is dated the 4th February, but has been travelling ever since. I request you to acknowledge it for me and that I will answer it when my Bridge is erected. With much affection to all my friends, and many wishes to see them again, I am, etc."

Washington received the Key at New York, along with this last letter, and on August 10, 1790, acknowledges Paine's "agreeable letters."

"It must, I dare say, give you great pleasure to learn by repeated opportunities, that our new government answers its purposes as well as could have been reasonably expected, that we are gradually overcoming the difficulties which presented in its first organization, and that our prospects in general are growing more favorable."

Paine is said by several biographers to have gone to Paris in the May of this year. No doubt he was missed from London, but it was probably because he had gone to Thetford, where his mother died about the middle of May. Gouverneur Morris reports interviews with him August 8th and 15th, in London. The beautiful iron bridge, 110 feet long, had been erected in June at Leasing-Green (now Paddington-Green) at the joint expense of Paine and Peter Whiteside, an American merchant in London. It was attracting a fair number of visitors, at a shilling each, also favorable press notices, and all promised well.

So Paine was free to run over to Paris, where Carlyle mentions him, this year, as among the English " missionaries." [1] It was a brief visit, however, for October finds him again in London, drawn probably by intimations of disaster to the interests of his Bridge. Whiteside had failed, and his assignees, finding on his books £620 debited to Paine's Bridge, came upon the inventor for the money ; no doubt unfairly, for it seems to have been Whiteside's investment, but Paine, the American merchants Cleggett and Murdoch becoming his bail, scraped together the money and paid it. Probably he lost through Whiteside's bankruptcy other moneys, among them the sum he had deposited to supply his mother with her weekly nine shillings. Paine was too much accustomed to straitened means to allow this affair to trouble him much. The Bridge exhibition went on smoothly enough. Country gentlemen, deputations from riverside towns, visited it, and suggested negotiations for utilizing the invention. The snug copyright fortune which the author had sacrificed to the American cause seemed about to be recovered by the inventor.

[1] " Her Paine ; rebellious Staymaker ; unkempt ; who feels that he, a single needleman, did, by his ' Common Sense ' pamphlet, free America ;— that he can and will free all this World ; perhaps even the other."—French Revolution.

But again the Cause arose before him ; he must part from all—patent interests, literary leisure, fine society—and take the hand of Liberty, undowered, but as yet unstained. He must beat his bridge-iron into a Key that shall unlock the British Bastille, whose walls he sees steadily closing around the people.

CHAPTER XX.

"THE RIGHTS OF MAN."

EDMUND BURKE'S " Reflexions on the Revolution in France" appeared about November 1, 1790. Paine was staying at the Angel inn, Islington, and there immediately began his reply. With his sentiment for anniversaries, he may have begun his work on November 4th, in honor of the English Revolution, whose centenary celebration he had witnessed three years before. In a hundred years all that had been turned into a more secure lease of monarchy. Burke's pamphlet founded on that Revolution a claim that the throne represented a perpetual popular franchise. Paine might have heard under his window the boys, with their

> " Please to remember
> The fifth of November,"

and seen their effigy of Guy Fawkes, which in two years his own effigy was to replace. But no misgivings of that kind haunted him. For his eyes the omens hung over the dark Past ; on the horizon a new day was breaking in morning stars and stripes. With the inspiration of perfect faith, born of the sacrifices that had ended so triumphantly in America, Paine wrote the book which, coming from such deep, the deeps answered.

Although Paine had been revising his religion, much of the orthodox temper survived in him; notably, he still required some kind of Satan to bring out his full energy. In America it had been George III., duly hoofed and horned, at whom his inkstand was hurled; now it is Burke, who appeared with all the seductive brilliancy of a fallen Lucifer. No man had been more idealized by Paine than Burke. Not only because of his magnificent defence of American patriots, but because of his far-reaching exposures of despotism, then creeping, snake-like, from one skin to another. At the very time that Paine was writing "Common Sense," Burke was pointing out that "the power of the crown, almost dead and rotten as prerogative, has grown up anew, with much more strength and far less odium, under the name of influence." He had given liberalism the sentence: "The forms of a free and the ends of an arbitrary government are things not altogether incompatible." He had been the intimate friend of Priestley and other liberals, and when Paine arrived in 1787 had taken him to his heart and home. Paine maintained his faith in Burke after Priestley and Price had re-marked a change. In the winter of 1789, when the enthusiastic author was sending out jubilant missives to Washington and others, announcing the glorious transformation of France, he sent one to Burke, who might even then have been preparing the attack on France, delivered early in the Parliament of 1790. When, soon after his return from Paris, Paine mingled with the mourners for their lost leader, he was informed that Burke had for some time been a "masked pensioner," to the extent of £1,500 per annum. This rumor Paine mentioned, and it was not denied, whether because true, or because Burke was looking forward to his subsequent pension of £2,500, is doubtful. Burke's book preceded the events in France which caused reaction in the minds of Wordsworth and other thinkers in England and America. The French were then engaged in adapting their government to the free principles of which Burke himself had long been the eloquent advocate. It was not without justice that Erskine charged him with having challenged a Revolution in England, by claiming that its hereditary monarchy was bound on the people by a compact of the previous century, and that, good or bad, they had no power to alter it. The power of Burke's pamphlet lay largely in his deftness with the methods of those he assailed. He had courted their company, familiarized himself with their ideas, received their confidences. This had been especially the case with Paine. So there seemed to be a *soupçon* of treachery in his subtleties and his disclosures.

But after all he did not know Paine. He had not imagined the completeness with which the struggle in America had trained this man in every art of controversy. Grappling with Philadelphia Tories, Quakers, reactionists, with aristocrats on the one hand and anarchists on the other, Paine had been familiarized beyond all men with every deep and by-way of the subject on which Burke had ventured. Where Burke had dabbled Paine had dived. Never did man reputed wise go beyond his depth in such a bowl as when Burke appealed to a revolution of 1688 as authoritative. If one revolution could be authoritative, why not another? How did the seventeenth century secure a monopoly in revolution? If a revolution in one century could transfer the throne from one family to another, why might not the same power in another transfer it to an elective monarch, or a president, or leave it vacant?

To demolish Burke was the least part of Paine's task. Burke was, indeed, already answered by the government established in America, presided over by a man to whom the world paid homage. To Washington, Paine's work was dedicated. His real design was to write a Constitution for the English nation. And to-day the student of political history may find in Burke's pamphlet the fossilized, and in Paine's (potentially) the living, Constitution of Great Britain.

For adequacy to a purpose Paine's "Common Sense" and his "Rights of Man" have never been surpassed. Washington pronounced the former unanswerable, and Burke passed the like verdict on the latter when he said that the refutation it deserved was "that of criminal justice." There was not the slightest confusion of ideas and aim in this book. In laying down first principles of human government, Paine imports no preference of his own for one form or another. The people have the right to establish any government they choose, be it democracy or monarchy,—if not hereditary. He explains with nicety of consecutive statement that a real Constitution must be of the people, and for

the people.   That is, for the people who make it;
they have no right, by any hereditary principle, to
bind another people, unborn.   His principle of the
rights of man was founded in the religious axiom of
his age that all men derived existence from a divine
maker.   To say men are born equal means that
they are created equal.   Precedent contradicts precedent, authority is against authority, in all our
appeals to antiquity, until we reach the time when
man came from the hands of his maker.   "What
was he then?   Man.   Man was his high and only
title, and a higher cannot be given him."   "God
said Let us make man in our own image."   No distinction between men is pointed out.   All histories,
all traditions, of the creation agree as to the unity
of man.   Generation being the mode by which
creation is carried forward, every child derives its
existence from God.   "The world is as new to him
as it was to the first man that existed, and his natural right to it is of the same kind."   On these natural rights Paine founds man's civil rights.   To
secure his natural rights the individual deposits
some of them—*e. g.* the right to judge in his own
cause—in the common stock of society.

Paine next proceeds to distinguish governments
which have arisen out of this social compact from
those which have not.   Governments are classified as
founded on—(1) superstition; (2) power; (3) the
common interests of society, and the common rights
of man : that is, on priestcraft, on conquest, on
reason.   A national constitution is the act of the
people antecedent to government; a government
cannot therefore determine or alter the organic law
it temporarily represents.   Pitt's bill to reform Par-

liament involves the absurdity of trusting an admittedly vitiated body to reform itself. The judges are to sit in their own case. " The right of reform is in the nation in its original character, and the constitutional method would be by a general convention elected for the purpose." The organization of the aggregate of rights which individuals concede to society, for the security of all rights, makes the Republic. So far as the rights have been surrendered to extraneous authority, as of priest-craft, hereditary power, or conquest,—it is Despotism.

To set forth these general principles was Paine's first design. His next aim was to put on record the true and exact history of events in France up to the year 1791. This history, partly that of an eyewitness, partly obtained from the best men in France—Lafayette, Danton, Brissot, and others,—and by mingling with the masses, constitutes the most fresh and important existing contribution to our knowledge of the movement in its early stages. The majority of histories of the French Revolution, Carlyle's especially, are vitiated by reason of their inadequate attention to Paine's narrative. There had been then few serious outbreaks of the mob, but of these Burke had made the most. Paine contends that the outrages can no more be charged against the French than the London riots of 1780 against the English nation ; then retorts that mobs are the inevitable consequence of misgovernment.

"It is by distortedly exalting some men, that others are distortedly debased. A vast mass of mankind are degradedly thrown into the background of the human picture, to bring forward, with greater glare, the puppet show of state and aristocracy. In the commencement of a revolution, those men are rather followers of the camp than of the standard of liberty, and have yet to be instructed how to use it."

Part I. of "The Rights of Man" was printed by Johnson in time for the opening of Parliament (February), but this publisher became frightened, and only a few copies bearing his name found their way into private hands,—one of these being in the British Museum. J. S. Jordan, 166 Fleet Street, consented to publish it, and Paine, entrusting it to a committee of his friends—William Godwin, Thomas Holcroft, and Thomas Brand Hollis— took his departure for Paris.[1] From that city he sent a brief preface which appeared with Jordan's first edition, March 13, 1791. Oldys (Chalmers) asserts that the work was altered by Jordan. This assertion, in its sweeping form, is disproved not only by Holcroft's note to Godwin, but by a comparison of the "Johnson" and "Jordan" volumes in the British Museum.[2]

[1] " I have got it—If this do not cure my cough it is a damned perverse mule of a cough—The pamphlet—From the row—But mum—We don't sell it—Oh, no—Ears and Eggs—Verbatim, except the addition of a short preface, which as you have not seen, I send you my copy—Not a single castration (Laud be unto God and J. S. Jordan!) can I discover—Hey for the New Jerusalem! The Millennium! And peace and eternal beatitude be unto the soul of Thomas Paine!"—C. Kegan Paul's "William Godwin." In supposing that Paine may have gone to Paris before his book appeared (March 13th), I have followed Rickman, who says the work was written " partly at the Angel, at Islington, partly in Harding Street, Fetter Lane, and finished at Versailles." He adds that " many hundred thousand more copies were rapidly sold." But I have no certain trace of Paine in Paris in 1791 earlier than April 8th.

[2] This comparison was made for me by a careful writer, Mr. J. M. Wheeler, of London, who finds, with a few corrections in spelling, but one case of softening: " P. 60, in Johnson Paine wrote 'Everything in the English government appears to me the reverse of what it ought to be' which in Jordan is modified to ' Many things,' etc."

The preface to which Holcroft alludes is of biographical interest both as regards Paine and Burke. As it does not appear in the American edition it is here inserted :

" From the part Mr. Burke took in the American Revolution, it was natural that I should consider him a friend to mankind ; and as our acquaintance commenced on that ground, it would have been more agreeable to me to have had cause to continue in that opinion, than to change it

" At the time Mr. Burke made his violent speech last winter in the English Parliament against the French Revolution and the National Assembly, I was in Paris, and had written him, but a short time before, to inform him how prosperously matters were going on. Soon after this I saw his advertisement of the Pamphlet he intended to publish. As the attack was to be made in a language but little studied, and less understood, in France, and as everything suffers by translation, I promised some of the friends of the Revolution in that country, that whenever Mr. Burke's Pamphlet came forth, I would answer it. This appeared to me the more necessary to be done, when I saw the flagrant misrepresentations which Mr. Burke's Pamphlet contains ; and that while it is an outrageous abuse of the French Revolution, and the principles of Liberty, it is an imposition on the rest of the world.

" I am the more astonished and disappointed at this conduct in Mr. Burke, as (from the circumstance I am going to mention) I had formed other expectations.

" I had seen enough of the miseries of war, to wish it might never more have existence in the world, and that some other mode might be found out to settle the differences that should occasionally arise in the neighbourhood of nations. This certainly might be done if Courts were disposed to set honestly about it, or if countries were enlightened enough not to be made the dupes of Courts. The people of America had been bred up in the same prejudices against France, which at that time characterized the people of England ; but experience and an acquaintance with the French Nation have most effectually shown to the Americans the falsehood of those prejudices ; and

I do not believe that a more cordial and confidential intercourse exists between any two countries than between America and France.

"When I came to France in the spring of 1787, the Archbishop of Thoulouse was then Minister, and at that time highly esteemed. I became much acquainted with the private Secretary of that Minister, a man of an enlarged benevolent heart; and found that his sentiments and my own perfectly agreed with respect to the madness of war, and the wretched impolicy of two nations, like England and France, continually worrying each other, to no other end than that of a mutual increase of burdens and taxes. That I might be assured I had not misunderstood him, nor he me, I put the substance of our opinions into writing, and sent it to him; subjoining a request, that if I should see among the people of England any disposition to cultivate a better understanding between the two nations than had hitherto prevailed, how far I might be authorised to say that the same disposition prevailed on the part of France? He answered me by letter in the most unreserved manner, and that not for himself only, but for the Minister, with whose knowledge the letter was declared to be written.

"I put this letter into the hands of Mr. Burke almost three years ago, and left it with him, where it still remains, hoping, and at the same time naturally expecting, from the opinion I had conceived of him, that he would find some opportunity of making a good use of it, for the purpose of removing those errors and prejudices which two neighbouring nations, from the want of knowing each other, had entertained, to the injury of both.

"When the French Revolution broke out, it certainly afforded to Mr. Burke an opportunity of doing some good, had he been disposed to it; instead of which, no sooner did he see the old prejudices wearing away, than he immediately began sowing the seeds of a new inveteracy, as if he were afraid that England and France would cease to be enemies. That there are men in all countries who get their living by war, and by keeping up the quarrels of Nations, is as shocking as it is true; but when those who are concerned in the government of a country, make it their study to sow discord, and cultivate prejudices between Nations, it becomes the more unpardonable.

"With respect to a paragraph in this work alluding to Mr. Burke's having a pension, the report has been some time in circulation, at least two months; and as a person is often the last to hear what concerns him the most to know, I have mentioned it, that Mr. Burke may have an opportunity of contradicting the rumour, if he thinks proper."

"The Rights of Man" produced a great impression from the first. It powerfully reinforced the "Constitutional Society," formed seven years before, which Paine had joined. The book was adopted as their new *Magna Charta*. Their enthusiasm was poured forth on March 23d in resolutions which Daniel Williams, secretary, is directed to transmit "to all our corresponding Constitutional Societies in England, Scotland, and France." In Ireland the work was widely welcomed. I find a note that "at a numerous meeting of the Whigs of the Capital [Dublin] on Tuesday the 5th of April, Hugh Crothers in the chair," a committee was appointed to consider the most effectual mode of disseminating Mr. Paine's pamphlet on "The Rights of Man."

In order to be uniform with Burke's pamphlet the earlier editions of "The Rights of Man," were in the three-shilling style. The proceeds enriched the Society for Constitutional Information, though Paine had been drained of funds by the failure of Whiteside. Gouverneur Morris, as appears by the subjoined extracts from his diary, is disgusted with Paine's "wretched apartments" in Paris, in which, however, the reader may see something finer than the diarist's luxury, which the author might have rivalled with the means devoted to his Cause. This

was perhaps what Morris and Paine's friend Hodges
agreed in deeming a sort of lunacy.

"April 8. Return home, and read the answer of Paine to
Burke's book ; there are good things in the answer as well as
in the book. Paine calls on me. He says that he found great
difficulty in prevailing on any bookseller to publish his book ;
that it is extremely popular in England, and, of course, the
writer, which he considers as one of the many uncommon
revolutions of this age. He turns the conversation on times
of yore, and as he mentions me among those who were his
enemies, I frankly acknowledge that I urged his dismissal
from the office he held of secretary to the Committee of
Foreign Affairs."

"April 16. This morning I visit Paine and Mr. Hodges.
The former is abroad, the latter is in the wretched apartments
they occupy. He speaks of Paine as being a little mad, which
is not improbable."

"April 25. This morning Paine calls and tells me that the
Marquis de Lafayette has accepted the position of head of
the National Guards."

"May 1. Dine with Montmorin. Bouinville is here. He
is just returned from England. He tells me that Paine's book
works mightily in England."

Up to this point Paine had, indeed, carried England with him,—for England was at heart with Fox
and the Opposition. When Burke made his first
attack on the French Revolution (February 9, 1790),
he was repeatedly called to order ; and Fox—with
tears, for their long friendship was breaking forever—overwhelmed Burke with his rebuke. Even
Pitt did not say a word for him. His pamphlet
nine months later was ascribed to inspiration of the
King, from whom he expected favors ; and although
the madmen under whom the French Revolution
fell presently came to the support of his case,

Burke personally never recovered his place in the esteem of England.   That the popular instinct was true, and that Burke was playing a deeper game than appeared, was afterwards revealed in the archives of England and France.[1]

There was every reason why Paine's reply should carry liberal statesmen with him.   His pamphlet was statesmanlike.   The French Constitution at that time was the inchoate instrument beginning with the " Declaration of Rights," adopted on Lafayette's proposal (August 26, 1789), and containing provisions contrary to Paine's views.   It recognized the reigning house, and made its executive power hereditary.   Yet so free was Paine from pedantry, so anxious for any peaceful advance, that it was at the expected inauguration of this Constitution he had consented to bear the American flag, and in his reply to Burke he respects the right of a people to establish even hereditary executive, the right of constitutional reform being retained. " The French constitution distinguishes between the king and the sovereign ; it considers the station of the king as official, and places sovereignty in the nation."   In the same practical way he deals with other survivals in the French Constitution—such as clericalism, and the property qualification for suffrage—by dwelling on their mitigations, while reaffirming his own principles on these points.

---

[1] " Thirty thousand copies of Burke's book were circulated in all the courts and among the European aristocracy as so many lighted brands to set Europe in flames.   During this time the author, by his secret correspondence, excited Queen Marie-Antoinette, the court, the foreigners, to conspire against the Revolution. ' No compromises with rebels !' he wrote ; ' appeal to sovereign neighbors ; above all trust to the support of foreign armies.' "—" Histoire de France," par Henri Martin, i., p. 151.

A very important part of Paine's answer was that which related to the United States. Burke, the most famous defender of American revolutionists, was anxious to separate their movement from that in France. Paine, with ample knowledge, proved how largely the uprising in France was due to the training of Lafayette and other French officers in America, and to the influence of Franklin, who was "not the diplomatist of a court, but of man." He also drew attention to the effect of the American State Constitutions, which were a grammar of liberty.[1] He points out that under this transatlantic influence French liberalism had deviated from the line of its forerunners,—from Montesquieu, "obliged to divide himself between principle and prudence"; Voltaire, "both the flatterer and satirist of despotism"; Rousseau, leaving "the mind in love with an object without describing the means of possessing it"; Turgot, whose maxims are directed to "reform the administration of government rather than the government itself." To these high praise is awarded, but they all had to be filtered through America.

[1] Dr. Franklin had these constitutions translated, and presented them in a finely bound volume to the King. According to Paine, who must have heard it from Franklin, Vergennes resisted their publication, but was obliged to give way to public demand. Paine could not allude to the effect of his own work, "Common Sense," which may have been the more effective because its argument against monarchy was omitted from the translation. But his enemies did not fail to credit his pen with the catastrophes in France. John Adams declares that the Constitution of Pennsylvania was ascribed wrongly to Franklin; it was written by Paine and three others; Turgot, Condorcet, and the Duke de la Rochefoucauld were enamored of it, and two of them "owed their final and fatal catastrophe to this blind love" (Letter to S. Perley, June 19, 1809). Whence Cheetham, dwelling on the enormity of the "single representative assembly," queries: "May not Paine's constitution of Pennsylvania have been the cause of the tyranny of Robespierre?"

And it goes without saying that it was not the reactionary America with which John Adams and Gouverneur Morris had familiarized Burke. "The Rights of Man" was the first exposition of the republicanism of Jefferson, Madison, and Edmund Randolph that ever appeared. And as this republicanism was just then in deadly struggle with reaction, the first storm raised by Paine's book occurred in America. It was known in America that Paine was about to beard the British lion in his den, and to expectant ears the roar was heard before its utterance.

"Paine's answer to Burke (writes Madison to Jefferson, May 1st) has not yet been received here [New York]. The moment it can be got, Freneau tells me, it will be published in Child's paper [*Daily Advertiser*]. It is said that the pamphlet has been suppressed, and that the author withdrew to France before or immediately after its appearance. This may account for his not sending copies to his friends in this country."

Mr. Beckley, however, had by this time received a copy and loaned it to Jefferson, with a request that he would send it to J. B. Smith, whose brother, S. H. Smith, printed it with the following Preface:

"The following Extracts from a note accompanying a copy of this pamphlet for republication is so respectable a testing of its value, that the Printer hopes the distinguished writer will excuse its present appearance. It proceeds from a character equally eminent in the councils of America, and conversant in the affairs of France, from a long and recent residence at the Court of Versailles in the Diplomatic department; and at the same time that it does justice to the writings of Mr. Paine, it reflects honor on the source from which it flows by directing the mind to a contemplation of that Republican firmness and Democratic simplicity which endear their possessor to every friend of the Rights of Man.

"After some prefatory remarks the Secretary of State observes :

" ' I am extremely pleased to find it will be reprinted, and that something is at length to be publickly said against the political heresies which have sprung up among us.

" ' I have no doubt our citizens will rally a *second* time round the *standard* of Common Sense.' "

As the pamphlet had been dedicated to the President,[1] this encomium of the Secretary of State (" Jefferson " was not mentioned by the sagacious publisher) gave it the air of a manifesto by the administration. Had all been contrived, Paine's arrow could not have been more perfectly feathered to reach the heart of the anti-republican faction. The Secretary's allusion to " political heresies " was so plainly meant for the Vice-President that a million hands tossed the gauntlet to him, and supposed it was his own hand that took it up. These letters, to *The Columbian Centinel* (Boston), were indeed published in England as by " John Adams," and in the trial of Paine were quoted by the Attorney-General as proceeding from " the second in the executive government " of America. Had it been generally known, however, that they were by the Vice-President's son, John Quincy Adams, the effect might not have been very different on the father. Edmund Randolph, in view of John Adams' past services, felt some regret at the attacks on him, and wrote to Madison : " I

---

[1] " Sir, I present you a small treatise in defence of those principles of freedom which your exemplary virtue hath so eminently contributed to establish. That the rights of men may become as universal as your benevolence can wish, and that you may enjoy the happiness of seeing the new world regenerate the old, is the prayer of, Sir, your much obliged, and obedient humble servant, THOMAS PAINE."

should rejoice that the controversy has been excited, were it not that under the character of [Publicola] he, who was sufficiently depressed before, is now irredeemable in the public opinion without being the real author." The youth, however, was only in his twenty-fourth year, and pretty certainly under his father's inspiration.

It is improbable, however, that John Adams could have written such scholarly and self-restrained criticisms on any work by Paine, mere mention of whom always made him foam at the mouth. Publicola's arguments could not get a fair hearing amid surviving animosities against England and enthusiasm for a republican movement in France, as yet not a revolution, which promised the prevalence of American ideas in Europe. The actual England of that era, whose evils were powerfully portrayed by Paine, defeated in advance any theoretical estimate of the advantages of its unwritten Constitution. America had, too, an inventor's pride in its written Constitution, as yet untried by experience. Publicola assailed, successfully as I think, Paine's principle that a vitiated legislature could never be trusted to reform itself. It was answered that there is no reason why the people may not delegate to a legislature, renewed by suffrage, the power of altering even the organic law. Publicola contends that the people could not act in their original character in changing a constitution, in opposition to an existing legislature, without danger of anarchy and war; that if the people were in harmony with their legislature it could be trusted to carry out their amendments; that

a legislature without such constitutional powers
would nevertheless exercise them by forced constructions; and that the difficulty and delay of
gathering the people in convention might conceiv-
ably endanger the commonwealth, were the power
of fundamental alteration not delegated to the
legislature,—a concurrent right being reserved by
the people.

This philosophical statement, interesting in the
light of French revolutions and English evolutions,
recoiled on Publicola from the walls of Paine's
real fortress.   This was built of the fact that in
England the majority was not represented even in
the Commons, and that the people had no representation at all in two branches of their government.   Moreover, Paine's plea had been simply
for such reconstitution of government as would
enable the people to reform it without revolution
or convulsion.   Publicola was compelled to admit
that the English people had no resort but the right
of revolution, so that it appeared mere Monarchism
to argue against Paine's plea for a self-amending
constitution in England.

Publicola's retort on the Secretary's phrase,
" political heresies " (infelicitous from a free-
thinker),—" Does he consider this pamphlet of
Mr. Paine's as the canonical book of political
scripture,"—hurt Jefferson so much that he supposed himself harmed.   He was indeed much
annoyed by the whole affair, and straightway wrote
to political leaders letters—some private, others to
be quoted,—in which he sought to smooth things
by declaring that his note was not meant for publi-

cation.   To Washington he writes (May 8th) the Beckley-Smith story, beginning :

" I am afraid the indiscretion of a printer has committed me with my friend Mr. Adams, for whom, as one of the most honest and disinterested men alive, I have a cordial esteem, increased by long habits of concurrence in opinion in the days of his republicanism ; and even since his apostasy to hereditary monarchy and nobility, though we differ, we differ as friends should do."

The " Jeffersonians " were, of course, delighted, and there is no knowing how much reputation for pluck the Secretary was gaining in the country at the very moment when his intimate friends were soothing his tremors.   These were increased by the agitation of the British representatives in America over the affair.   The following re-enforcement was sent by Madison on May 12th :

" I had seen Paine's pamphlet, with the Preface of the Philadelphia edition.   It immediately occurred that you were brought into the frontispiece in the manner you explain.   But I had not foreseen the particular use made of it by the British partizans.   Mr. Adams can least of all complain.   Under a mock defence of the Republican constitutions of his country he attacked them with all the force he possessed, and this in a book with his name to it, while he was the Representative of his country at a foreign Court.   Since he has been the second magistrate in the new Republic, his pen has constantly been at work in the same Cause ; and though his name has not been prefixed to his anti-republican discourses, the author has been as well known as if that formality had been observed.   Surely if it be innocent and decent in one servant of the public thus to write attacks against its Government, it cannot be very criminal or indecent in another to patronize a written defence of the principles on which that Government is founded.   The sensibility of Hammond [British Minister] and Bond [British Consul-General] for the indignity to the British Constitution is truly ridiculous. If offence could be justly taken in that quarter, what would France have a right to say to Burke's pamphlet, and the countenance given to it and its author, particularly by the King himself? What, in fact, might not the United States say, when revolutions and democratic Governments come in for a large charge of the scurrility lavished on those of France ?"

One curious circumstance of this incident was that the fuss made by these British agents was about a book concerning which heir government, under whose nose it was published, had not said a word. There was, indeed, one sting in the American edition which was not in the English, but that does not appear to have been noticed.[1] The resentment shown by the British agents was plainly meant to aid Adams and the partisans of England in their efforts to crush the republicans, and bring Washington to their side in hostility to Jefferson. Four years later they succeeded, and already it was apparent to the republican leaders that fine engineering was required to keep the Colossus on their side. Washington being at Mount Vernon, his secretary, Tobias Lear, was approached by Major Beckwith, an English agent (at Mrs. Washington's reception), who undertook to lecture through him the President and Secretary of State. He expressed surprise that Paine's pamphlet should be dedicated to the President, as it contained re-

---

[1] It has already been stated that the volume as printed by Jordan (London) in March, contained one single modification of that which Johnson had printed in February, but declined to publish. The American edition was printed from the Johnson volume ; and where the English were reading "Many things," etc, the Americans read : "Every thing in the English government appears to me the reverse of what it ought to be, and of what it is said to be."

marks "that could not but be offensive to the British government." The Major might have been embarrassed if asked his instructions on the point, but Lear only said that the President had not seen the pamphlet, nor could he be held responsible for its sentiments. "True," said Beckwith, "but I observe, in the American edition, that the Secretary of State has given a most unequivocal sanction to the book, as *Secretary of State;* it is not said as Mr. Jefferson." Lear said he had not seen the pamphlet, "but," he added, "I will venture to say that the Secretary of State has not done a thing which he would not justify." Beckwith then remarked that he had spoken only as "a private character," and Lear went off to report the conversation in a letter to Washington (May 8th), and next day to Attorney-General Randolph. Lear also reports to Washington that he had heard Adams say, with his hand upon his breast: "I detest that book and its tendency, from the bottom of my heart." Meanwhile the Attorney-General, after conversation with Beckwith, visited Jefferson, and asked if he had authorized the publication of his note in Paine's pamphlet.

"Mr. Jefferson said that, so far from having authorized it, he was exceedingly sorry to see it there ; not from a disavowal of the approbation which it gave the work, but because it had been sent to the printer, with the pamphlet for republication, without the most distant idea that he would think of publishing any part of it. And Mr. Jefferson further added that he wished it might be understood, that he did not authorize the publication of any part of his note."

These words of Lear to Washington, written no doubt in Randolph's presence, suggest the delicacy of the situation. Jefferson's anxiety led him to write Vice-President Adams (July 17th) the Beckley-Smith story.

"I thought [he adds] so little of the note that I did not even keep a copy of it, nor ever heard a tittle more of it till, the week following, I was thunderstruck with seeing it come out at the head of the pamphlet. I hoped that it would not attract. But I found on my return from a journey of a month, that a writer came forward under the name of Publicola, attacking not only the author and principles of the pamphlet, but myself as its sponsor by name. Soon after came hosts of other writers, defending the pamphlet and attacking you by name as the writer of Publicola. Thus our names were thrown on the stage as public antagonists."

Then follows some effusiveness for Adams, and protestations that he has written none of these attacks. Jefferson fully believed that Publicola was the Vice-President, and had so informed Monroe, on July 10th. It was important that his lieutenants should not suspect their leader of shrinking, and Jefferson's letters to them are in a different vein. "Publicola," he tells Monroe, "in attacking all Paine's principles, is very desirous of involving me in the same censure with the author. I certainly merit the same, for I profess the same principles ; but it is equally certain I never meant to have entered as a volunteer in the cause. My occupations do not permit it." To Paine he writes (July 29th) : "Indeed I am glad you did not come away till you had written your Rights of Man. A writer under the signature of Publicola has attacked it, and a host of champions has entered the arena immediately in your defence." It is added that the controversy has shown the people

firm in their republicanism, " contrary to the assertions of a sect here, high in name but small in
numbers," who were hoping that the masses were
becoming converted " to the doctrine of King,
Lords, and Commons."

In the letter to which this was a reply, Paine had
stated his intention of returning to America in the
spring.[1] The enthusiasm for Paine and his principles elicited by the controversy was so overwhelm-
ing that Edmund Randolph and Jefferson made an
effort to secure him a place in Washington's Cabinet. But, though reinforced by Madison, they
failed.[2] These statesmen little knew how far
Washington had committed himself to the British
government. In October, 1789, Washington, with
his own hand, had written to Gouverneur Morris,

---

[1] " I enclose you a few observations on the establishment of a Mint. I
have not seen your report on that subject and therefore cannot tell how
nearly our opinions run together ; but as it is by thinking upon and talking
subjects over that we approach towards truth, there may probably be something in the enclosed that may be of use.—As the establishment of a Mint
combines a portion of politics with a knowledge of the Arts, and a variety
of other matters, it is a subject I shall very much like to talk with you
upon. I intend at all events to be in America in the Spring, and it will
please me much to arrive before you have gone thro' the arrangement."—
Paine to Jefferson, dated London, September 28, 1790.

[2] Madison to Jefferson, July 13th,—" I wish you success with all my heart
in your efforts for Paine. Besides the advantage to him which he deserves,
an appointment for him at this moment would do public good in various
ways."

Edmund Randolph to Madison, July 21st.—" I need not relate to you,
that since the *standard* of republicanism has been erected, it has been
resorted to by a numerous corps. The newspapers will tell you how much
the crest of aristocracy has fallen. .   .   . But he [Adams] is impotent, and
something is due to past services. Mr. J. and myself have attempted to
bring Paine forward as a successor to Osgood [Postmaster-General]. It
seems to be a fair opportunity for a declaration of certain sentiments. But
all that I have heard has been that it would be too pointed to keep a
vacancy unfilled until his return from the other side of the water."

desiring him in "the capacity of private agent, and on the authority and credit of this letter, to converse with His Britannic Majesty's ministers on these points ; viz., whether there be any, and what objections to performing those articles in the treaty which remained to be performed on his part, and whether they incline to a treaty of commerce with the United States on any, and what terms ?"   This was a secret between Washington, Morris, and the British Cabinet.[1] It was the deepest desire of Washington to free America from British garrisons, and his expectation was to secure this by the bribe of a liberal commercial treaty, as he ultimately did.   The demonstration of the British agents in America against Paine's pamphlet, their offence at its dedication to the President and sanction by the Secretary of State, were well calculated. That it was all an American *coup*, unwarranted by any advice from England, could not occur to Washington, who was probably surprised when he presently received a letter from Paine showing that he was getting along quite comfortably under the government he was said to have aggrieved.

"LONDON, July 21, 1791 — DEAR SIR. — I received your favor of last August by Col : Humphries since which I have not written to or heard from you.   I mention this that you may know no letters have miscarried.   I took the liberty of addressing my late work ' Rights of Man,' to you ; but tho' I left it at that time to find its way to you, I now request your acceptance of fifty copies as a token of remembrance to yourself and my Friends.   The work has had a run beyond anything that has been published in this Country on the subject of Government, and the demand continues.   In Ireland it

---

[1] " Diary of Gouverneur Morris," i., p. 310.

has had a much greater. A letter I received from Dublin, 10th
of May, mentioned that the fourth edition was then on sale.
I know not what number of copies were printed at each edition, except the second, which was ten thousand. The same
fate follows me here as I *at first* experienced in America,
strong friends and violent enemies, but as I have got the ear
of the Country, I shall go on, and at least shew them, what is
a novelty here, that there can be a person beyond the reach
of corruption.

"I arrived here from france about ten days ago. M. de la
Fayette is well. The affairs of that Country are verging to a
new crisis, whether the Government shall be Monarchical and
heredetary or wholly representative? I think the latter
opinion will very generally prevail in the end. On this
question the people are much forwarder than the National
Assembly.

"After the establishment of the American Revolution, it
did not appear to me that any object could arise great enough
to engage me a second time. I began to feel myself happy in
being quiet; but I now experience that principle is not confined to Time or place, and that the ardour of seventy-six is
capable of renewing itself. I have another work on hand
which I intend shall be my last, for I long much to return to
America. It is not natural that fame should wish for a rival,
but the case is otherwise with me, for I do most sincerely wish
there was some person in this Country that could usefully and
successfully attract the public attention, and leave me with a
satisfied mind to the enjoyment of quiet life : but it is painful
to see errors and abuses and sit down a senseless spectator.
Of this your own mind will interpret mine.

"I have printed sixteen thousand copies ; when the whole
are gone of which there remain between three and four thousand I shall then make a cheap edition, just sufficient to bring
in the price of the printing and paper as I did by Common
Sense.

"Mr. Green who will present you this, has been very much
my friend. I wanted last October to draw for fifty pounds on
General Lewis Morris who has some money of mine, but as he
is unknown in the Commercial line, and American credit not
very good, and my own expended, I could not succeed,

especially as Gov'r Morris was then in Holland. Col:
Humphries went with me to your Agent Mr. Walsh, to whom
I stated the case, and took the liberty of saying that I knew
you would not think it a trouble to receive it of Gen. Morris
on Mr. Walsh's account, but he declined it. Mr. Green afterwards supplied me and I have since repaid him. He has a
troublesome affair on his hands here, and is in danger of
losing thirty or forty thousand pounds, embarked under the
flag of the United States in East India property. The persons
who have received it withhold it and shelter themselves under
some law contrivance. He wishes to state the case to Congress not only on his own account, but as a matter that may
be nationally interesting.

" The public papers will inform you of the riots and tumults
at Birmingham, and of some disturbances at Paris, and as Mr.
Green can detail them to you more particularly than I can do
in a letter I leave those matters to his information. I am, etc."

Nine months elapsed before Washington answered this letter, and although important events
of those months have yet to be related, the answer
may be here put on record.

" PHILADELPHIA, 6 May, 1792.—DEAR SIR.—To my friends,
and those who know my occupations, I am sure no apology is
necessary for keeping their letters so much longer unanswered,
than my inclination would lead me to do. I shall therefore
offer no excuse for not having sooner acknowledged the receipt of your letter of the 21st of June [July]. My thanks,
however, for the token of your remembrance, in the fifty
copies of ' *The Rights of Man,*' are offered with no less cordiality, than they would have been had I answered your letter
in the first moment of receiving it.

" The duties of my office, which at all times, especially
during the session of Congress, require an unremitting attention, naturally become more pressing towards the close of it ;
and as that body have resolved to rise tomorrow, and as I
have determined, in case they should, to set out for Mount
Vernon on the next day, you will readily conclude that the

present is a busy moment with me ; and to that I am persuaded your goodness will impute my not entering into the
several points touched upon in your letter. Let it suffice,
therefore, at this time, to say, that I rejoice in the information
of your personal prosperity, and, as no one can feel a greater
interest in the happiness of mankind than I do, that it is the
first wish of my heart, that the enlightened policy of the
present age may diffuse to all men those blessings, to which
they are entitled, and lay the foundation of happiness for
future generations.—With great esteem, I am, dear Sir &c.

"P. S. Since writing the foregoing, I have received your
letter of the 13th of February, with the twelve copies of your
new work, which accompanied it, and for which you must
accept my additional thanks."

There is no lack of personal cordiality in this
letter, but one may recognize in its ingenious
vagueness, in its omission of any acknowledgment
of the dedication of Paine's book, that he mistrusts
the European revolution and its American allies.

CHAPTER XXI.

FOUNDING THE EUROPEAN REPUBLIC.

IT has already been mentioned that John Adams had been proclaimed in France the author of "Common Sense." [1] The true author was now known, but, as the anti-monarchal parts of his work were expurgated, Paine, in turn, was supposed to be a kind of John Adams—a revolutionary royalist. This misunderstanding was personally distasteful, but it had the important compensation of enabling Paine to come before Europe with a work adapted to its conditions, essentially different from those of America to which "Common Sense" was

[1] "When I arrived in France, the French naturally had a great many questions to settle. The first was, whether I was the famous Adams. 'Ah, le fameux Adams.' In order to speculate a little upon this subject, the pamphlet 'Common Sense' had been printed in the 'Affaires de l'Angleterre et de l'Amerique,' and expressly ascribed to Mr. Adams, 'the celebrated member of Congress.' It must be further known that although the pamphlet 'Common Sense' was received in France and in all Europe with rapture, yet there were certain parts of it that they did not dare to publish in France. The reasons of this any man may guess. 'Common Sense' undertakes to prove that monarchy is unlawful by the Old Testament. They therefore gave the substance of it, as they said ; and paying many compliments to Mr. Adams, his sense and rich imagination, they were obliged to ascribe some parts of it to republican zeal. When I arrived at Bordeaux all that I could say or do would not convince anybody but that I was the fameux Adams. 'C'est un homme célèbre. Votre nom est bien connu ici.' "—" Works of John Adams," vol. iii., p. 189. This was in 1779, and when Adams entered on his official duties at Paris the honors thrust upon him at Bordeaux became burdensome.

addressed in 1776. It was a matter of indifference to him whether the individual executive was called "King" or "President." He objected to the thing, not the name, but as republican superstition had insisted on it in America there was little doubt that France would follow the example. Under these circumstances Paine made up his mind that the republican principle would not be lost by the harmonizing policy of preserving the nominal and ornamental king while abolishing his sovereignty. The erection of a tremendous presidential power in the United States might well suggest to so staunch a supporter of ministerial government that this substance might be secured under a show of royalty. Dr. Robinet considers it a remarkable "prophecy" that Paine should have written in 1787 of an approaching alliance of "the Majesty of the Sovereign with the Majesty of the Nation" in France. This was opposed to the theories of Jefferson, but it was the scheme of Mirabeau, the hope of Lafayette, and had not the throne been rotten this prudent policy might have succeeded. It was with an eye to France as well as to England that Paine, in his reply to Burke, had so carefully distinguished between executive sovereignty subject to law and personal monarchy.

When the last proof of his book was revised Paine sped to Paris, and placed it in the hand of his friend M. Lanthenas for translation. Mirabeau was on his death-bed, and Paine witnessed that historic procession, four miles long, which bore the orator to his shrine. Witnessed it with relief, perhaps, for he is ominously silent concerning Mirabeau.   With others he strained his eyes to see the Coming Man ; with others he sees formidable Danton glaring at Lafayette ; and presently sees advancing softly between them the sentimental, philanthropic—Robespierre.

It was a happy hour for Paine when, on a day in May, he saw Robespierre rise in the National Assembly to propose abolition of the death penalty. How sweet this echo of the old " testimonies " of Thetford Quaker meetings. " Capital punishment," cries Robespierre, " is but a base assassination— punishing one crime by another, murder with murder.   Since judges are not infallible they have no right to pronounce irreparable sentences."   He is seconded by the jurist Duport, who says impressively : " Let us at least make revolutionary scenes as little tragic as possible !   Let us render man honorable to man ! "   Marat, right man for the rôle, answered with the barbaric demand " blood for blood," and prevailed.   But Paine was won over to Robespierre by this humane enthusiasm.   The day was to come when he must confront Robespierre with a memory of this scene.

That Robespierre would supersede Lafayette Paine could little imagine.   The King was in the charge of the great friend of America, and never had country a fairer prospect than France in those beautiful spring days.   But the royal family fled. In the early morning of June 21st Lafayette burst into Paine's bedroom, before he was up, and cried : " The birds are flown ! "   " It is well," said Paine ; " I hope there will be no attempt to recall them." Hastily dressing, he rushed out into the street, and found the people in uproar.   They were clamoring as if some great loss had befallen them.   At the Hôtel de Ville Lafayette was menaced by the crowd, which accused him of having assisted the King's flight, and could only answer them : " What are you complaining of ?   Each of you saves twenty sous tax by suppression of the Civil List."   Paine encounters his friend Thomas Christie.   " You see," he said, " the absurdity of monarchical governments ; here will be a whole nation disturbed by the folly of one man." [1]

Here was Marat's opportunity.   His journal, *L'Ami du Peuple*, clamored for a dictator, and for the head of Lafayette.   Against him rose young Bonneville, who, in *La Bouche de Fer*, wrote : " No more kings !   No dictator !   Assemble the People in the face of the sun ; proclaim that the Law alone shall be sovereign,—the Law, the Law alone, and made for all !"

Bonneville's words in his journal about that time were apt to be translations from the works of his friend Paine, with whom his life was afterwards so closely interwoven.   The little group of men who had studied Paine, ardent republicans, beheld a nation suddenly become frantic to recover a king who could not be of the slightest value to any party in the state.   The miserable man had left a letter denouncing all the liberal measures he had signed since October, 1789, which sealed his doom as a monarch.   The appalling fact was revealed that the most powerful revolutionists—Robespierre and

---

[1] The letter of Christie (Priestley's nephew), written June 22d, appeared in the *London Morning Chronicle*, June 29th.

Marat especially—had never considered a Republic, and did not know what it was.

On June 25th, Paine was a heavy-hearted spectator of the return of the arrested king.   He had personal realization that day of the folly of a people in bringing back a king who had relieved them of his presence.   He had omitted to decorate his hat with a cockade, and the mob fell on him with cries of " Aristocrat ! à la lanterne ! " After some rough handling he was rescued by a Frenchman who spoke English, and explained the accidental character of the offence. Poor Paine's Quaker training had not included the importance of badges, else the incident had revealed to him that even the popular rage against Louis was superstitious homage to a cockade. Never did friend of the people have severer proofs that they are generally wrong.   In America, while writing as with his heart's blood the first plea for its independence, he was " shadowed " as a British spy ; and in France he narrowly escapes the aristocrat's lantern, at the very moment when he was founding the first republican society, and writing its declaration.

This " Société Républicaine," as yet of five members, inaugurated itself on July 1st, by placarding Paris with its manifesto, which was even nailed on the door of the National Assembly.

" Brethren and fellow citizens :

" The serene tranquillity, the mutual confidence which prevailed amongst us, during the time of the late King's escape, the indifference with which we beheld him return, are unequivocal proofs that the absence of a King is more desirable than his presence, and that he is not only a political superfluity, but a grievous burden, pressing hard on the whole nation.

"Let us not be imposed upon by sophisms ; all that concerns this is reduced to four points.

"He has abdicated the throne in having fled from his post. Abdication and desertion are not characterized by the length of absence ; but by the single act of flight. In the present instance, the act is everything, and the time nothing.

"The nation can never give back its confidence to a man who false to his trust, perjured to his oath, conspires a clandestine flight, obtains a fraudulent passport, conceals a King of France under the disguise of a valet, directs his course towards a frontier covered with traitors and deserters, and evidently meditates a return into our country, with a force capable of imposing his own despotic laws.

"Whether ought his flight to be considered as his own act, or the act of those who fled with him ? Was it a spontaneous resolution of his own, or was it inspired into him by others ? The alternative is immaterial ; whether fool or hypocrite, idiot or traitor, he has proved himself equally unworthy of the important functions that had been delegated to him.

"In every sense that the question can be considered, the reciprocal obligation which subsisted between us is dissolved. He holds no longer any authority. We owe him no longer obedience. We see in him no more than an indifferent person ; we can regard him only as Louis Capet.

"The history of France presents little else than a long series of public calamity, which takes its source from the vices of the Kings ; we have been the wretched victims that have never ceased to suffer either for them or by them. The catalogue of their oppressions was complete, but to complete the sum of their crimes, treason yet was wanting. Now the only vacancy is filled up, the dreadful list is full ; the system is exhausted ; there are no remaining errors for them to commit, their reign is consequently at an end.

"What kind of office must that be in a government which requires neither experience nor ability to execute? that may be abandoned to the desperate chance of birth, that may be filled with an idiot, a madman, a tyrant, with equal effect as by the good, the virtuous, and the wise ? An office of this nature is a mere nonentity : it is a place of show, not of use. Let France then, arrived at the age of reason, no longer be deluded by the sound of words, and let her deliberately examine, if a King, however insignificant and contemptible in himself, may not at the same time be extremely dangerous.

"The thirty millions which it costs to support a King in the eclat of stupid brutal luxury, presents us with an easy method of reducing taxes, which reduction would at once release the people, and stop the progress of political corruption. The grandeur of nations consists, not, as Kings pretend, in the splendor of thrones, but in a conspicuous sense of their own dignity, and in a just disdain of those barbarous follies and crimes, which, under the sanction of royalty have hitherto desolated Europe.

"As to the personal safety of Louis Capet, it is so much the more confirmed, as France will not stoop to degrade herself by a spirit of revenge against a wretch who has dishonored himself. In defending a just and glorious cause, it is not possible to degrade it, and the universal tranquillity which prevails is an undeniable proof, that a free people know how to respect themselves." [1]

Malouet, a leading royalist member, tore down the handbill, and, having ascertained its author, demanded the prosecution of Thomas Paine and Achille Duchâtelet. He was vehemently supported by Martineau, deputy of Paris, and for a time there was a tremendous agitation. The majority, not prepared to commit themselves to anything at all,

---

[1] "How great is a calm, couchant people! On the morrow men will say to one another, 'We have no king, yet we slept sound enough.' On the morrow Achille Duchâtelet, and Thomas Paine, the rebellious needleman, shall have the walls of Paris profusely plastered with their placard, announcing that there must be a republic."—Carlyle.

Dumont ("Recollections of Mirabeau") gives a particular account of this paper, which Duchâtelet wished him to translate. "Paine and he, the one an American, the other a young thoughtless member of the French nobility, put themselves forward to change the whole system of government in France." Lafayette had been sounded, but said it would take twenty years to bring freedom to maturity in France. "But some of the seed thrown out by the audacious hand of Paine began to bud forth in the minds of many leading individuals." (*E. g.*, Condorcet, Brissot, Pétion, Clavière.)

voted the order of the day, affecting, says Henri Martin, a disdain that hid embarrassment and inquietude.

This document, destined to reappear in a farther crisis, and the royalist rage, raised Paine's Republican Club to vast importance.   Even the Jacobins, who had formally declined to sanction republicanism, were troubled by the discovery of a society more radical than themselves.   It was only some years later that it was made known (by Paine) that this formidable association consisted of five members, and it is still doubtful who these were.   Certainly Paine, Achille Duchâtelet, and Condorcet; probably also Brissot, and Nicolas Bonneville.   In order to avail itself of this tide of fame, the Société Républicaine started a journal,—*The Republican.*[1] The time was not ripe, however; only one copy appeared; that, however, contained a letter by Paine, written in June, which excited considerable flutter.   To the reader of to-day it is mainly interesting as showing Paine's perception that the French required instruction in the alphabet of republicanism; but, amid its studied moderation, there was a paragraph which the situation rendered pregnant :

" Whenever the French Constitution shall be rendered conformable to its declaration of rights, we shall then be enabled to give to France, and with justice, the appellation of a *Civic Empire ;* for its government will be the empire of laws, founded on the great republican principles of *elective representation* and the rights of man.   But monarchy and hereditary succession are incompatible with the *basis* of its Constitution."

[1] " Le Républicain ; on le défenseur du gouvernement Représentatif ; par une Société des Républicains. À Paris. July 1791. No. 1."

Now this was the very constitution which Paine, in his answer to Burke, had made comparatively presentable; to this day it survives in human memory mainly through indulgent citations in "The Rights of Man." Those angels who, in the celestial war, tried to keep friendly with both sides, had human counterparts in France, their constitutional oracle being the Abbé Sieyès. He had entered warmly into the Revolution, invented the name "National Assembly," opposed the veto power, supported the Declaration of Rights. But he had a superstitious faith in individual executive, which, as an opportunist, he proposed to vest in the reigning house. This class of "survivals" in the constitution were the work of Sieyès, who was the brain of the Jacobins, now led by Robespierre, and with him ignoring republicanism for no better reason than that their title was "Société des Amis de la Constitution."[1] Sieyès petted his constitution maternally, perhaps because nobody else loved it, and bristled at Paine's criticism. He wrote a letter to the *Moniteur*, asserting that there was more liberty under a monarchy than under a republic. He announced his intention of maintaining monarchical executive against the new party started into life by the King's flight. In the same journal (July 8th,) Paine accepts the challenge "with pleasure."[2] Paine himself was something of an opportunist; as in

[1] The club, founded in 1789, was called "Jacobin," because they met in the hall of the Dominicans, who had been called Jacobins from the street St. Jacques in which they were first established, anno 1219.

[2] It was probably this letter that Gouverneur Morris alludes to in his "Diary," when, writing of a Fourth of July dinner given by Mr. Short (U. S. Chargé d'Affaires), he mentions the presence of Paine, "inflated to the eyes and big with a letter of Revolutions."

America he had favored reconciliation with George
III. up to the Lexington massacre, so had he desired a *modus vivendi* with Louis XVI. up to his
flight.[1]   But now he unfurls the anti-monarchical
flag.

"I am not the personal enemy of Kings. Quite the contrary. No man wishes more heartily than myself to see them
all in the happy and honorable state of private individuals ;
but I am the avowed, open, and intrepid enemy of what is
called monarchy ; and I am such by principles which nothing
can either alter or corrupt—by my attachment to humanity ;
by the anxiety which I feel within myself for the dignity and
honor of the human race ; by the disgust which I experience
when I observe men directed by children and governed by
brutes ; by the horror which all the evils that monarchy has
spread over the earth excite within my breast ; and by those
sentiments which make me shudder at the calamities, the exac-
tions, the wars, and the massacres with which monarchy has
crushed mankind : in short, it is against all the hell of monarchy that I have declared war."

In reply Sieyès used the terms "monarchy" and
"republic" in unusual senses. He defines "republic" as a government in which the executive
power is lodged in more than one person, "monarchy" as one where it is entrusted to one only.
He asserted that while he was in this sense a mon-
archist Paine was a "polycrat." In a republic all
action must finally lodge in an executive council
deciding by majority, and nominated by the people

---

[1] In this spirit was written Part I. of "The Rights of Man" whose
translation by M. Lanthenas, with new preface, appeared in May. Sieyès
agreed that "hereditaryship" was theoretically wrong, "but," he said,
"refer to the histories of all elective monarchies and principalities : is there
one in which the elective mode is not worse than the hereditary succession ?"
For notes on this incident see Professor F. A. Aulard's important work,
"Les Orateurs de l'Assemblée Constituante," p. 411. Also Henri Martin's
"Histoire de France," i., p. 193.

or the National Assembly. Sieyès did not, however, care to enter the lists. "My letter does not announce that I have leisure to enter into a controversy with republican *polycrats*."

Paine now set out for London. He travelled with Lord Daer and Etienne Dumont, Mirabeau's secretary. Dumont had a pique against Paine, whose republican manifesto had upset a literary scheme of his,—to evoke Mirabeau from the tomb and make him explain to the National Assembly that the King's flight was a court plot, that they should free Louis XVI. from aristocratic captivity, and support him. But on reading the Paine placard, "I determined," says Dumont, "for fear of evil consequences to myself, to make Mirabeau return to his tomb."[1] Dumont protests that Paine was fully convinced that the world would be benefited if all other books were burned except " The Rights of Man," and no doubt the republican apostle had a sublime faith in the sacred character of his "testimonies" against kings. Without attempting to determine whether this was the self-reliance of humility or egoism, it may be safely affirmed that it was that which made Paine's strokes so effective.

It may also be remarked again that Paine showed a prudence with which he has not been credited. Thus, there is little doubt that this return to London was in pursuance of an invitation to attend a celebration of the second anniversary of the fall of the Bastille. He arrived at the White Bear, Piccadilly, the day before (July 13th), but on finding that there was much excitement

---

[1] " Souvenirs sur Mirabeau." Par Étienne Dumont.

about his republican manifesto in France he concluded that his presence at the meeting might connect it with movements across the Channel, and did not attend. Equal prudence was not, however, displayed by his opponents, who induced the landlord of the Crown and Anchor to close his doors against the advertised meeting. This effort to prevent the free assemblage of Englishmen, and for the humane purpose of celebrating the destruction of a prison whose horrors had excited popular indignation, caused general anger. After due consideration it was deemed opportune for those who sympathized with the movement in France to issue a manifesto on the subject. It was written by Paine, and adopted by a meeting held at the Thatched House Tavern, August 20th, being signed by John Horne Tooke, as Chairman. This "Address and Declaration of the Friends of Universal Peace and Liberty," though preceded by the vigorous "Declaration of the Volunteers of Belfast," quoted in its second paragraph, was the earliest warning England received that the revolution was now its grim guest.

"Friends and Fellow Citizens : At a moment like the present, when wilful misrepresentations are industriously spread by partizans of arbitrary power and the advocates of passive obedience and court government, we think it incumbent upon us to declare to the world our principles, and the motives of our conduct.

"We rejoice at the glorious event of the French revolution. If it be asked, 'What is the French revolution to us?' we answer as has already been answered in another place, 'It is much—much to us as men ; much to us as Englishmen. As men, we rejoice in the freedom of twenty-five millions of men.

We rejoice in the prospect which such a magnificent example opens to the world.'

"We congratulate the French nation for having laid the axe to the root of tyranny, and for erecting government on the sacred hereditary rights of man ; rights which appertain to all, and not to any one more than another.

"We know of no human authority superior to that of a whole nation ; and we profess and claim it as our principle that every nation has at all times an inherent and indefeasable right to constitute and establish such government for itself as best accords with its disposition, interest, and happiness.

" As Englishmen we also rejoice, because we are immediately interested in the French Revolution.

"Without inquiring into the justice, on either side, of the reproachful charges of intrigue and ambition which the English and French courts have constantly made on each other, we confine ourselves to this observation,—that if the court of France only was in fault, and the numerous wars which have distressed both countries are chargeable to her alone, that court now exists no longer, and the cause and the consequence must cease together.   The French therefore, by the revolution they have made, have conquered for us as well as for themselves, if it be true that this court only was in fault, and ours never.

" On this side of the case the French revolution concerns us immediately : we are oppressed with a heavy national debt, a burthen of taxes, an expensive administration of government, beyond those of any people in the world.

" We have also a very numerous poor ; and we hold that the moral obligation of providing for old age, helpless infancy, and poverty, is far superior to that of supplying the invented wants of courtly extravagance, ambition, and intrigue.

" We believe there is no instance to be produced but in England, of seven millions of inhabitants, which make but little more than one million families, paying yearly seventeen millions of taxes.

" As it has always been held out by the administrations that the restless ambition of the court of France rendered this expences necessary to us for our own defence, we consequently rejoice, as men deeply interested in the French revolution ; for that court, as we have already said, exists no longer, and

consequently the same enormous expences need not continue
to us.

" Thus rejoicing as we sincerely do, both as men and Englishmen, as lovers of universal peace and freedom, and as
friends to our national prosperity and reduction of our public
expences, we cannot but express our astonishment that any
part or any members of our own government should reprobate
the extinction of that very power in France, or wish to see it
restored, to whose influence they formerly attributed (whilst
they appeared to lament) the enormous increase of our own
burthens and taxes. What, then, are they sorry that the pretence for new oppressive taxes, and the occasion for continuing
many old taxes, will be at an end ? If so, and if it is the
policy of courts and court government to prefer enemies to
friends, and a system of war to that of peace, as affording
more pretences for places, offices, pensions, revenue and taxation, it is high time for the people of every nation to look
with circumspection to their own interest.

" Those who pay the expences, and not those who participate in the emoluments arising from them, are the persons
immediately interested in inquiries of this kind. We are a
part of that national body on whom this annual expence of
seventeen millions falls ; and we consider the present opportunity of the French revolution as a most happy one for
lessening the enormous load under which this nation groans.
If this be not done we shall then have reason to conclude that
the cry of intrigue and ambition against other courts is no
more than the common cant of all courts.

" We think it also necessary to express our astonishment
that a government desirous of being called FREE, should prefer
connexion with the most despotic and arbitrary powers in
Europe. We know of none more deserving this description
than those of Turkey and Prussia, and the whole combination
of German despots.

" Separated as we happily are by nature from the tumults of
the continent, we reprobate all systems and intrigues which
sacrifice (and that too at a great expence) the blessings of our
natural situation. Such systems cannot have a natural origin.

" If we are asked what government is, we hold it to be nothing more than a national association ; and we hold that to be

the best which secures to every man his rights and promotes the greatest quantity of happiness with the least expence. We live to improve, or we live in vain ; and therefore we admit of no maxims of government or policy on the mere score of antiquity or other men's authority, the old whigs or the new.

" We will exercise the reason with which we are endued, or we possess it unworthily. As reason is given at all times, it is for the purpose of being used at all times.

" Among the blessings which the French revolution has produced to that nation we enumerate the abolition of the feudal system, of injustice, and of tyranny, on the 4th of August, 1789. Beneath the feudal system all Europe has long groaned, and from it England is not yet free. Game laws, borough tenures, and tyrannical monopolies of numerous kinds still remain amongst us ; but rejoicing as we sincerely do in the freedom of others till we shall haply accomplish our own, we intended to commemorate this prelude to the universal extirpation of the feudal system by meeting on the anniversary of that day (the 4th of August) at the Crown and Anchor : from this' meeting we were prevented by the interference of certain unnamed and sculking persons with the master of the tavern, who informed us that on their representation he would not receive us. Let those who live by or countenance feudal oppressions take the reproach of this ineffectual meanness and cowardice to themselves : they cannot stifle the public declaration of our honest, open, and avowed opinions. These are our principles, and these our sentiments ; they embrace the interest and happiness of the great body of the nation of which we are a part. As to riots and tumults, let those answer for them who by wilful misrepresentations endeavour to excite and promote them ; or who seek to stun the sense of the nation, and lose the great cause of public good in the outrages of a mis-informed mob. We take our ground on principles that require no such riotous aid.

" We have nothing to apprehend from the poor for we are pleading their cause ; and we fear not proud oppression for we have truth on our side.

" We say and we repeat it that the French revolution opens to the world an opportunity in which all good citizens must rejoice, that of promoting the general happiness of man, and that it moreover offers to this country in particular an opportunity of reducing our enormous taxes : these are our objects, and we will pursue them."

A comparative study of Paine's two republican manifestos—that placarded in Paris July 1st, and this of August 20th to the English—reveals the difference between the two nations at that period. No break with the throne in England is suggested, as none had been declared in France until the King had fled, leaving behind him a virtual proclamation of war against all the reforms he had been signing since 1789. The Thatched House address leaves it open for the King to take the side of the Republic, and be its chief. The address is simply an applied " Declaration of Rights." Paine had already maintained, in his reply to Burke, that the English monarch was an importation unrelated to the real nation, " which is left to govern itself, and does govern itself, by magistrates and juries, almost on its own charge, on republican principles." His chief complaint is that royalty is an expensive " sinecure." So far had George III. withdrawn from his attempt to govern as well as reign, which had ended so disastrously in America. The fall of the French King who had aided the American " rebellion " was probably viewed with satisfaction by the English court, so long as the revolution confined itself to France. But now it had raised its head in England, and the alarm of aristocracy was as if it were threatened with an invasion of political cholera.

The disease was brought over by Paine. He

must be isolated. But he had a hold on the people, including a large number of literary men, and Nonconformist preachers. The authorities, therefore, began working cautiously, privately inducing the landlords of the Crown and Anchor and the Thatched House to refuse their rooms to the "Painites," as they were beginning to be called. But this was a confession of Paine's power. Indeed all opposition at that time was favorable to Paine. Publicola's reply to "The Rights of Man," attributed to Vice-President Adams, could only heighten Paine's fame ; for John Adams' blazing court-dress, which amused us at the Centenary (1889), was not forgotten in England ; and while his influence was limited to court circles, the entrance of so high an official into the arena was accepted as homage to the author. The publication at the same time of the endorsement of Paine's "Rights of Man" by the Secretary of State, the great Jefferson, completed the triumph. The English government now had Paine on its hands, and must deal with him in one way or another.

The closing of one door after another of the usual places of assembly to sympathizers with the republican movement in France, being by hidden hands, could not be charged upon Pitt's government ; it was, however, a plain indication that a free expression through public meetings could not be secured without risk of riots. And probably there would have been violent scenes in London had it not been for the moderation of the Quaker leader. At this juncture Paine held a supremacy in the constitutional clubs of England and Ireland equal to that of Robespierre over the Jacobins of Paris. He had the giant's strength, but did not use it like a giant. He sat himself down in a quiet corner of London, began another book, and from time to time consulted his Cabinet of Reformers.

His abode was with Thomas Rickman, a bookseller, his devoted friend. He had known Rickman at Lewes, as a youthful musical genius of the club there, hence called "Clio." He had then set some song of Paine's to music, and afterwards his American patriotic songs, as well as many of his own. He now lived in London with wife and children— these bearing names of the great republicans, beginning with Thomas Paine,—and with them the author resided for a time. A particular value, therefore, attaches to the following passages in Rickman's book :

"Mr. Paine's life in London was a quiet round of philosophical leisure and enjoyment. It was occupied in writing, in a small epistolary correspondence, in walking about with me to visit different friends, occasionally lounging at coffee-houses and public places, or being visited by a select few. Lord Edward Fitzgerald, the French and American ambassadors, Mr. Sharp the engraver, Romney the painter, Mrs. Wolstonecraft, Joel Barlow, Mr. Hull, Mr. Christie, Dr. Priestley, Dr. Towers, Col. Oswald, the walking Stewart, Captain Sampson Perry, Mr. Tuffin, Mr. William Choppin, Captain De Stark, Mr. Horne Tooke, &c. &c. were among the number of his friends and acquaintance ; and of course, as he was my inmate, the most of my associates were frequently his. At this time he read but little, took his nap after dinner, and played with my family at some game in the evening, as chess, dominos, and drafts, but never at cards ; in recitations, singing, music, &c ; or passed it in conversation : the part he took in the latter was always enlightened, full of information, entertainment, and anecdote. Occasionally we visited enlightened friends, indulged in domestic jaunts and recreations from home, frequently lounging at the White Bear, Picadilly, with his old friend the walking Stewart, and other clever travellers from France, and different parts of Europe and America. When by ourselves we sat very late, and often broke in on the morning hours, indulging the reciprocal interchange of affectionate and confidential intercourse. 'Warm from the heart and faithful to its fires' was that intercourse, and gave to us the 'feast of reason and the flow of soul.'"

"Mr. Paine in his person was about five feet ten inches high, and rather athletic ; he was broad shouldered, and latterly stooped a little. His eye, of which the painter could not convey the exquisite meaning, was full, brilliant, and singularly piercing ; it had in it the 'muse of fire.' In his dress and person he was generally very cleanly, and wore his hair cued, with side curls, and powdered, so that he looked altogether like a gentleman of the old French school. His manners were easy and gracious ; his knowledge was universal and boundless ; in private company and among his friends his conversation had every fascination that anecdote, novelty and truth could give it. In mixt company and among strangers he said little, and was no public speaker."

Paine does not appear to have ever learned that his name had been pressed for a place in Washington's Cabinet, and apparently he did not know until long after it was over what a tempest in Jefferson's teapot his book had innocently caused. The facts came to him while he was engaged on his next work, in which they are occasionally reflected. In introducing an English friend to William Short, U. S. Chargé d'Affaires at Paris, under date of November 2d, Paine reports progress :

"I received your favour conveying a letter from Mr. Jefferson and the answers to Publicola for which I thank you. I had John Adams in my mind when I wrote the pamphlet and it has hit as I expected.

"M. Lenobia who presents you this is come to pass a few days at Paris. He is a bon republicain and you will oblige me much by introducing him among our friends of bon foi. I am again in the press but shall not be out till about Christmas, when the Town will begin to fill. By what I can find, the Government Gentry begin to threaten. They have already tried all the under-plots of abuse and scurrility without effect ; and have managed those in general so badly as to make the work and the author the more famous ; several answers also have been written against it which did not excite reading enough to pay the expence of printing.

"I have but one way to be secure in my next work which is, to go further than in my first. I see that *great rogues* escape by the excess of their crimes, and, perhaps, it may be the same in honest cases. However, I shall make a pretty large division in the public opinion, probably too much so to encourage the Government to put it to issue, for it will be rather like begging them than me.

"By all the accounts we have here, the french emigrants are in a hopeless condition abroad ; for my own part I never saw anything to fear from foreign courts—they are more afraid of the french Revolution than the revolution needs to be of them ; and the same caution which they take to prevent the french principles getting among their armies, will prevent their sending armies among the principles.

"We have distressing accounts here from St. Domingo. It is the natural consequence of Slavery and must be expected every where. The Negroes are enraged at the opposition made to their relief and are determined, if not to relieve themselves to punish their enemies. We have no new accounts from the East Indies, and people are in much doubt. I am, affectionately yours, THOMAS PAINE."

The " scurrility " referred to may have been that of George Chalmers, elsewhere mentioned. Two days after this letter to Short was written Paine received a notable ovation.

There was a so-called " Revolution Society " in London, originally formed by a number of prominent dissenters. The Society had manifested its existence only by listening to a sermon on the anniversary of the Revolution of 1688 (November 4th) and thereafter dining together. It had not been supposed to interest itself in any later revolution until 1789. In that year the annual sermon was delivered by Dr. Richard Price, the Unitarian whose defence of the American Revolution received the thanks of Congress. In 1776 Price and Burke stood shoulder to shoulder, but the sermon of 1789 sundered them. It was " On the Love of our Country," and affirmed the constitutional right of the English people to frame their own government, to choose their own governors, and to cashier them for misconduct. This was the " red rag " that drew Burke into the arena. Dr. Price died April 19, 1791, and his great discourse gathered new force from the tributes of Priestley and others at his grave. He had been a staunch friend of Paine, and at the November festival of this year his place was accorded to the man on whom the " Constitutionalists " beheld the mantle of Price and the wreath of Washington. The company at this dinner of 1791, at the London Tavern, included many eminent men, some of them members of Parliament. The old Society was transformed— William and Mary and 1688 passed into oblivion before Thomas Paine and 1791. It was probably for this occasion that the song was written (by whom I know not)— " Paine's Welcome to Great Britain."

"He comes—the great Reformer comes !
  Cease, cease your trumpets, cease, cease your drums !
  Those warlike sounds offend the ear,
  Peace and Friendship now appear :
  Welcome, welcome, welcome, welcome,
  Welcome, thou Reformer, here !

"Prepare, prepare, your songs prepare,
  Freedom cheers the brow of care ;
  The joyful tidings spread around,
  Monarchs tremble at the sound !
  Freedom, freedom, freedom, freedom,—
  Rights of Man, and Paine resound ! "

Mr. Dignum sang (to the tune of " The tear that
bedews sensibility's shrine.")

"Unfold, Father Time, thy long records unfold,
  Of noble achievements accomplished of old ;
  When men, by the standard of Liberty led,
  Undauntedly conquered or chearfully bled :
  But now 'midst the triumphs these moments reveal,
  Their glories all fade and their lustre turns pale,
  While France rises up, and proclaims the decree
  That tears off their chains, and bids millions be free.

"As spring to the fields, or as dew to the flowers.
  To the earth parched with heat, as the soft dropping showers,
  As health to the wretch that lies languid and wan,
  Or rest to the weary—is Freedom to man !
  Where Freedom the light of her countenance gives,
  There only he triumphs, there only he lives ;
  Then seize the glad moment and hail the decree
  That tears off their chains, and bids millions be free.

"Too long had oppression and terror entwined
  Those tyrant-formed chains that enslaved the free mind ;
  While dark superstition, with nature at strife,
  For ages had locked up the fountain of life ;
  But the dæmon is fled, the delusion is past,

And reason and virtue have triumphed at last ;
Then seize the glad moments, and hail the decree,
That tears off their chains, and bids millions be free.

" France, we share in the rapture thy bosom that fills,
While the Genius of Liberty bounds o'er thy hills :
Redundant henceforth may thy purple juice flow,
Prouder wave thy green woods, and thine olive trees grow !
While the hand of philosophy long shall entwine,
Blest emblems, the laurel, the myrtle and vine,
And heaven through all ages confirm the decree
That tears off their chains, and bids millions be free ! "

Paine gave as his toast, " The Revolution of the World," and no doubt at this point was sung " A New Song," as it was then called, written by Paine himself to the tune of " Rule Britannia " :

" Hail, Great Republic of the world,
　　　The rising empire of the West,
　Where famed Columbus, with a mighty mind inspired,
　　　Gave tortured Europe scenes of rest.
　　　　Be thou forever, forever great and free,
　　　　The Land of Love and Liberty.

" Beneath thy spreading mantling vine,
　　　Beside thy flowery groves and springs,
　And on thy lofty, thy lofty mountains' brow,
　　　May all thy sons and fair ones sing.
　　　　　　　　　　Chorus.

" From thee may rudest nations learn
　　　To prize the cause thy sons began ;
　From thee may future, may future tyrants know
　　　That sacred are the Rights of Man.

" From thee may hated discord fly,
　　　With all her dark, her gloomy train ;
　And o'er thy fertile, thy fertile wide domain
　　　May everlasting friendship reign.

" Of thee may lisping infancy
         The pleasing wondrous story tell,
   And patriot sages in venerable mood
         Instruct the world to govern well.

" Ye guardian angels watch around,
         From harm protect the new-born State ;
   And all ye friendly, ye friendly nations join,
         And thus salute the Child of Fate.
           Be thou forever, forever great and free,
           The Land of Love and Liberty ! "

Notwithstanding royal tremors these gentlemen were genuinely loyal in singing the old anthem with new words :

     " God save the Rights of Man !
         Give him a heart to scan
             Blessings so dear ;
         Let them be spread around,
         Wherever Man is found,
         And with the welcome sound
             Ravish his ear ! "

No report is preserved of Paine's speech, but we may feel sure that in giving his sentiment " The Revolution of the World " he set forth his favorite theme—that revolutions of nations should be as quiet, lawful, and fruitful as the revolutions of the earth.

CHAPTER XXII.

THE RIGHT OF EVOLUTION.

THE Abbé Sieyès did not escape by declining to
stand by his challenge of the republicans. In the
second part of " The Rights of Man " Paine considers the position of that gentleman, namely, that
hereditary monarchy is an evil, but the elective
mode historically proven worse. That both are
bad Paine agrees, but " such a mode of reasoning
on such a subject is inadmissible, because it finally
amounts to an accusation of providence, as if she
had left to man no other choice with respect to
government than between two evils." Every now
and then this Quaker Antæus touches his mother
earth—the theocratic principle—in this way ; the
invigoration is recognizable in a religious serious-
ness, which, however, makes no allowance for the
merely ornamental parts of government, always so
popular. " The splendor of a throne is the corruption of a state." However, the time was too serious
for the utility of bagatelles to be much considered
by any. Paine engages Sieyès on his own ground,
and brings historic evidence to prove that the wars
of succession, civil and foreign, show hereditary a
worse evil than elective headship, as illustrated by
Poland, Holland, and America. But he does not

defend the method of either of these countries, and clearly shows that he is, as Sieyès said, a " poly-crat," so far as the numerical composition of the Executive is concerned.[1]   He affirms, however, that governing is no function of a republican Executive. The law alone governs.   " The sovereign authority in any country is the power of making laws, and everything else is an official department."

More than fifty thousand copies of the first part of " The Rights of Man " had been sold, and the public hungrily awaited the author's next work.   But he kept back his proofs until Burke should fulfil his promise of returning to the subject and comparing the English and French constitutions.   He was disappointed, however, at finding no such comparison in Burke's " Appeal from the New to the Old Whigs."   It did, however, contain a menace that was worth waiting for.

" Oldys " (Chalmers) says that Paine was disappointed at not being arrested for his first pamphlet on " The Rights of Man," and had, " while fluttering on the wing for Paris, hovered about London a whole week waiting to be taken."   It is, indeed, possible that he would have been glad to elicit just then a fresh decision from the courts in favor of freedom of speech and of the press, which would strengthen faint hearts.   If he had this desire he was resolved not to be disappointed a second time.

---

[1] " I have always been opposed to the mode of refining government up to an individual, or what is called a single Executive.   Such a man will always be the chief of a party.   A plurality is far better.   It combines the mass of a nation better together.   And besides this, it is necessary to the manly mind of a republic that it lose the debasing idea of obeying an individual."— Paine MS.

A publisher (Chapman) offered him a thousand guineas for the manuscript of Part II. Paine declined ; " he wished to reserve it in his own hands." Facts afterwards appeared which rendered it probable that this was a ministerial effort to suppress the book.[1]

Paine's Part Second was to appear about the first of February, or before the meeting of Parliament. But the printer (Chapman) threw up the publication, alleging its " dangerous tendencies," whereby it was delayed until February 17th, when it was published by Jordan. Meanwhile, his elaborate scheme for reducing taxes so resembled that which Pitt had just proposed in Parliament that the author appended his reasons for believing that his pages had been read by the government clerk, Chalmers, and his plan revealed to Pitt. " Be the case, however, as it may, Mr. Pitt's plan, little and diminutive as it is, would have made a very awkward appear-

---

[1] Paine may, indeed, only have apprehended alterations, which he always dreaded. His friends, knowing how much his antagonists had made of his grammatical faults, sometimes suggested expert revision. " He would say," says Richard Carlile, " that he only wished to be known as he was, without being decked with the plumes of another."

At the time (September) when Chapman began printing Paine's Part II., George Chalmers brought to the same press his libellous " Life of Pain." On learning that Chapman was printing Paine, Chalmers took his book away. As Chalmers was a government employé, and his work larger, Chapman returned Paine's work to him half printed, and the Chalmers book was restored to him. As Chapman stated in his testimony, and so wrote to Paine (January 17, 1792), that he was unwilling to go on with the printing because of the dangerous tendency of a part of it, his offer of a thousand guineas for it could only have contemplated its expurgation or total suppression. That it was the latter, and that the money was to be paid by the government, is rendered probable by the evidences in Chalmers' book, when it appeared, that he had been allowed the perusal of Paine's manuscript while in Chapman's hands. Chalmers also displays intimate knowledge of Chapman's business transactions with Paine.

ance had this work appeared at the time the printer
had engaged to finish it."

In the light of Pitt's subsequent career it is a
significant fact that, in the beginning of 1792, he
should be suspected of stealing Paine's thunder !
And, indeed, throughout Paine's Part Second the
tone towards Pitt implies some expectation of
reform from him.   Its severity is that which English agitators for constitutional reform have for a
half century made familiar and honorable.   The
historical student finds mirrored in this work the
rosy picture of the United States as seen at its
dawn by the disfranchised people of Europe, and
beside that a burdened England now hardly credi-
ble.   It includes an historical statement of the powers
claimed by the crown and gradually distributed
among non-elective peers and class-elective commoners, the result being a combination of all three
against admission of the people to any degree of
self-government.   Though the arraignment is heavy,
the method of reform is set forth with moderation.
Particular burdens are pointed out, and England is
warned to escape violent revolution by accommo-
dating itself to the new age.   It is admitted that
no new system need be constructed.   " Mankind
(from the long tyranny of assumed power) have had
so few opportunities of making the necessary trials
on modes and principles of government, in order to
discover the best, *that government is but now beginning to be known*, and experience is yet wanting to
determine many particulars."   Paine frankly retracts
an old opinion of his own, that the legislature
should be unicameral.   He now thinks that, though

there should be but one representation, it might secure wiser deliberation to divide it, by lot, into two or three parts. " Every proposed bill shall first be debated in those parts, by succession, that they may become hearers of each other, but without taking any vote; after which the whole representation to assemble, for a general debate, and determination by vote." The great necessity is that England shall gather its people, by representation, in convention and frame a constitution which shall contain the means of peaceful development in accordance with enlightenment and necessity.

In Part I. Paine stated his general principles with some reservations, in view of the survival of royalty in the French constitution. In Part II. his political philosophy is freely and fully developed, and may be summarized as follows :

1. Government is the organization of the aggregate of those natural rights which individuals are not competent to secure individually, and therefore surrender to the control of society in exchange for the protection of all rights.

2. Republican government is that in which the welfare of the whole nation is the object.

3. Monarchy is government, more or less arbitrary, in which the interests of an individual are paramount to those of the people generally.

4. Aristocracy is government, partially arbitrary, in which the interests of a class are paramount to those of the people generally.

5. Democracy is the whole people governing themselves without secondary means.

6. Representative government is the control of a nation by persons elected by the whole nation.

7. The Rights of Man mean the right of all to representation.

Democracy, simple enough in small and primitive societies, degenerates into confusion by extension to large populations. Monarchy, which originated amid such confusion, degenerates into incapacity by extension to vast and complex interests requiring "an assemblage of practical knowledges which no one individual can possess." "The aristocratical form has the same vices and defects with the monarchical, except that the chance of abilities is better from the proportion of numbers."

The representative republic advocated by Paine is different from merely epitomized democracy. "Representation is the delegated monarchy of a nation." In the early days of the American republic, when presidential electors were independent of the constituents who elected them, the filtration of democracy was a favorite principle among republicans. Paine evidently regards the representative as different from a delegate, or mere commissioner carrying out instructions. The representatives of a people are clothed with their sovereignty ; that, and not opinions or orders, has been transferred to them by constituencies. Hence we find Paine, after describing the English people as "fools" (p. 260), urging representation as a sort of natural selection of wisdom.

"Whatever wisdom constituently is, it is like a seedless plant ; it may be reared when it appears, but it cannot be voluntarily produced. There is always a sufficiency somewhere in the general mass of society for all purposes ; but, with respect to the parts of society, it is continually changing place. It rises in one today, in another tomorrow, and has most probably visited in rotation every family of the earth, and again withdrawn. As this is the order of nature, the order of government must follow it, or government will, as we see it does, degenerate into ignorance. The hereditary system therefore, is as repugnant to human wisdom as to human rights ; and is as absurd as unjust. As the republic of letters brings forward the best literary productions, by giving to genius a fair and universal chance, so the representative system is calculated to produce the wisest laws, by collecting wisdom where it can be found."

We have seen that " Publicola " (John Quincy Adams) in his answer to Paine's Part I. had left the people no right to alter government but the right of revolution, by violence ; Erskine pointed out that Burke's pamphlet had similarly closed every other means of reform. Paine would civilize reformation :

" Formerly, when divisions arose respecting governments, recourse was had to the sword, and civil war ensued. That savage custom is exploded by the new system, and reference is had to national conventions. Discussion and the general will arbitrate the question, private opinion yields with a good grace, and order is preserved uninterrupted."

Thus he is really trying to supplant the right of revolution with the right of evolution :

" It is now towards the middle of February. Were I to take a turn in the country the trees would present a leafless wintery appearance. As people are apt to pluck twigs as they go along, I perhaps might do the same, and by chance might observe that a single bud on that twig had begun to smell. I should reason very unnaturally, or rather not reason at all to suppose this was the only bud in England which had this appearance. Instead of deciding thus, I should instantly conclude that the same appearance was beginning, or about to begin, everywhere ; and though the vegetable sleep will continue longer on some trees and plants than others, and though some of them may not blossom for two or three years, all will be in leaf in the summer, except those which are rotten. What pace the political summer may keep with the natural, no human foresight can determine. It is, however, not difficult to perceive that the Spring is begun. Thus wishing, as I sincerely do, freedom and happiness to all nations, I close the Second Part."

Apparently the publisher expected trouble. In the *Gazetteer*, January 25th, had appeared the following notice :

"MR. PAINE, it is known, is to produce another book this season. The composition of this is now past, and it was given a few weeks since to two printers, whose presses it was to go through as soon as possible. They printed about half of it, and then, being alarmed by *some intimations*, refused to go further. Some delay has thus occurred, but another printer has taken it, and in the course of the next month it will appear. Its title is to be a repetition of the former, 'The Rights of Man,' of which the words 'Part the Second' will shew that it is a continuation."

That the original printer, Chapman, impeded the publication is suggested by the fact that on February 7th, thirteen days after the above announcement, Paine writes : "Mr. Chapman, please to deliver to Mr. Jordan the remaining sheets of the Rights of Man." And that "some intimations" were received by Jordan also may be inferred from the following note and enclosure to him :

"February 16, 1792.—For your satisfaction and my own, I send you the enclosed, tho' I do not apprehend there will be any occasion to use it.   If, in case there should, you will immediately send a line for me under cover to Mr. Johnson, St. Paul's Church-Yard, who will forward it to me, upon which I shall come and answer personally for the work.   Send also to Mr. Horne Tooke.—T. P."

"February 16, 1792.—Sir: Should any person, under the sanction of any kind of authority, enquire of you respecting the author and publisher of the Rights of Man, you will please to mention me as the author and publisher of that work, and shew to such person this letter.   I will, as soon as I am made acquainted with it, appear and answer for the work personally.—Your humble servant,

"THOMAS PAINE.

" Mr. Jordan,
      No. 166 Fleet-street."

Some copies were in Paine's hands three days before publication, as appears by a note of February 13th to Jefferson, on hearing of Morris' appointment as Minister to France :

"Mr. Kennedy, who brings this to New York, is on the point of setting out.   I am therefore confined to time.   I have enclosed six copies of my work for yourself in a parcel addressed to the President, and three or four for my other friends, which I wish you to take the trouble of presenting.

"I have just heard of Governeur Morris's appointment.   *It is a most unfortunate one ;* and, as I shall mention the same thing to him when I see him, I do not express it to you with the injunction of confidence.   He is just now arrived in London, and this circumstance has served, as I see by the french papers, to increase the dislike and suspicion of some of that nation and the National Assembly against him.

"In the present state of Europe it would be best to make no appointments."

Lafayette wrote Washington a strong private protest against Morris, but in vain.   Paine spoke frankly to Morris, who mentions him on Washington's birthday :

"February 22. I read Paine's new publication today, and tell him that I am really afraid he will be punished. He seems to laugh at this, and relies on the force he has in the nation. He seems to become every hour more drunk with self-conceit. It seems, however, that his work excites but little emotion, and rather raises indignation. I tell him that the disordered state of things in France works against all schemes of reformation both here and elsewhere. He declares that the riots and outrages in France are nothing at all. It is not worth while to contest such declarations. I tell him, therefore, that as I am sure he does not mean what he says, I shall not dispute it. Visit the Duchess of Gordon, who tells me that she supposes I give Paine his information about America, and speaks very slightly of our situation, as being engaged in a civil war with the Indians. I smile, and tell her that Britain is also at war with Indians, though in another hemisphere."

In his appendix Paine alludes vaguely to the book of George Chalmers (" Oldys ").

" A ministerial bookseller in Picadilly, who has been employed, as common report says, by a clerk of one of the boards closely connected with the Ministry (the board of Trade and Plantations, of which Lord Hawkesbury is president) to publish what he calls my Life (I wish his own life and that of the Cabinet were as good,) used to have his books printed at the same printing office that I employed."

In his fifth edition Chalmers claims that this notice of his work, unaccompanied by any denial of its statements, is an admission of their truth. It looks as if Paine had not then seen the book, but he never further alluded to it. There was nothing in Chalmers' political or orthographical criticisms requiring answer, and its tar and feathers were so adroitly mixed, and applied with such a masterly hand, that Paine had to endure his literary lynching in silence. " Nothing can lie like the truth."[1]   Chalmers' libels were so ingeniously interwoven with the actual stumbles and humiliations of Paine's early life, that the facts could not be told without dragging before the public his mother's corpse, and breaking treaty with his divorced wife.   Chalmers would have been more successful as a government employé in this business had he not cared more for himself than for his party.   By advertising, as we have seen (Preface, xv), his first edition as a "Defence" of Paine's writings he reaped a pecuniary harvest from the Painites before the substitution of " Review" tempted the Burkites. This trick probably enraged more than it converted. The pompous pseudonym covered a vanity weak enough to presently drop its lion skin, revealing ears sufficiently long to expect for a government clerk the attention accorded to a reverend M.A. of the University of Pennsylvania.   This degree was not only understood in England with a clerical connotation, but it competed with Paine's " M.A." from the same institution.   The pseudonym also concealed the record of Chalmers as a Tory refugee from Maryland, and an opponent of Burke, long enough to sell several editions.   But the author was known early in 1792, and was named in an important pamphlet by no means altogether favorable to Paine.   After rebuking Paine for personalities towards men whose station prevents reply, this

---

[1] Not that Chalmers confines himself to perversions of fact.   The book bore on its title-page five falsehoods : " Pain," instead of " Paine " ; " Francis Oldys " ; " A. M." ; " University of Pennsylvania " ; " With a Defence of his Writings."   There is a marked increase of virulence with the successive editions.   The second is in cheap form, and bears at the back of its title this note : " Read this, and then hand it to others who are requested to do likewise."

writer also disagrees with him about the Constitution. But he declares that Paine has collected the essence of the most venerated writers of Europe in the past, and applied the same to the executive government, which cannot stand the test.

" The Constitution will ; but *the present mode of administering that Constitution* must shrink from the comparison. And this is the reason, that foolish Mr. Rose of the Treasury trembles on the bench, and the crafty clerk in Lord Hawkesbury's office, carries on his base attacks against Paine by sap, fights him under the mask of a Philadelphia parson, fit disguise for the most impudent falsehoods that ever were published, and stabs him in the dark. But, of this upstart clerk at the *Cockpit*, more hereafter." [1]

George Chalmers being mentioned by name in this and other pamphlets, and nothing like a repudiation coming from him or from " Oldys " in any of his ten editions, the libel recoiled on the government, while it damaged Paine. The meanness of meeting inconvenient arguments by sniffing village gossip for private scandals was resented, and the calumnies were discounted. Nevertheless, there was probably some weakening in the " Painite " ranks. Although this " un-English " tracking of a man from his cradle, and masked assassination angered the republicans, it could hardly fail to intimidate some. In every period it has been seen that the largest interests, even the liberties, of English peoples may be placed momentarily at the mercy of any incident strongly exciting the moral sentiment. A crafty clerk accuses Paine of mal-

[1] " Paine's Political and Moral Maxims, etc. By a Free-Born Englishman. London. Printed for H. D. Symonds, Paternoster Row, 1792." The introductory letter is dated May 15th.

treating his wife ; the leader's phalanx of friends is for one instant disconcerted ; Burke perceives the opportunity and points it out to the King ; Pitt must show equal jealousy of royal authority ; Paine is prosecuted. There is little doubt that Pitt was forced to this first step which reversed the traditions of English freedom, and gave that Minister his historic place as the English Robespierre of counter-revolution.[1]

On May 14th Paine, being at Bromley, Kent, learned that the government had issued summons against Jordan, his publisher. He hastened to London and assumed the expense of Jordan's defence. Jordan, however, privately conpromised the affair by agreeing to plead guilty, surrender his notes relating to Paine, and receive a verdict to the author's prejudice—that being really the end of the government's business with the publisher. On May 21st a summons was left on Paine at his London lodgings (Rickman's house) to appear at the Court of King's Bench on June 8th. On the same day issued a royal proclamation against seditious writings. On May 25th, in the debate on the Proclamation, Secretary Dundas said in the House of Commons that the proceedings against Jordan were instituted because Mr. Paine could not be found. Thereupon Paine, detecting the unreality of the prosecution of his publisher, addressed a letter to the Attorney-General. Alluding to the remark of Dundas in Parliament, he says :

[1] " Pitt ' used to say,' according to Lady Hester Stanhope, ' that Tom Paine was quite in the right, but then he would add, what am I to do ? As things are, if I were to encourage Tom Paine's opinions we should have a bloody revolution."—Encyclop. Britannica.

" Mr. Paine, Sir, so far from secreting himself never went a step out of his way, nor in the least instance varied from his usual conduct, to avoid any measure you might choose to adopt with respect to him. It is on the purity of his heart, and the universal utility of the principles and plans which his writings contain, that he rests the issue ; and he will not dishonour it by any kind of subterfuge. The apartments which he occupied at the time of writing the work last winter, he has continued to occupy to the present hour, and the solicitors of the prosecution know where to find him ; of which there is a proof in their own office, as far back as the 21st of May, and also in the office of my own attorney.—But admitting, for the sake of the case, that the reason for proceeding against the publication was, as Mr. Dundas stated, that Mr. Paine could not be found, that reason can now exist no longer. The instant that I was informed that an information was preparing to be filed against me as the author of, I believe, one of the most useful and benevolent books ever offered to mankind, I directed my attorney to put in an appearance ; and as I shall meet the prosecution fully and fairly, and with a good and upright conscience, I have a right to expect that no act of littleness will be made use of on the part of the prosecution towards influencing the future issue with respect to the author. This expression may, perhaps, appear obscure to you, but I am in the possession of some matters which serve to show that the action against the publisher is not intended to be a *real* action."

He then intimates that, if his suspicions should prove well-founded, he will withdraw from his intention of defending the publisher, and proposes that the case against Jordan be given up. At the close of his letter Paine says :

"I believe that Mr. Burke, finding himself defeated, has been one of the promoters of this prosecution ; and I shall return the compliment by shewing, in a future publication, that he has been a masked pensioner at £1500 per annum for about ten years. Thus it is that the public money is wasted, and the dread of public investigation is produced."

The secret negotiations with the publisher being thus discovered, no more was heard of Jordan, except that his papers were brought out at Paine's trial.

The Information against Paine, covering forty-one pages, octavo, is a curiosity.   It recites that

"Thomas Paine, late of London, gentleman, being a wicked, malicious, seditious, and ill-disposed person, and being greatly disaffected to our said Sovereign Lord the now King, and to the happy constitution and government of this kingdom . . . and to bring them into hatred and contempt, on the sixteenth day of February, in the thirty-second year of the reign of our said present Sovereign Lord the King, with force and arms at London aforesaid, to wit, in the parish of St. Mary le Bone, in the Ward of Cheap, he, the said Thomas, wickedly, maliciously and seditiously, did write and publish, and caused to be written and published, a certain false, scandalous, malicious, and seditious libel, of and concerning the said late happy Revolution, and the said settlements and limitations of the crown and regal governments of the said kingdoms and dominions . . . intituled, 'Rights of Man, Part the Second, Combining principle and practice.'   . . .   In one part thereof, according to the tenor and effect following, that is to say, 'All hereditary government is in its nature tyranny.   An heritable crown' (meaning, amongst others, the crown of this kingdom) 'or an heritable throne,' (meaning the throne of this kingdom), 'or by whatother fanciful name such things may be called, have no other significant explanation than that mankind are heritable property.   To inherit a government is to inherit the people, as if they were flocks and herds.' . . .   'The time is not very distant when England will laugh at itself for sending to Holland, Hanover, Zell, or Brunswick, for men' (meaning the said King William the Third, and King George the First) 'at the expence of a million a year, who understood neither her laws, her language, nor her interest, and whose capacities would scarcely have fitted them for the office of a parish constable. If government could be trusted to such hands, it must be some easy and simple thing indeed ; and materials fit for all the purposes may be found in every town and village in England.' In contempt of our said Lord the now King and his laws, to the evil example of all others in like case offending, and against the peace of our said Lord the King, his crown and dignity. Whereupon the said Attorney General of our said Lord the King, who for our said Lord the King in this behalf, prosecuteth for our said Lord the King, prayeth the consideration of the court here in the premises, and that due process of law may be awarded against him, the said Thomas Paine, in this behalf, to make him answer to our said Lord the King, touching and concerning the premises aforesaid.

" To this information the defendant hath appeared, and pleaded Not Guilty, and thereupon issue is joined."

The specifications and quotations in the Information are reiterated twice, in one case (Paine's note on William and Mary centenary), three times.[1] It is marvellous that such an author, martial with "force and arms," could still walk freely about London. But the machinery for suppressing thought had always a tendency to rust in England ; it had to be refurbished. To the royal proclamation against seditious writings corporations and rotten boroughs responded with loyal addresses. In the

---

[1] " I happened to be in England at the celebration of the centenary of the Revolution of 1688. The characters of William and Mary have always appeared to me detestable ; the one seeking to destroy his uncle, the other her father, to get possession of power themselves ; yet, as the nation was disposed to think something of the event, I felt hurt at seeing it ascribe the whole reputation of it to a man who had undertaken it as a job ; and who besides what he otherwise got, charged six hundred thousand pounds for the expense of the little fleet that brought him from Holland. George the First acted the same close-fisted part as William had done, and bought the Duchy of Bremen with the money he got from England, two hundred and fifty thousand pounds over and above his pay as King ; and, having thus purchased it at the expense of England, added it to his Hanoverian dominions for his own private profit. In fact every nation that does not govern itself is governed as a job. England has been the prey of jobs ever since the Revolution."

debate on that proclamation (May 25th) Secretary Dundas and Mr. Adam had arraigned Paine, and he addressed an open letter to the Secretary (June 6th) which was well received.   Mr. Adam had said that

" He had well considered the subject of constitutional publications, and was by no means ready to say that books of science upon government though recommending a doctrine or system different from the form of our constitution were fit objects of prosecution ; that if he did, he must condemn Harrington for his Oceana, Sir Thomas More for his Utopia, and Hume for his Idea of a Perfect Commonwealth. But the publication of Mr. Paine reviled what was most sacred in the Constitution, destroyed every principle of subordination, and established nothing in their room."

The real difficulty was that Paine *had* put something in the room of hereditary monarchy—not a Utopia, but the representative system of the United States. He now again compares the governmental expenses of England and America and their condition. He shows that the entire government of the United States costs less than the English pension list alone.

" Here is a form and system of government that is better organized than any other government in the world, and that for less than one hundred thousand pounds, and yet every member of Congress receives as a compensation for his time and attendance on public business, one pound seven shilings per day, which is at the rate of nearly five hundred pounds a year. This is a government that has nothing to fear. It needs no proclamations to deter people from writing and reading. It needs no political superstition to support it. It was by encouraging discussion and rendering the press free upon all subjects of government, that the principles of government became understood in America, and the people are now enjoying their present blessings under it. You hear of no riots, tumults and disorders in that country; because there exists no cause to produce them. Those things are never the effect of freedom, but of restraint, oppression, and excessive taxation."

On June 8th Paine appeared in court and was much disappointed by the postponement of his trial to December. Lord Onslow having summoned a meeting at Epsom of the gentry·in Surrey, to respond to the proclamation, receives due notice. Paine sends for presentation to the gentlemen one hundred copies of his " Rights of Man," one thousand of his " Letter to Dundas." The bearer is Horne Tooke, who opens his speech of presentation by remarking on the impropriety that the meeting should be presided over by Lord Onslow, a bed-chamber lord (sinecure) at £1,000, with a pension of £3,000. Tooke, being cut short, his speech was continued by Paine, whose two letters to Onslow (June 17th and 21st) were widely circulated.[1] On June 20th was written a respectful letter to the Sheriff of Sussex, or other presiding officer, requesting that it be read at a meeting to be held in Lewes. This interesting letter has already been quoted in connection with Paine's early residence at Lewes. In these letters the author reinforces his accused book, reminds the assemblies of their illegal conduct in influencing the verdict in a pending matter, taunts them with their meanness in

---

[1] To this noble pensioner and sinecurist he says : " What honour or happiness you can derive from being the principal pauper of the neighborhood, and occasioning a greater expence than the poor, the aged, and the infirm for ten miles round, I leave you to enjoy. At the same time I can see that it is no wonder you should be strenuous in suppressing a book which strikes at the root of these abuses."

seeking to refute by brute force what forty pamphlets had failed to refute by argument.

The meeting at Lewes, his old town, to respond
to the proclamation occurred on the fourth of
July. That anniversary of his first cause was celebrated by Paine also. Notified by his publisher
that upwards of a thousand pounds stood to his
credit, he directed it to be all sent as a present to
the Society for Constitutional Information.[1]

A careful tract of 1793 estimates the sales of
'The Rights of Man" up to that year at 200,000
copies.[2] In the opinion of the famous publisher
of such literature, Richard Carlile, the king's proclamation seriously impeded the sale. "One part
of the community is afraid to sell, and another to
purchase, under such conditions. It is not too much
to say that, if 'Rights of Man' had obtained two
or three years' free circulation in England and
Scotland, it would have produced a similar effect
to that which 'Common Sense' did in the United
States." However, the reign of terror had not
yet begun in France, nor the consequent reign of
panic in England.

[1] *The Argus,* July 6, 1792. See "Biographia Addenda," No. vii., London, 1792. To the same society Paine had given the right to publish his
"Letter to Dundas," "Common Sense," and "Letter to Raynal" in new
editions.

[2] "Impartial Memoirs of the Life of Thomas Paine," London, 1793.
There were numbers of small "Lives" of Paine printed in these years, but
most of them were mere stealings from "Oldys."

CHAPTER XXIII.

THE DEPUTY FOR CALAIS IN THE CONVENTION.

THE prosecution of Paine in England had its counterpart in a shrine across the channel. The *Moniteur*, June 17, 1792, announces the burning of Paine's works at " Excester," and the expulsion from Manchester of a man pointed out as Paine. Since April 16th his " Rights of Man," sympathetically translated by M. Lanthenas, had been in every French home. Paine's portrait, just painted in England by Romney and engraved by Sharpe, was in every cottage, framed in immortelles. In this book the philosophy of visionary reformers took practical shape. From the ashes of Rousseau's " Contrat Social," burnt in Paris, rose " The Rights of Man," no phœnix, but an eagle of the new world, with eye not blinded by any royal sun.[1] It comes to tell how by union of France and America—of Lafayette and Washington — the " Contrat Social " was framed into the Constitution of a happy and glorious new earth, over it a new heaven unclouded by priestly power or superstitions. By that book of Paine's (Part I),

[1] L'Esprit du Contrat Social ; suivi de l'Esprit de Sens Commun de Thomas Paine. Présenté a la Convention. Par le Citoyen Boinvilliers, Instituteur et ci-devant Membre de plusieurs Sociétés Littéraires. L'an second.

347

the idea of a national convention was made the purpose of the French leaders who were really inspired by an "enthusiasm of humanity." In December, 1791, when the legislature sits paralyzed under royal vetoes, Paine's panacea is proposed.[1]

On the tenth of August, 1792, after the massacre of the Marseillese by the King's Swiss guards, one book, hurled from the window of the mobbed palace, felled an American spectator — Robert Gilmor, of Baltimore—who consoled himself by carrying it home. The book, now in the collection of Dr. Thomas Addis Emmet, New York, was a copy of "The Thirteen Constitutions," translated by Franklin's order into French (1783) and distributed among the monarchs of Europe.[2] What a contrast between the peace and order amid which the thirteen peoples, when the old laws and authorities were abolished, formed new ones, and these scenes in France! "For upwards of two years from the commencement of the American war," wrote Paine, "and a longer period, in several of the American States, there were no established forms of government. The old governments had been abolished, and the country was too much occupied in defence to employ its attention in establishing new governments; yet, during this interval, order and harmony were preserved as inviolate as in any coun-

[1] "*Veto* after *Veto;* your thumbscrew paralysed! Gods and men may see that the Legislature is in a false position. As, alas, who is in a true one? Voices already murmur for a National Convention."—Carlyle.

[2] "Constitutions des Treize États-Unis de l'Amérique." The French king's arms are on the red morocco binding, and on the title a shield, striped and winged; above this thirteen minute stars shaped into one large star, six-pointed. For the particulars of Franklin's gift to the monarchs see Sparks' "Franklin," x., p. 39. See also p. 290 of this volume.

try in Europe." When Burke pointed to the first riots in France, Paine could make a retort: the mob is what your cruel governments have made it, and only proves how necessary the overthrow of such governments. That French human nature was different from English nature he could not admit. Liberty and equality would soon end these troubles of transition. On that same tenth of August Paine's two great preliminaries are adopted: the hereditary representative is superseded and a national convention is called. The machinery for such convention, the constituencies, the objects of it, had been read in "The Rights of Man," as illustrated in the United States and Pennsylvania, by every French statesman.[1] It was the American Republic they were about to found; and notwithstanding the misrepresentation of that nation by its surviving courtiers, these French republicans recognized their real American Minister: Paine is summoned.

On August 26, 1792, the National Assembly, on proposal of M. Guadet, in the name of the "Commission Extraordinaire," conferred the title of French citizen on "Priestley, Payne, Benthom, Wilberforce, Clarkson, Mackintosh, David Williams, Gorani, Anacharsis Clootz, Campe, Cormelle, Paw, N. Pestalozzi, Washington, Hamilton, Maddison, Klopstoc, Kosciusko, Gilleers." Schiller

---

[1] "Théorie et Pratique des Droits de l'Homme. Par Thomas Paine, Sécrétaire du Congres au Département des Affaires Étrangeres pendant la guerre d'Amérique, auteur du 'Sens Commun,' et des Réponses à Burke. Traduit en Français par F. Lanthenas, D.M., et par le Traducteur du "Sens Commun." À Paris: Chez les Directeurs de l'Imprimerie du Cercle Social, rue du Théâtre Français, No. 4. 1792. L'an quatrième de La Liberté."

was afterwards added, and on September 25th the *Patriote* announces the same title conferred on Thomas Cooper, John Horne Tooke, John Oswald, George Boies, Thomas Christie, Dr. Joseph Warner, Englishmen, and Joel Barlow, American.[1]

Paine was elected to the French Convention by three different departments—Oise, Puy-de-Dôme, and Pas-de-Calais. The votes appear to have been unanimous.

Here is an enthusiastic appeal (Riom, le 8 Septembre) signed by Louvet, "auteur de la Sentinelle," and thirty-two others, representing nine communes, to Paine, that day elected representative of Puy-de-Dôme :

"Your love for humanity, for liberty and equality, the useful works that have issued from your heart and pen in their defence, have determined our choice. It has been hailed with universal and reiterated applause. Come, friend of the people, to swell the number of patriots in an assembly which will decide the destiny of a great people, perhaps of the human race. The happy period you have predicted for the nations has arrived. Come! do not deceive their hope !"

But already Calais, which elected him September 6th, had sent a municipal officer, Achille Audibert, to London, to entreat Paine's acceptance. Paine was so eager to meet the English government in court, that he delayed his answer. But his friends had reason to fear that his martyrdom might be less mild than he anticipated, and urged his acceptance. There had been formed a society of the " Friends of Liberty," and, at its gathering of September 12th, Paine appears to have poured forth

[1] " Life and Letters of Joel Barlow," etc., by Charles Burr Todd, New York, 1886, p. 97.

"inflammatory eloquence." At the house of his friend Johnson, on the following evening, Paine was reporting what he had said to some sympathizers, among them the mystical William Blake, who was convinced that the speech of the previous night would be followed by arrest. Gilchrist's account of what followed is here quoted:

"On Paine's rising to leave, Blake laid his hand on the orator's shoulder, saying, 'You must not go home, or you are a dead man,' and hurried him off on his way to France, whither he was now in any case bound to take his seat as a legislator. By the time Paine was at Dover, the officers were in his house, [he was staying at Rickman's, in Marylebone] and, some twenty minutes after the Custom House officials at Dover had turned over his slender baggage, narrowly escaped from the English Tories. Those were hanging days! Blake on the occasion showed greater sagacity than Paine, whom, indeed, Fuseli affirmed to be more ignorant of the common affairs of life than himself even. Spite of unworldliness and visionary faculty, Blake never wanted for prudence and sagacity in ordinary matters." [1]

Before leaving London Paine managed to have an interview with the American Minister, Pinckney, who thought he could do good service in the Convention.

Mr. Frost, who accompanied Paine and Audibert, had information of certain plans of the officials. He guided them to Dover by a circuitous route—Rochester, Sandwich, Deal. With what emotions does our world-wanderer find himself in the old town where he married and suffered with his first love, Mary Lambert, whose grave is near! Nor is he so far from Cranbrook, where his wife receives her mysterious remittances, but since their separa-

---

[1] "Life of William Blake," by Alexander Gilchrist, p. 94.

tion "has not heard of" this said Thomas Paine, as her testimony goes some years later. Paine is parting from England and its ghosts forever. The travellers find Dover excited by the royal proclamation. The collector of customs has had general instructions to be vigilant, and searches the three men, even to their pockets. Frost pretended a desire to escape, drawing the scent from Paine. In his report (September 15th) of the search to Mr. Dundas, Paine says :

"Among the letters which he took out of my trunk were two sealed letters, given into my charge by the American minister in London [Pinckney], one of which was addressed to the American minister at Paris, the other to a private gentleman ; a letter from the president of the United States, and a letter from the secretary of State in America, both directed to me, and which I had received from the American minister, now in London, and were private letters of friendship ; a letter from the electoral body of the department of Calais, containing the notification of my being elected to the National Convention ; and a letter from the president of the National Assembly informing me of my being also elected for the department of the Oise [Versailles]. . . . When the collector had taken what papers and letters he pleased out of the trunks, he proposed to read them. The first letter he took up for this purpose was that from the president of the United States to me. While he was doing this I said, that it was very extraordinary that General Washington could not write a letter of private friendship to me, without its being subject to be read by a custom-house officer. Upon this Mr. Frost laid his hand over the face of the letter, and told the collector that he should not read it, and took it from him. Mr. Frost then, casting his eyes on the concluding paragraph of the letter, said, I will read this part to you, which he did ; of which the following is an exact transcript—'And as no one can feel a greater interest in the happiness of mankind than I do, it is the first wish of my heart that the enlightened policy of the present age may diffuse to all men those blessings to which they are entitled and lay the foundation of happiness for future generations.'"

So Washington's nine months' delay (p. 302) in acknowledging Paine's letter and gift of fifty volumes had brought his letter in the nick of time. The collector quailed before the President's signature. He took away the documents, leaving a list of them, and they were presently returned. Soon afterward the packet sailed, and "twenty minutes later" the order for Paine's arrest reached Dover. Too late! Baffled pursuers gnash their teeth, and Paine passes to his ovation.

What the ovation was to be he could hardly anticipate even from the cordial, or glowing, letter of Hérault Séchelles summoning him to the Convention,—a fine translation of which by Cobbett is given in the Appendix. Ancient Calais, in its time, had received heroes from across the channel, but hitherto never with joy. That honor the centuries reserved for a Thetford Quaker. As the packet sails in a salute is fired from the battery; cheers sound along the shore. As the representative for Calais steps on French soil soldiers make his avenue, the officers embrace him, the national cockade is presented. A beautiful lady advances, requesting the honor of setting the cockade in his hat, and makes him a pretty speech, ending with Liberty, Equality, and France. As they move along the Rue de l'Égalité (late Rue du Roi) the air rings with "*Vive Thomas Paine!*" At the town hall he is presented to the Municipality, by each member embraced, by the Mayor also addressed. At the meeting of the Constitutional

Society of Calais, in the *Minimes*, he sits beside the president, beneath the bust of Mirabeau and the united colors of France, England, and America. There is an official ceremony announcing his election, and plaudits of the crowd, " *Vive la Nation !* " " *Vive Thomas Paine !* "   The *Minimes* proving too small, the meeting next day is held in the church, where martyred saints and miraculous Madonnas look down on this miraculous Quaker, turned savior of society.   In the evening, at the theatre, a box is decorated "For the Author of 'The Rights of Man.'"

Thus for once our wayfarer, so marked by time and fate, received such welcome as hitherto had been accorded only to princes.   Alas, that the aged eyes which watched over his humble cradle could not linger long enough to see a vision of this greatness, or that she who bore the name of Elizabeth Paine was too far out of his world as not even to know that her husband was in Europe.   A theatrical La France must be his only bride, and in the end play the rôle of a cruel stepmother.   When Washington was on his way to his inauguration in New York, passing beneath triumphal arches, amid applauding crowds, a sadness came over him as he reflected, so he wrote a friend, how easily all this enthusiasm might be reversed by a failure in the office for which he felt himself so little competent. But for Paine on his way to sit in the Convention of a People's representatives—one summoned by his own pen for objects to which his life was devoted, for which he had the training of events as well as studies,—for him there could be no black star hovering over his welcome and his triumphal pathway to Paris. For, besides his fame, there had preceded him to every town rumors of how this representative of man—of man in America, England, France—had been hunted by British oppressors down to the very edge of their coast. Those outwitted pursuers had made Paine a greater power in France than he might otherwise have been. The *Moniteur* (September 23d) told the story, and adds: " Probably M. Payne will have been indemnified for such injustices by the brilliant reception accorded him on his arrival on French soil."

Other representatives of Calais were Personne, Carnat, Bollet, Magniez, Varlet, Guffroy, Eulard, Duquesnoy, Lebas, Daunon. It could hardly be expected that there should be no jealousy of the concentration of enthusiasm on the brilliant Anglo-American. However, none of this yet appeared, and Paine glided flower-crowned in his beautiful barge, smoothly toward his Niagara rapids. He had, indeed, heard the distant roar, in such confused, hardly credited, rumors of September massacres as had reached London, but his faith in the National Convention was devout. All the riots were easily explained by the absence of that charm. He had his flask of constitutional oil, other representatives no doubt had theirs, and when they gathered on September 21st, amid equinoctial gales, the troubled waters would be still.

Paine reached White's Hotel, Paris, September 19th ; on the 20th attends a gathering of the " Conventionnels "; on the 21st moves in their procession to the Tuileries, for verification of credentials by the expiring Assembly, repairing with them for work in the Salle du Manége. He was introduced by the Abbé Grégoire, and received with acclamations.

On September 21st, then, the Year One opens. It greets mankind with the decree: "Royalty is from this day abolished in France."

September 22d, on a petition from Orleans, Danton proposes removal of the entire administrative corps, municipal and judicial, to prevent their removal by popular violence. Paine (through Goupilleau) suggests postponement for more thorough discussion. Having got rid of kings they must be rid of royal hirelings; but if partial reforms are made in the judiciary system those institutions cannot possess coherence; for the present persons might be changed without altering laws; finally, justice cannot be administered by men ignorant of the laws. Danton welcomes Paine's views, and it is decreed that the administrative bodies be renewed by popular election; but the limitations on eligibility, fixed by the Constitution of 1791, are abolished—the judge need not be a lawyer, nor the municipal officer a proprietor.

On September 25th appears Paine's letter to his " Fellow Citizens," expressing his " affectionate gratitude" for his adoption and his election. " My felicity is increased by seeing the barrier broken down that divided patriotism by spots of earth, and limited citizenship to the soil, like vegetation." The letter is fairly "floreal" with optimistic felicities. " An over-ruling Providence is regenerating the old world by the principles of the new." "It is impossible to conquer a nation determined to be free." "It is now the cause of all nations against the cause of all courts." "In entering on this great scene, greater than any nation has been called to act in, let us say to the agitated mind, be calm! Let us punish by instruction, rather than by revenge. Let us begin the new era by a greatness of friendship, and hail the approach of union and success."

October 11th, a committee to frame a constitution is appointed, consisting of Sieyès, Paine, Brissot, Pétion, Vergniaud, Gensonne, Barrère, Danton, Condorcet. Supplementary—Barbaroux, Hérault Séchelles, Lanthenas, Débry, the Abbé Fauchet, Lavicourterie. Paine was placed second to his old adversary, Sieyès, only because of his unfamiliarity with French. At least four of the committee understood English—Condorcet, Danton, Barrère, and Brissot. Paine had known Brissot in America, their friendship being caused by literary tastes in common, and the zeal of both for negro emancipation.

On October 25th was written for *Le Patriote Français* (edited by Brissot) an address by Paine arguing carefully the fallacies of royalism. He tersely expresses the view now hardly paradoxical, that "a talented king is worse than a fool."

" We are astonished at reading that the Egyptians set upon the throne a stone, which they called king. Well! such a monarch was less absurd and less mischievous than those before whom nations prostrate themselves. At least he deceived no one. None supposed that he possessed qualities or a character. They did not call him Father of his People; and yet it would have been scarcely more ridiculous than to give such a title to a blockhead *(un étourdi)* whom the right of succession crowns at eighteen. A dumb idol is better than one animated." [1]

In this letter Paine adroitly prepares the way for his purpose of saving the life of Louis XVI., for whose blood the thirst is growing. "It is little," he says, "to overthrow the idol; it is the pedestal which must especially be beaten down. It is the kingly *office*, rather than the officer, that is destructive *(meurtrière)*. This is not seen by every one."

In those who sympathized with the human spirit of his views Paine inspired deep affection. A volume might be filled with the personal tributes to him. In Paris he was the centre of a loving circle, from the first. "I lodge," writes Lord Edward Fitzgerald to his mother (October 30th), "with my friend Paine—we breakfast, dine, and sup together. The more I see of his interior, the more I like and respect him. I cannot express how kind he is to me; there is a simplicity of manner, a goodness of heart, and a strength of mind in him, that I never knew a man before possess." [2]

Paine was chosen by his fellow-deputies of Calais to offer the Convention the congratulations of their department on the abolition of monarchy. This letter, written October 27th, was on that day read in Convention, in French.

---

[1] "Father of his People" was a title of Geo. III. "Father of his Country" was applied to Peyton Randolph, first president of Congress. Paine's essay, quoted above, which is not included in the editions of Paine's works, was printed by James Watson in London, 1843, the translation being by W. J. Linton, who, while editing the *National*, also wrote the same year, and for the same publisher, a small but useful "Life of Paine."

[2] Moore's "Life and Death of Lord Edward Fitzgerald."

"CITIZEN PRESIDENT : In the name of the deputies of the department of Pas de Calais, I have the honor of presenting to the Convention the felicitations of the General Council of the Commune of Calais on the abolition of royalty.

"Amid the joy inspired by this event, one can not forbear some pain at the folly of our ancestors, who have placed us under the necessity of treating seriously *(solennellement)* the abolition of a phantom.

"THOMAS PAINE, Deputy, etc."[1]

The *Moniteur*, without printing the letter, says that applause followed the word "*fantôme*." The use of this word was a resumption of Paine's effort to save the life of the king, then a prisoner of state, by a suggestion of his insignificance.[2] But he very soon realizes the power of the phantom, which lies not only in the monarchical Trade Union of Europe but in the superstition of monarchy in those who presently beheaded poor Louis. Paine was always careful to call him Louis Capet, but the French deputies took the king seriously to the last. The king's divine foot was on their necks in the moment when their axe was on his. But Paine feared a more terrible form which had arisen in place of the royal prisoner of the Temple. On the fourth day of the Convention Marat arose with the words, " It seems a great many here are my enemies," and received the shouted answer, " All ! all !" Paine had seen Marat hypnotize the Convention, and hold it subdued in the hollow of his hand. Here was King Stork ready to succeed King Log.

[1] This letter I copied and translated in the Historical Exhibition of the Revolution, in Paris, 1889. This letter of the "*philosophe anglais*," as he is described in the catalogue, is in the collection of M. Charavay, and was framed with the Bonneville portrait of Paine.

[2] In his republican manifesto at the time of the king's flight he had deprecated revenge towards the captured monarch.

But what has the Convention to do with deciding about Louis XVI., or about affairs, foreign or domestic? It is there like the Philadelphia Convention of 1787; its business is to frame a Constitution, then dissolve, and let the organs it created determine special affairs. So the committee work hard on the Constitution; "Deputy Paine and France generally expect," finds Carlyle, "all finished in a few months." But, alas, the phantom is too strong for the political philosophers. The crowned heads of Europe are sinking their differences for a time and consulting about this imprisoned brother. And at the same time the subjects of those heads are looking eagerly towards the Convention.[1]

The foreign menaces had thus far caused the ferocities of the revolution, for France knew it was worm-eaten with enemies of republicanism. But now the Duke of Brunswick had retreated, the French arms were victorious everywhere; and it is just possible that the suicide of the Republic—the Reign of Terror—might never have been completed but for that discovery (November 20th) of secret papers walled up in the Tuileries. These papers compromised many, revealed foreign schemes, and made all Paris shriek "Treason!" The smith (Gamain) who revealed the locality of that invisible iron press which he had set under the wainscot, made a good deal of history that day.

---

[1] "That which will astonish posterity is that at Stockholm, five months after the death of Gustavus, and while the northern Powers are leaguing themselves against the liberty of France, there has been published a translation of Thomas Paine's " Rights of Man," the translator being one of the King's secretaries!"—*Moniteur*, Nov. 8, 1792.

A cry for the king's life was raised, for to France he was the head and front of all conspiracy.

How everybody bent under the breath of those days may be seen in the fact that even Gouverneur Morris is found writing to Lord Wycombe (November 22d) : " All who wish to partake thereof [freedom] will find in us (ye French) a sure and certain ally. We will chase tyranny, and, above all, *aristocracy*, off the theatre of the Universe." [1]

Paine was living in the " Passage des Pétites Pères, No. 7."   There are now two narrow passages of that name, uniting near the church " Notre Dame des Victoires," which still bears the words, " Liberté, Égalité, Fraternité."   No. 7 has disappeared as a number, but it may have described a part of either No. 8 or No. 9,—both ancient.   Here he was close to a chapel of the Capucines, unless, indeed, it had already been replaced by this church, whose interior walls are covered with tablets set up by individuals in acknowledgment of the Virgin's miraculous benefits to them.   Here he might study superstition, and no doubt did ; but on November 20th he has to deal with the madness of a populace which has broken the outer chains of superstition with a superstition of their own, one without restraints to replace the chains.   Beneath his window the Place des Victoires will be crowded with revolutionists, frantic under rumors of the discovered iron press and its treasonable papers.   He could hardly look out without seeing some poor human scape-goat

---

[1] " Diary and Letters."   The letter was probably written with knowledge of its liability to fall into the hands of the French Committee.   It could not deceive Wycombe.

seeking the altar's safety. Our Lady will look on him from her church the sad-eyed inquiry : " Is this, then, the new religion of Liberty, with which you supplant the Mother and Babe ? "

Paine has carried to success his anti-monarchical faith. He was the first to assail monarchy in America and in France. A little more than a year before, he had founded the first Republican Society in Europe, and written its Declaration on the door of the National Assembly. Sieyès had denounced him then as a " polyarchist." Now he sat with Sieyès daily, framing a republican Constitution, having just felicitated the Convention on the abolition of the phantom—Royalty. And now, on this terrible night of November 20th, this unmaker of kings finds himself the solitary deputy ready to risk his life to save the man whose crown he had destroyed. It is not simply because the old Quaker heart in him recoils from bloodshed, but that he would save the Republic from the peril of foreign invasion, which would surely follow the execution of Louis, and from disgrace in America, whose independence owed much to the fallen monarch.

In his little room, the lonely author, unable to write French, animated by sentiments which the best of the French revolutionists could not understand—Danton reminding him that " revolutions are not made of rose-water "—must have before the morrow's Convention some word that shall control the fury of the moment. Rose-water will not answer now. Louis must pass his ordeal ; his secret schemes have been revealed ; the treachery of his submissions to the people exposed. He is guilty, and the alternatives are a calm trial, or death by the hands of the mob. What is now most needed is delay, and, that secured, diversion of national rage from the individual Louis to the universal anti-republican Satan inspiring the crowned heads of Europe. Before the morning dawns, Paine has written his letter to the president. It is translated before the Convention meets, November 21st, and is read to that body the same day.[1] Louis XVI., he says, should be tried. The advice is not suggested by vengeance, but by justice and policy. If innocent, he may be allowed to prove it ; if guilty, he must be punished or pardoned by the nation. He would, however, consider Louis, individually, beneath the notice of the republic. The importance of his trial is that there is a conspiracy of "crowned brigands" against the liberties not only of France, but of all nations, and there is ground for suspecting that Louis XVI. was a partner in it. He should be utilized to ferret out the whole gang, and reveal to the various peoples what their monarchs, some of whom work in secret for fear of their subjects, are doing. Louis XVI. should not be dealt with except in the interest of all Europe.

"If, seeing in Louis XVI. only a weak and narrow-minded man, badly reared, as all like him, subject, it is said, to intemperance, imprudently re-established by the Constituent Assembly on a throne for which he was unfit,—if we hereafter show him some compassion, this compassion should be the effect of national magnanimity, and not a result of the burlesque notion of pretended inviolability."[2]

---

[1] "L' Histoire Parlémentaire," xx., p. 367.

[2] This essay has suffered in the translation found in English and American editions of Paine. The words "national magnanimity" are omitted. The phrase "brigands couronnés" becomes "crowned robbers" in England, and

Lamartine, in his history of the Girondists, reproaches Paine for these words concerning a king who had shown him friendship during the American war.   But the facts were not well explored in Lamartine's time.   Louis Blanc recognizes Paine's intent.[1]   " He had learned in England that killing a monarch does not kill monarchs."   This grand revolutionary proposal to raise the inevitable trial from the low plane of popular wrath against a prisoner to the dignity of a process against European monarchy, would have secured delay and calmer counsels.   If the reader, considering the newly discovered papers, and the whole situation, will examine critically Paine's words just quoted, he will find them meriting a judgment the reverse of Lamartine's.   With consummate art, the hourly imperilled king is shielded from

"crowned ruffians" in America.   Both versions are commonplace, and convey an impression of haste and mere abuse.   But Paine was a slow writer, and weighed his words even when " quarelling in print."   When this letter was written to the Convention its members were reading his Essay on Royalty, which filled seven columns of Brissot's *Patriote Français* three weeks before.   In that he had traced royalty to the bandit-chief.   " Several troops of banditti assemble for the purpose of upsetting some country, of laying contributions over it, of seizing the landed property, of reducing the people to thraldom.   The expedition being accomplished, the chief of the gang assumes the title of king or monarch.   Such has been the origin of royalty among all nations who live by the chase, agriculture, or the tending of flocks.   A second chieftain arriving obtains by force what has been acquired by violence.   He despoils his predecessor, loads him with fetters, puts him to death, and assumes his title.   In the course of ages the memory of the outrage is lost ; his successors establish new forms of government ; through policy, they become the instruments of a little good ; they invent, or cause to be invented, false genealogical tables ; they employ every means to render their race sacred ; the knavery of priests steps in to their assistance ; for their body-guard they take religion itself ; then it is that Royalty, or rather Tyranny, becomes immortal.   A power unjustly usurped is transformed into a hereditary right."

[1] " Hist. de la Révolution," etc., vol. vii., p. 396.

vindictive wrath by the considerations that he is *non compos*, not responsible for his bringing up, was put back on the throne by the Assembly, after he had left it, acknowledging his unfitness, and that compassion for him would be becoming to the magnanimity of France. A plea for the King's immunity from trial, for his innocence or his virtues, would at that juncture have been fatal. As it was, this ingenious document made an impression on the Convention, which ordered it to be printed. [1]

The delay which Paine's proposal would involve was, as Louis Blanc remarks, fatal to it. It remains now only to work among the members of the Convention, and secure if possible a majority that will be content, having killed the king, to save the man ; and, in saving him, to preserve him as an imprisoned hostage for the good behavior of Europe. This is now Paine's idea, and never did man toil more faithfully for another than he did for that discrowned Louis Capet.

[1] "Convention Nationale. Opinion de Thomas Payne, Deputé du Département de la Somme, concernant le jugement de Louis XVI. Précedé de sa lettre d'envoi au Président de la Convention. Imprimé par ordre de la Convention Nationale. À Paris. De l'imprimerie Nationale." It is very remarkable that, in a State paper, Paine should be described as deputy for the Somme. His votes in the Convention are all entered under Calais. Dr. John Moore, who saw much of Paine at this time, says, in his work on the French Revolution, that his (Paine's) writings for the Convention were usually translated into French by the Marchioness of Condorcet.

CHAPTER XXIV

OUTLAWED IN ENGLAND.

WHILE Paine was thus, towards the close of 1792, doing the work of a humane Englishman in France, his works were causing a revolution in England—a revolution the more effectual because bloodless.

In Paine's letter to Secretary Dundas (Calais, September 15th), describing the examination of his papers at Dover, a "postscript" states that among the papers handled was "a printed proof copy of my Letter to the Addressers, which will soon be published." This must have been a thumbscrew for the Secretary when he presently read the pamphlet that escaped his officers. In humor, freedom, and force this production may be compared with Carlyle's "Latter Day Pamphlets." Lord Stormont and Lord Grenville having made speeches about him, their services are returned by a speech which the author has prepared for them to deliver in Parliament. This satirical eulogy on the British constitution set the fashion for other radical encomiums of the wisdom of the king and of the peers, the incorruptibility of the commons, beauty of rotten boroughs, and freedom of the people from taxes, with which prosecuting attorneys were unable to

deal.   Having felicitated himself on the circulation
of his opinions by the indictment, and the adver-
tisements of his books by loyal " Addresses," Paine
taunts the government for its method of answering
argument.   It had been challenging the world for
a hundred years to admire the perfection of its
institutions.   At length the challenge is taken up,
and, lo, its acceptance is turned into a crime, and
the only defence of its perfection is a prosecution !
Paine points out that there was no sign of prosecution until his book was placed within reach of the
poor.   When cheap editions were clamored for by
Sheffield, Leicester, Chester, Warwickshire, and
Scotland, he had announced that any one might
freely publish it.   About the middle of April he
had himself put a cheap edition in the press.   He
knew he would be prosecuted for that, and so
wrote to Thomas Walker.[1]   It was the common
people the government feared.   He remarks that
on the same day (May 21st) the prosecution was
instituted and the royal proclamation issued—the
latter being indictable as an effort to influence the
verdict in a pending case.   He calls attention to
the " special jury," before which he was summoned.
It is virtually selected by the Master of the Crown
Office, a dependant on the Civil List assailed in his
book.   The special jury is treated to a dinner, and
given two guineas for a conviction, and but one
guinea and no dinner for acquittal.   Even a fairly

[1] At the trial the Attorney-General admitted that he had not prosecuted
Part I. because it was likely to be confined to judicious readers ; but this
still more reprehensible Part II. was, he said, with an industry incredible,
ushered into the world in all shapes and sizes, thrust into the hands of subjects of every description, even children's sweetmeats being wrapped in it.

selected local jury could not justly determine a constitutional issue affecting every part of the empire. So Paine brings under scrutiny every part of the legal machinery sprung on him, adding new illustrations of his charges against the whole system. He begins the siege, which Bradlaugh was to carry forward in a later time, against the corrupt Pension List, introducing it with his promised exposure of Edmund Burke. Near the end of Lord North's administration Burke brought in a bill by which it was provided that a pension or annuity might be given without name, if under oath that it was not for the benefit of a member of the House of Commons. Burke's pension had been taken out under the name of another man; but being under the necessity of mortgaging it, the real pensioner had to be disclosed to the mortgagee.[1] For the rest, this " Address to the Addressers," as it was popularly called,—or " Part Third of the Rights of Man," as one publisher entitled it,—sowed broadcast through England passages that were recited in assemblies, and sentences that became proverbs.

[1] This disclosure, though not disproved, is passed over silently by most historians. Nevertheless it was probably that which ended Burke's parliamentary career. Two years later, at the age of sixty-two, he retired with an accumulation of pensions given at the king's request, amounting to £3,700 per annum. His reputation had been built up on his supposed energy in favor of economy. The secret and illegal pension (£1,500) cast light on his sudden coalition with Lord North, whom he once proposed to impeach as a traitor. The title of "masked pensioner" given by Paine branded Burke. Writing in 1819 Cobbett says: "As my Lord Grenville introduced the name of Burke, suffer me, my Lord, to introduce that of the man [Paine] who put this Burke to shame, who drove him off the public stage to seek shelter in the pension list, and who is now named fifty million times where the name of the pensioned Burke is mentioned once."

"It is a dangerous attempt in any government to say to a Nation, *Thou shalt not read.*"

"Thought, by some means or other, is got abroad in the world, and cannot be restrained, though reading may."

"Whatever the rights of the people are, they have a right to them, and none have a right either to withhold or to grant them."

"The project of hereditary Governors and Legislatures was a treasonable usurpation over the rights of posterity."

"Put a country right, and it will soon put government right."

"When the rich plunder the poor of his rights, it becomes an example to the poor to plunder the rich of his property."

"Who are those that are frightened at reform? Are the public afraid their taxes should be lessened too much? Are they afraid that sinecure places and pensions should be abolished too fast? Are the poor afraid that their condition should be rendered too comfortable?"

"A thing moderately good is not so good as it ought to be."

"If to expose the fraud and imposition of monarchy, and every species of hereditary government—to lessen the oppression of taxes—to propose plans for the education of helpless infancy, and the comfortable support of the aged and distressed—to endeavour to conciliate nations with each other—to extirpate the horrid practice of war—to promote universal peace, civilization, and commerce—and to break the chains of political superstition, and raise degraded man to his proper rank—if these things be libellous, let me live the life of a Libeller, and let the name of Libeller be engraven on my tomb."

Two eminent personages were burnt in effigy in Europe about this time, one in France, the other in England: Paine and the Pope.

Under date of December 19th, the American minister (Morris) enters in his diary: "Several Americans dine with me. Paine looks a little down at the news from England ; he has been burned in effigy."

This was the reply of the Addressers, the noblemen and gentry, to Paine's " Letter." It is said that on the Fifth of November it was hinted to the boys that their Guy Fawkes would extort more pennies if labelled " Tom Paine," and that thenceforth the new Guy paraded with a pair of stays under his arm. The holocaust of Paines went on through December, being timed for the author's trial, set for the eighteenth. One gets glimpses in various local records and memoirs of the agitation in England. Thus in Mrs. Henry Sandford's account of Thomas Poole,[1] we read in Charlotte Poole's journal :

"December 18, 1792.—John dined with Tom Poole, and from him heard that there was a great bustle at Bridgwater yesterday—that Tom Paine was burnt in Effigy, and that he saw Richard Symes sitting on the Cornhill with a table before him, receiving the oaths of loyalty to the king, and affection to the present constitution, from the populace. I fancy this could not have been a very pleasant sight to Tom Poole, for he has imbibed some of the wild notions of liberty and equality that at present prevail so much ; and it is but within these two or three days that a report has been circulated that he has distributed seditious pamphlets to the common people of Stowey. But this report is entirely without foundation. Everybody at this time talks politicks, and is looking with anxiety for fresh intelligence from France, which is a scene of guilt and confusion."

In Richardson's " Borderer's Table Book " is recorded : " 1792 (Dec.)—This month, Thomas Paine, author of the ' Rights of Man,' &c. &c., was burnt at most of the towns and considerable

---

[1] " Thomas Poole and his Friends." By Mrs. Henry Sandford. New York : Macmillan, 1888.

villages in Northumberland and Durham." No doubt, among the Durham towns, Wearmouth saw at the stake an effigy of the man whose iron bridge, taken down at Paddington, and sold for other benefit than Paine's, was used in spanning the Wear with the arch of his invention; all amid shouts of "God save the King," and plaudits for the various public-spirited gentlemen and architects, who patriotically appropriated the merits and patent of the inventor. The *Bury Post* (published near Paine's birthplace) says, December 12th :

"The populace in different places have been lately amusing themselves by burning effigies. As the culprit on whom they meant to execute this punishment was Thomas Paine, they were not interrupted by any power civil or military. The ceremony has been at Croydon in Surrey, at Warrington, at Lymington, and at Plymouth."

January 9, 1793 :

"On Saturday last the effigy of Thomas Paine was carried round the town of Swaffham, and afterwards hung on a gibbet, erected on the market-hill for that purpose. In the evening his remains were committed to the flames amidst acclamations of God save the King, etc."

The trial of Paine for high treason was by a Special Jury in the Court of King's Bench, Guildhall, on Tuesday, December 18, 1792, before Lord Kenyon.[1] The "Painites" had probably little

---

[1] *Special Jury:* John Campbell, John Lightfoot, Christopher Taddy, Robert Oliphant, Cornelius Donovan, Robert Rolleston, John Lubbock, Richard Tuckwell, William Porter, Thomas Bruce, Isaac Railton, Henry Evans. *Counsel for the Crown:* Sir Archibald Macdonald (Attorney-General), Solicitor-General, Mr. Bearcroft, Mr. Baldwin, Mr. Wood, Mr. Percival. *Counsel for the Defendant:* The Hon. Thomas Erskine, Mr. Piggot, Mr. Shepherd, Mr. Fitzgerald, Mr. F. Vaughan. *Solicitors:* For the Crown, Messrs. Chamberlayne and White ; for Defendant, Mr. Bonney.

hope of acquittal. In Rickman's journal (manuscript) he says: "C. Lofft told me he knew a gentleman who tried for five or six years to be on the special juries, but could not, being known to be a liberty man. He says special juries are packed to all intents and purposes." The reason for gathering such powerful counsel for defence must have been to obtain from the trial some definitive adjudication on the legal liabilities of writers and printers, and at the same time to secure, through the authority of Erskine, an affirmation of their constitutional rights. Lord Loughborough and others vainly tried to dissuade Erskine from defending Paine. For himself, Paine had given up the case some time before, and had written from Paris, November 11th, to the Attorney-General, stating that, having been called to the Convention in France, he could not stay to contest the prosecution, as he wished.

"My necessary absence from your country affords the opportunity of knowing whether the prosecution was intended against Thomas Paine, or against the Rights of the People of England to investigate systems and principles of government; for as I cannot now be the object of the prosecution, the going on with the prosecution will show that something else was the object, and that something else can be no other than the People of England. . . . But I have other reasons than those I have mentioned for writing you this letter; and however you chuse to interpret them they proceed from a good heart. The time, Sir, is becoming too serious to play with Court prosecutions, and sport with national rights. The terrible examples that have taken place here upon men who, less than a year ago, thought themselves as secure as any prosecuting Judge, Jury, or Attorney-General can do now in England, ought to have some weight with men in your situation.

That the Government of England is as great, if not the greatest perfection of fraud and corruption that ever took place since governments began, is what you cannot be a stranger to ; unless the constant habit of seeing it has blinded your sense. But though you may not chuse to see it, the people are seeing it very fast, and the progress is beyond what you may chuse to believe. Is it possible that you or I can believe, or that reason can make any other man believe, that the capacity of such a man as Mr. Guelph, or any of his profligate sons, is necessary to the government of a nation ? I speak to you as one man ought to speak to another ; and I know also that I speak what other people are beginning to think. That you cannot obtain a verdict (and if you do it will signify nothing) without *packing a Jury*, and we *both* know that such tricks are practised, is what I have very good reason to believe. . . . Do not then, Sir, be the instrument of drawing away twelve men into a situation that may be injurious to them afterwards. I do not speak this from policy, but from benevolence ; but if you chuse to go on with the process, I make it my request that you would read this letter in Court, after which the Judge and the Jury may do what they please. As I do not consider myself the object of the prosecution, ·neither can I be affected by the issue one way or the other, I shall, though a foreigner in your country, subscribe as much money as any other man towards supporting the right of the nation against the prosecution ; and it is for this purpose only that I shall do it. As I have not time to copy letters, you will excuse the corrections."

A month after this awful letter was written, Paine no doubt knew its imprudence. It was sprung on the Court by the Attorney-General, and must alone have settled the verdict, had it not been foregone. Erskine, Paine's leading counsel, was Attorney-General for the Prince of Wales—foremost of " Mr. Guelph's profligate sons,"—and he was compelled to treat as a forgery the letter all felt to be genuine. He endeavored to prevent the reading of it, but Lord Kenyon decided that "in prosecutions for high treason, where overt acts are laid, you may prove overt acts not laid to prove those that are laid. If it [the letter] goes to prove him the author of the book, I am bound to admit it." Authorship of the book being admitted, this was only a pretext. The Attorney-General winced a good deal at the allusion to the profligate sons, and asked :

"Is he [Paine] to teach human creatures, whose moments of existence depend upon the permission of a Being, merciful, long-suffering, and of great goodness, that those whose youthful errors, from which even royalty is not exempted, are to be treasured up in a vindictive memory, and are to receive sentence of irremissible sin at His hands ?"

It may be incidentally remarked here that the Attorney-General could hardly have failed to retort with charges against the author, had not Paine's reputation remained proof against the libellous "biography" by the government clerk, Chalmers.

The main part of the prosecution was thus uttered by Paine himself. While reading the letter the prosecutor paused to say : "If I succced in this prosecution he shall never return to this country otherwise than *in vinculis*, for I will outlaw him." [1]

[1] 22 Howell's State Trials 357. Other reports are by Joseph Gurney and "by an eminent advocate." The brief evidence consisted mainly of the notes and statements of Paine's publishers already mentioned in connection with the publication of the indicted work. The Attorney-General cited effectively the reply to Paine which he attributed to Vice-President Adams. Publicola's pamphlet gave great comfort to Paine's prosecutors. Mr. Long writes to Mr. Miles, agent in Paris (December 1st), about this "book by the American Adams, which is admirable, proving that the American government is not founded upon the absurd doctrine of the pretended rights of man, and that if it had been it could not have stood for a week."

Erskine's powerful defence of the constitutional rights of thought and speech in England is historical. He built around Paine an enduring constitutional fortress, compelling Burke and Fox to lend aid from their earlier speeches. The fable with which he closed was long remembered.

"Constraint is the natural parent of resistance, and a pregnant proof that reason is not on the side of those who use it. You must all remember, gentlemen, Lucian's pleasant story: Jupiter and a countryman were walking together, conversing with great freedom and familiarity upon the subject of heaven and earth. The countryman listened with attention and acquiescence, while Jupiter strove only to convince him; but happening to hint a doubt, Jupiter turned hastily around and threatened him with his thunder. 'Ah, ha !' says the countryman, 'now, Jupiter, I know that you are wrong; you are always wrong when you appeal to your thunder.'

"This is the case with me. I can reason with the people of England, but I cannot fight against the thunder of authority."

Mr. Attorney-General arose immediately to reply to Mr. Erskine, when Mr. Campbell (the foreman of the jury) said: "My Lord, I am authorized by the jury here to inform the Attorney-General that a reply is not necessary for them, unless the Attorney-General wishes to make it, or your Lordship." Mr. Attorney-General sat down, and the jury gave in their verdict—Guilty.

Paine was outlawed.

The eye of England followed its outlaw before and after his trial. In the English state archives is a note of G. Munro to Lord Grenville, September 8th, announcing "Mr. Payne's" election for the Département de l'Oise. Earl Gower announces, on information of Mr. Mason, that "Tom Payne is on his road to take his seat." On September 22d a despatch mentions Paine's speech on the judiciary question. "December 17, 1792. Tom Payne is in the country unwell, or pretending to be so." The most remarkable of the secret despatches, however, are two sent from Paris on the last day of the year 1792. One of these alludes to the effect of Paine's trial and outlawry on the English radicals in Paris:

"Tom Payne's fate and the unanimity of the English has staggered the boldest of them, and they are now dwindling into nothing. Another address was, however, proposed for the National Convention; this motion, I understand, was made by Tom Payne and seconded by Mr. Mery; it was opposed by Mr. Frost, seconded by Mr. McDonald."

The second allusion to Paine on December 31st deserves to be pondered by historians:

"Tom Payne has proposed banishing the royal family of France, and I have heard is writing his opinion on the subject; his consequence seems daily lessening in this country, and I should never be surprised if he some day receives the fate he merits."

It thus seems that whatever good deed Paine was about, he deserves death. Earl Gower, and the agents he left on his departure (September) in Paris, must have known that Paine's proposal was the only alternative of the king's execution, and that if his consequence was lessening it was solely because of labors to save the lives of the royal family. This humane man has the death-sentence of Robespierre on him anticipated by the ambassador of a country which, while affecting grief for Louis XVI., was helping on his fate.[1]

Danton said to Count Theodore de Lameth :

" I am willing to try and save the King, but I must have a million of money to buy up the necessary votes, and the money must be on hand in eight days. I warn you that although I may save his life I shall vote for his death ; I am quite willing to save his head, but not to lose mine."

The Count and the Spanish Ambassador broached the matter to Pitt, who refused the money.[2] He was not willing to spend a few thousands to save the life of America's friend, though he made his death a pretext for exhausting his treasury to deluge Europe with blood.

Gouverneur Morris, whose dislike of Paine's republicanism was equally cynical,[3] was intimate with Earl Gower, and no doubt gave him his information. Morris was clear-headed enough to per-

[1] After September it was, as Talleyrand says, " no longer a question that the king should reign, but that he himself, the queen, their children, his sister, should be saved. It might have been done. It was at least a duty to attempt it. At that time France was only at war with the Emperor [Austria], the Empire [the German states], and Sardinia. Had all the other states concerted themselves to offer their mediation by proposing to recognise whatever form of government France might be pleased to adopt, with the sole condition that the prisoners in the Temple should be allowed to leave the country and retire wherever they liked, though such a proposal, as may be supposed, would not have filled the demagogues with delight, they would have been powerless to resist it."—Memoirs of the Prince de Talleyrand. New York, 1891, i., p. 168.

[2] Taine's " French Revolution " (American ed.), iii., p. 135. See also the " Correspondence of W. A. Miles on the French Revolution," London, 1890, i., p. 398. The Abbé Noel, a month before the king's death, pointed out to this British agent how he might be saved.

[3] In relating to John Randolph of Roanoke Paine's exposure of Silas Deane, Morris regards it as the prevention of a fraud, but nevertheless thinks Paine deserved punishment for his " impudence " !

ceive that the massacres in France were mainly due to the menaces of foreign monarchs, and was in hearty sympathy with Paine's plan for saving the life of Louis XVI. On December 28th he writes to Washington that a majority of the Convention

"have it in contemplation not only to refer the judgment to the electors of France, that is, to her people, but also to send him and his family to America, which Paine is to move for. He mentioned this to me in confidence, but I have since heard it from another quarter."

On January 6, 1793, Morris writes to Washington concerning Genêt, the new Minister to the United States, who had been introduced to him by Paine, and dined with him. At the close he says :

"The King's fate is to be decided next Monday the 14th. That unhappy man, conversing with one of his council on his own fate, calmly summed up the motives of every kind, and concluded that a majority of the Council [Convention] would vote for referring his case to the people, and that in consequence he should be massacred. I think he must die or reign."

Paine also feared that a reference to the populace meant death. He had counted a majority in the Convention who were opposed to the execution. Submission of the question to the masses would thus, if his majority stood firm, be risking the life of Louis again. Unfortunately this question had to be determined before the vote on life or death. At the opening of the year 1793 he felt cheerful about the situation. On January 3d he wrote to John King, a retreating comrade in England, as follows :

"Dear King,—I don't know anything, these many years, that surprised and hurt me more than the sentiments you published in the Courtly HERALD, the 12th December, signed John King, Egham Lodge. You have gone back from all you ever said. When I first knew you in Ailiffe-street, an obscure part of the city, a child, without fortune or friends, I noticed you ; because I thought I saw in you, young as you was, a bluntness of temper, a boldness of opinion, and an originality of thought, that portended some future good. I was pleased to discuss with you, under our friend Oliver's lime-tree, those political notions which I have since given the world in my ' Rights of Man.'

"You used to complain of abuses as well as me. What, then, means this sudden attachment to *Kings ?* this fondness of the English Government, and hatred of the French ? If you mean to curry favour, by aiding your Government, you are mistaken ; they never recompence those who serve it ; they buy off those who can annoy it, and let the good that is rendered it be its own reward. Believe me, KING, more is to be obtained by cherishing the rising spirit of the People, than by subduing it. Follow my fortunes, and I will be answerable that you shall make your own.—THOMAS PAINE."[1]

This last sentence may even now raise a smile. King must subsequently have reflected with satisfaction that he did not "follow the fortunes" of Paine, which led him into prison at the end of the year. A third letter from him to Paine appeared in the *Morning Herald*, April 17, 1793, in which he says :

[1] "Mr. King's Speech, at Egham, with Thomas Paine's Letter," etc. Egham, 1793. In his reply, January 11th, King says : "Such men as Frost, Barlow, and others, your associates, show the forlornness of your cause. Our respectable citizens do not go to you," etc. Writing February 11th, King expresses satisfaction at Paine's vote on the King's fate : " the imputation of cruelty will not now be added to the other censures on your character ; but the catastrophe of this unhappy Monarch has shewn you the danger of putting a nation in ferment."

" ' If the French kill their king, it will be a signal for my departure, for I will not abide among such sanguinary men.' These, Mr. Paine, were your words at our last meeting ; yet after this you are not only with them, but the chief modeller of their new Constitution."

Mr. King might have reflected that the author of the " Rights of Man," which he had admired, was personally safer in regicide France than in liberticide England, which had outlawed him.

END OF VOL. I.

www.ingramcontent.com/pod-product-compliance
Lightning Source LLC
Chambersburg PA
CBHW051526100726
47898CB00005B/1588